ART AND MURDER

Jack Taggart Mysteries

ART AND MURDER

A Jack Taggart Mystery

Don Easton

DUNDURN
TORONTO

Project Editor: Shannon Whibbs
Editor: Maryan Gibson
Design: Laura Boyle
Cover Design: Laura Boyle
Front Cover Image: © Littleny | Dreamstime.com
Printer: Webcom

Library and Archives Canada Cataloguing in Publication

Easton, Don, author
    Art and murder / Don Easton.
(A Jack Taggart mystery)
Issued in print and electronic formats.
ISBN 978-1-4597-3069-4 (pbk.).--ISBN 978-1-4597-3070-0 (pdf).--
ISBN 978-1-4597-3071-7 (epub)

I. Title. II. Series: Easton, Don. Jack Taggart mystery.
PS8609.A78A78 2015   C813'.6   C2015-901264-3
                                        C2015-901265-1

1   2   3   4   5   19   18   17   16   15

We acknowledge the support of the **Canada Council for the Arts** and the **Ontario Arts Council** for our publishing program. We also acknowledge the financial support of the **Government of Canada** through the **Canada Book Fund** and **Livres Canada Books**, and the **Government of Ontario** through the **Ontario Book Publishing Tax Credit** and the **Ontario Media Development Corporation**.

Care has been taken to trace the ownership of copyright material used in this book. The author and the publisher welcome any information enabling them to rectify any references or credits in subsequent editions.

— *J. Kirk Howard, President*

The publisher is not responsible for websites or their content unless they are owned by the publisher.

Printed and bound in Canada.

VISIT US AT
Dundurn.com | @dundurnpress | Facebook.com/dundurnpress | Pinterest.com/dundurnpress

Dundurn
3 Church Street, Suite 500
Toronto, Ontario, Canada
M5E 1M2

To those who serve and protect us …

Chapter One

"Hey!" Brandy yelled. "What the …?" She stared open-mouthed at Klaus as she sat naked on the edge of the hotel room bed.

Klaus stood glowering down at her. Somewhere in his early thirties, he was taller than most men. At the moment he was only wearing his underwear and it was apparent from his muscular build that he lifted weights on a regular basis. His head was shaved and he had a large tattoo of a scorpion on the centre of his chest, the creature's claws reaching up each side of his neck.

At the moment he was drunk and Brandy wondered if his slap to her face was intended to be playful. She put her fingertips to her nose and saw a smear of blood. "You … you hurt me," she stammered, then looked at the other two men in the room, hoping for support.

Clive and Liam were completely naked. Clive, a guy of average height and build with well-trimmed brown hair, pretended not to notice what Klaus had done.

She glanced at Liam. He was a short, skinny guy with close-cropped red hair and freckles all over his body. He was swaying on his feet and, despite having achieved orgasm moments earlier, still had an erection.

"Hey, look at this, baby!" Liam sniggered while gripping his penis and fixating his gaze on her breasts. "These little blue pills really work!"

Brandy hoped her voice didn't portray her fear. "That's it, I'm outta here," she said, getting to her feet.

"Like fuck you are," Klaus said, shoving her back down on the bed. "We're not done with you yet ... are we, guys?"

"Hell no," Liam said. "This is my stag an' I'm gonna party all night long!"

"I'll scream," Brandy threatened. "Now let me —"

Klaus grabbed her with one hand around her throat, choking off her words. "Listen, bitch! You co-operate and we'll let you go in a little while. You don't and ... well, let's not talk about that. Okay?"

Brandy was twenty-four years old and as far as her parents knew, she worked as a cocktail waitress in a high-end lounge. What they didn't know was that she moonlighted as a call girl.

All her life Brandy had been told how beautiful she was. Her bottom price for sex was a thousand dollars and she had a steady clientele willing to pay. Men had always treated her like she was a princess ... but her beauty and self-worth were slipping away as her addiction to cocaine increased.

Clive was her connection and usually rewarded her with cocaine in exchange for sex. Tonight was different. He had rented a hotel room, but when she'd arrived and discovered two other men were to be included, she'd balked at the idea. An ounce of cocaine and $2,000 in cash for one hour of her time convinced her otherwise.

Besides the money and cocaine, there was one other reason she wanted to please Clive. She owed someone a favour. A favour that required Clive to trust her more.

She had now been in the room for three hours. Her earlier protest at the time had been met with promises of more cocaine.

"You listenin' to me?" Klaus asked as his fingers tightened around her windpipe.

Panic flooded her brain. She needed oxygen. She stared into his eyes. *He'll kill me if I don't do as he says! Maybe he still will…*: She nodded quickly.

Klaus slowly released his grip and she fell sideways onto the bed, gasping and clutching her throat.

He smiled sarcastically. "Now … tell me what a naughty girl you are. Tell me the things you would like us to do to you."

"I … I …"

"You do have naughty thoughts, don't you?" Klaus continued. "It's okay," he added softly. "You can tell me." He smiled reassuringly.

"Please," Brandy begged. "I'm not like … into the rough stuff. I … I have never been with more than one guy at once before. I don't want …"

Klaus scowled and raised the back of his hand, and Brandy immediately cowered, protecting her face with her hands.

"Easy, big guy." Clive chuckled, patting Klaus on the shoulder before looking at Brandy. "Relax. Klaus didn't mean to hit you that hard. It was an accident. Come on, we're having fun. I'll see that you get an extra-big tip."

"Yeah, startin' with *my* tip," chortled Liam, waving his penis at her.

Clive glanced at Liam, then looked back at Brandy. "He's teasing … sort of. I promise I'll reward you big when we're done."

Brandy swallowed and self-consciously rubbed her neck as she stared up at Clive.

"Besides, there's a first time for everything," he added.

"Yeah," Liam said, "I wish it was the other way around. Three of you and only one of me." He turned to Klaus. "That's always been one of my fantasies."

Klaus laughed. "You're too ugly for three women."

"Fuck you!" Liam grinned.

Brandy interjected. "Let me go to the bathroom and clean up before we start again."

Klaus gave her a hard look. "Yeah, go ahead." Then he smiled slightly and added, "I'll light up a smoke while you do."

As Brandy got up, Klaus looked at Clive and said, "Go with her. Make sure she doesn't do something stupid, like try to lock herself in."

Moments later Brandy dabbed at her face over the bathroom sink while Clive stood beside her. She caught a reflection in the mirror outside the bathroom and saw Klaus go into her purse and take the $2,000 back. She pretended not to notice. She was too afraid of what would happen if she said anything. All she wanted was to get out … and get out fast.

"Hey, we're not payin' you to stand and look at yourself in a mirror!" Klaus hollered.

Brandy focused on her image in the bathroom mirror and gripped the sink with both hands in an effort to keep herself from trembling. The image she saw was no longer one of confidence and beauty. *Mascara under my eyes ... my cheek bruised and starting to swell. Why would they treat me like this? I just don't get it.*

She thought about the man she owed the favour to. His name was Jack. *He promised to protect me ... but will he?*

Brandy had met Jack a month ago. It was the week before Christmas when he'd come into the lounge where she worked. She'd guessed him to be in his late thirties or early forties, but despite the age difference, she was attracted to him and hoped their relationship would develop further than the friendly banter. She also hoped he would never find out she was a call girl ... or perhaps *had* been a call girl, because after meeting him, she intended to quit.

It turned out he already knew. Any thought she had of developing a personal relationship with him dissolved when she sat beside him in the lounge that night at closing time and sold him an ounce of cocaine. He did not pay her for the cocaine, opting instead to flash his badge and tell her she had two choices. Either be arrested or become his informant.

She started to cry. It was a response that worked with most men.

"Cut the crap," he said harshly, "and listen."

Most men, not all. She quit crying instantly and listened. He promised that if she became his informant, he would protect her. Nobody else would know, with the exception of his partner, to whom he'd introduce her if she agreed. He said he wanted her to help him catch her cocaine connection.

Her mind had felt numb. "I'm not sure what to say," she replied.

"You don't have a criminal record yet," Jack said. "Someday you'll probably have a family. How do you tell your children that you can't ever take them to Disneyland because you're a convicted drug dealer?"

Brandy slumped in her chair. When she spoke, her voice came out as a whisper. "Okay … I guess."

"You guess?"

"I'll do what you want."

"There is one more thing to keep in mind before you say anything," said Jack. "If you ever lie to me … ever … I will find out and all deals are off. Understood?"

Brandy nodded. "I won't lie, but I only know him as Clive."

Jack reached into his pocket and pulled out a mug shot. It was Clive.

"You already knew," she said, confused. "Why are you hassling me if —"

"I need help catching him. I don't even know where he lives."

"I don't know, either," she protested, fearing that Jack wouldn't believe her, "but he told me he was going to Mexico for Christmas."

"Do you know who he went with?"

"Nope, but he sort of joked about taking me with him."

"To mule-back coke?"

Brandy stared momentarily at Jack, then said, "He hinted at that once. Said he could provide me with a fake passport so that if I had a record, customs would wave me through. I told him I don't have a record, but I know enough about Mexican jails that I would never chance it. Did you ever see that movie where a guy went to jail in —"

"Where does he get the passports?"

"I don't know," Brandy replied indignantly. "It's not something you ask."

Jack met her gaze. "Who else does he hang with?"

Brandy sighed loudly. She disliked being questioned. When she saw Jack frown, she said, "I've only seen him with one other person."

"Who?"

"I don't think it's who you're looking for. This guy doesn't strike me as the type to take orders from Clive, let alone mule coke."

"What's his name? What's does he look like?"

"I only know him as Klaus. Steroid monkey with a tat on his neck. Dresses like a gangster with all the bling. He's got a shaved head, wears a ball cap sideways — the thing's too big." Brandy shook her head to show her distaste. "Makes him look like a pinhead. I like guys who can protect me, but not if they look stupid."

"Keep going," said Jack.

"You know, the typical loose pants that show the crack of his ass."

"I get the picture, but what's the tattoo on his neck?"

"Oh, that. I only saw the top of it poking up above his collar. Looked like a crab claw, so maybe he's a Cancer. You know, like in the horoscope. I'm a Virgo. What are you?"

Jack ignored her question. "Do you have a contact number for Clive?"

"I did, but it's not working now. He's always changing phones. I'll have to wait until he comes in to get his new number."

Jack gave her a long, cold stare, then said, "I'll give you my numbers. Write them on a piece of paper. I don't want you carrying my business card. If either Clive or Klaus come in, call me immediately. I want to follow them and find out where they live."

"Okay."

"When he's not in Mexico, how often do you see him?"

"About once a week."

"How much coke do you get from him?"

"Usually an ounce, sometimes more."

"And what do you pay for it?"

"I, uh, pay about …"

"I warned you once what will happen if you lie," Jack said.

Brandy felt dismayed. "You know about that, too, don't you."

"That you're hooking and trade sex for coke," he said flatly.

Brandy sighed. "Yes, but there's something about Clive I don't like. I was going to break it off with him. He gives me bad vibes."

"How many times have you, uh, been with him?" Jack asked.

"Maybe a dozen, but he's becoming nasty in the way he treats me."

"For my purposes, could you handle another session with him if you had to?"

Brandy grimaced. "I guess so. He is generous. He gives me an ounce each time we, uh, spend an hour alone together."

"An ounce of coke for an hour … you must be good."

At that, Brandy had felt a little surge of optimism. "If you'd like to find out, the first one's on me. Actually, not just the first one. I could see you being my boy —"

"Time for you to meet my partner." Jack had nodded in the direction of a woman sitting at the bar.

* * *

Brandy knew that time for reflection in the mirror was over when Klaus entered and gave her a solid smack on her backside.

"I told you to hurry up," he snarled.

She gasped when he grabbed her by the back of the neck and propelled her out and onto the bed. She glimpsed the clock. *One-twenty-five. Will Jack answer if I call?*

Klaus sneered down at her. "Okay, bitch, time to really earn what we paid you."

It has to be now … or never.

Chapter Two

In Paris, France, it was ten-twenty-five in the morning, nine hours ahead of Vancouver time, when Kerin Bastion ordered a coffee. It was only ten degrees Celsius, but the sun shone in a clear blue sky, giving a feeling of warmth and optimism.

Kerin was particularly optimistic, albeit nervous, as he looked out the café window. He was on the most exciting case of his career in the seven years he had been with the Police nationale, and today would be a pivotal moment in the investigation.

Three months earlier he had been selected to go undercover. The French judiciary had only recently approved the use of an undercover agent, or *agent provocateur,* as a lawful means to collect evidence.

Unlike North America, where criminals were familiar with undercover tactics, the criminals in France were naive by comparison. The top echelon of the Police nationale hoped to take advantage of the situation.

To impress their political watchdogs, the Police nationale picked an impressive target to illustrate the benefit of such a tool. An international crime ring had operated out of several European countries for years. Its members were known to have committed armed robberies of jewellery stores, armoured trucks, financial institutions, and various other businesses.

The crimes were often investigated as individual cases, and many jurisdictions had not come to realize the big picture. When the police did pick up their scent, the criminals moved elsewhere and were usually forgotten when more active cases surfaced.

Over the years arrests had been made, but only of low-end criminals who had contracted their talents out to the gang. Efforts to find where the stolen goods were going or identify the real bosses had met with little success — until recently.

A year earlier a French informant managed to ally himself with some local criminals associated with the gang. It was this informant who alerted the police that they were dealing with an international crime ring.

The informant said the criminal empire was not large. Perhaps fewer than fifty people, counting the street criminals who worked for the gang in different countries. He said the criminals he met in Paris were controlled by a man by the name of Roche Freulard. He was also told that Roche had a boss whose real identity was unknown to any of the local criminals.

Four months ago the informant was invited to a party and had a chance to meet Roche. What caught the rapt attention of the police was the informant's telling them that one thug at the party let it slip that the gang was responsible for the high-profile murder of an art collector, and also that some of the stolen paintings were for the personal gallery of Roche's boss.

A couple of months before that, a respected and well-known art collector in Paris by the name of Philippe Petit had been found bludgeoned to death in his home. Seven of his paintings were stolen, but to date none had been located.

Two days after the party, both the informant and the thug who'd let the information slip were found shot to death in an alley.

That action prompted a premature start to Kerin's undercover assignment, even though it would be another two months before judicial approval was officially given.

Kerin managed to befriend Roche by passing himself off as a high-class criminal who operated a car-theft ring that moved stolen cars, as well as other merchandise, around the world. When Roche asked *what* other merchandise, Kerin smiled and twirled a diamond ring around his finger. It was enough to bait the hook.

Roche began to confide in Kerin more and more with the idea of bringing him into the gang as an equal. He spoke of working for someone he referred to as the Ringmaster. Kerin had laughed at the title, but Roche shrugged it off. He said they were like a circus, with multiple troupes playing in different countries and moving frequently. He said the secrecy of their identities helped keep them safe from the police. That and using disposable phones.

"And do you have a title?" Kerin asked.

"Actually, I do," Roche replied. "I'm known as the juggler, or sometimes the French juggler. I'm responsible for recruiting people to do the dirty work, as well as looking after the distribution of the goods in France. Sometimes I need to store them until it is safe, while other times the situation calls for a speedier distribution."

"Hence the juggling act," Kerin said. "Are there many jugglers in your, uh, company?"

"It varies. At the moment, there are five of us, counting my brother."

"Anton is a juggler?" Kerin was surprised. "You once mentioned he was a cabinetmaker."

"You've got a good memory," Roche noted. "Yes, it is a recent development that he was brought into the fold."

"I see."

"Keep what I told you in confidence," warned Roche. "The Ringmaster and the jugglers meet once a year to go over what we have done and see what we can do to help each other. That meeting should be happening soon. If you are accepted, you will meet the others then."

Kerin smiled. *That is an opportunity I don't want to miss.*

Despite Roche's apparent trust, Kerin was still subjected to an electronic search for hidden transmitters once in a while. Roche would apologize each time and say he was simply following procedure. As a result, Kerin never wore a transmitter, but meticulously made notes of all his conversations with Roche immediately afterwards.

Recently Roche had mentioned that the Ringmaster's birthday was coming up, so Kerin gave him a gold watch to pass along, acting like it was a trivial item. The truth was, the cost of the watch had cut a big hole in the investigative funds allotted.

The watch had a dual purpose. Besides gaining the favour of the Ringmaster, the watchband had a unique pattern of gold and silver. Unique enough, Kerin had convinced his bosses, that the man wearing it might be spotted and thus identified.

Unfortunately subsequent surveillance of Roche did not identify anyone wearing the watch, but today Kerin had a chance to please his disgruntled bosses back at headquarters.

A week ago Roche said he thought he might be garnering police attention. Kerin expressed concern, knowing full well that surveillance teams were targeting Roche. Fortunately it had an unexpected benefit. Roche blamed the police attention on the informant, who had allied himself to the gang and had been murdered prior to Kerin's arrival. He then asked Kerin if he would be interested in temporarily replacing him as a safety precaution and suggested Kerin might be able to use his own connections to move stolen goods.

Kerin could barely contain the exhilaration he felt. He remained silent.

"I have heard that many stolen cars from Europe or North America end up in Arab countries," Roche said. "Is that true?"

"My best clients happen to be Arab," Kerin replied.

"Those are countries where we would like to expand. Are you willing to help?"

Kerin hesitated, pretending to consider the offer.

"I can assure you that you will be well paid," Roche said.

"Well paid?"

"Contingent upon your meeting with the Ringmaster for final approval."

"I see."

"Are you interested?" Roche prodded him.

"Yes, it sounds like it could be beneficial."

Kerin was told that he would only meet the Ringmaster face to face once. After that, all communication would be made through Roche. Subsequent arrangements were made for Roche to meet Kerin today at a café, where he'd introduce the Ringmaster.

It was deemed unlikely that the Ringmaster would say anything to Kerin about the murders during the meeting, but identifying the Ringmaster would be a big step forward in the investigation. Once that was done, physical and electronic surveillance could be utilized, along with whatever other police investigative means were needed.

* * *

Kerin was pleased when he saw Roche parking his black Peugeot in front of the café, and a moment later greeted him when he walked inside. Roche declined to sit down and told Kerin that they would walk to another location to meet the Ringmaster.

A half-hour stroll later, they came to a park. During the stroll, Kerin had caught the occasional glimpse of his long-time partner, Maurice Leblanc, who followed on the sidewalk across the street.

Maurice was a tall, slender man with a black Fu Manchu moustache that grew to the bottom of his jaw. Kerin grinned to himself when he imagined that moustache twitching as it always did when Maurice was worried. *It's okay, Maurice, the meeting is still on.*

Kerin caught the odd glimpse of other colleagues. They had divided up their eight-person surveillance team, leaving drivers in four cars while the others followed on foot. Two of the team members who'd been in the café switched back to their cars.

Once at the park, Roche received a call. After hanging up, he said, "The Ringmaster is coming, but is nervous about meeting you. I need you to answer a question."

Kerin frowned. "What?"

"We can walk around the park as we talk," Roche suggested.

Kerin fell in step with Roche. and waited for him to speak. Finally, Roche asked, "Where do you come up with your stolen property?"

Kerin stopped and faced Roche. "Jesus! You're asking me about that again? I told you about one of the heists in advance!" In reality, the heist was not genuine but a ruse to gain Roche's trust. A co-operative jeweller had agreed to say he was robbed and the police had released a fake news release.

Roche gave a sympathetic smile. "Do not be angry with me, my friend. I trust you completely — otherwise you would not be here. That was simply a question I was told to put to you. The Ringmaster will be along shortly. Please be patient."

Kerin nodded, unaware that the Ringmaster was already watching with binoculars. Every look and gesture Kerin made was being closely scrutinized.

Chapter Three

In the hotel room in Vancouver, Brandy sat up after Klaus had flung her onto the bed. She did her best to smile at Liam. "You know, seeing as it is your stag, maybe I could help you fulfill your fantasy of having three girls at once."

Liam looked up from a Scotch he was pouring. "Really?"

"I know two other girls. They're really pretty ... classy-looking. What d'you say I give them a call and get this party really rocking?"

Liam looked at Klaus and Clive. "That's a great idea!"

Klaus was skeptical. "Why are you offering to do this?" he asked. "What is it you really —"

"You guys have worn me out," Brandy said. "Two extra girls will give me a break and it will be better for everyone." She shrugged. "If you don't like the looks of them, you don't have to let 'em in."

Klaus looked at Brandy suspiciously. "I'm not sure if —"

"Yeah, yeah," Brandy continued. "It will cost a little more, but I'm sure cash or blow isn't a problem for you guys." She gave a nod toward Liam. "Let's make his night really special." *It's not like you plan on paying, anyway.*

"Yeah, Klausie," Liam slurred. "Like she says, it's my night. Come on, it'll be a blast!"

Klaus thought for a moment, then bent over so he was nose to nose with Brandy. "Okay, give them a call ... but if things don't turn out good, I'll break your fucking neck and haul you out in a suitcase. You got that?"

I believe you. I've seen Pulp Fiction *like ten times. I know people do stuff —*

"I said you got that?" Klaus demanded again.

Brandy nodded, then went and picked up her purse. When she found the slip of paper, Klaus grabbed it from her and looked at the number, then used her phone and dialled it himself.

Brandy swallowed nervously. "Ask for Jackie."

She was relieved when Klaus handed her the phone and said, "It's ringing. You talk to her."

She did her best to give Klaus a reassuring smile as she sat in a chair and held the phone tight to her ear.

* * *

It was one-thirty in the morning when Corporal Jack Taggart grabbed the phone on the bedside table before it started the second ring. It was a common occurrence and he reacted quickly, hoping not to disturb his wife. It did, but Natasha was used to the calls and started to doze off again.

Jack was an undercover police operative who worked on an intelligence unit with the Royal Canadian Mounted Police in Vancouver. Along with his partner, Constable Laura Secord, they were like a constant open sore on the side of established organized crime families. For crime families that were not as well established, the sore was often fatal.

Undercover operations were only one of the tools they used in their battle against organized crime. Wiretaps were also used, but their most important tool was informants. To protect their own identities and those of their informants, undercover operators on the intelligence unit seldom went to court. It was up to their discretion if what they learned would be turned over to other units to further the investigation for court purposes.

Jack had an exceptional ability to gain the trust of informants. It was a trust that was well deserved. He protected his informants like a mother bear with her cubs.

"Jackie, it … it's me … Brandy."

Jackie? Jack heard the strain in her voice and knew she was in trouble. "I told you not to call me direct when you want to speak to Jackie," Jack said, while turning on the bedside light and prodding Natasha with his foot. "Besides, I hate phones. You never know who could be listening." He got ready to hand the phone to Natasha if need be.

Natasha sat up in bed. She was still groggy, but from the concern on Jack's face, she knew something was amiss. "I'm Jackie?" she whispered.

Jack put his finger to his lips for her to be quiet. "You hear what I'm sayin' about the listenin' bit?"

"You're okay," replied Brandy, "which is why I called to let you in on a good thing. I'm in a room at the Emerald Hotel. Top floor, corner … uh …" She hesitated. "Room 1201. Got three guys looking to party." She then lowered her voice as if speaking in confidence and said, "These guys are loaded. Think you and Laura would like in on it?"

"Three guys…. Do they have guns?" Jack asked.

"I don't think so … but …"

Jack heard her panting for breath and knew she was starting to hyperventilate. "Are you in immediate danger?" he asked.

"Not immediately … but soon," Brandy replied, as if repeating someone else's words. "You should get here as soon as possible. Like within the hour."

"Is there anything else you can tell me about these guys?" Jack asked. "Say yes when I hit it right. Are they —"

"I think I told you about him … he's really rich. You said I had all the luck and you wished you could meet him."

"You're with Clive?"

"Yes … but you need to meet him. He's really good-looking. So's his friend. Not a fat guy, either. He works out."

"Klaus is there too?"

"You bet. These guys are real gentlemen and will treat you good."

"We're on our way. Forty-five minutes tops."

* * *

Brandy hung up and glanced at Clive as he turned up the music on the radio. Liam lay on his back on the bed and gestured with his finger for her to come to him. When she stood up, he pulled his penis back to expose his scrotum.

"While we're waiting, give my boys a good licking, will you, darlin."

Brandy nodded nervously, then got on her knees between his legs and complied with his request, unaware that Klaus was twirling a pillowcase behind her to use as a gag so that further, more painful acts could be performed without her screams being heard.

Chapter Four

"Who's Jackie?" Natasha asked as soon as Jack hung up.

"Me." Jack pushed the speed dial to call Laura.

"Then who was I supposed to be?"

"A hooker."

"Kick me like that again," Natasha said, "and I might start charging you. Can I go back to sleep now?"

Jack nodded and turned his attention to the phone when Laura answered. His instructions were brief and terse.

"Got it," said Laura. "You'll be here in what ... twenty-five minutes?"

"Fifteen," Jack replied and hung up. As he reached for his clothes, his brain nagged him about what Brandy had gotten herself into. *Or more like what I got her into.*

He shoved his Smith and Wesson 9mm pistol into his belt at the back of his pants, then hesitated before going to the closet to retrieve an issue twelve-gauge Bushmaster shotgun with a metal folding stock and pistol grip. It could be held under his jacket without being seen.

He heard Natasha suck in a mouthful of air. "Trouble?" she asked.

"Not for me. The guys I'm about to meet won't be happy."

Natasha exhaled and nodded knowingly. "Remember I love you. Same goes for Mike and Steve."

* * *

Laura was waiting at the curb and climbed in when Jack pulled up in a black SUV. "I'll put my makeup on as you drive," she said, "but how do I look?"

Jack glanced at her quickly.

"You said to look like a high-class hooker," Laura continued, "if there is such a thing."

"You look perfect. More than I could afford."

Laura smiled. "You got that right."

Jack's moment of humour didn't last. His face darkened and he stepped on the gas, causing the tires to squeal when he pulled away from the curb.

"Watch it, will ya?" Laura said. "I have to live in this neighbourhood."

"You didn't hear her voice," Jack said. "She's really scared."

"Three of them, you say? But no guns?"

"No guns that she saw. Clive and Klaus are there for sure. Some other guy, too, but I didn't get a name."

"Fill me in a bit. If we burst in there, aren't you worried about burning her?"

"No. That's why you're a hooker tonight."

"I thought that was just to get them to open the door. What happens then?" She glanced at Jack and realized what he was going to do. "Oh, man," she muttered. "You're going to pretend to be her pimp."

"You got a better idea?"

"No, but a real pimp would probably mess them up."

"Probably," Jack agreed.

"We're cops, remember?"

"I remember." Jack glanced at her. "Don't worry. I brought the shotgun. If I stick that in their faces it'll scare them enough."

"So we go in. You wave the gun to scare them, then we collect Brandy and leave. Right?"

"You got it. It'll be a cakewalk."

I've heard that one before, Laura thought.

Jack drove in silence for a few minutes and tried to imagine what was going on in the hotel. "Damn it, whatever they're doing to her is my fault," he said bitterly as he swung into an oncoming lane to pass a car. "She told me Clive was becoming nastier and said she didn't want to go with him anymore. It was because of me that —"

"This isn't her first time with him," Laura said, no doubt hoping to ease his guilt.

"And what's this business with three guys?" Jack muttered. "I didn't think she was into that type of action." He slammed his hand on the steering wheel. "Bet she's doing it because of me."

"Maybe it's a money issue," Laura suggested. "I hope she isn't calling us over that. Can't say as I want to be charged with pimping."

"I'm sure that's not it. She was so scared she was starting to hyperventilate."

Jack thought about the reason he'd pushed Brandy into the situation. *Is Clive worth it?* He went over what he knew. Another informant had told him that Brandy had bragged to her about receiving ounces of cocaine from Clive in lieu of payment for sexual favours. Brandy had said that Clive was a big player who provided his smugglers with fake passports. It was the passports that caught Jack's attention. If a drug dealer had access to those, perhaps some terrorist could also get access to them. He later identified a known cocaine importer by the name of Clive Dempsey, and when Brandy became his informant, she confirmed that it was the Clive she knew.

Jack ignored a red light and the angry blast of a horn as he stepped on the gas. A moment later he pulled into the hotel parking lot. Forty minutes had passed since Brandy called him. He glanced up at the top floor of the hotel, wondering what awaited them, then gave a nod to Laura and they both thought the same thing.

It's showtime.

Chapter Five

In room 1201 at the Emerald Hotel, Brandy closed her eyes and tried to project her mind outside of the nightmare she was in. She was straddling Liam, who now sat naked on the chair under her. He was covered in sweat and grunting like a pig, but was apparently too tired to thrust his buttocks upward, relying on her to pump up and down on his penis.

"He keeps slipping out. Clamp him tighter," Klaus ordered as he stood behind her. Searing pain on her rear caused her to cry out, but her voice was muffled with the gag.

She heard Klaus suck on the cigarette. She tensed her buttocks and bit the gag in anticipation of more pain to come, but a knock on the door caused the men to stop and look at each other.

"Fresh meat," Liam said with a smirk.

Clive, who had been sitting in another chair watching, was the only one wearing a hotel robe. He plodded to the door and looked out the peephole.

An attractive woman with auburn hair smiled at him from the hallway. She was wearing feathered earrings and had on the perfect amount of makeup to make her look sexy without looking trashy. She slowly unzipped her raincoat to reveal a red silk blouse unbuttoned enough to expose plenty of cleavage that was barely constrained in a black lacy push-up bra. "I'm Laura," she said sweetly. "I was invited to a party here."

Clive fumbled in his haste to open the door. "Welcome to the par —"

Jack rammed the shotgun into his gut and literally ran him backward into the room as Laura stepped in and closed the door behind her.

Jack saw Brandy staring at him from where she was straddling a man on a chair. She was gagged and one eye was swollen shut. Her butt was peppered with cigarette burns.

Klaus's mouth dropped open and his cigarette fell to the floor.

"You fucking bastards!" Jack ran across the floor and pivoted the shotgun with his hands, smashing the butt end into Klaus's mouth. The man's head snapped back with a sickening sound of breaking teeth, and he fell to the floor like a wet bag of cement.

Liam, whose eyes were as big as his gaping mouth, shoved Brandy onto the floor and started to rise from his chair, but Jack spun around and rammed the barrel of the shotgun onto his forehead, forcing him back down.

"Jack! Don't!" Laura cried. "You can't —" She stopped as Clive tried to make a run for the door and dropped him with a kick to the groin.

A vein on Jack's temple throbbed with rage as he stared at Liam before slowly stepping back. "Okay, none of you fuckers move unless I say so," he ordered. The smell of fecal matter from Liam indicated that he wouldn't be a problem.

Klaus hadn't moved and Jack stared at his motionless body. *Is he dead? I didn't mean to kill him, just…* A feeling of panic gripped him. *Wait a minute, his chest is moving. He's alive!*

Jack took a deep breath and glanced at Clive, who was curled up in a fetal position on the floor, holding his groin with both hands and moaning.

Laura's eyes met Jack's and her voice was barely audible. "Is he …?" She gave a worried nod toward Klaus.

Jack could see the angst in Laura's eyes. He felt awful about the position he had put her in. He knew he had over-reacted and would face severe consequences if charged criminally. He regained his composure enough to play the role he intended. "Not yet. The fucker's still breathing." He caught the fleeting look of relief on Laura's face, quickly replaced by a glare. "I barely tapped him," Jack continued. "He must have a glass jaw or something." He hoped a little humour would lighten the situation. "I've heard about guys like that."

Laura frowned at Jack, unsure if she felt like laughing or screaming in response. Her attention was diverted when Brandy lurched to her feet and mumbled through the gag. Seeing the battered face, Laura decided she didn't feel like laughing or screaming. Tears of frustration and compassion clouded her vision when she thought of what human beings could do to one another.

"Take her to the bathroom while I take care of these guys," Jack ordered.

"Please don't kill us!" Liam wailed.

His shrill voice aroused Klaus, who sat up, cupping his broken jaw with the palm of his hand. A broken tooth emerged from between his fingers and fell to the carpet. He looked at Jack and growled, "Who the fuck are you?"

Jack glared at him. *First of all, you beat and torture a young woman, then scare the crap out of me because I thought I'd busted your neck. I really do hate you.* "I'm with hotel security," Jack snarled. "I'm here because the music is too loud." He then pointed the shotgun at Klaus's head and said, "You dumb piece of shit! Who the hell do you think I am?"

Klaus gingerly felt his broken teeth with his fingers, before picking out another broken piece and tossing it on the floor. The glower he gave Jack was meant to intimidate.

Jack acted like he didn't notice, just shook his head and muttered, "I can't believe what you did to my girl."

"I'm sorry," Liam spouted. "Things got a little carried away. We'll make it up —"

"Shut the fuck up!" Jack snapped. He turned his attention back to Klaus and said, "Hasn't anyone told you that you have really bad teeth? Don't you ever go to the dentist?"

Klaus's look turned to pure hatred.

"Lie face down on the floor and put your hands behind your back," Jack ordered.

"I'll kill you," Klaus spluttered.

"Trying to tell me I should kill you first?" said Jack menacingly.

Klaus decided to obey, arching his shoulders to rest his forehead on the carpet before putting his hands behind his back. His movements were slow, but Jack didn't know if it was in defiance or due to pain.

Jack gestured at Clive and Liam with the shotgun. "You two goofs, lie face down on each side of your buddy with your heads in the opposite direction."

"The opposite direction to who?" Liam asked as he got out of the chair and meekly crawled forward on his hands and knees.

"To your stupid friend who won't be eating any corn on the cob for a while. Who do you think I meant?"

"Please, don't hurt us." Clive hobbled, bow-legged, across the floor while holding his scrotum with one hand. "We can make it up to you … honest."

"No more talking from any of you," Jack said. "If I hear as much as a whisper I'll waste the three of you."

Jack saw Laura go to a closet to retrieve a hotel robe. When she glanced at him he said, "Give her the robe, then come out and cover me."

Jack used pillowcases to blindfold the men before yanking the belts from their pants and tying their hands behind their backs. Despite the loud music, he could hear Brandy crying as he worked. It did nothing to alleviate the anger he felt.

When he was finished securing the men, he took the shotgun back from Laura and placed the muzzle of the barrel on the base of Klaus's scull. "I'm going to talk to my girl and find out what you maggots did to her. I'll be able to see the three of you from the bathroom door. If any one of you so much as hiccups, you're all dead."

"Maybe you should gag them," whispered Laura once they were out of earshot.

Jack shook his head. "Klaus might suffocate if I do. It's not only the blood, but a broken jaw means a loss of support for the tongue. Call me an old softie, but we should keep an eye on him."

"Yeah, it's always been a concern of mine that you're a little too soft on people," Laura muttered.

As soon as Jack opened the bathroom door, Brandy rushed toward him and wrapped her arms around him. "I was afraid you wouldn't come!"

"Keep your voice down. Of course we came. I told you I would protect you." He patted her on the back to calm her, then said, "Start from the beginning. Tell me everything."

Between sobs, Brandy told Jack and Laura what she had endured. Jack knew that her physical injuries were not life-threatening, but emotionally, she would have nightmares for years to come. "Why didn't you call me as soon as Clive contacted you?" he asked.

"It was late when he called for me to meet him. He told me to hurry because he had some friends coming over after. I thought I would only be an hour and was going to call you when I left."

Jack nodded. "And it was Klaus who stole the money from your purse?"

"Yes. I should also have an ounce of blow. I don't know if he took that, as well."

"Go into the room and get your money back."

As soon as Brandy left the bathroom, Laura whispered, "Are you sure you should let her do that? We could already go down for assault. Armed robbery makes it worse."

"It's her money."

"Tell that to a judge. Even if we weren't convicted, we'd lose our jobs. Let's take Brandy and leave."

"A real pimp wouldn't go yet. He'd have his rep' to consider. He'd want to scare these guys so badly that not only wouldn't they ever do it again, but they would also be too afraid to retaliate. Right now, Klaus needs an attitude adjustment. If these assholes ever figure out who we really are, they'll kill her. Besides, maybe I can shake Clive up enough to learn something. I'll go back in and see if I can remember the lines from all the tough-guy movies I've ever seen."

"Oh, man. Don't you think he's already shook up —" Laura fell silent as Brandy returned to the bathroom with a fistful of money and her purse.

"You two stay in here," ordered Jack loudly. "This could get messy."

Jack returned to the room and ripped the pillowcases off Clive's and Liam's heads, then gestured at them with the shotgun. "Do either of you two dumb fucks know what an Italian silencer is?"

They both shook their heads.

"It's a way to muffle noise," said Jack. "You're in for a special treat because you've got the best view of Act One of three acts. Watch this," he said as he knelt behind Klaus. "The only bad part is cleaning the barrel after."

Klaus lurched and tried to squeeze his ass tight when Jack slowly pushed the tip of the shotgun barrel between the cheeks.

The looks on Clive's and Liam's faces were ones of absolute horror. Klaus's head jerked and he gave a pitiful moan from inside the pillowcase. Any thoughts he had of being defiant had evaporated.

"I can't believe what you did to her," said Jack angrily. "Eye swollen shut, burns on her ass ... she won't be able to work for at least a month!"

Klaus cried out in response, *"Mein Gott, mein Gott!"*

"Too late to be praying to some god," said Jack. "Besides, I'm an atheist." He gave Clive a hard look. "How about you? Do you believe in some god? Wanna meet him?"

Clive shook his head as panic clouded his ability to speak. He stared at Liam, who was babbling and pleading for his life.

"Hey, big nuts, quit staring at the bawl-baby and watch." With that, Jack locked eyes with Clive's once more.

Clive's jaw twitched, but no words came out. He panted twice, then said, "Please, I can make all this up to you. How about I give you a half-pound of coke? High quality ... totally uncut."

Jack did not want to appear anxious. He was hoping to get a lead on the fake passports, but knew he couldn't bring up that topic himself. He looked at Clive and hesitated, then ripped the pillowcase off of Klaus's head. "What do you think? Should I take him up on his offer?"

Klaus coughed and sputtered, blood drooling out of his mouth, as Jack turned back to Clive. "What makes you think I'd be interested in coke?"

"How about diamonds? Full carats!" Clive offered.

Diamonds? Didn't expect that. Probably glass or zircons. "You've been watching too much television. Who the fuck do you think I am? Some goof who walks around with gold chains and eighteen-carat fucking diamonds stuck in his ear? Yeah, cops, here I am. Come and bust me."

Clive spoke rapidly, stumbling over his words. "Sorry, I ... I'm sorry. I didn't mean it that way. I can see you got more class than that."

"You're damn right I do. A lot more class than to be bought off with a half-pound of blow. What else can you offer?"

"Coke or diamonds is all I can get. How about I make it a full pound?"

It wasn't the answer Jack was hoping for, but he knew it would get him in the door. "How long will it take to get it?" he asked.

"I delivered it to these guys this morning. I can go get it. Forty minutes there and forty minutes back."

"What makes you think they still have it?"

"Oh, they got it all right," replied Clive, sounding relieved that Jack appeared interested. "If you wait here, I'll be back in an hour and a half."

"Like fuck you will. If you think I'm letting you go on your own, think again!"

Klaus looked at Clive and mumbled, "Don't take 'im there. There has to be another way."

Jack pointed the barrel of the shotgun at Klaus's face and said, "Shut the fuck up! When I want your opinion, I'll politely ask for it."

"Please," Clive said. "Let me make a phone call and maybe I can get them to deliver it."

"Not a chance," Jack replied. "No phone calls. I'm not setting myself up to be whacked or to walk into some ambush. Take me to them, and no tipoffs that we're coming!"

Clive looked at Klaus, who shook his head. "Do we have a choice?" snapped Clive in response. He then looked at Jack. "I'll do whatever you want."

"Okay, I'll have a word with the girls. Same as before — don't move and don't talk!"

Jack passed the shotgun to Laura and then blindfolded the men again, before picking up their pants and going through the pockets. He found their driver's licences. One licence had been issued in Germany to Klaus Eichel, and the other two were Canadian licences, issued to Clive Dempsey and Liam Quinn respectively.

Laura stood guard while Jack went into the bathroom and closed the door.

A call to the telecommunications centre said there was nothing on Klaus in Canada, but Liam was listed as being of interest to the Major Crimes Unit in regard to several armed robberies. Jack did not bother with Clive's name, as he already knew he had a previous charge for drug trafficking that had been dismissed in court.

Jack opened the door and motioned for Laura to return so they could confer. After telling her in a whisper about Liam's criminal background, he said, "I'm going to get Clive to take me to the guys he delivered the coke to. If we took all three of them, these guys we're meeting would likely get the drop on us."

"You want me to stay here with Klaus and Liam?" Laura asked.

"Yes. Clive's a wimp so I can handle him okay." He gave a half-smile. "Although a lot of guys get wimpy when you kick 'em in the nuts."

"That was nothing compared to what you did to Klaus," said Laura, sounding defensive. "If anyone is wimpy, it should be him."

"Yeah, Klaus." Jack's tone was serious. "Watch that guy — and not just for breathing difficulties. He's more than a sadist. He's evil."

"I know," agreed Laura. "I can see it in his eyes."

"Liam won't be a problem. He shit himself earlier and is still babbling."

"What if Clive sets you up? He may be bullshitting about the coke."

"I don't think he is. That was his reason for going to Mexico. I'm sure there's a lot more than a pound at the stash, which is why Klaus doesn't want me to know where it is. If things turn ugly, Klaus and Liam can be used as bargaining chips."

"Bargaining chips," repeated Laura. "That's a polite term for kidnapping."

"Kidnapping? Nah, I simply think of it as being a little slow at reading them their rights. As far as my safety goes, they only know I have a shotgun. It might be better if Clive doesn't think I'm armed when he takes me. Whoever I'm meeting will be more inclined to talk first rather than shoot first. I want you to do a little scenario out there about your being worried about my safety."

"I *am* worried about your safety," replied Laura seriously.

"Good, you won't have to pretend." Jack then eyed Brandy and said, "I'd like an extra pair of eyes to help Laura watch these guys while I'm gone. Are you okay to stay? Or do you think you should get to a hospital?"

"I'd like a doctor to check out my burns, but I'm okay for now," replied Brandy. "I would like to have a shower, though."

"Make it quick," said Jack.

Brandy frowned, then said, "I hope I don't get scars or something. I mean, how would I explain that if I was to get married?"

Jack and Laura didn't reply and returned to the main room. Jack tore off the blindfolds again. He then prodded Clive in the ribs with his foot while holding their driver's licences in one hand and the shotgun in the other. "You, big nuts … or I guess your name is Clive," he said, glancing at the driver's licences. "Do you guys have wheels at the hotel?"

"Klaus and I do," Clive answered. "Liam came with Klaus."

Laura looked at Jack. "I'm worried about you taking off with this jerk and leaving me the gun. What if he —"

"I don't need a gun to handle this little hemorrhoid," said Jack gruffly. "We'll go in his car and he'll drive. You'll need the blaster to cover these other two turds. If I get held hostage, flip a coin and kill one of them, then exchange me with the other guy."

"Somebody might hear the gunshot," Laura cautioned.

"Not if you shove the barrel far enough up their asses. It will muffle the sound."

Klaus and Liam looked at each other as they thought of their chances with a coin toss.

"One more thing for you guys to know." Jack smiled grimly. "I texted your names and addresses to a good friend of mine. He's not as nice as I am. Clive and Liam, I see you each have a P.O. box for an address. Klaus, your address is in Germany. It doesn't matter where you guys live. If anything happens to me, you'll be tracked down." He looked at Clive. "Get dressed. You're taking me for a drive."

Once Clive was dressed and they were about to leave, Jack looked at Laura and said, "While you're waiting, clean your prints from the room. If you don't hear from me within an hour, kill 'em both and fuck off."

"Oh, God!" Liam cried. "Please … an hour…. What if that's not enough?"

"No talkin," Jack snarled.

Chapter Six

Outside in the hotel parking lot, Jack had Clive give him the keys to his car and asked, "Which one is it?"

"Over there." Clive pointed. "The white Beamer."

Once in the car, Jack returned the keys to Clive and told him to drive.

"Where we going?" asked Jack.

"They live on an acreage out in Fort Langley."

"They?"

"Klaus and two of his buddies rent the place."

"And you're sure they'll still have a pound?"

"I delivered it to them this morning. I'm pretty sure they still got it."

"Pretty sure?" said Jack harshly.

"Well, uh, I mean, I mean … there's always other stuff. I know they got lots of jewellery."

"I told you how I feel about wearing that," replied Jack. "Do they have anything else I might be interested in?"

"Not really, unless you're interested in some fake IDs."

"You mean driver's licences?"

"No, I'm talking passports."

"Passports? Yeah, right." Jack ladled on the sarcasm. "A buddy of mine could sure use one, but these days you'd never be able to cross a border with a fake passport."

"These aren't fake," Clive protested. "They're real. I've, uh, got … know people using them. Your friend would have to pretend to be from Romania, but everything about the passport itself is authentic."

"How the hell did they end up with Romanian passports? If they robbed some tourists, the passports will light up the customs' computer like the Vegas strip."

"They didn't take them from anyone using them. They're basically blank. These guys have a connection. All they need is a passport photo to make one up."

"Really? That sounds interesting. If you're giving me the straight goods, I'd like to get one for myself, as well as my friend."

"I'll ask them," Clive said.

"How well do you know these guys where we're going?"

"I met Klaus a while back at a nightclub. He introduced me to his two friends later. Him I know really well, but the other two are a little more standoffish."

Jack knew he couldn't ask many more questions without arousing suspicion. The rest of the trip was relatively quiet, but the closer they got to their destination, the more jittery Clive became.

After driving down some back-country roads, they arrived at a property surrounded by a high, chain-link fence. Jack hadn't seen a sign to indicate what road they were on, but texted a rough location to Laura when Clive parked in front of an electric gate and pushed the intercom button. Eventually a sleepy voice said, "Who's there?"

"Clive. I gotta talk to you. It's urgent."

The gate opened and they drove down a driveway lined on both sides by large cedar trees. Motion-sensor lights illuminated the roadway, and Jack saw a birdhouse on a tree that faced down the driveway. *Closed-circuit television camera? What have I gotten into?* The 9mm pistol tucked in the back of his belt usually felt uncomfortable, but not now.

They arrived in a yard illuminated with floodlights and parked in front of a modest, ranch-style house. Nearby was a storage building with a large sliding door on the front. Two men came out of the house and approached them as Clive turned off the ignition.

"You sure these are the only two guys here?" asked Jack. "I really hate surprises."

"I think so, but ... uh, they're heavy-duty and won't like it that I brought you along. Better just let me do the talking."

As soon as they stepped out of the car, one of the men gestured with his thumb at Jack. "Who the fuck is this?" he asked Clive. He had a French accent, Jack noticed.

"It's okay, Anton. He, uh, his name is Jack." Clive paused, then glanced at the other man. "Hey, Bojan. Sorry to wake you guys up, but I, uh, was ..." He paused again and looked at Jack nervously. "Well, me and Klaus and Liam were sort of being rough with one of this guy's, uh, lady friends. To compensate for hurting her I agreed to give him a pound of coke."

"You brought a pimp here ... to this place," said Anton. His voice was cold and ominous.

He whispered something to Bojan, who looked at Clive and asked, "Did you search him?"

"Yes, of course," Clive lied. "He's not packing. I know he's cool."

"But you brought him here," Bojan said, the anger in his voice almost palpable.

"I, uh, made him keep his head down below the dash, so he doesn't know where he is," responded Clive with another nervous glance at Jack.

Jack nodded, pretending to agree. *Actually, I don't really know where I am.*

"Uh, but, there's a problem," said Clive.

"I'll say there's a problem." Bojan's tone was menacing.

"No, I mean the reason I agreed to bring him," Clive continued. "He … a couple of his ladies are holding Klaus and Liam in a hotel room until he gets the pound."

"Holding Klaus?" Anton said incredulously. "What are you talking about?"

With a nod toward Jack, Clive said, "He burst into the room and smacked Klaus in the face with a shotgun and got the drop on us. Right now, Klaus and Liam are both naked, tied up and blindfolded. His ladies are guarding them with a shotgun."

Anton looked at Jack in amazement, then yelled, "Your whores are holding my friend Klaus with a fucking shotgun and you have the balls to come here?"

"Only holding them as collateral until I get my pound," replied Jack calmly. "I am not looking to hurt them. Once I'm compensated, everyone can be on their way."

Anton stepped forward and scrutinized Jack's face closely. "Everyone wait. I'll be right back."

A few minutes passed with Bojan staring silently at Clive while Jack pretended to walk around and nonchalantly admire Clive's car. In reality, he wanted to use the car for protection if Anton returned with a gun and the intent to kill him.

Eventually Anton returned empty-handed and gave a subtle shake of his head at Bojan, then slammed Clive in the chest with both hands and watched him stumble backward.

"What the —"

"You were told never to bring anyone here!" Anton shouted at Clive.

"What choice did I have?" whined Clive. "I'm saving Klaus's life. Liam's too. You know we'll pay it back."

"You're a fucking idiot!" retorted Anton. "So is Klaus!"

As Clive stood meekly without responding, Jack glanced at his watch and said, "Listen, boys, I don't have all night. If I don't make a phone call soon, some poor maid is going to have a hell of a mess to clean up."

Bojan looked at Anton, then said, "You better call your brother."

Anton nodded, then took a phone out of his pocket and walked a short distance away to make the call. As he did, Clive took the opportunity to whisper to Jack, "Be calm. Everything will be okay. They're pissed off, but really, I don't see what the big deal is."

Jack looked at the enraged faces of Anton and Bojan. *Something's a big deal. A really big deal.*

Chapter Seven

It was approaching one o'clock in the afternoon in Paris, and Kerin was becoming more anxious as he sat on a bench with Roche in the park. Roche had received a call saying that the Ringmaster would arrive at twelve-thirty, but there had been no calls since then to explain the delay.

Kerin was aware that the sunshine had brought office workers into the park to stroll around during their lunch break, but now the park was clearing out, leaving his cover team more exposed. "This is ridiculous," he complained. "We've been here for almost two hours. Where is he?"

Roche did not tell Kerin that the delay was for counter-surveillance. Instead, he said, "You're right. I will check with the Ringmaster. Wait one moment and —" He looked startled as one of his phones vibrated. "My emergency phone," he muttered as he fished it out of his pocket. "From … my brother in Canada."

Canada? Kerin listened as Roche spoke to his brother. He saw a look of concern cross Roche's face and heard the name *Clive Dempsey* before Roche hung up.

"Everything okay?" Kerin asked.

Roche shook his head. "If you become a juggler for our organization, what would you do if one of the people who work for you brought a stranger to the stash house at quarter-to-four in the morning, wanting to get a pound of cocaine?"

"Cocaine?" Kerin looked puzzled.

"I know, I know," replied Roche. "It is a new commodity that I chose to venture into on my own. A decision I may come to regret. But back to the question, what would you do? Especially when the person had been warned never to tell anyone about it."

"Is this happening in Canada right now?"

Roche nodded.

"I … I'm not sure," Kerin stammered, not wanting to promote murder but at the same time not wanting to appear weak and hinder his chance of being accepted.

"You're not sure?"

"Without knowing the full circumstances," Kerin explained. "An unknown person … perhaps the Ringmaster should be consulted before any drastic action is taken. Time may be needed to find out who he is."

"Time is not an option they have. Still, I agree that the Ringmaster should be consulted."

"In Canada …," said Kerin, becoming increasingly worried as the possibility of a more serious concern entered his mind. "I know the police there are allowed to portray themselves as criminals. Are you afraid that the person he brought is police?"

"No, no, don't worry." Roche smiled. "The stranger is only a pimp. Quite ... dispensable." He got to his feet. "I'll be back in ten minutes," he said, then left while thumbing his phone.

* * *

The Ringmaster continued to watch. *Who was Roche talking to? Kerin appears nervous ... looking across the park. The man on the far side in a blue windbreaker is watching him. Kerin is tapping his watch....*

The Ringmaster studied the man in the windbreaker. *A droopy moustache, and it's twitching. Looks like a tarantula dancing on his lip,* mused the Ringmaster before refocusing on Kerin. *He's getting up....*

* * *

Kerin stepped into the public washroom. He glanced under the cubicle doors and saw that he was alone. Roche had told him that he was not to make any phone calls before meeting the Ringmaster, but he took out his phone and called his boss, Yves Charbonneau, to quickly outline what was happening in Canada.

"I didn't think they were involved with drugs," Yves said.

"Roche said it's a venture he got into on his own. Forget the drugs. Two men in Canada might be murdered!"

"Who cares if two criminals in Canada are murdered? Focus on what you are doing."

"Criminals or not, shouldn't we try to stop it? How will it look in court if I am questioned and say we did nothing to prevent it?"

"Yeah, yeah, okay," grumbled Yves. "I'm having lunch with a friend at the moment. When I return to the office I will contact Interpol. It's not like anyone could stop it, but you're right, it will look better if we appear to make an effort."

* * *

The Ringmaster answered Roche's call and listened as he explained the situation in Canada, then asked, "Are you sure the man with Clive is a pimp?"

"Yes. Klaus, Clive, and Liam were abusing the whore when the pimp showed up with another whore and beat Klaus with a shotgun."

"Klaus," the Ringmaster muttered. "I shouldn't be surprised. I'm glad the pimp beat him. Why was he with the other two?"

"The whore was a present for Liam. He is getting married next week and Klaus thought it would promote a better relationship by —"

"Don't give me that shit. Klaus is an ass. The whore was for him as much as anyone. I know what he likes to do to women."

"So what should I tell Anton to do?"

"I can't believe the timing," the Ringmaster grumbled. "Years spent tracking down a rumour … then finding out the rumour was true."

"The ship sales from Vancouver in three weeks," Roche said.

"You needn't remind me. I've been counting the days …
and now this. What if the pimp is caught by the police and
tells them about the drugs? Or worse yet, decides to gather
a few friends and come back and steal everything? For my
Pierrot to fall into the hands of a pimp is too disgusting to
contemplate. What will he do? Hang it in some brothel?"

"The painting's well hidden," said Roche.

"Do you trust Anton not to talk under torture? Look
what the pimp did to Klaus."

Roche didn't respond. The idea of his brother being
tortured was too horrific to imagine.

"Your silence answers that," said the Ringmaster. "I'm
not particularly fond of pimps, let alone someone stupid
enough to bring him there. Would Liam be a problem if
Clive was permanently removed?"

"No."

"Then let Liam live, but tell Anton to dispose of Clive
and the pimp immediately."

"There could be an investigation," warned Roche.

"I doubt a missing pimp will cause the police to do
anything … but no matter, tell them to hide the bodies
and leave Clive's car parked at an airport or a train station. If the police do look into their disappearances, it will
throw them off-track. Once my Pierrot is onboard ship,
tell Anton it is time for them to return to Europe."

"He will be pleased. I know he is homesick."

"Good. Once you receive confirmation that Liam and
the pimp have been taken care of, ensure he disposes of
the phone, which is what I will be doing when we are
done talking."

"Naturally, but …"

"But what?"

"Will we abandon North America completely?"

The Ringmaster smiled. "I will soon retire. That is a decision which will be left up to you or one of the other jugglers."

"You have hinted at retirement before, but I did not realize your decision was imminent," said Roche in surprise.

"I've made enough," replied the Ringmaster. "Besides, I am becoming bored. It is time to move on."

"Who were you thinking of to —"

"I have given the matter much thought. Although I am inclined to think it should be you who replaces me, it is important that the other three receive a fair voice. I am not counting your brother, as he is too new."

"By fair voice?"

"I want there to be harmony in the decision. If there are any objections or reasons to oppose you, it needs to be discussed. That is better than someone sticking a knife in your back later."

"When will this take place?"

"Our Italian juggler happens to be in Germany at the moment meeting with our man there. Tomorrow we will have a meeting in Frankfurt to give everyone time to think about it and then come to a final decision in a month or so."

"I am truly grateful that you favour me to take over."

The Ringmaster focused the binoculars on Roche's face. "Good. The day I hang the Pierrot in my gallery will be the day I step aside." The concern was evident on Roche's face. The task of handling the situation in Canada was now of utmost importance to him, as well.

"Are you ready to meet Kerin?" asked Roche, anxious to get matters taken care of.

"I have some concern in that regard. Did you say anything to him about your call from Canada?"

"I mentioned that someone had brought a stranger to our stash house and asked him what he would do about it if he were the juggler."

"And his response?"

Roche chuckled. "At first he was worried that it might be a cop. I assured him it was only a pimp."

"And why would he worry if it was a cop? Especially in Canada?"

Roche was silent as he thought about it.

The Ringmaster continued, "There is more. After you left, Kerin may have signalled to a man in the park."

"What man?" Roche looked cautiously around.

"He is wearing a blue windbreaker and has a droopy moustache. Kerin made eye contact with him and then tapped his watch and opened his hand twice."

"I told him I would be back in ten minutes," said Roche sombrely.

"He then went to the public washroom for a few minutes. Nobody went in with him, but he may have used his phone. I also think you are being followed, although I am not sure."

"My God! I trusted him."

"I warned you that your trust in him seemed rushed."

"I can't believe it. If this is true …"

"Don't worry about it. This is one of the reasons we take the precautions we do."

"What should I do?" asked Roche.

"I want to confirm my suspicions. Tell him our people in Canada have discovered that the pimp really is an *agent provocateur*. Then say you are to meet me in a couple of minutes at the café across the street to discuss whether they should both be disposed of. Tell Kerin to wait where he is, then go to the café."

Roche glanced around again, taking note of the people he saw, then said, "If what you suspect is happening, should the two men in Canada be killed?"

"It is of more concern to me if the pimp lives. He may return with others and find the stash before we can move it. I will sleep better knowing they are dead."

"And the two whores the pimp has guarding Klaus and Liam?"

"What can they do? At best, tell the police they are whores who kidnapped and beat two people ... or as it will turn out, more likely murdered the two people they held captive. I am fed up with Klaus and don't care what happens to him. Either way, the whores aren't going to tell the police about it."

"And the situation here?" asked Roche. "If Kerin is working for the police ... or with the recent approval of an *agent provocateur,* perhaps he is a cop."

"His concern that the pimp in Canada could be an undercover agent would tell me the guy likely is. An informant wouldn't care that much about what is happening in Canada." The Ringmaster paused. "The French police have never been allowed to use such measures before. So how would you know? If they set Kerin up to meet you, they would have had to start prior to receiving their new powers. This may be an opportunity to persuade the French justice system that their new investigative tool should be taken away. I will deal with him."

"You will deal with him yourself? Now?"

The Ringmaster laughed. "Why not? It will be fun. Like a magician doing slight of hand, all eyes will be on you and not where they should be. For me, I will treat it like the last performance I give ... before taking my final bow and leaving the stage."

Roche smiled. "And the stage may soon be in my hands."

"Precisely. If my suspicions are true and things go as I suspect, meet me tonight in Frankfurt. If you are detained by the police, contact me when you are free or through your lawyer and we will set another time."

Roche glanced around the park yet again. Most people had left. Who was staying? A couple walking a dog seemed legitimate ... but a man and a woman staring at a flower bed seemed to be taking far too long to enjoy the beauty, and they did not appear particularly fond of each other. Another man was taking an inordinate amount of time to tie his shoe. *The Ringmaster has a sharp eye....*

"If you are right, then I likely will be arrested," said Roche, sounding matter-of-fact. "I have made certain statements to him, including today."

"Arrested on what evidence?" replied the Ringmaster. "Especially if there is no witness to testify against you. Telling fairy tales to impress someone you thought was a gangster may have been childish, but it is hardly grounds to convict you of anything. You would be released in time for supper."

"I suppose you're right," Roche allowed.

"Tell Anton to tidy up the loose ends in Canada, then talk to Kerin and tell him what I told you to say. If my suspicions are right, I am certain I will see some activity to confirm."

Roche hung up and called Anton, giving him the order to kill Clive and the pimp.

"And what about Klaus and Liam?" asked Anton.

"If you can think of a way to save them, fine. If not, don't worry about it."

Upon hanging up, Roche walked over and stood before Kerin, who was sitting on the bench.

"Did you speak with the Ringmaster?" asked Kerin.

"Yes, but I also spoke to our people in Canada. They grabbed who they thought was a pimp and searched him. They found a badge."

"He's a police officer!" exclaimed Kerin.

"I'm meeting the Ringmaster in the café across the street in a few minutes to talk about it face to face. I'm certain I'll be told to have our men kill him and the idiot who brought him there."

"Are you sure that's wise?" asked Kerin. "Other officers could be watching him."

"They don't think the cop has had any way to tell anyone where he is. That's why I'm sure the Ringmaster will order it done immediately." He smiled and put his hand on Kerin's shoulder. "It's okay, my friend. Wait here while I go to the café. With what is going on, I don't know if the Ringmaster will still want to see you today."

Roche had barely turned to walk to the café when Kerin headed for the public washrooms again. He knew he didn't have much time. On his way he texted a short message to the surveillance team:

RF meeting Ring in café across from park. My meet may be put off.

With the four members of the surveillance team who were on foot, Kerin knew it would look better if a couple of them were already in the café when Roche arrived. As he neared the washrooms, he glanced back and was pleased to see two of the team enter the café before Roche. The other two took up positions on the sidewalk.

As he made his way around to the front of the washrooms, any elation he had at the prospect of meeting the Ringmaster was gone. A police officer's life was at stake and he had a sickening feeling that there wouldn't be enough time to save him.

Chapter Eight

Jack saw Clive swallow nervously as they leaned against the front of the car. Anton had told them to wait as he was expecting a call back.

Anton and Bojan stood a short distance away with their arms folded across their chests, watching. Tension was high, and the silence made every minute seem like ten.

Jack was conscious of the floodlight above his head, but under the situation he did not see much choice. As he waited, he noticed a close-circuit television camera mounted on the corner of the house and another one on the outbuilding. Finally, he saw Anton answer his phone and speak briefly, before hanging up and whispering to Bojan.

"So what's the story, guys?" Jack asked.

Anton glared at Jack. "I've been told to give you what you ask for, but once it is in your hands, Klaus and Liam must be released before you go."

"I don't like that idea," Jack said. "There's no reason for me to hold the two of them once I'm away from here. I'll let them go then."

"Also no reason for you not to kill them," said Bojan.

"That is the only way we can do it," added Anton. He pointed his finger at Clive. "You are responsible for this and will pay us back before the day is over!"

"Not a problem," Clive said. "My money is in a safety deposit box. I'll get it as soon as the bank opens."

Anton nodded, then turned his attention to Jack. "Under the circumstances, given what they did to your lady, we have no quarrel with you."

"Okay, but I want to see the coke in my hand before they're released," said Jack.

"That is not a problem. You will see that it is high quality. Wait here and I will get it."

Anton went to the outbuilding, entering through a side door, and flicked on the lights. A few minutes later he beckoned for them to come inside.

Jack entered and saw that the building was being used as a workshop. There was a table saw in the room, along with piles of lumber and partially built pieces of furniture. Some of the furniture was clamped for gluing and resting on sawhorses. Another piece of furniture on a workbench was wrapped in bubble wrap.

An open door at the far end of the workspace led into another room, and Jack caught a glimpse of a band saw and another workbench, with tools hanging on the wall above it.

"Over there," said Anton, pointing to a set of weigh scales on the nearby bench. On the scales was a clear plastic bag containing a brick of white powder. "Check it out, it's yours."

Jack checked the weight. It was slightly more than a pound. Anton had broken a kilo in two and was not concerned that he was offering more than had been bargained for. He picked up the bag and examined it. "Looks good," he said. "The weight is a little over."

"Consider it a tip to get you the hell out of here and never come back," replied Anton. "First, though, call your women and tell them to release my guys and tell Klaus to call me as soon as they're free."

* * *

It was quarter after four when Laura took the call from Jack. When he explained the situation, she freed Klaus and Liam and, still holding the shotgun on them, allowed them to get dressed.

"Now get out," she said coldly.

Klaus hesitated and glared back at Laura, until she pointed the shotgun at his face. Then he turned and, holding his jaw and mouth with one hand, followed Liam out the door. Once in the hotel parking lot he turned to Liam and mumbled, "You able to drive?"

Liam glanced nervously back at the hotel. "Yeah, that kind of sobered me up."

Klaus tossed his car keys to Liam, and once inside the car, with his free hand he retrieved a pistol he had hidden under the dash.

"Want to go back and do the whores?" asked Liam.

Klaus glanced up at the hotel, then down at his pistol as he rethought his actions. *Go up against two whores waiting in a room with a shotgun ... maybe not such a good idea. Besides, it's not them I want.* He took his hand away from his mouth and looked at the blood on his fingers. "No, not the whores. I want the fucker who did this to me. Speaking of which, I better phone my friends."

* * *

Anton answered the call from Klaus and walked toward the end of the workshop so he could talk without being overheard. "You free?" he asked.

"Yeah, Liam and me are driving away from the hotel," said Klaus, "but the fucking pimp ... I'm sure he broke my jaw. I'm in a lot of pain. Also busted most of my teeth and my lips are all cut up. I'm spittin' blood everywhere."

"Get Liam to take you to a hospital."

"What about the pimp?"

"Orders are for me to do him and Clive as soon as I hang up."

"Wish you could keep the pimp alive until I get there," Klaus said. "Can't you gut-shoot him or something?"

"I'll see what I can do."

"As soon as I'm out of Emergency, I'll take Liam home and be right over," Klaus said. "If the pimp's still alive, I'm going to use every tool we got in the shop on him."

Anton hung up and looked at Jack and smiled, then motioned with his finger for Clive to approach him. "I need to tell you exactly how you will repay us."

Clive had taken a few steps forward when Anton raised a .32-calibre pistol and pointed it directly at his face. "You will pay with your life," said Anton calmly.

Clive's mouth opened to scream as Anton pulled the trigger.

The bullet entered Clive's face beside his nose before ricocheting around inside his skull, turning his brain to mush. He was dead before his body hit the floor.

Chapter Nine

Roche saw the man and long-haired woman hurry into the café ahead of him. Earlier he had spotted them strolling around the park and ostensibly admiring every flower bed they came to. Another man he had seen in the park was a short distance away staring at a display case in a nearby store window.

Roche silently cursed himself for having been fooled by Kerin, then entered the café and took a seat.

* * *

Kerin entered the public washroom and a peek under the stalls told him he was alone. This time he made his call direct to dispatch and quickly explained the problem. He tapped his foot nervously as he waited while dispatch placed an urgent call to Interpol.

The feel of cold metal behind his ear told him he was no longer alone. He froze as a Latex-gloved hand reached for his phone. He released his grip on the phone and slowly turned around, facing the muzzle of a pistol.

The sound of police radios and voices from dispatch could be heard over the phone, then a dispatcher said, "We've connected with Interpol in Canada. They want to speak to you directly."

For a brief moment Kerin clung to the hope that he was only being robbed, but that hope evaporated when his eyes shifted from the pistol to a watch with a gold-and-silver band being dangled in front of him.

Kerin knew he was going to die as he stared at the smiling face taunting him from behind the watch.

"Are you there?" came the dispatcher's voice over the phone.

"*You're* the Ringmaster!" Kerin yelled. "It's —"

He was interrupted by the gunshot. Several urgent requests from the dispatcher for him to respond went unanswered.

* * *

In the café across from the park, Roche watched the couple who had entered shortly before he did. The woman flicked her long hair out of the way and placed her hand over her ear. She appeared to be listening intently. Her face registered panic, and a comment she made to her companion sent them both running from the café. Two men who'd been outside on the sidewalk joined them as they raced to the park.

Roche waited a moment, then went to the doorway to look. At the park near the washrooms he heard a woman's screams. Another couple who had been walking a dog stood staring at the commotion. Other people bolted from parked cars and ran toward the washrooms.

Roche apologized to the waitress and told her to cancel the tea he'd ordered. Then he left.

Chapter Ten

Constable Jane Martin, on duty at the Interpol office in Ottawa, tried to calm the panic rising in her throat when she received the information from Paris that an undercover police officer in Canada was about to be murdered. Given the time of the call, she deduced that British Columbia was the most likely location. Her line to the dispatch office in Paris was still open, but she was already typing two names into the Canadian Police Information Computer as she waited to be connected with the officer who'd made the original report.

The name *Anton Roche* on CPIC did not yield a response, but *Clive Dempsey* popped up as being of interest to Corporal Jack Taggart in the Intelligence Unit in Vancouver. "Listen," Jane said, "I've got a lead on the name Dempsey. Does your officer know if —"

"We think someone shot our agent!" screamed the French dispatcher in heavily accented English. She then yelled in French to someone in the background. "I don't know … I don't know! I heard the shot. He's not answering.

He yelled, *the Ringmaster!* Then I heard … yes, it sounded like a shot. I'm certain it was. The line is dead now."

Seconds later Constable Martin called the telecommunications centre in Vancouver. They were unaware of any undercover operation taking place, but had her wait while they called Corporal Jack Taggart, first on the air and then at home.

Jane's heart sank when the dispatcher said, "His wife was reluctant to say much, but she did say he was called out to work about 1:30 a.m. I tried his cell but it went to voice mail. I'm calling his boss, Staff-Sergeant Rose Wood. I'll give her your number, as well."

* * *

Natasha felt uneasy after the call from someone purporting to be from the telecommunications centre. *A certain urgency in the caller's voice. Then again, with Jack, there always seems to be an urgency.*

When she received a call from Rose moments later, she was really worried. Rose would not be involved at this time of the night unless something serious was going on.

She got out of bed and went into Mike and Steve's room and gave each of her sons a kiss on the cheek. She thought about trying to call Jack herself, but if he was in an undercover situation it might not be appreciated. *Besides, Rose would have already tried.*

She went back to bed and turned on the light to try to read. She knew it would be another long night as she clung to the hope of what he had once told her: that he was very good at what he did. He said if he had to rewire a lamp he would probably kill himself, but undercover was his forte.

Natasha believed him. She had to. To think otherwise was unbearable.

* * *

Laura felt relieved when her phone rang. Now that Klaus and Liam had left, she was expecting Jack to call and say he was on his way back, but the call display told her it was Rose.

Oh, man. Why is she up? Laura took a deep breath and slowly exhaled as she answered.

"Laura, are you working?" Rose asked immediately.

"Yes. We got called out unexpectedly."

"So you're with Jack?"

"Not at the moment," Laura said as she eyed Brandy, who was walking around the hotel room with one high-heeled shoe in her hand as she searched for the other one.

"Can we talk? Are you with someone?" Rose asked.

"Yes, but go ahead."

"What's my middle name?"

"Alice," replied Laura. "I'm with a source, not with any bad guys."

"I'm trying to reach Jack. I called Natasha, who said he got called out and that she heard him call you. I tried his cell but he didn't answer. Are you working undercover?"

"Yes, we're in the middle of a UC, but I spoke to him a few minutes ago," Laura replied as her gaze took in the bloody pillow case that had been on Klaus's head. "He's probably with someone and doesn't want to answer. I'm expecting to hear from him any minute. Do you want me to have him call you?"

"Is he with Clive Dempsey?" Rose asked tersely.

Oh, man. How did she know that? "Yes."

"I got a call from Interpol via France," Rose said. "A French undercover operative heard an order directing someone in Canada to kill Clive Dempsey and an undercover police officer with him. It sounds like they searched Jack and found his badge."

"Oh, no ... no," Laura moaned, bile rising in her throat as she fought her panic.

"Focus!" Rose demanded. "Can you contact them? Do you know where they are, who they went to see?"

"I don't know who they went to meet or exactly where he is." Laura struggled to maintain her professionalism. "He's near Fort Langley. He texted me rough coordinates. He's between 232nd and 264th streets and somewhere north of the Number One, but south of River Road."

"That covers a lot of area. Where are you?"

"Still in the city ... at the Emerald Hotel. Jack left with Dempsey almost two hours ago. Some other bad guys were here too, but they, uh, left a couple of minutes ago. I'm not even sure if they're out of the hotel parking lot yet. I was expecting Jack to call again any minute."

"That may not be happening," Rose said more to herself than Laura.

"Don't say that! I ... I need to concentrate." Laura desperately tried to come up with an idea. "What else do the French have for us to go on? Is there some way you could find out who Dempsey was taking Jack to meet? Anything at all that would help?"

"No. The French telecom's centre was receiving the information through a call from their operative a few minutes ago. Then their dispatch —"

"Was receiving?" Laura asked. "What do you mean?"

"As the operative was talking, dispatch heard what sounded like a gunshot at close range. No word from their man since then."

"Oh, my God." Laura looked at her phone like it wasn't real, then put it back to her ear. She felt like she wanted to vomit and tears clouded her vision.

"They've got a cover team checking now to … hang on. Gotta put you on hold. Incoming call."

Laura swallowed a couple of times to clear the bile in her throat and sat in stunned silence until Rose came back on line. "It's confirmed," she said. "The French officer was shot in the head by an unidentified person. They have a rough description of the man who did it, but so far there've been no arrests."

Laura fought back the tears, not knowing what to say.

"Can your source help us?" Rose asked.

"No."

"Then get clear and call me."

"I'll call in a couple of minutes," Laura said. As soon as she hung up, she dialled Jack and as the phone rang, she looked at Brandy. "Get a move on! We're outta here!"

"I'm ready. Where we going?" Brandy asked. "What's going on?"

Laura's call went to voice message. She thought of Klaus as her mind filled with rage. "What's going on is I'm going to the nearest emergency room."

"I don't need to," Brandy said. "They worked me over pretty good, but I want to go home and —"

"It's not for you." Laura's tone was harsh. "I'll drop you off a block or two away as soon as it's safe. You can call a cab."

"Oh, you're going to follow Klaus away from the hospital," Brandy said.

I don't have time to follow him, Laura thought, tucking the shotgun under her jacket. Immediate persuasion would be needed. *When I find him, he'll phone and beg for Jack's life as if it was his own … if I'm not too late.*

Chapter Eleven

When Anton shot Clive, Jack dropped the bag of cocaine and ducked behind the table saw.

Anton stepped over Clive's body as he approached and waved his .32 Beretta back and forth, pointing it at each side of the saw. "Come out, come out, wherever you are!" He exchanged a grin with Bojan.

"Want to play games?" Jack said. "Well, guess what, asshole, my gun is bigger than yours."

Neither Anton nor Bojan were smiling when they glimpsed a 9mm pistol pointing at them from above the table saw and Jack's face peeking out from behind. "Drop it!" Jack barked, "or I will sure as hell drop the both of you!"

Anton must have known he was an easy target and lowered his gun.

"I said drop it! If I intended to kill you, you'd both be dead already."

Anton dropped the gun.

"The both of you, no talking, put your hands over your head and turn around and take three steps," Jack demanded.

Anton and Bojan nervously complied. Jack came out, scooped up the Beretta, and stuck it in his waistband before making them lean against the wall to be searched. He took a phone from Bojan's pocket and two phones from Anton. He then had them both lie face down on the floor. He was going to use their belts to tie them up, but spotted a roll of duct tape and a box cutter lying on a pile of bubble wrap.

He ordered Anton to tape Bojan's hands behind his back and bind his ankles. When he was finished, Jack had Anton bind his own ankles and then lie face down on the floor again while he tied his hands behind his back.

After checking to ensure that Bojan was secure, he yelled, "Where's the rest of the stash hidden?"

"You got what we had left," Anton said.

"That's a lie." Jack ground the side of Anton's face into the cement floor with the sole of his shoe. "The brick I have was busted off a kilo. Where's the rest?"

"That was all of it," Anton protested. "I swear on my mother's grave."

"Okay, I tried to be nice," Jack said. "Looks like we have to do it the hard way."

Anton and Bojan glanced at each other in panic while Jack wrapped duct tape over their mouths. He then dragged Anton by the ankles into the room at the back of the shop.

Once Jack had Anton out of Bojan's view, he started the band saw and let it run for a moment, then shut it off. "Fuck it, too messy."

Anton's body twitched when Jack fired a shot into a pile of wood near his head before walking back to talk to Bojan. As he did, he felt his phone vibrate. He had received two calls earlier, starting when he ducked behind the table saw. He decided to ignore this call, as well, so as not to lose the momentum of fear he'd induced in the two men. Instead, he ripped the tape off Bojan's mouth. "I know the stash is here someplace. I'll find it one way or another, so why not make it easy on yourself and tell me where it is?"

"There is no stash," Bojan insisted. "Besides, you're going to kill me, anyway, so even if there was a stash, why should I tell you where it is?"

Jack's phone vibrated again and he saw it was Laura's number. He hesitated, then shoved the phone back in his pocket and put his gun to Bojan's temple.

Bojan shut his eyes tight and a few seconds ticked by, then Jack muttered, "Too easy for you. Messy or not, let's see how the band saw works. If you don't talk in the next ten seconds, I *will* use it."

He grabbed the tape around Bojan's ankles and slowly dragged him toward the back room while counting down from ten. By the time he reached four, they heard Anton's muffled voice through his gag. Jack silently cursed to himself, then dragged Bojan the rest of the way and laid him face down beside Anton. "I decided to give you guys one more chance to tell me where the stash is. Think about it while I make a call." He speed-dialled Laura's number.

She answered right away. "Are you okay?"

"Yes. Sorry to take so long to get back to you."

Laura took a deep breath and slowly exhaled. "Damn you," she muttered.

"I know you've been calling, but I was too busy to pick up. The two guys here tried to kill us. I'm okay, but things didn't turn out so well for Clive."

"In what way?"

"The dead way. But everything's under control now, so relax. Both guys are hog-tied and kissing the concrete." He gave Bojan a nudge in the ribs with his foot. "Their stash is around here someplace. I've got a band saw, and if they don't tell me where it is, I'm going to use it. Once I find out where I am, I'll need you to come over here with some heavy duty garbage bags."

Laura understood that Jack was in earshot of the men who were trussed up, but her stress over the situation was still running high. A situation Jack knew nothing about.

"We'll need to talk," Jack continued.

"No shit we need to talk!"

Jack realized how stressed she still was. "Did something happen there?"

"Not here, but ... I'm with Brandy and driving out of the hotel parking lot. I'll drop her off in a moment and call you back."

"What's going on, Laura?"

Laura felt sick. "Oh, man ... call Rose immediately, then call me back. I'll be clear by then."

"Rose?" Jack questioned. *What the hell does she want at this hour?*

"She called because of what you're doing. That's all I can say at the moment ... except call her!"

Jack hung up, but hesitated before calling Rose. *How did she find out?* He looked at Anton and Bojan and then over at Clive's body in the main part of the shop. *Okay, so*

I've got a body … and two bad guys hog-tied. Everything is under control.

* * *

Halfway around the world Maurice Leblanc stared at the lifeless body of his partner on the floor of the public washroom. Kerin was sprawled on his back with his eyes staring at the ceiling. A man's gold-and-silver watch and a .32 Beretta pistol lay alongside his head. Maurice felt like his chest was being crushed in a vice. *Two years ago I was best man at his wedding. Gabrielle is pregnant. How do I tell her she no longer has a husband?*

Chapter Twelve

"Thank God! Are you okay?" Rose asked when Jack called.

"Of course I'm okay," he replied. "Why wouldn't I be?" He tried to sound casual.

"Are you with someone?"

"Yes. Give me a sec." He walked to the front of the workshop so he could talk while still watching his captives. "Okay, Rose Alice Wood, I'm clear."

"Your life is in danger," she said. "I received word that the guys you're with are going to kill you."

"You received word?"

"I don't know if I have time to explain. What's your situation?"

"The situation you are no doubt referring to has been rectified," Jack said.

"Rectified? How? What the hell is going on?"

"Rose, how did you —"

"I'll explain, but first tell me what you're doing."

"Well, uh, I'm with three bad guys, but one has a bullet in his head and I've hog-tied the other two."

"You killed one them?" Rose asked.

"No, let me start at the beginning." Jack paused a moment, wondering what the staff-sergeant could possibly know and whether it included his antics in the hotel room.

"I'm listening," she prodded.

"An informant called me tonight. She needed help after meeting with a client I had asked her to report on."

"A client?"

"The informant's a hooker."

"Was this client, by chance, Clive Dempsey?"

"Yes." Jack felt a little nervous that Rose knew.

"Keep talking," Rose said.

"Dempsey and two others, Klaus and Liam, had her in a hotel room and were torturing her. Laura and I intervened. I pretended I was her pimp to protect her as an informant."

"Go on."

"Well, when we went in, her eye was swollen shut and I saw that Klaus had been burning her butt with a cigarette." He let the anger show in his voice.

"Damn it, Jack, is it Klaus who has a bullet in his head?"

"No. Why are you angry with me?"

"Because I know how protective you are of your informants and how you feel about men who abuse women."

"Sure, I would've loved to put a bullet in him, but I didn't."

"So they did kill Clive Dempsey." The staff-sergeant sounded matter-of-fact.

"You already knew he was going to be whacked?"

"Yes."

"How —"

"I'll get back to that. What did you do to Klaus? I know you would have done something."

"I, uh … he may be roughed up a little, but I didn't kill him and —"

"That's a relief."

"Yeah, well … and as far as Dempsey goes, he was shot by one of the guys I have hog-tied."

"Okay, starting from when you roughed up Klaus a little, what happened?"

"Dempsey volunteered to compensate me with a pound of coke. I left Laura and our informant to guard Klaus and Liam. Dempsey then drove me to where I am, and I met two guys called Anton and Bojan. After Anton spoke on the phone a couple of times, he gave me the coke and I had Laura cut Klaus and Liam free. Then Anton shot Dempsey. I got the drop on them and tied them up. That's when I called Laura and she said to call you. I don't want to report Dempsey's murder because it'll burn my informant."

"Christ, you want to hide a murder?"

"These guys killed Dempsey just for bringing me here. Imagine what they'd do to my informant." When Rose didn't respond, Jack went on, "They also have access to blank passports. That, combined with Anton talking on the phone before killing Dempsey … and trying to kill me, I'm sure I'm on to something bigger than the two yokels I've got here."

"You're right that you're on to something big," Rose stated flatly.

"So fill me in," Jack said.

Her hesitation, Jack guessed, was because she was a bit afraid of how he'd respond.

"What's going on, Rose?" he pressed her quietly.

"You're not safe, Jack. How long do you think you have before Klaus and Liam show up? We better get the troops over to where you are before they do."

"Forget the troops. That would burn everything. Besides, I have reason to believe they won't show up for at least a few hours, so quit stalling. Tell me what's going on."

At last the words spilled out of her. She told Jack about her calls from Interpol and everything the French knew about the Ringmaster, leading up to their undercover officer being murdered.

Jack wanted to cry out in both pain and rage, but managed to remain stoic as Anton and Bojan watched him from the far end of the building.

"You there, Jack? Speak to me," said Rose softly.

"Yeah ... I'm here," he replied. "Something doesn't add up. These guys never searched me or found my badge. There's no way they think I'm a cop."

"Then it doesn't make sense."

"It does if they were testing Kerin," Jack said. *And he failed the test big time, all because of me.* He swallowed, then asked, "Was he married?"

"I don't know. A moment ago I got a call direct from Paris telling me about their investigation into the Ringmaster. We didn't know if you'd been killed, too. I'm expecting another call any minute from a Maurice Leblanc. He was Kerin's partner and he's at the scene."

Jack knew it was not a good idea to take his eyes off his captives, but he turned away briefly and pretended to cough as he wiped the moisture from his eyes with his knuckles. "And they don't have any idea who this Ringmaster is?" he asked, sounding croaky.

"A witness heard the shot and saw a man running from the washroom, but there haven't been any arrests. The killer left a watch behind, along with a pistol. The French are not optimistic that Forensics will come up with anything."

"What kind of pistol?"

"I don't know yet. The person I spoke with wasn't at the scene."

"What about the guy they call the juggler? Is he in custody?"

"No, Roche Freulard slipped away during the commotion … although then the officer I was speaking with changed it and said they didn't have any grounds to arrest him, so they let him go."

"Yeah, let him go without any surveillance on him. Meaning whoever you spoke with was too embarrassed to say they lost him."

"They're pretty upset."

"No more than me." Jack was bitter.

"No, but imagine the panic. Roche took second seat to finding the killer."

A plan began to formulate in Jack's mind. "I'm glad Roche slipped away."

"Why?"

"I don't want him arrested. I want the Ringmaster."

"Nobody knows who he is."

"I've got Anton. He might know. He's Roche's brother, after all."

"Possible, but the French say only the higher echelons know his real name and that Anton reports to Roche."

"All the more reason not to arrest Roche," Jack said.

"You've already got some sort of plan, don't you."

"I'm working on it."

"What are you thinking?" Rose asked.

Jack paused, then said, "Will you let me handle this the way I want?"

"Depends on what your plan is," Rose replied firmly.

"To start with, I have to protect the informant."

"Will she accept Witness Protection?"

"It shouldn't be offered. She's young and not all that bright. Her parents and siblings live here, and even if she agreed, I know she'd back out or turn around and return to her family later. That's if her family's still alive. These guys seem vengeful."

"I agree with you on that," said Rose.

"It's not only the Europeans we have to worry about," Jack went on. "We have our local hoods involved, as well. Liam was crying like a baby tonight, but I saw what they were doing to my informant for fun. Imagine how they'd retaliate if they found out she was an informant." He paused, then added, "Besides, I gave her my word that I would protect her."

"I understand."

Good. Then there's no need to explain to you the judicial repercussions if defence discovered I was a cop. Smacking a guy's teeth down his throat and letting Brandy clean out a wallet while I shove a shotgun up a guy's ass would likely not go over well.

"So what do you want to do?" asked Rose.

"To continue my undercover role and find out who he is," Jack said determinedly.

"But you've got a murder victim where you are," Rose replied "You can't get around that without blowing your cover."

"I can if I don't report it."

"You can't do that! You witnessed a murder. You'll have to report it."

"Okay, so how about I delay reporting it until I feel it is safe for my informant?"

"When would that be?"

"I'm not sure yet. How and when I do it depends on what happens in the next few hours."

"For the sake of your informant, I might agree to stall," Rose conceded.

"Might?"

"Depends on what your plan is — and don't tell me you haven't already thought of something. I know you better than you think. How do you plan on getting in with them?"

"At the moment I don't know. I want to stall for a couple of hours to figure out my best options."

"A couple of hours?"

"Yes. During that time I want you to find out every detail you can about this organization, including getting a translation of all of Kerin's undercover notes."

"I doubt I could get the notes that fast."

"Then have them read the notes to you over the phone so you can record them."

"I'll try."

"Explain that I'm going undercover into the group, as well. What I learn could be critical to how I go about getting in."

"I'll do my best."

"I also need to know Roche's level of sophistication," Jack said.

"From what I was told, he's sophisticated. Travels internationally."

"By sophistication, I meant lifestyle. Bikers are international, too, but not the sort to hang out at cocktail parties. Find out his tastes in wine, clothing, cars, women ... whatever. I need to know whether to continue on as a pimp or figure out a way to change my image."

"But you have a body and two bad guys trussed up. There —"

"— isn't much time. Exactly. I also need you to find Klaus and set up surveillance on him and report his movements back to me."

"Yes, Klaus." Rose paused, then, "Why, as you said, are you fairly certain that he and Liam aren't going straight to where you are?"

"I think Klaus will be going to Emergency. Try VGH — it's the closest hospital."

"You said you roughed him up *a little.*"

"I brought it to his attention that he has bad teeth and should get them looked at."

Rose's sigh was audible. "Hang on, I've got another call."

Jack waited for about a minute, then Rose came back on line. "That was Maurice Leblanc — Kerin's partner. He's glad you're alive and wanted to know what we knew about the guys here. I told him we hadn't even heard of them until tonight."

"And?"

He heard Rose swallow. "Kerin was married. His wife's name is Gabrielle."

"Children?" Jack asked.

"First one due next month."

Jack felt his stomach knot and swallowed the acrid taste of bile that burned up the back of his throat and into his mouth. *How would Natasha get along if it was me?*

"Jack ... I'm sorry."

"Sorry enough to support me," he said coldly, while staring at his prisoners.

"Yes. I'll do what I can, starting with calling Special 'O' to watch Klaus."

Jack felt a little relieved. Special "O" was an elite surveillance team that was in high demand. *Rose is onside ... at least for now.*

"Anything else?" Rose asked.

"Not at the moment. I'll call Laura and tell her to meet me here."

"And here being?"

"I'll get back to you on that. The address is difficult to explain. I don't have time."

"Time for what?"

To tell you that I'm about to do an illegal search.

"Or is it that you won't give it to me until you find out if the brass will approve Homicide not getting involved until you okay it?"

"That would be insolent. I need to call Laura for security reasons. I don't know who else might show up. Every second I spend talking to you could be putting me at risk."

He heard Rose sigh with exasperation. He knew she was thinking he always had an excuse.

"And as far as the brass goes," he said, "let's wait a couple of hours and see what I come up with. It's not like they could do anything at the moment, so why bother waking them?"

"Okay, but after you call Laura, sit tight and don't do anything until I call you back."

"Well, there is one thing I'll be doing," Jack said.

"And what is that?" Rose snapped.

"I'll be calling Roche to have a little chat."

Chapter Thirteen

Jack's first call was to Natasha. "Hi, I'm okay," he said quietly. "Thought you might be awake. I heard that telecoms and Rose called you."

He heard Natasha take a deep breath, then slowly exhale. "I'm lying in bed reading."

"Sorry about that."

"You're whispering. I take it whatever you're doing is not over yet?"

"It's far from over ... but I wanted you to know I'm okay."

"You sound unhappy. Are you really okay?"

"I'm okay. Very tired and busy. Hopefully I'll be home for supper and I'll explain then. Go back to sleep."

He heard her yawn. "The boys will be up soon."

"Sorry, I have to go. I love you."

"I love you, too."

"Yeah? Well, I love you six." Jack hoped a little humour would provide assurance to Natasha that he really was okay, but she'd hung up. His next call was to Laura.

"You heard?" she asked glumly.

"Yes. Get over here."

"I need directions."

"Hang on a sec." Jack walked to the rear of the shop and kicked Bojan in the knee. "Hey. I've got a friend coming to pick me up, but she needs directions. You two can figure out a way to untie yourselves after I'm gone."

The optimism on Bojan's face was evident as he quickly gave directions.

"You get that?" said Jack into the phone.

"Got it," replied Laura. "Should be there in thirty minutes."

Jack hung up and glanced around the workshop. The building was open to the roof and long and narrow, with windows on the sides. The floor was a cement slab and the walls were covered in sheets of plywood. A long workbench was under the windows in the front section of the building, and another workbench was on the end wall in the room at the rear. The end wall did not have any windows, and rows of tools hung above the workbench.

Jack used his knuckles to rap on the end wall. As he did, Anton glanced at Bojan and gave an exaggerated roll of his eyes, as if to say Jack was an idiot to search there.

That's encouraging. He knocked a few more times and detected a section that sounded hollow where a stud should have been. A tug on a support bracket holding a row of screwdrivers caused the section to open like a door to reveal that a false wall had been built over the end of the building.

Inside, Jack saw kilos of cocaine stacked up, along with a cardboard box and a narrow wooden crate. He hauled the cocaine and the cardboard box out and placed them on the workbench, then smiled at Anton. "You're a bad boy, Anton. Telling me there was no more cocaine. I count thirty-one and a half kilos. Guess it must have slipped your mind."

Anton's mouth was still wrapped in duct tape but his eyes revealed his anger.

Jack opened the cardboard box and saw an assortment of jewellery, two passports, and four cellphones. The passports were both Romanian and the numbers were in sequence. The photograph in each one was of the same woman, but the names were different, as was her date of birth, although both dates put her age at twenty.

He looked at the phones and saw that a felt pen had been used to scrawl a number on the back of each phone, running in sequence from four to seven. He retrieved the two phones he had taken from Anton's pocket and saw that one had the number three on it.

Next he slid the crate out and pried the top off. Inside he felt the edge of a picture frame that had been wrapped in bubble wrap. Anton and Bojan were watching intently, but when Jack glanced at them, they both looked away with an obviously feigned lack of interest. *Something important, boys?*

Jack left the picture as it was and picked up Anton's phone with the number three. He gave a grim smile as he pushed redial.

"It's about time," Roche said in French.

"So, you're a Frenchman," Jack said harshly. "Do you speak English?"

"Who is this?" Roche replied frostily in English.

"My name is Jack. I'm the guy you ordered Anton to kill."

A gasp was followed by a moment of silence, then Roche said, "I've never heard of you and I don't know what you're talking about. You must have the wrong number."

"Perhaps you would like to speak to Anton. Personally, I hate talking on phones, but with what happened, I'm presuming this call is okay. I'll let him explain the situation to you," he said, then ripped the duct tape from Anton's mouth.

Roche listened in shock as Anton spoke and then Jack took the phone away.

"Okay, I think he's explained the situation to you enough," said Jack.

Roche remained silent as he tried to figure out what to say or do.

"I take it very personally what you tried to do to me," Jack continued, letting the anger show in his voice. *And a lot more personally for what you did to Kerin Bastion.*

Jack knew if he took the stash, there would be no reason for the bad guys to continue to contact him. He had to think of another solution and cleared this throat. "I have located something valuable … but not exactly something I can take to the bank. Still, it's enough collateral for me to give you incentive to find a way to reimburse me, even if I do kill these two idiots."

"Please, don't harm them," Roche begged.

"That will depend on you," Jack said. "I will give you two hours to decide on what you can offer to rectify the wrong you've committed. If I don't hear from you at exactly seven-thirty, don't bother calling later because there won't be anyone who could answer. Same thing if you phone anyone to try to rescue them. If I or my associates see someone, I'll kill these two idiots immediately and take what's in front of me."

"I don't have Klaus's number!" Roche's voice revealed his panic. "He lives there and will be coming home after he sees the doctor."

Jack remained silent.

"Please, don't hurt them," said Roche again, speaking rapidly. "I'm sure we can come to some form of —"

Jack hung up. *Let the games begin.*

Chapter Fourteen

Jack turned his attention back to the crate and caught the worried look Bojan gave Anton as he slid the painting out and unwrapped it. It was an image of a clown with a white face and a teardrop under one eye. It reflected his own emotions.

He realized he'd been lost in his own thoughts when he became aware that both Anton's and Bojan's gazes were fixed on him. "Why are you staring at me?" he yelled. "You thinking of trying something?"

"No," replied Anton. "I was only watching what —"

"Shut up!" Jack put the duct tape back over Anton's mouth and then over his and Bojan's eyes, before using his phone to photograph the painting, passports, and jewellery. He then sent the photos to Rose, along with a text telling her he'd contacted Roche and that he was expecting to hear back from him at seven-thirty.

Jack was placing the painting back into the crate when Laura called to say she had arrived at the front gate. He ripped the tape off Bojan's mouth, then put a gun to his head, saying, "You have a choice. Give me the number for the keypad at the front gate or I'll ram it open with you tied to the front bumper."

Moments later, Laura entered and parked behind the workshop as Jack had directed. The first thing she saw upon entering the workshop was Clive's body on the floor.

"Back here!" Jack called.

Laura walked into the back room and saw two men lying hog-tied on the floor. Next to them stood Jack, who gestured to a stack of cocaine, along with a cardboard box and a flat wooden crate. "Take a look," he said.

His voice sounded hollow and Laura knew he was hurting inside. She fought the urge to tell him the French police officer's murder wasn't his fault. Her eyes met his and she saw the muscle in his jaw ripple. His eyes flashed anger as he put his finger to his lips.

Laura nodded. *Message received.*

"Got thirty-two kilos of coke and enough jewellery to keep you happy for a lot of birthdays," said Jack, continuing to play the role he'd set out for himself.

Laura looked at the cocaine stacked on the workbench alongside several phones and a couple of passports. She then looked in the cardboard box and saw it was filled with expensive watches and cloth bags no doubt containing diamond rings and gold jewellery. She looked at the two captives again, then at Jack. *A dead police officer in Paris, a dead dope dealer here … and this?* She made a palms-up gesture, silently asking, *What should we do?*

* * *

Jack's phone went off, and he held up a hand indicating Laura to wait while he answered the call. It was Rose. He left Laura to watch the captives as he moved to the opposite end of the building.

"What have you got?" he asked abruptly.

"Special 'O' located Klaus at VGH. He's sitting with Liam in the waiting area. They said he's rocking back and forth and holding his jaw and moaning, but the waiting room's full. I doubt he will be clear before noon."

"Good. What else?"

"I called Paris and told them you were talking directly to Roche in an undercover capacity. That caught their attention. I'll be getting a copy of Kerin's notes any minute."

"Thank you," Jack said.

"I haven't had time to check into the jewellery or the painting yet, other than to ask the French about it, and they say the painting doesn't match any of the stolen ones they know about. What did you say to Roche?"

"I let his brother explain the situation to him, although at this point I can't let on that I know they're brothers. I then told him I wanted compensation other than what I found and would hold the stash and the two guys as collateral. Besides the photos I sent you, I also have thirty-two kilos of coke."

"Great. I also presume it was all in plain sight for you to see?"

"It was when I photographed everything."

"That's what I was afraid of," said Rose sternly.

"It isn't like I had time to get a warrant," replied Jack tersely. "I'm surprised Roche hadn't already tossed his phone. Probably waiting for a confirmation call. I needed all the ammo I could find and to call him as quickly as possible. Besides, I don't have any intention of charging these guys with dope trafficking or stolen property."

Rose decided to drop the subject of a search warrant. "You also found two passports made out to the same person with different names. I asked the French about that, too, but they said the issue of fake passports has never come up before."

"The woman on the passports is probably a courier," Jack said. "If they're handing out passports to dope runners, I hate to think who else might be getting them."

"Makes the rest of what you found seem insignificant in comparison."

"It's all insignificant when compared to a policeman being murdered." Again, feelings of guilt and self-doubt clouded his mind.

"I know, I know," Rose said. She paused, uncertain of how to respond, then asked, "How did Roche react?"

"I didn't give him time to talk. The reason I stalled for two hours was to figure out what my strategy should be. Did the French give you something?"

Rose took a deep breath and slowly exhaled. She knew that today would be a long one, followed by a sleepless night. "Okay, according to the French, Roche is a high roller. Sharp dresser, expensive restaurants, high-class hookers, and he owns a villa on the outskirts of Paris."

"Which means his boss, or the Ringmaster as they call him, will be similar or even more so. Is drugs their main thing?"

"No, from what Kerin learned, that was a venture that Roche was doing on his own. Stolen property appears to be what the Ringmaster has made a living out of. Roche had also hinted that the Ringmaster might retire and hopes *he'll* become Ringmaster."

Jack thought about that. "The Ringmaster must be busy if he's in charge of different crime rings operating out of different countries."

"I expect he travels a lot, but we're talking Europe. EU nationals can hop in and out of different countries without even showing a passport."

Sounds like a lonely life, Jack thought, recalling all the times he was away from home and missing his family. "Do we know if the Ringmaster's married?"

"They don't know. They said he's like a ghost. They only know it was the Ringmaster who killed him because of what Kerin said before he was shot. They still have no idea who he is or what he looks like."

"What about the witness who saw him run from the washroom?"

"The men's washroom adjoins the women's. A lady heard the shot and at first thought someone had banged a stall door really hard, but when she walked out, a man burst past her from out of the men's side. She suspected then that it wasn't a door banging she'd heard. So she peaked inside and saw the body."

"Did she see the killer's face?"

"No, he had his hand up to the side of his face when he ran past. After that she only saw him from behind. She was too rattled to remember what he was wearing. She described him as having a stocky build, collar-length black hair, and said that his hand had lots of black hair on it."

"That describes a lot of men."

"I know. She did add that he was agile. Apparently he jumped a waist-high stone wall without using his hands. Made her think the guy was an acrobat."

"Some circus act," said Jack cynically.

Rose paused, then asked, "What do you want to do?"

"The French appear to be onboard with us," Jack noted.

"How about you give me Roche's number and I'll pass it on to them?" Rose suggested. "Maybe they'll be able to triangulate the call to know where he is."

"I'll text it to you, but these guys are phone savvy. His number will continually change."

"You're probably right. They say he barely used the phone that Kerin had the number for."

"I don't expect he ever will. You'll have to work hand in hand with the French and use my number to backtrack from so the French can triangulate Roche's new phone and location on their end."

"Agreed, but we're still investigating a murder here. I know you witnessed it, but we need to get evidence on whoever ordered it. I'll need you to sign the paperwork so we can record your conversation with Roche. It would be nice to implicate him right away."

"I'll sign the form when I return to the office."

"Then text me permission," Rose said, "and I'll get the ball rolling."

Jack didn't know what he would have to do to convince Roche to do what he wanted, but would do whatever it took ... and he didn't want that recorded.

His silence told Rose that she would not be getting permission anytime soon. *Damn you, Jack.*

"Back to the French tracing the call," Jack said at last. "Remind them that any chance there is of me getting to the Ringmaster will be lost if Roche spots any heat."

"Yes, and did you hear me when I told you to text me permission to record you?"

Jack sighed. "A police officer died trying to save my life, so give me room to operate."

Rose felt her stomach knot. *Okay, Jack. I'll forget about recording your calls for now.* "After what happened, I'm sure they're all too aware of having their surveillance burned."

"Next question. Are you willing to let me take this all the way?"

Rose was silent for a moment as she thought about the potential fallout when the Integrated Homicide Investigation Team found out that Jack had witnessed a murder and didn't report it immediately.

"What are you thinking?" Jack asked.

"What about Clive Dempsey? We're going to have to notify I-HIT sometime and they'll call Forensics. You won't get away with a UC for more than a couple of hours."

"I'll need a lot longer than that. When I called Roche, I caught him off guard. Once he's had time to think, he'll be more paranoid about me."

"Thinking that your UC might not work?"

"I'm not saying that. Only that I may have to come up with some unorthodox means to gain his trust."

"Unorthodox?"

Jack waited a beat, then said, "I guess you have to ask yourself a question. Do you want to arrest someone today for killing a dope dealer, or delay that so we can catch a cop killer later?"

Rose was silent.

"Well?" Jack asked.

"Even if I support you, it doesn't mean that everyone will. I-HIT will come unglued when they find out. There's no way we can keep it under wraps. Not with what just happened and the involvement of the French. For you to be at the actual scene and not call in Forensics to do a proper investigation is —"

"I can't take a chance on that. I don't know who else could show up. As far as Dempsey goes, I'll help out I-HIT by delivering his body to them personally."

"Oh, God," Rose groaned. "They'll go nuts."

"I've fought with them before to protect an informant. Remember that serial rapist?"

"Yes, but this is murder."

"Damn right it is. Murder of a cop … a husband … a father."

"You don't need to tell me that!" Rose snapped. "I'm hurting too. We all are. What I'm saying is that Paris isn't I-HIT's jurisdiction. I was referring to Dempsey. There is another consideration. Whoever you have there who killed Dempsey will probably flee to some other country if you let him go."

"He probably will," conceded Jack. "Still, I'll see what I-HIT has to say. Who knows what the future might bring? I'll make sure I identify these guys. We'll find them again if need be." *Provided they aren't already using fake passports.*

"I better call the brass," said Rose. "Considering that a foreign officer was murdered trying to save one of us, I suspect they'll eventually go along with you doing an undercover op."

"Eventually being the key word. For my UC plan to work, I need to act now. It's almost 6:00 a.m. The brass will be at work at 8:30. Call them then to make an appointment. That will give me time to come up with more results to support my actions."

"Your actions," Rose echoed. "I don't even want to ask what those are."

"I'm flying by the seat of my pants. I'm not sure what I'll do."

"Like I believe that," muttered Rose. "Maybe I should at least try to clear it with I-HIT to give them a heads-up."

"And risk having them call the brass ... who will then put everything on hold? For my plan to work, I have to act immediately."

"So you do have a plan."

"Only an initial plan to keep the door open with Roche."

"I see." Rose sounded skeptical.

"Let me deal with I-HIT," Jack said.

"When do you plan on doing that?"

"Between nine and ten o'clock this morning if all goes according to plan."

"Which is when you want me to tell the brass," said Rose.

"Exactly."

"If you do a UC, can you still protect your informant if you do discover who the Ringmaster is?"

"I expect I'll be going to Europe. Depending on the laws of some of those countries, my real identity may not need to be divulged. It could even appear like I'm an informant — or worst-case scenario, the police involved in any arrests will be told that I'm the informant, which will take the heat off the real informant."

Rose ran the situation through her head again.

"So? Do I at least have your backing?" asked Jack.

"You really think you can get Roche to tell you who the Ringmaster is?"

"Tell me who he is?" Jack's tone was harsh. "I'll be meeting the bastard face to face."

Rose slowly breathed out. "Do what you have to do."

Chapter Fifteen

After texting Roche's number to Rose, Jack left Laura to guard their captives and went to the house. It was a three-bedroom home with a den. The three bedrooms all contained men's clothes and he found a passport in each room. One was a Bulgarian passport made out to Bojan Buchvarov, one was a German passport made out to Klaus Eichel, and the last one was a French passport for Anton Freulard.

He photographed the passports and sent the information to Rose, asking her to run Klaus's and Bojan's names past the French police. After that he checked the den where the monitors were located for the CCTV cameras mounted around the property, along with an alarm system. It didn't surprise him that there wasn't a recorder hooked up to record the camera images. The bad guys didn't want to be identified, either.

A plan was forming in his head, but he knew that he and Laura couldn't do it on their own. He decided to phone someone he could trust and sat in the den to make the call.

Sammy Crofton was a trained undercover operative who worked in Drug Section. He sounded groggy when he answered — he must've been sleeping — but upon hearing that an undercover policeman had been murdered, he sounded alert.

Jack outlined exactly what he wanted, but said it would be better if Sammy could bring someone else with him.

"I have someone who'd be good," Sammy said.

"Nobody can know about this," Jack replied, "until I say otherwise."

"What about my own boss?"

"Not even him. Make note that I am telling you Assistant Commissioner Isaac has approved this, but it is on a need-to-know basis only."

The lie was to protect Sammy down the road, and he knew Sammy understood that.

"So who's your guy?" Jack said.

"Benny."

"Benny?"

"Benny Saunders. He's an operator and a good friend of mine. A stocky little fucker with a real pockmarked face. Ugly as the day is long. Couldn't attract a hooker if he had a fist full of hundreds."

"I've never worked with him," Jack said.

"I trust him," Sammy said

"That's good enough for me," Jack replied.

"One quick question. I've got a goatee. You said you wanted us to wear suits and ties, so want me to take the whiskers off?"

"No, your goatee will enhance the appearance I want. One more thing, if you have time, grab a computer flash stick for me if you've got one handy, but if not, don't waste time getting one."

"I'll bring one from home. Gotta hustle if I'm gonna grab the surveillance van before anyone shows up for work."

"Try and be here by eight-thirty this morning."

After talking with Sammy, Jack looked at the computer in front of him. It had been left on, so he moved the mouse and the screen opened to reveal a series of surveillance photographs taken of Clive Dempsey and people associated with him.

It was then Jack realized why Anton had gone back into the house when he and Clive had first arrived, then come back and shaken his head at Bojan. *He was checking to see if I was on file.*

He opened the computer desk drawer and his question as to who had taken the surveillance photos was answered. He found an invoice from a private investigation firm in Vancouver called Big Joe Investigations.

It was seven-thirty when Jack headed back to the workshop and felt Anton's phone vibrate as he entered the building. The display number was different from the recall number he had used earlier. *Paranoia setting in, Roche?*

Jack let the phone ring a few times as he walked to the back room, then answered. "Glad you can tell time," he said.

"Yes, whoever you are, you asked me to call you for some reason," said Roche.

Jack noted the change in Roche's voice, bordering on arrogance in a psychological bid to gain control. "For some reason?" replied Jack. "Are you suffering from Alzheimer's? I have two reasons laid out before me that you should be interested in, but soon there'll only be one."

Jack ignored whatever response Roche made as he put the phone on the workbench and ripped the tape off Anton's and Bojan's faces, then said to Laura, "Stand back. I want to look into their eyes before deciding which one to shoot."

Anton and Bojan lay on the floor begging as Jack pointed his gun, first at Bojan's face and then at Anton's.

Roche's voice yelled over the phone, "Wait! Wait!"

Jack ignored the plea as he fired a shot into the cement floor beside Anton's head. Fragments of lead and cement peppered the side of Anton's face and neck as he cried out in terror.

"Oops, I don't usually miss," Jack grumbled. "Damn it, Anton, hold your head still, will you?"

Roche's voice could be heard screaming over the phone, "Please! Don't kill him! Don't kill him!"

Jack hesitated, then picked up the phone. "Why not?"

"He's my brother!" Roche cried.

Jack was silent for a moment, then said, "So ... Anton is your brother, is he? What's *your* first name?"

"Roche. It's Roche," he stammered, trying to calm his terror at the thought he may have been responsible for his brother's death.

"Nice to meet you, Mr. Roche Freulard. Has your memory come back?"

"Yes ... it's just ... I don't know who I'm really talking to."

"And if I'm reimbursed to my satisfaction, there is no need for you to know."

Jack's words gave Roche a measure of relief. *Perhaps everything will work out. The Ringmaster will approve things, the pimp will be paid, and the problem will be resolved.* He glanced at his watch and winced when he thought of how he would explain what happened to the Ringmaster.

"Are you listening to me?" Jack asked.

"Yes, but … please, I need more time to prepare a, uh, compensation for you. Five or six hours is all I ask."

Jack was pleased. *At least I don't have to come up with a reason to stall.* "Five or six hours," he said, as if contemplating the request.

"Please," Roche begged. "If I could simply have the time I ask for. Then I will be in a better position to offer you something substantial. You must realize that what you have found is valuable, except for the painting, of course, which is simply a copy."

He's hoping I'll leave it behind. Jack glanced at the kilos of cocaine and boxes of jewellery. *The coke is worth close to a million even if they sell it by the kilo, the jewellery looks like it would be a couple hundred thousand, so what's with the painting?*

"I will do my utmost to make up for what happened, but I need time," Roche went on.

Time to shed the pimp image. "Unfortunately, I haven't had time to examine the painting closely, but collecting art is a pastime of mine," Jack said.

Roche gasped. "It is?"

"Yes, I travel extensively for the various corporations I contract out to, and am proud to say I have managed to gather a fairly impressive collection." Jack waited for Roche to respond. *These guys have stolen paintings. Maybe I'll be put on their list of potential buyers.*

"The corporations you work for?"

Jack ignored his question. "It is unfortunate if it is a copy, because quite frankly, as far as the rest of the stuff goes, I wouldn't even know who to sell it to. I was going to give the pound I was promised to the young woman who was abused. Although I barely know her, she does not strike me as the type to have the connections I would need to sell the rest."

"Well, I'm sure that, uh, something could be worked out with me."

"There is another problem. Your brother and his friend have created a mess. I don't trust them to properly clean it up. It would have a very adverse effect on my reputation if I were to become entangled with the law due to their incompetence. I need time to tidy up. Call me back in an hour, say, quarter to nine my time — I realize from your area code that you're nine hours ahead, yes?"

"You want me to call you back again?"

"Yes, but if I don't pick up … well, I think you know what will have happened."

"Please, I am doing my best. Don't —"

Jack hung up and squatted beside Bojan, then tapped the side of his skull with the barrel of his pistol. "Tell me, if I take what I found and leave, what will you and Anton do with the body in the next room?"

"We'd look after it, of course." Bojan's voice showed optimism that he might be left alive.

"How?"

"We'd dig a pit out back in the bush behind the building," Anton said eagerly.

"Exactly what I thought you would do." Jack stood up. "You guys really are stupid." He glanced at Laura and muttered, "I hate talking to stupid people. It wastes my time." He then looked at Anton and asked incredulously, "You would actually bury a body on property that you live on?"

"We only rent it," Bojan said.

"Yes, tell that to the cops if it was discovered." Jack punched out a number on his cell phone. "Tell me, Sammy's Janitorial Service, how far away are you?"

"Thirty minutes," Sammy replied.

"Good. Call me when you're at the gate."

Jack shook his head in disgust at Anton and Bojan, then blindfolded them again with duct tape and gestured for Laura to follow him to the front of the workshop to talk.

"You scared me," said Laura. "For a second, I thought you really did shoot him."

"Forget Anton, he deserves what I did. Let me fill you in."

Jack told her what was happening, then sent her back to watch the captives while he texted Rose a priority message:

> *Check out painting asap. Line up a curator or art specialist to see if genuine. I will arrange delivery.*

Jack then used his phone to take pictures of Clive Dempsey's body from all angles, as well as the rest of the shop, including the workbench with the scales and the bag of cocaine he'd dropped when he dove for cover after Anton shot Clive.

Next he took Clive's keys and placed the crate with the painting in the trunk of Clive's car. He then went back inside the workshop as Sammy called to say they were at the gate. He surveyed the room once more. *Okay. I'm not as good as Forensics, but I-HIT will have to live with it.*

Chapter Sixteen

Jack gave Sammy the entry code, then dragged Anton and Bojan one at a time out to the main area and ripped the tape from their faces again. They watched as Jack slid the large door open and motioned for a green van to back inside.

Seconds later, Anton and Bojan exchanged puzzled looks when two men, both dressed in suits and ties, stepped out. One man stroked his goatee as he glanced at them, then looked at Dempsey's body. "Shouldn't take long," he said gruffly.

The newcomers opened the rear doors of the van and put on coveralls, followed by latex gloves. Next, they unrolled a large sheet of plastic in the back of the van, before picking Dempsey's body up and tossing it inside.

Anton cringed when the man with the goatee gestured at him with his thumb and asked, "What about them two? Want us to dispose of them at the same time?"

"I'm expecting a call in that regard in a couple of minutes," Jack replied.

The man with the goatee shrugged, then he and the other man took a jug of bleach and a mop and pail out of the van and proceeded to mop the floor where Dempsey had been lying.

Jack received his call three minutes later, but for Anton and Bojan, it seemed much longer.

"Is this phone okay?" asked Jack as soon as he answered. "I see you changed yours."

Roche waited a beat, then said, "There are other phones there. There is a number on the back of the phones. Use the next one in sequence and I will call you back."

"Glad I'm not dealing with an imbecile," Jack said.

Several minutes passed, then the phone marked number four rang. Jack answered and said, "Would you like to talk to your brother so that you know he's okay?"

"Yes ... please," Roche agreed.

Jack knelt and held the phone for Anton, who spoke rapidly in French while his eyes darted from the van to Jack and then to Sammy and Benny. When he was finished talking, he looked at Jack. "He wants to talk to you."

Jack took the phone and said, "You understand the problems you've caused me? I have had to employ a janitorial service to clean up the mess your brother made. I expect to be compensated for that, as well."

"Who are you?" asked Roche in a voice barely above a whisper.

"What do you mean, who am I? I told you, my name is ... Oh, wait a moment. You probably think I'm a pimp, don't you."

"Well, uh ... that's what I was told."

"The young woman your men abused was hired by me

a month ago when I arranged for her to meet an important executive. She convinced him to take her for dinner two days from now when he returns to Vancouver. This would have allowed me access to his briefcase in his hotel room, the contents of which are of interest to a corporate client. The executive would not appreciate being seen with a woman who looks like she's being beaten. I know that when he sees her, he'll find an excuse to cancel the date. If that happens, I could stand to lose a lot of money."

"Corporate client?"

"I provide a consulting service to select companies to reduce risk and improve profit, but what I do is irrelevant. I am simply saying that I am not a pimp. In fact, I detest pimps and I can't say as I favour the company of drug dealers, either, but one must make ends meet." Jack paused, then said, "But I digress. Back to the matter at hand. How do you propose compensation?"

"Uh —"

"And don't tell me to take the dope. I don't want to enter that business."

"I told you, I need more time to confer with someone. A few more hours."

"I'm a reasonable man," Jack said. "I do have business to take care of on another matter, so call me back at one o'clock my time. I should be free by then." *Providing I-HIT doesn't arrest me.*

"If you were to release Anton, I could arrange for him to pick up the money," Roche suggested. "You would still have Bojan as, uh, collateral."

"Releasing anyone to get the money is not necessary. When negotiations are agreed on, I will provide you with my bank account number in the Grand Caymans, along with the name of my consulting company for you to do a wire transfer."

* * *

Roche heard the click as Jack hung up, but stared at his phone in a daze as a feeling of impending doom entered his brain. Moments later he clutched his boarding pass and nodded to the flight attendant as she directed him to his seat.

Chapter Seventeen

Jack had Sammy and Benny blindfold and gag Anton and Bojan again, then drag them to the back room, out of sight of anyone entering the main area of the shop.

"That's good," said Jack, when Anton and Bojan were done with. "Dispose of the package in the van, but then return in case I decide to give you two more packages."

Anton and Bojan had both been wriggling in an attempt to get comfortable, but stopped instantly. As Sammy and Benny strode off, Jack turned to Laura. "I'm going to take a look around. Kill them if they make any noise or try to move."

"Not a problem," Laura replied.

Jack then went to the front of the shop to speak with Sammy and Benny. "Stay here in case Klaus shows up," he said as Sammy passed him the keys to the van. "I hope to be back before noon, but it might take longer. You know what the brass are like. I'm sure they'll want to rehash every detail and ask a bunch of questions."

"Yeah, I'm sure they'll have lots of questions for you." Sammy shook his head. "Hopefully they don't start by reading you the charter of rights."

Jack eyed Sammy, then said, "What? You doubt my sincerity when I told you I had permission?"

Sammy smirked. "Don't think I should answer that one."

Jack gave Sammy the keys to Dempsey's car. "These are for the car outside. I've put what I am sure is a valuable painting in the trunk. Hang on to it."

Moments later, Jack drove away in the van and called Rose. "You about to meet Isaac?" he asked.

"He's in another meeting. I'm scheduled for nine-thirty."

"Perfect. I'm on my way to I-HIT with a package for them. I spoke to Roche and he asked for more time so he could talk to someone. I'm betting it's the Ringmaster."

"I spoke with Paris. They didn't get the paperwork through in time to trace the call back to wherever he is."

"No worries. The next call isn't until one o'clock. Hopefully they'll have their ducks in a row by then."

* * *

It was 9:45 a.m. when Jack arrived at the I-HIT office. Moments later, Inspector Dyck waved him in with a friendly smile. "Take a seat. What can I do for you?" he asked.

"Have you received a call from Assistant Commissioner Isaac today?"

"No." Dyck looked puzzled.

"You will," Jack said.

"In regards to what?"

"In regards to a body I've got in the back of a van out in your parking lot."

"Yeah, right." Dyck shook his head. "Sorry, I don't mean to be rude, but I'm short of time. What is it you'd like?"

"For you to take me seriously," Jack replied sombrely. "Let me explain what happened. I'll start by telling you that a policeman was murdered last night for trying to save my life."

Insp. Dyck realized by the haggard look on Jack's face and his tone of voice that he wasn't joking. "My God, I haven't even heard about it."

"Few people know."

"So you really do have a body in a van outside?" Dyck said.

"Yes."

"Is it the person who killed the officer?"

"I wish. The killer got away and is unidentified. I am doing a UC at the moment to identify him. The body in the van is another victim — he was a dope dealer." Jack glanced at his watch. "I need to be out of here within half an hour to avoid complications. Perhaps I could give you the keys to the van so you could have someone take a look while I explain the situation."

The inspector leaned back in his chair, his mind no doubt reeling at what he was told.

Jack held the keys up. "The bad guys have never had any contact with the van, so it's only the body you need to be concerned with. I've got it wrapped in plastic."

"I'm not touching them," Dyck said, jerking his hands back. "How about you give them to Corporal Crane? She's worked with you before."

"Yeah, Connie will like this one," Jack said dryly.

"Was the officer one of ours?" Dyck asked as he phoned for Connie Crane to come to his office.

"No. It was a French police officer who was murdered while trying to warn me that *I* was about to be murdered. It's a little complicated. I'll start at the beginning."

Jack started to explain when Connie arrived, so he held the keys out to her and said, "Brought you an easy one to do. Take a look in the back of the green surveillance van parked in visitors' parking."

"An easy what?" Connie asked.

"A murder. The evidence is wrapped in plastic in the back, but it'd be better if you saw it with your own eyes."

She threw Jack a questioning look.

"I'm short on time," he explained, "and I don't want to start from the beginning again."

Connie looked at Dyck for help. But the inspector simply gestured with his hand for her to take the keys, then addressed Jack. "So you were in a hotel room with a hooker and three bad guys. You were pretending to be a pimp and one of them volunteered to take you to get some cocaine so you wouldn't kill them. Then what happened?"

Connie rolled her eyes, snatched the keys from Jack's hand, and muttered to herself as she left the office.

Jack had barely finished what he was willing to share with Inspector Dyck when Connie burst back into the office.

"Jesus H. Christ! You won't believe this! He's got a body in the back of the van — some guy shot in the head!"

Dyck's eyes remained focused on Jack.

"That's the situation." Jack nodded as he stared back. "I expect you'll be getting a call from Isaac soon."

"You haven't told me where this acreage is," Dyck said.

"First, I was hoping to have everyone's support, so as not to jeopardize my UC. As I said, I've taken photos of the crime scene and the person who did it, including his passport."

"Who you're doing an undercover scenario with to find out who this Ringmaster is."

"Basically, yes."

"Was he married?"

"Sir?"

"The policeman who was murdered."

"Oh, Jesus," Connie put in. "The guy is one of us?"

Jack glanced at her. "Not the one in the van. That's another murder in relation to the policeman's murder."

"Another murder?" Connie mumbled.

Jack nodded. "I almost forgot to tell you. The murder weapon for the guy in the van was a .32 Beretta. I put it under the front seat. His wallet and identification is still in his pocket. Inspector Dyck can fill you in after I leave."

"After you leave?" Connie looked outraged. "Where the hell do you think you're going?"

Jack ignored her, looked at Dyck, and replied, "Yes, he was married. No children, but his wife is due next month. Rose is meeting with Isaac right now and telling him what happened."

Dyck nodded. "I don't know what Isaac will say, but you have my support for the time being. What can we do to help?"

"At the moment, all I need is a car. I need to get going."

"You can take one from our unit."

"Thank you, sir."

As Jack left, he overheard Connie exclaim, "Sir? Did you hear what I said? He brought a body to our office. He can't take off! We need details. It's not like he popped in and dropped off a pizza, for Christ's sake! What's going on?"

Jack headed for the parking lot. *What's going on is we have a cop killer to catch, and I want to be the first one to get my hands on him.*

Chapter Eighteen

Jack was pulling away from the I-HIT office when Rose called. "Had my meeting with Isaac," she said, sounding matter-of-fact.

"And how did our dear assistant commissioner take it?"

"He isn't happy with your method of handling a crime scene."

"Is he is trying to put the kybosh on this?"

"No, but he's perceptive enough to know that you delivered Dempsey to circumvent any negative response to your plan. He made it clear that what you did should have been his decision."

"So he's upset with me," Jack said. *No surprise.*

"No, with me. I told him I authorized you to do it."

"You didn't need to stick your neck out for me."

"What you do is ultimately my responsibility," Rose said. "He made it clear that you better get results to compensate."

"I just left I-HIT. Inspector Dyck is being supportive."

"Good. I'm sure Isaac is on the phone to him. Are you on your way back to the acreage?"

"Yes. Do you have anything on Klaus or Bojan?"

"The French don't know them, and as far as Anton goes, they knew he was Roche's brother, but up until today they thought he was a cabinetmaker and not involved."

"I would say he's involved," Jack replied. "He was the one who shot Dempsey. There's furniture being built in a workshop at the place. Bet that's how they planned to smuggle their goods. Anything else?"

"I don't have anything on the jewellery yet, but I hit pay dirt on the painting. It was stolen during a home invasion in Burnaby less than a month ago."

"How'd you find that out so fast?"

"By staying on top of things. Did you know we have a national art crime enforcement unit?"

"No."

"It was formed by the Sureté du Québec, who work in collaboration with two of our members. I sent them the photo you took and they responded immediately. Providing it isn't a copy of the one stolen, it was appraised recently by a professional art authentication agency in Vancouver. It was painted in the early seventeen hundreds by a famous artist and is considered priceless."

"Perfect. Peaks and valleys. Looks like we hit a peak."

"I haven't spoken with the investigator out of Burnaby yet, but I'll call her when I hang up. I was told the painting is basically an undiscovered piece of work, as far as the art world goes, but the clown in it is well-known and has been portrayed by several artists. It'll have to be authenticated to confirm it's the original."

"Is it more valuable than thirty-two keys of coke and all the jewellery?"

"They told me that a recently discovered painting by the same artist sold for fifteen million Euros."

Jack blew out a breath. "You've got to be kidding. That's about twenty million in our money. Who's the artist?"

"How much do you know about art?" Rose asked.

"Not much. When I was a kid, I used to eat my crayons, instead of drawing with them. My colourful creations were all flushed down the toilet."

"Ever hear of Jean-Antoine Watteau?"

"No."

"If you hadn't eaten your crayons when you were a kid, you probably would've. The guy's right up there with Rembrandt and Van Gogh."

"Okay, I've heard of those guys and I get the picture, but I'm short on time. Give me the nutshell version. Maybe I can use it as part of my UC."

"The painting you have is known as *The Sad Clown*. It depicts a clown called Pierrot, which was the stage name for a clown performing in a seventeenth-century Italian troupe of actors. In the play, Pierrot had his heart broken by a woman who left him for another."

"Earlier you said the Ringmaster was behind the murder of an art collector in Paris and kept some of the paintings for his own gallery. How many people collect expensive paintings? There must be some way of coming up with a suspect or at least someone who bought some of the stolen paintings."

"There are many unscrupulous art collectors whose fanatical desire to own a certain piece of art far outweighs any sense of morality. These people don't advertise who they are."

"I'd like to assemble an art piece myself," Jack said, "by emulating Picasso and using the Ringmaster's body parts."

"Jack, I know how you feel, but —"

"Perhaps you can imagine it —" Jack's tone was harsh "— but you don't really know how I feel, so don't say that. A husband and soon-to-be father died trying to save my life tonight. Unless you've had that experience, you don't —"

"I know, I know. I'm sorry."

Jack breathed deeply, until he felt calmer. "This painting may be my way to get in."

"You can buy Pierrot prints online really cheap, but none like the one you have. I would still like to have it validated. Can you get it to me?"

"I'll text Sammy Crofton and have him bring it to you within the hour."

"You've got him involved?"

"Him and Benny Saunders, also from Drug Section. I needed someone I could trust until things were approved."

"I take it I'm not in that category," Rose sniffed.

"Actually, you are. I simply didn't want you sticking your neck out."

"Thanks, but that's why I get paid the big bucks," she said. "I'll line up a member from Burnaby to take it from Sammy so that Sammy can hustle back to help you when Klaus arrives. Speaking of which, you can't hold these guys forever."

"I know. My next chat with Roche is crucial. He's already curious about me, but I need to bait the hook to gain his trust — or at least ensure he maintains contact with me."

"And how will you do that? Or dare I ask?"

"I'm still formulating a plan."

"In other words, I should … hang on. I'm being told that Klaus is about to leave the hospital and was overheard telling Liam that he would drop him off at home.

"Good," Jack said. "Tell Special 'O' to break off."

"So they don't follow him to where you are? I told you, Isaac has approved it."

"No, because these guys may know enough to do proper heat checks. Special 'O' are good, but even they've been burnt on occasion. I found out that these guys hired a private investigation firm to check out some of the guys working for them."

"Holy smoke."

"Exactly. The firm is called Big Joe Investigations. I'd like you to make discreet inquiries to see what they're about. In the mean time, if Klaus detects surveillance, my UC will be blown out of the water. I've strung them along by thinking I had Sammy and Benny dispose of Dempsey's body, but coming up with a surveillance team this quickly on Klaus is pushing it too far. It could scare them away permanently."

"If I pull 'O' off, we may not know where Liam lives. Are you sure?"

"Positive. Liam is bottom end and not worth worrying about. As far as Klaus goes, I'll be there to welcome him home. He'll be another poker chip to raise the ante."

Rose was silent and Jack sensed she was troubled. "Something wrong?" he asked.

"I know you hate Klaus for what he did to your informant."

"He's a sadistic animal," Jack said.

"Yes, but ..."

"But what?" He knew he sounded sarcastic.

"From the medical attention Klaus needed at the hospital, which I'm told resulted in a plate screwed into his jaw over a fracture and will include implants, root canals, new crowns and —"

"So much for doctor-patient confidentiality," Jack muttered. "Hope your inquiries don't get back to Klaus."

"A Special 'O' member's wife is a nurse there. Don't you, of all people, give me any crap about privacy concerns. I was also told that he needed stitches to his lip and will only be able to swallow puréed foods through a straw for the next while."

"You know, now that you mention it, I thought he had bad teeth." Jack was being deliberately obtuse. "I seem to recall telling him he should get them checked. I thought I'd mentioned that to you."

Rose wasn't amused. "You know what I'm saying," she warned.

"Okay … I hear you. Don't worry. My emotions are in check. I'll point a shotgun at his face and scare him into submission."

"Call me once you have him under control so I don't need to worry."

"Don't worry. Besides Laura, I have two narcs helping me. Klaus shouldn't be expecting anything."

"It isn't you I'm worried about, it's Klaus."

"I promise I'll be gentle and tie him up alongside his buddies."

"Good. Also, how long did you plan to detain these guys? If it ever comes out —"

"We're allowed to arrest someone and detain them for twenty-four hours without charge."

"Arrest?"

"Yeah, so I haven't had time to inform them of their rights and bring them in yet."

"Which you have no intention of doing," Rose stated flatly.

"The situation may be rectified when Roche calls me back at one o'clock."

"There can't be any *may* about it. I want them freed by then. You don't know where it'll end up. Down the road some defence lawyer is liable to charge you with kidnapping and assault."

"Okay, okay, damn it," said Jack in frustration. "I'll let them go as soon as I'm done talking to Roche. I need him to get to the Ringmaster. I'll also text you permission to record my conversation, as well as the phone numbers for the remaining phones I found."

"That's nice to hear. How will you try to ingratiate yourself with them?"

"I think I've caught their attention with what has happened."

"That is an understatement," said Rose dryly. "You've caught everyone else's attention, too."

"I need to portray myself as having similar characteristics to the Ringmaster."

"Tough to do when we don't know anything about him."

"I know he's professional enough to hire a private investigator to check people out. I also know he collects art, may be retiring soon, travels extensively, and is not a drug dealer. Like I said before, I'll have to wing it, but I have enough to point me in the right direction."

"Good luck," Rose said.

"Thanks."

"There's one more characteristic the Ringmaster has that you didn't mention." Rose paused. "He murders people."

Jack snorted. "Yes ... that, too."

Chapter Nineteen

Klaus parked his car in front of the workshop. When he got out, he heard the sound of the band saw from inside and saw that the side door was open. As he stepped inside, he said, "Hey! Hope that fucking pimp is alive so I can saw a chunk off him!"

"Don't move, shithead!" yelled Jack as he and Sammy appeared from behind him.

Klaus spun around and saw Jack pointing the shotgun at his face.

Most people would not have moved. What Jack hadn't counted on was that Klaus thought Anton and Bojan were dead and believed he was next. He lunged forward in a panicked attempt to grab the shotgun by the barrel. Jack took half a step back and pivoted the shotgun, using the butt once more to smack him in the mouth. Combined with the momentum Klaus had when he was lunging forward, the blow knocked him sideways, landing him face first on the concrete floor. Seconds later, he moaned and looked back up at Jack.

"What are you? Crazy?" Jack aimed the shotgun at his face. "Don't move, I said!"

Klaus gurgled and coughed pieces of broken teeth onto the floor. The plate screwed into his jaw to cover the first fracture remained in place, but now his jaw was fractured on the opposite side. Luckily for him, his mouth was still frozen from surgery, and the pain, for the moment, was minimal.

Jack eyed Klaus, who remained sitting on the floor as he held his jaw with the palm of his hand. *Damn it. Rose won't ever believe this.* He looked at Sammy, who rolled his eyes in response. Jack then locked eyes with Klaus and said, "That's what you get for being stupid. Also, don't ever call me a pimp. I hate pimps!"

Klaus sullenly stared back at him.

"Get up and walk to the back of the shop," Jack ordered. "We're going to tie you up alongside your two friends."

"They're alive?" Klaus moaned.

"See for yourself. Get moving!"

Moments later Klaus was bound and blindfolded with duct tape, and lay beside Bojan and Anton. Unlike the other two, he was not gagged due to his mouth injuries. During Klaus's capture, Jack had detailed Benny to remain in the den to monitor the closed-circuit television cameras. Now Jack, Laura, and Sammy stepped into the main area of the shop to talk in private.

"What are you going to do?" Laura asked.

"Roche will be calling me in an hour," Jack replied. "I'll leave you and Sammy here on guard duty while I go back to the house. I need to use the Internet."

"You said Rose wants us to cut these guys loose after you talk with Roche." Laura glanced at the captives in the back of the shop. "That could prove interesting. I have a sneaking suspicion they won't be too happy with us. Particularly Klaus. Did you really have to smack him again?"

"He tried to grab the shotgun!" Jack looked at Sammy for corroboration.

Sammy pretended to look surprised at Jack's comment, but then smiled and nodded.

"Bet you broke his jaw again, which means I need to make sure he doesn't suffocate," Laura said. "If he does, you can be the one to do CPR. I'm not."

"It's not like he has any teeth left to bite you," Jack replied.

"Yeah, good point." Laura could see that Jack's mind was elsewhere and knew he was trying to decide a course of action. "Go," she said. "Find a quiet place to think and come up with a game plan. I've got Sammy for company."

Jack made his way to the house and sat at the kitchen table, then grimaced as he called Rose. "Klaus arrived and is tied up alongside his two buddies," he said as soon as she answered.

"Good. Without problem I take it?"

"I was as gentle as the situation allowed. I even assisted in lowering him to the floor, but his mouth appears to be bothering him."

"I'm sure it is. I can only imagine how he'll feel when the freezing wears off."

"Are the French set to go with the phone taps?" Jack wanted to change the topic.

"I'm expecting to hear back any minute."

"I should go," Jack said. "I need to figure out how I'm going to play this."

After hanging up, Jack glanced around the kitchen. He

thought of the fun he had with his own family over dinners and tried to imagine what it would be like for Gabrielle raising a child without a father. *A father who died trying to save me. What can I ever say to her? Any words I come up with will be trivial against the pain she feels.*

He glanced at his watch. *I have less than an hour.* He pushed the image of a dead policeman and his pregnant widow to the recesses of his brain. *Who is the Ringmaster? What do I have that I can use? Roche didn't seem overly concerned about the drugs and jewellery....*

He brooded for a moment about why the head of an organization would risk committing the murder himself. It didn't match the behaviour of other criminal kingpins he knew. *Those jobs are usually assigned to some flunky. The meeting with Kerin could easily have been postponed for such a purpose.*

Then Jack came to a chilling conclusion. *The Ringmaster enjoyed doing it. He's a sociopath. What do I know about him? He likes art and murder. I know about murder, and I need to think about art. Telling someone I used to eat crayons won't cut it.*

He used his own phone to go on the Internet to find out what he could learn about a sad clown by the name of Pierrot. He discovered that the clown was a lovable but hapless fool who was in love with a character by the name of Columbina. She left Pierrot for another clown by the name of Harlequin.

Harlequin? So that's where the name came from for those romance novels. His thoughts went back to the painting. *Why is it so important? Is it all about the money? Or does it represent something else ... something personal to the Ringmaster?*

Chapter Twenty

It was nine o'clock at night in Frankfurt, Germany, when the Ringmaster entered Roche's room and listened in shock at what he had to say.

"He can't have my Pierrot," the Ringmaster said vehemently. "Anything else, but not that!"

"I told him it was only a copy. Worthless, but ..." Roche paused, uncertain how best to break the news.

"But what?"

Roche swallowed. "He said he's an art collector."

The Ringmaster looked at him sharply.

"Only as a hobby," Roche hastened to say.

"Who is this man?" the Ringmaster demanded.

"I don't know. He told me his name was Jack."

"Obviously not some pimp ... like you led me to believe."

"That was what Anton thought, but as I told you, he said he does consulting work for international companies. He wants me to wire money to an account in the Caymans."

"I can only imagine what kind of consulting he does. Disposing of a body in that manner and cleaning away the bloodstains — by men in suits?"

"Anton said they put on coveralls, but yes."

"I would surmise that his consulting work is for the Mafia or drug cartels. Perhaps he does corporate spying, as well, with assassination thrown in."

"My thoughts, too," Roche said.

"He is an interesting man." The Ringmaster sounded thoughtful.

"Dangerous is more like it," Roche said.

"Negotiate with him. I do not care if he takes everything else, but the painting is mine." The Ringmaster was emphatic. "You better ensure that I get it."

Roche swallowed again. Hard. "I have tried my best. He does not seem particularly interested in the cocaine or the jewellery."

"I understood it was cocaine that brought him there to start with."

"Yes, but apparently that was simply to reimburse the whore for what Klaus and the others did to her. For the rest he said he wouldn't know what to do with it."

"With his connections? I'm sure that's just a ploy to get more money from us."

"Perhaps."

"Is there not someone we can call to deal with him — personally?"

"Not immediately. Anton and Bojan are his prisoners. That leaves Klaus, but I don't have his number. I fear he may have returned home to an ambush."

"Yes … Klaus. The man responsible for this whole mess.

We knew he was a sadistic animal in the true sense of the word, but you assured me that Anton would keep him in line."

"I was basing part of my trust on the recommendation of our man here in Frankfurt."

"It was Wolfgang who initially sponsored him, that is true," the Ringmaster said.

"Despite his sadistic quirks, or perhaps because of them, Klaus could always be counted on to terminate those who interfered or talked too much."

"His ability appears amateurish, compared to this Jack," the Ringmaster noted.

"I agree, but Wolfgang's original assessment and recommendation to use Klaus made sense at the time. Until now, I've never heard of anyone the likes of Jack."

"Wolfgang has been a juggler for many years," the Ringmaster said. "He is experienced and was able to control Klaus. It is my fault, as well. I knew Anton was inexperienced. I should not have sent Klaus to work for him. If Klaus is not dead, once this is settled, I'll order him back to Germany and tell Wolfgang to cut him loose."

"Klaus will be upset."

"Upset? He is lucky I don't put a bullet in his brain."

Roche nodded respectfully.

The Ringmaster eyed him silently for a moment, then said, "I warned you about the drug trade. It is filled with whores and addicts who are more than willing to sell you out or cut your throat and rob you."

"I would never deal with those types of people." Roche wrinkled his nose.

"Not directly, but eventually it will lead back to you. It already has. You ignored my advice and you must pay.

Use whatever you need from your thirty-two kilos to pay him off."

"I'll try, but he made it clear that he is neither a pimp nor a drug trafficker."

"That can work to our advantage. If he actually doesn't know where to dispose of the drugs, he may be forced to come to us. Have him hold the drugs as collateral, then buy them back."

"What if he mentions the painting?"

"It is not negotiable. He must be made to know that."

"I understand," Roche replied.

"Make the call, but keep it short. I'll sit beside you to listen."

"Surely you don't think he has the capabilities to trace my call, do you?"

"I do not know what to think. As always, it is best to be cautious."

Roche nodded. "And if he does take the painting? He said he is an art collector."

"If he does that, find him, find my painting … and kill him."

Chapter Twenty-One

At quarter to one, Rose called Jack to say that the French had fulfilled their judicial requirements for the wiretap and gave him a reminder to keep Roche on the line for as long as possible while they traced the call.

"Did they give you any more info on the Ringmaster or Roche that could help me out?" Jack asked.

"No, what you have is what there is," Rose replied. "Although I did find out that the murder weapon was a .32 Beretta."

"Same thing Anton shot Dempsey with. Not overly noisy, and small enough to conceal."

"Maybe a trace of the gun will give them something."

"I wouldn't hold my breath. Probably stolen during one of their robberies."

"What's your plan on dealing with Roche when he calls?"

"I'm going to focus on the painting," Jack replied, "but bring up the passports as a side issue. I'm hoping they'll want to negotiate on the painting, but if they don't, I'll use the passport angle. If I get the feeling they don't want to meet me in the future, I'll emphasize that I'm a specialized business consultant and see if I can convince them to hire me. After what's happened, they may want to use my services."

"You could tell them that you'd do a better job than Big Joe Investigations," Rose suggested.

"I don't want them to know that I know about Big Joe. If they do bring me on board, they may use him to check me out. If they put me under surveillance, it'll be a good opportunity to enhance my cover story."

"Gotcha. Good luck. We'll be listening."

"Hope the French don't blow it," Jack said.

* * *

At one o'clock, Roche called Jack. "We are happy to let you take everything you found for collateral except —"

"Except the painting," Jack interjected. He was sitting at the kitchen table.

"Uh, yes … and my men will buy the other items back from you over the next week or two at a price I'm sure you will agree is generous."

"Are you not interested in what happened to Klaus when he got home?"

"Oh, uh, yes. I had forgotten about him," Roche admitted.

They couldn't care less if he's alive or dead. The painting is their top priority. "Well, to let you know, he's resting in the same circumstance as Anton and Bojan."

"I see. That's fine." Roche was dismissive. "About our offer, I am sure you will be pleased with the amount we are willing to pay for —"

"Actually, I'm not interested in receiving any money from you," said Jack.

"You're not?"

"I told you I'm an art collector. I've since examined the painting carefully and can hardly believe my eyes."

"It is a good replica."

"Replica?" Jack chuckled. "I believe it's an original. In fact, I have never even seen a copy of it before … which, for me, makes it more precious. I will be keeping it." He kept his tone matter of fact.

"No!" blurted Roche. "You can't do that!"

"You are hardly in a position to tell me what I can or cannot do."

"Yes, of course, but …"

"But what?" prodded Jack.

"For you the painting is a piece of art, but, uh, for a close friend of mine it has great emotional value. You will be paid handsomely for it."

Emotional value? A painting of a sad clown who's considered a fool and has lost his love? I don't see the Ringmaster thinking of himself as a fool … or has he lost someone he loves?

Jack took a deep breath. *Time to lay it on thick … and hope it works.* "It's as if a special angel guided it to my hand," he said wistfully. "It was meant for me. It's my destiny to have it."

"Your destiny?" Roche sounded confused.

"Yes. Do you know I have another painting of Pierrot in my collection?"

"You do?" asked Roche. Jack could hear panic in his voice.

"It is only a copy, of course," continued Jack. "Unlike this one. It is also the only copy I have, as the rest of my collection are originals. Do you know why that is?"

"Uh, no."

"Pierrot grips my heart with a passion you could never understand. I lost someone. Someone who, like Pierrot, was naive and too trusting of the world. Perhaps, like Pierrot, even considered by some to be a fool. But I loved her. There will never be another ... but it is as if she comes alive every time I look at Pierrot."

* * *

Roche watched the Ringmaster, who was sitting close enough to overhear, recoil in shock. *They have experienced an identical tragedy. Fate was playing a cruel trick by bringing them together, both with a blind passion to own the same painting. "Mon Dieu,"* he muttered.

"What was that?" asked Jack. "Did you say 'my God'?"

"I ... I, uh," Roche stammered, "understand that you like the painting, but I am willing to pay you —"

"Like? Mr. Roche, you have no idea what love is, do you? You cannot put a price on it." Jack sounded scornful.

"I am sorry to disappoint you, but I believe what you have is only a forgery, albeit a very good one."

"Good, then I am sure you do not mind my taking it."

Roche paused, uncertain what to say as his panic rose.

"At a loss for words?" Jack said, his voice dripping with contempt. "You are not a very accomplished liar, so don't insult my intelligence by trying it. Besides, do you really think I would concede to letting this painting hang amongst some gaudy collection the likes of which a drug trafficker like you would own? Likely placed with a grouping of velvet paintings of naked women?"

"My friend is not a drug dealer," Roche said lamely.

Jack continued as if he hadn't heard. "I've often been hired by the likes of you to do consulting work. Sure, I admit that some of my clients live in fabulous mansions. Maybe you do, too, but I've never met any who had a real appreciation of fine art. For them it is only a facade of civilization. A way to impress people. For me, my paintings are for my eyes only. I will not have strangers cast their eyes on and make uncultured comments about what I treasure."

Roche felt the tap on his wristwatch and nodded to the Ringmaster. "I must get off this phone," he said, "but please, I will call you back in —"

"There is some good news," said Jack.

"There is?"

"I will leave the rest of the stuff for your men on one condition."

Roche paused as he looked at the Ringmaster. "Are you there?" asked Jack.

"Uh, yes. What condition?"

"I found two passports made out to the same person. One never knows what the future holds. I plan to retire soon, perhaps even in your country."

"You're thinking of moving here?" Roche was truly surprised. Who *was* this man?

"Possibly," Jack replied. "The French really do have an exquisite collection of art, although I think Italy rivals you in that regard. Do you go to the museums yourself?"

"No, but please, quickly, what is it you want? As a safety precaution, I need to hang up."

"This will only take a second. I might find it useful to have a passport under a different name for my own use. How about we make a gentlemen's agreement? I will leave everything except the painting and later you will provide me with my own passport."

"Uh, I'm not sure what to say. I really should hang —"

"You would not need to contact me again," Jack interrupted. "I could make arrangements with your brother to deliver it to me. Naturally, I have some concerns that when he and his two buddies are released they may act like idiots and continue their quest to kill me. Arrangements will have to be made to ensure that doesn't happen, and any future interactions, such as the one where I provide your brother with a passport photo, can be done through a mail drop."

"No, uh, please wait," Roche replied as the Ringmaster whispered instructions.

"You do not wish to do that?" Jack asked.

"Yes, but ..."

"But what?"

"We can discuss the passport with you at another time, but more than that, we may be interested in your consulting services."

"My consulting services?" It's was Jack's turn to sound surprised. "If I thought you were genuine, I would consider it, but under the circumstances, what with trying to kill me, you must understand why I am skeptical about your sincerity."

"We *are* sincere," Roche said. "But please, I need to hang up and use one of the other phones you found."

"One of the others?"

"Yes. Use the number five and I will call you back in one hour."

"An hour? Why so long?"

"To ensure security for where I am," Roche replied hastily.

"Glad to hear you are cautious. So am I."

"Also, if you let me speak to my brother when I call back, I will instruct him to consider you a friend."

"A friend! After he tried to kill me? And on your orders?"

"We thought you were a pimp."

"Believe me, I'm not some parasitic pimp who lives off human flesh," Jack said with disdain.

"We realize that now, which is why we would like to hire you. I will call you in one hour."

* * *

Jack smiled grimly as he hung up and used his own phone to call Rose. "You heard?"

"Yes," she replied.

"I'm not cutting these guys loose before the next call." Jack was adamant.

"Take it easy," Rose said. "After what I heard, you've got the extension."

"Thanks … sorry."

"Listening to your call, I never knew you could be so passionate about a painting!" No doubt Rose hoped to lighten the moment, relieve his stress a little.

"I'm passionate when it comes to murdered cops," Jack said bluntly. "Roche was with someone. I bet it was the

Ringmaster."

"I agree. Hopefully the French were successful."

"I doubt they will be. That's why he wants to call me back in an hour. He'll be switching locations. If they did trace the call, he'll be gone before they get there."

"Maybe, but it sounds to me like you played him well," the staff-sergeant said. "They obviously want to maintain — Hold on, incoming call, let me put you on hold."

Jack drummed his fingers on the kitchen table as he waited. He was pleased that Roche had brought up the idea to use him for consulting services. *But how do I maintain credibility? They know I wouldn't blindly walk into a trap.*

* * *

Seconds later, Rose said, "They've traced the call. Your man is in Frankfurt, Germany. The coordinates put him at a place called the Steigenberger Airport Hotel." She paused. "So. Your call. What do you want done?"

"Bet he's already left to check into another hotel," Jack said. "Frankfurt is a big city. Damn it, even if he stays around the airport, there'll be lots of other hotels to choose from." He clenched his fist in frustration, then took a breath and told Rose what he wanted her to do.

Chapter Twenty-Two

In Frankfurt, Detective Otto Reichartinger listened intently as the officer in their Interpol bureau relayed the information from the French police.

Otto commanded a specialized surveillance unit, and his team was in the office doing reports and wrapping up the end of their shift before going home. But on hearing what had happened earlier that day in Paris, he ordered his team back to work.

Moments later copies of Roche's picture had been given to everyone in his unit, along with the description of a man known only as the Ringmaster. The only details were that he was acrobatic and had collar-length black hair and exceptionally hairy hands.

Although the murdered policeman was French, Otto was told that his current orders were at the discretion of an undercover policeman from Canada. The instructions were clear. Try to identify the Ringmaster — provided there was zero chance of surveillance being spotted.

The same condition applied to making inquiries. If a hotel staff member seemed even remotely suspicious, then that hotel was not to be approached. Members of Otto's team were to lose the subjects, rather than alert them to any police presence.

If any other players could be identified, so much the better, but the priority of Otto's team was to identify anyone fitting the description of the Ringmaster.

Otto glanced at the hair on his hands. *Hairy hands. Black hair. That narrows it down to damn near half the men in the country, especially anyone of Mediterranean or Mideastern descent. And acrobatic? How do they expect us to see that? Not a lot of trampolines and trapezes around. And this bullshit of making sure there's zero chance of surveillance being spotted, give me a break. There's always a chance.*

Counting himself, there were eight people on the team — and dozens of hotels in the vicinity of the airport besides the Steigenberger. Fortunately, many of them were clustered together so that a person at the wrong hotel could get to the right hotel within minutes. *Provided we have minutes,* Otto thought.

He had his team split up to try to cover the various hotel clusters. For himself, he decided to head for a location northeast of the airport, where there were about three dozen hotels, most of which were in walking distance of one other.

He put a hand on his stomach as he drove. *I've become soft. Too many years spent sitting on my ass drinking Victoria Bitter. If I have to get out and hustle tonight, the exercise will do me good.*

He glanced at his watch and saw that there was less than fifteen minutes before the next call was to be made. He swore as a motorist slammed on his brakes when he cut him off and blasted his horn behind him.

One other question plagued Otto's mind. He was not given the name of the policeman in Canada, but whoever it was had asked for him by name. *Strange, considering I have never met a policeman from Canada.*

Chapter Twenty-Three

Jack returned to the workshop. He motioned for Laura to meet him at the front so he could tell her what happened.

"You told them the painting represents a lost love?" Laura frowned.

"I had to come up with some reason for why they simply couldn't pay me for it. I think it struck a chord with him."

"It strikes a chord with me, too," Laura said. "Sounds to me like you cut me out of the equation. If you'd pretended I was your girlfriend, I would've been able to cover you."

"You're still in as one of my people," Jack replied. "Same for Sammy and Benny. It doesn't mean you're cut out of anything."

"Where have I heard that one before." Her tone was stony.

"Look, a policeman was murdered for trying to save me," said Jack, "so I'll play it the best way I know how. If I do have to cut you out, then so be it."

"I'm trying to look out for your best interests, is all," Laura retorted. "Two dead cops won't help the situation, either."

Jack frowned. "I know you're thinking of my best interests. I won't take any chances that aren't necessary."

"Oh, no, you would never do that." She didn't bother to hide her sarcasm.

"I'm older. I've got a family and —"

"Yeah, yeah." Laura shook her head. "As long as you understand where I'm coming from."

"I do … and I appreciate it," Jack said.

"Good." Laura reached over to give him an affectionate squeeze on the arm. "That being said, there is one more thing. You requested the police in Frankfurt try and find him. You're already taking a chance. What if the bad guys spot the heat? If they do, it'll be game over."

"Remember that UC we did where we ended up in Koh Samui — that island off the coast of Thailand?"

"Yes. We stayed at Bill Resort. Who could forget? I'd love to go back to that place for a holiday."

"Remember the detective from Frankfurt we met there? He was there the whole time we were, but we never told him who we really were."

Laura stared blankly at Jack.

"He was friends with the people we met from Norway — Terje, Inger Siri, Eirik, and Trine," Jack added. "When he was with them, he drank Heineken, but at the Outback Bar in Lamai he usually drank Victoria Bitter."

"Oh, yeah, now I remember him. Funny you'd remember him for the beer he drank. I remember him for his eyes. They were almost mesmerizing. A metallic blue."

"That's the guy. His name was Otto."

"I've never met anyone else with eyes like his," Laura said.

"You do remember him. Quite well, I would say," Jack teased.

Laura studied Jack briefly. She could see sadness in his face and realized that Kerin's death must be weighing heavy on his mind. She knew that humour could alleviate stress, so she decided to play along, even though Jack knew she was devoted to her husband. "Well, he was kind of charming," she replied, sighing wistfully sigh. "Quick to smile, and he could melt you with those eyes of his."

"Yes, and like you, he enjoyed a good joke." Jack grinned, appreciating Laura's effort.

"And he mentioned he worked with a special surveillance unit," she added.

"He's in charge of it," Jack said. "The guy is smart. I trust him not to screw things up. I requested him by name."

"Think we'll be going to Frankfurt?"

"This morning I thought we might be going to Paris ... so I have no idea."

"I'll keep my passport handy," Laura said, "in the event you don't cut me out."

Jack nodded, then walked to the rear of the shop and had Sammy peel the tape from their captives' faces and let them sit up. The skin on their faces had become inflamed, wide red stripes where the tape had been repeatedly ripped off. Klaus was still drooling blood and a new temporary crown lay on the floor. He glanced at it and then glared up at Jack.

"You know, you really do have bad teeth," said Jack. "Too much candy, I suspect. I wonder if all that sugar makes you stupid, as well." He knew it was wrong to torment his prisoner, but the hatred he felt for Klaus after what he did to Brandy overrode his conscience.

Klaus's response was in German, but Jack had the distinct feeling it wasn't polite. He turned his attention to Anton. "Your brother should be calling. I'll let you speak to him."

Jack retrieved the phone marked with the number five and returned to the house to wait. He wanted to keep Roche on the phone for as long as possible, and walking back to the workshop to let him talk to Anton would use up some time.

Roche called at two o'clock and Jack saw that he had switched phones again.

"Let me speak to my brother," said Roche, "and I will give him instructions on how to contact you. We don't mind that you're keeping the painting and are pleased that you are willing to leave the rest."

You really are a terrible liar, Jack thought. "That's great. I'm glad you feel that way. Not that you have any choice."

"Your response is more than generous," Roche said. "We are also serious about using your, uh, consulting services."

Time to play hard to get. "I wouldn't feel safe working for you, considering that you ordered your men to kill Dempsey and me. Let's leave it that your brother gets me the passport. As much as I don't like the idea of meeting your brother again, I presume I'll have to, so that I can sign the forms with whatever name I'll be using. But once that takes place, I don't see us doing business together." *Wish I could be with you in person to watch you sweat over that comment.*

Roche took a couple of deep breaths. He was about to make the biggest gamble of his life. As cagey as Jack apparently was, learning more about him in a one-time meeting might not work. He knew he had to play his last card. "As a gesture of goodwill to prove that you can trust me, I have something to tell you."

"I'm listening."

"The passports are no longer available."

"They're not?" *Damn. Now what do I say?*

"No," Roche went on. "Five were obtained, but an audit discovered their disappearance. Anyone using them would be arrested."

"Can you get more later?"

"Unfortunately not. The ones we have would pass scrutiny if used within a country's borders, but you would be arrested if they were checked or cross-referenced by customs. In the European Union, it is not necessary to check passports when travelling between member countries, but Romania is not a member country."

"Good of you to tell me that the passports were no longer of any use," Jack said. "I appreciate your honesty." He sounded sincere. "You're risking that I might take everything and disappear."

"I know. We would like to meet with you to discuss what you could offer our organization. We are impressed and intrigued with the way you present yourself and how you, uh, cleaned up the mess there. My telling you about the passports is a gesture to prove that we wish you no harm and would like to hire you."

Or maybe you just don't want me arrested and put where you can't get your hands on me. "I didn't expect that," Jack said. "I'm not sure what to tell you. I need to think about it."

"Are you at least willing to give my brother a contact number for you?"

"Yes, I'll do that. Perhaps I could have one for you, as well?"

"My brother will give you an email address where contact can be made. Please let me speak to him. I will talk with him in English so you can listen in and understand."

"Sure, but hang on. I'm in the house and he's in the workshop. I'll go there right now."

"Okay, I'll hang up and call you back in ten minutes," said Roche.

"Hardly necessary. It will only take me —" Jack quit talking when he heard Roche hang up.

Ten minutes later Roche called back from a different phone, and Jack held his phone for Anton to speak while he listened in. The conversation was brief, but Roche told Anton that the Ringmaster wished to hire Jack to do consulting and made it clear that under no circumstances was he to be harmed.

Anton was ready to accept any proposal that would save his life. He told Bojan and Klaus the news. Bojan smiled in response, but Klaus gave Jack a cold, hard stare.

Roche then spoke to Jack. "You will not have a problem when you release them."

"I trust you will understand if I decide to be a little cautious about how I do that," said Jack. "And who the hell is the Ringmaster? Are you guys running a circus?"

"No, it is simply a code name we use for the president of the company," Roche explained. "The majority of the people who work for us do not know the real identities of anyone beyond their immediate superior."

"And what is your code name?"

"If you decide to work for us, I will tell you then."

"Sounds like you guys do know what you're doing," Jack allowed. "By the animals you had working for you who were mistreating that young lady, I'd thought otherwise."

"Yes … Klaus, Liam, and Clive. Let me assure you that Liam will never work for us again. As for Klaus, he will be summoned back and fired upon arrival, but I would ask you to keep that to yourself."

"Understood," Jack replied. "With that in mind, give me a moment to go where I can talk to you in private."

"Please make it quick. I am running out of phones."

Jack walked outside and said, "Generally, my consultation service involves checking out employees to see who should be trusted and who shouldn't. I provide further services such as the janitorial work you are aware of, but usually that is only after I'm satisfied with my background inquiries as well. It is not only the executive of a company I wish to protect; obviously there is a need to protect myself as well. Generally people who commit crimes are of lower intelligence, and although needed on occasion, for some, their potential to damage an organization outweighs their short-term value. Risk sometimes exists for those who do have brains. The trick is to figure out who would make a suitable employee and who wouldn't."

"And how do you analyze that?"

"It depends on what my client's willing to pay. I can provide a basic background check on an individual, or one that would include close associates. Or I could go all the way and include a psychological profile, which would necessitate a written test, coupled with a personal interview. The latter being one that many of my clients select for those in executive positions. The analysis would indicate the type that's emotionally needy, the kind of person who brags about his exploits in an attempt to impress people. It could also indicate if he's the type to talk if approached in, shall we say, a hostile takeover."

"You have a background in psychology?"

"Not officially, but I employ people who do."

"What you offer … are you able to do that on an international level?"

"I have worked for international companies that are usually capable of getting me the information or the contacts I seek. Generally, they have been more than happy to assist me as they know I'll reciprocate. Working with different organizations also allows me to act as a facilitator to promote smoother transactions between different organizations or help settle territorial disputes."

"Sounds impressive," Roche said.

"I would also probe anyone bent on doing harm to your organization, particularly on the legal front. An added service I've provided on occasion is to recommend certain investment opportunities. For that, my fee is based on a percentage of the profit you make."

"Remarkable. You also appear capable of cleaning up certain messes."

"Tying up loose ends is a service I occasionally provide, but with proper guidance it would become less necessary."

"So how do you feel about working for us? You would be paid very well."

"If I were to do consulting work for your organization, my working relationship would have to be at the executive level. I will not risk garnering unwanted attention by associating with scum like Klaus and his pals."

"Believe me, we, too, were extremely upset to discover how they behaved. We would welcome the services you described. It would add a new level of professionalism."

"It would allow you to sleep better," Jack said.

"So, you are interested?"

"I have to admit, Europe does intrigue me."

"Ah, yes. You mentioned that you plan to retire soon and perhaps move to Europe."

"Exactly, although as yet, I have not settled on where to buy a villa, but would like to do so soon. I already have most of my belongings in bonded storage — which is where the painting will soon be if I sense you are trying to lure me into some sort of trap."

"Definitely not!" Roche sounded emphatic.

Yeah, act surprised, show concern, and deny, deny, deny. "I simply thought I should warn you. I will not be shipping my belongings to Europe until I feel safe. If I die, the painting will be given to a museum, so with that in mind, do you still wish to hire me?"

"Of course," replied Roche. He paused and Jack could hear him whisper something before saying, "If you were to work for us, you would have time to scout out a villa while we pay your expenses as part of the agreement."

"That sounds generous, but as I said, I am unsure which country I will retire in."

"We have, uh, branches in several countries. If you were to consult for us, travel would be necessary for you to meet our people. You could … What is your expression? Kill two birds with the same rock?"

"With the same stone," Jack said. "I must say, your offer is tempting. Under the circumstances, providing your brother and his two friends don't try to extract some sort of revenge on me, you have piqued my interest."

"And you have piqued ours." Roche sounded sincere.

"I would prefer to speak to you in person before making a decision," Jack went on. "Considering what has transpired, I would want that to be on Canadian soil."

"Can you give me a moment, please?" said Roche.

"Take all the time you need."

Jack could hear Roche in a quiet conversation with someone. The only word he could make out was *Canada*. At last Roche came back on the line. "Jack, are you there?"

"Yes."

"Unfortunately, it would not be wise for me to meet you in Canada."

"Why not? I thought money was not a problem."

"It's not the cost, it's me. I have recently been involved in some legal difficulties. I do not want to risk bringing you unwanted attention. It is for your own protection that I think I should decline."

"I am thankful for your concern. I don't know what legal difficulties you're facing, but that's normally something I would be able to assist with."

"We have taken care of the problem, but there could be some aftermath. Nothing of real concern. Simply more of a temporary nuisance."

"It is too bad we hadn't met before last night. My service tends to preclude legal difficulties."

"Which is what we would like to discuss with you," Roche said.

"Still, considering that you tried to murder me a few hours ago, do you really expect me to come to your backyard?"

"No, uh —"

Another voice came on the phone. "I will come to Canada and meet you."

The man had a German accent and spoke with confidence. Jack made a conscious effort to keep the excitement out of his voice. "Who the hell are you?" he asked, feigning annoyance.

"The person who will be paying you, should you decide to work for us."

"And you are willing to come here to discuss it with me in person?"

"Leave your contact information with Anton. I will arrive early next week, if that is suitable."

"That is suitable. So who am I talking —"

The line went dead. Jack stared at the phone in his hand. *I want nothing better than to welcome you to Canada. We have many beautiful parks, well equipped with washrooms....*

Chapter Twenty-Four

Ten minutes after he and Jack disconnected, Detective Otto Reichartinger received a message through his wireless earpiece, which was part of a cellphone-conferencing system set up for officers who were on surveillance.

"We traced the call to the Dormero Hotel."

"Room?" Otto asked.

"Don't know. They hung up before we could find out"

Guess it doesn't matter, Otto thought. *They've probably left.* He cursed and screeched out into the traffic. The Dormero Hotel was only a couple of minutes away from where he was, but situated the farthest away from his closest team member. His instructions to lose the subjects, rather than risk them spotting the surveillance, was prevalent on his mind. Unlike movies and television, one-car surveillances did not remain unnoticed for long.

He was half a block from the hotel when he saw three men approaching a parked car. One man whom he recognized as Roche was getting into the back seat. A large, husky man with short blond hair was getting into the driver's seat, but it was the third man who attracted Otto's close attention as he drove past. This man had a swarthy complexion and collar-length black hair. He was also wearing a heavy gold chain, and a reflection from the streetlight indicated rings on the fingers of his right hand. It was too dark for Otto to see if his hands were hairy. Given the man's complexion, they might be.

"I've got the number-two target getting into the back seat of a red Porsche Panamera," Otto said into his cellphone. He glanced in his rear-view mirror and saw the car pull out and head in the opposite direction. "Two men are with him. The front-seat passenger may be our number-one target. They're eastbound on Europa-Allee."

"Ten minutes away," radioed Ulrich, Otto's closest team member. "Plate?"

"Don't have it," Otto muttered, "but the car looks new." He described the suspects, including that the number-one target wore several rings.

"On his fingers?" another team member asked.

"What do you think I mean? A Prince Albert?"

"Thought I should confirm," came the haughty reply.

"Hey, Otto," Ulrich asked, "you got a Prince Albert?"

"If I ever get drunk enough to put a ring in my dick, I want you to shoot me," Otto replied as he swung his car around and hit the gas to catch up to the Porsche. When he did, he tried to maintain three cars between him and his target.

Five minutes later, with his team still a few minutes away, the Porsche slowed down in the red-light district, then turned into a narrow passageway that led to one of the more popular brothels, called Eroscenter. The problem was, Otto knew, the small parking area behind led to numerous other brothels and exits. It was also not the type of area where you would leave a new Porsche unattended, especially at midnight.

"They pulled in behind Eroscenter 47 Elbe," he reported.

Ulrich chuckled. "Don't you have a membership at that place?"

"What's your ETA, funny man?" Otto asked.

"About four minutes."

"I'm going in on foot," Otto said, fearing that to drive in immediately behind the Porsche would alert them to the fact that they were being followed.

One thing was in Otto's favour. Parking stalls around the brothels did not remain occupied long and he quickly found a place to park. Moments later he ignored the friendly hello from a hooker on a balcony overlooking the passageway and hustled through.

It didn't take him long to find the Porsche, which was parked and empty. Six men were talking in a cluster a short distance away, and he was able to make out Roche as being one of them. *So far, so good.*

He decided to use the opportunity to get the licence plate from the Porsche, but as he neared, someone grabbed him by the shoulder. "What are you doing?" said a man with a deep, gravelly voice.

They were in the shadows, but Otto could see that the man had a broad chest and thick-muscled arms. He also had a broad nose and a short, black beard. It was the nose that caught Otto's attention and caused his pulse to quicken. *I know this face.*

"I said —"

"Lookin' for a place to puke," Otto slurred.

"Puke near this car and I'll wipe your face in it." The man shoved Otto backward. "If you so much as touch it, I'll break both your fucking arms. Get lost!"

Otto swayed on his feet as he caught a glimpse of the man's left hand. Half of the index finger was missing. *It's him!*

Not the Ringmaster, but a thug known as Nine-finger Joe, currently the subject of one of the most intensive manhunts Germany had ever seen. Nine-finger Joe had escaped prison a month earlier after being sentenced to sixteen years for the violent hijacking of a truck full of liquor.

"Okay, okay. Sorry," Otto mumbled. He managed to catch a glimpse of the plate before staggering back out the passageway to the street. He had intended to return to his own car, but the sound of men's voices following him out the passageway changed his mind.

He elected, instead, to stand on the sidewalk and engage the hooker on the balcony in idle chatter as he watched. The six men he'd seen in a cluster moments before talked briefly with Nine-finger Joe at the end of the passageway, then made their way toward him. *What's the matter, Joe? Afraid to come out in the light?*

As the six men neared, Otto caught a glimpse of Roche and the driver of the Porsche. They and two others had their backs to him as they proceeded to an outdoor café beside the brothel. The remaining two men left the group and were headed his way.

"I've never been to Canada, have you?" he heard one man say to the other as they passed.

Both were about thirty and had the hardened look of street criminals. Neither paid any attention to him as they continued on.

"So, you telling me you don't have twenty euros?" the hooker yelled down to him.

Otto waved his hand dismissively at the prostitute as Ulrich drove past. While Ulrich searched for a place to park, Otto returned to his own car and used his phone. "Targets are sitting out front of Café Elbe beside the Eroscenter," he reported.

His team responded and he was pleased to hear they were all nearby. "Have some more information for you," he added. "I just saw Nine-finger Joe in the back. He's somehow connected to these guys."

"Are you serious?" Ulrich asked. "Rumour was that he fled to Thailand."

"I'm very serious."

"Nine-finger Joe?" another member of the surveillance team exclaimed. "Are you sure? His real name is Manfred —"

"Yes, it's him," Otto stated. "He's grown a beard now, but there's no doubt. He's working for whoever it is we're following."

"There's eight of us. We can go in and arrest him!" This from Ulrich.

"No, we're not doing that," Otto said.

"You're right," Ulrich agreed. "Want me to call the Special Response Unit?"

"No! We're not to do anything that could alert the targets."

"But —"

"Nine-finger Joe's day will come, just not today."

"Hope whatever Canada is working on is worth letting him go." There was disappointment in Ulrich's voice.

"A policeman was murdered in Paris today," Otto told him. "Catching that person is worth a hundred guys like Nine-finger Joe."

"You're right, sorry."

"In the meantime, let's all make certain we don't do something that will get another policeman murdered in Canada. Everyone clear on that?"

After a round of affirmative replies came through his earpiece, Otto checked the license plate on the Porche. It was registered to a Wolfgang Menges with a local apartment address.

He used his binoculars to look at the four men in the café. The two men with Roche and Wolfgang looked like thugs, but neither was the man with the swarthy complexion.

You son of a bitch! Where did you go? Are you with Ninefinger Joe? Otto radioed his team to alert them that the unidentified man was missing. Moments later the two thugs left the café and disappeared back down the passageway.

To avoid jeopardizing the surveillance, Otto opted not to have anyone follow them, and the team remained to watch Roche and Wolfgang. Thirty minutes later Wolfgang drove Roche to the Sheraton Frankfurt Airport Hotel, where Roche doubtless booked a room. Wolfgang returned to his own apartment.

Otto checked his watch. *Quarter to two. Must be quarter to five in the afternoon in Canada. Who is the undercover cop there who asked for me, and what does he want done?*

He had been given a contact number for a Staff-Sergeant Wood, the cop's boss in Canada. As he opened his notebook, his phone vibrated. He looked at the 604 prefix on the call display, which matched the prefix of the number in his notebook. *What? Are you reading my mind?*

Chapter Twenty-Five

Again, Jack ripped the tape off Anton, who winced. His skin was more sensitive than ever. "Get to your feet," Jack ordered.

Anton complied, glancing nervously at Jack, Laura, Sammy, and Benny while massaging his wrists.

"What had you planned on doing with Dempsey's car?" asked Jack gruffly.

"We were going to leave it at the Vancouver Airport to throw the cops off."

Jack shook his head. "Security cameras are all around the airport — you don't need that headache. We're only minutes from the Fort Langley Airport, which is small and alongside the Fraser River. My guys will leave it near there. The cops won't know if he left on a small plane or went into the river. Either way, it's better than your idea."

"Hadn't thought of that," Anton said. "I don't know the area all that well."

Jack gave the keys for the car I-HIT had lent him to Benny and told him to follow Sammy in Dempsey's car and leave it where he said. He then turned to Anton again. "You're coming with me."

"Where are you taking me?" Anton's voice was shrill.

"I'm going to drop you off about two minutes away, then you can walk back and free your two buddies. I will also give you my number. I want to know when to schedule a meeting with whoever's coming to see me. I travel a lot, so let me know as soon as you find out. Give me a number for you, as well, in the event I need to contact you."

* * *

It was four in the afternoon when Jack and Laura arrived at their office. They immediately went to see Rose.

"Good news," Rose said as they took a seat. "The painting you found has been confirmed as the original that was stolen from the home in Burnaby. It is now stored in the vault at the Burnaby Detachment."

"Bet the owner will be glad to get it back," Laura said.

"The original investigator is away on holiday, but they brought us the file. It's on your desk if you want to look at it."

"Did you read it?" asked Jack.

"Yes," Rose replied. "Apparently, it was a real break-in. The painting wasn't insured, so that rules out an insurance scam."

"Not insured?" Jack was surprised.

"The owner is in his eighties. He only discovered it in his attic recently."

Jack nodded. "I'll look at the file later. In the meantime, I've got a phone number for Anton. I would like someone to apply for an emergency wiretap on it."

"What about Bojan and Klaus?" asked Rose. "Don't you have their numbers?"

"I do, but legislation requires they be notified later if we do electronic surveillance on them. Before Kerin's murder, the French police didn't know about Bojan and Klaus. In theory, only I do, so that would jeopardize the informant if they found out that wiretaps were applied for today. Later, if a wiretap shows Anton calling them, we could do it then."

"Klaus and Bojan are low-level hoods," Laura stated. "Roche doesn't deal with them, regardless."

Rose nodded. "As far as Anton goes, I've spoken with Inspector Dyck, and he said Corporal Crane is at your disposal to get that going."

"Wonder how she feels about that," Jack said. "I don't think she was happy with the delivery I made for her."

"She seemed okay when she called me earlier. She wants a written statement from the both of you describing everything that happened to use as grounds for the wiretap."

"Good. What about Kerin's notes?"

"The French police are transcribing them and say we'll have a full transcript by tomorrow. Everything else I've been told about their investigation is in this file." Rose gestured at a file on her desk. "If you wish to review it again, be my guest."

"And Germany?" Jack picked up the file. "What's going on there? Did they ever find out where Roche was when he called me the last time?"

"Haven't heard." Rose glanced at her watch. "It's one-forty in the morning there. Maybe they didn't come up with anything and shut it down."

"I think Otto is professional enough that he would let us know," Jack said. "Give me his number and I'll call him."

"And your statement for Connie?"

"I'll call her right after talking with Otto and give her the statement before I go home."

"You could probably wait and do your statement tomorrow morning," Rose suggested.

Jack shook his head. "It's not like I'll be able to sleep tonight."

* * *

"Yes, hello," Otto answered in perfect English.

"Detective Otto Reichartinger," Jack said, "this is Bart from the Outback Bar in Lamai, Koh Samui, Thailand, calling. You left without paying for your last bottle of Victoria Bitter."

Otto grinned. "I apologize. Some Canadian I was drinking with said he would buy it for me after I paid for the previous round. You know how cheap they are. He must have skipped out without paying."

"Must've," Jack said.

"Who are you really?" asked Otto seriously.

"Jack Taggart. My partner, Laura Secord, and I are both undercover operatives with the Royal Canadian Mounted Police. We were on assignment and met you at Bill Resort in Koh Samui a couple of years ago."

"Ah, so it was you!" Otto laughed.

"We never told you who we really were, but spent a bit of time partying with you and some Norwegians."

"Terje, Inger Siri, Eirik, and Trine," said Otto. "They are good friends of mine. Oh, yes, I remember the two of you. So Laura wasn't really your girlfriend?"

"No."

"Fine time to tell me." Otto pretended to be angry. "You knew I was single."

"She's married," Jack said. "So am I."

"Too bad!" Otto exclaimed.

"About her or me?"

Otto chuckled. "With you I don't care."

After a bit more reminiscing, Jack explained everything that had happened since his informant had called him.

Otto then updated Jack on his surveillance of Roche Freulard, Wolfgang Menges, and the unidentified man with the swarthy complexion. "By his looks, I would say he's either a Spaniard or an Italian." Otto paused. "I'm sorry I lost him."

"It happens. Better than burning the surveillance. I'm really happy you found out as much as you did."

"There is something else." Otto told Jack about seeing Nine-finger Joe.

"Sounds like I put you into a nest of some very nasty people," Jack replied. "Do you think the two bad guys who passed you on the sidewalk and mentioned never having been to Canada were planning on coming here?"

"I couldn't tell from the little I heard. They could have been talking about someone else, or perhaps the others who were at the café."

"Would you recognize all these men if you were to see them again?"

"Yes."

"I'll put in a request for you to come to Canada. Considering the kind of people we're dealing with, I'd like to have someone who knows their faces."

"Not a problem. Roche and Wolfgang appear to have gone to bed within the last few minutes. Do you want us to stay on them?"

"Could you break off, then be back on them by seven o'clock your time?"

"Yes," Otto said. "That should give me time for about four hours' sleep."

"Seems to me that's about all you ever got in Thailand." Jack stifled a yawn. "In the meantime, I'll put in that request."

"I'll pack my snowshoes."

"Good. Carry them on your back. That way you'll blend in with everyone else if we end up dodging in and out of the igloos."

Otto smiled as he hung up.

* * *

Jack's next call was to Connie Crane. "Hey, CC, you pissed off at me?" he asked as soon as she answered.

"Not after hearing the circumstances." She paused. "Only you would pull a stunt like that, though."

"Thought you would appreciate me delivering a take-out order. Save you the legwork of leaving the office."

"Very funny," she said sarcastically. "So who's the murderer? Or dare I ask?"

"Anton Roche. I've got his number for you to get an emergency wiretap, but I don't want him put under physical surveillance or arrested until I say so."

"Yeah, with you, I'm sure you don't want the bad guys being watched when you're dealing with them."

"What are you implying?"

"That not all murder victims are delivered to our office in a van."

"What the hell? I —"

"Never mind the bullshit," said Connie gruffly. "Give me the number and then I want a written statement from you and Laura to corroborate my request for the authorization."

* * *

It was eight-thirty at night when Jack and Laura finished writing their statements. They'd been working for nineteen hours straight, which wasn't unusual, but what with the stress they'd been under, both were exhausted.

Nevertheless, Laura wanted to peruse Jack's statement about what had happened at the acreage prior to her arrival.

As Jack waited, he skimmed through the investigational file from Burnaby regarding the stolen painting. The eighty-one-year-old victim, Mr. Herman Jaiger, lived alone in a small house. He was awakened at night by two men wearing ski masks and latex gloves. One man was exceptionally tall, spoke with a German accent, and may have had a tattoo on his neck. *Klaus,* Jack said to himself as he turned a page. The other man was described as being small and thin. *Probably Liam.* The thieves demanded to know the whereabouts of a painting.

Jack continued to read. One particular statement caught his attention: "During the home invasion, Mr. Jaiger was tied to a chair and questioned about the whereabouts of the painting. At first he denied having it, but when the larger of the two men burnt his eyelid with a lit cigarette, he quickly told them it was stored in his attic. The man continued to burn his face while the smaller man retrieved the painting."

The file went on to say that Mr. Jaiger had inherited the home when his father passed away years before. Last year, Mr. Jaiger found the painting in the attic, along with an envelope stuck in the back of the frame with the name *Mr. Guri L. Sacher* and a Paris address. Inside the envelope was a document of authentication from the Goldman Art Verification Agency in Paris, dated in 1933.

Herman Jaiger had the painting appraised in Vancouver and discovered it was worth millions. He told the investigator that his father was a German SS officer in the Second World War, and he believed his father had stolen the painting. Upon discovering it, he wanted to return it to its rightful owner and made some inquires. He learned that the Goldman Agency in Paris had disappeared during the war and that the home of Mr. Guri L. Sacher had been turned into a school.

Herman then contacted a museum in Paris. The curator told him that an art collector living in Paris had once lent the museum another painting by the same artist. They suggested he contact the collector to see if he could assist. The collector's name was Philippe Petit, so Herman wrote him a letter and sent a picture of the painting, but as yet, had not heard back.

The name sounded familiar to Jack and he flipped open the file Rose had made from what she had been told. *Philippe Petit was the art collector murdered in Paris and the catalyst that started Kerin's undercover investigation. Explains why he didn't reply.*

Jack removed some photos from a manila envelope and looked at Herman Jaiger's face. A half-dozen burn marks were evident, including one that caused his eyelid to puff up, leaving only a slit for him to peer out of.

Jack scowled as he leaned back in his chair. *Perhaps Connie has a point. I really don't want anyone watching me the next time I meet up with Klaus.*

Chapter Twenty-Six

Jack's phone woke him at three o'clock in the morning.

"*Guten Morgen*, Herr Taggart."

"*Guten Morgen* to you too, Otto." Jack glanced at the clock. "Or should I say good afternoon where you are. What's up?"

"Roche is at the airport and has booked an Air France flight departing for Paris. It's scheduled to arrive in Paris at one-thirty this afternoon."

"That was short and sweet," Jack said. "How about Wolfgang? What's he been up to?"

"Followed him to a mall this morning where he had a doctor's appointment. Knowing the area he hangs out in, he likely has a venereal disease. After that he returned home and has probably gone back to bed."

"And Roche wasn't seen meeting with anyone?"

"No. He had breakfast alone at the hotel and doesn't look happy. Do you want me to notify Paris and have them follow him from that end?"

"No, let him go," replied Jack. "I'm hoping his boss will be coming to see me in a few days. I don't want to chance heating anyone up. Are you able to stay on Wolfgang?"

"Sure, but it'll cost you a beer next time I see you."

* * *

At eight-thirty in the morning, Jack arrived at work and Rose spotted him in the hall as he passed her door. "You!" she said, pointing her finger at him. "Take a seat!" She gestured to a chair in front of her desk.

Oh, crap, what now? Jack sat down as directed.

"I found out where Klaus Eichel went yesterday as soon as he was freed," said Rose, glaring at Jack.

"Oh?"

"Don't give me that innocent look! You told me you didn't hurt him!"

"I didn't say that. I said I was as gentle as the situation allowed. He tried to grab my shotgun. My only other alternative was to shoot him."

"You told me you even assisted in lowering him to the floor!"

"I did, but had to use the butt of the shotgun to do it."

"Are you trying to be funny?"

"Not really. Did you look at the photos of the victim who had his painting stolen?"

"Yes, I did," replied Rose evenly.

"There's nothing funny about it. It was Klaus who did that to him."

"That doesn't give you the right to dispense justice," Rose snapped.

Jack stared silently back at her.

"Damn it, Jack, I know Klaus is a sadist and was abusing your informant, but you don't take the law into your own hands."

"I didn't. It was simply a situation where I had no other choice."

"Both sides of his jaw are fractured and he hardly has any teeth left."

"Maybe next time he won't try to grab a shotgun from me."

"There better not be a next time," warned Rose.

"Did you read that he continued to burn Mr. Jaiger with a cigarette even after he told them where the painting was?" asked Jack.

"You don't know for sure it was Klaus. Not one hundred percent."

"Really? Not one hundred percent? Maybe I'm better at math than you."

"Don't be impertinent," she said. "That's not the point. Even if it was, it doesn't give you the right to attack him."

"It was him who tried to attack me. If you don't believe me, call Sammy. He saw it."

Rose stared at Jack a moment, then said, "I want to make myself clear. I won't stand for unnecessary violence."

"You made yourself clear." Jack tried not to let the anger he felt show in his voice. "I only use as much force as necessary. Is there anything else?"

Rose paused. "Yes, two things. I have a translated copy of all of Kerin Bastion's undercover notes, including notes from his partner, Maurice Leblanc, who was on surveillance across the street from the park when the murder took place."

Jack clenched his jaw.

Rose caught the look. "It wasn't your fault," she said quietly. "You were doing your job and he was doing his. It happens."

"You said you had two things. What's the other?"

Rose studied Jack. Anger was a natural step on his road to recovery. It was how he dealt with his anger that concerned her. She decided to let it go for now. "The other thing I have is about who spied on Clive Dempsey for the bad guys."

"Big Joe Investigations," said Jack with sudden interest. "What have you got?"

"The company is owned by a Joe Hershey, who works out of his house. He's an ex-member from the Prairies who was stationed in a variety of plainclothes units."

"I don't know him," Jack said.

"He didn't have a good rep. Apparently, he would fabricate stories to make himself look good while making his colleagues look bad. He wasn't particularly gifted when it came to intelligence."

"Not someone I would trust to work with us," noted Jack.

"For sure," agreed Rose.

"Going by the name of his company, I take it he's a large man?"

"The person I spoke to said he weighed about two hundred kilos and that there wasn't a gram of muscle in his whole body. He said you could tell what police cars he drove because if they had bucket seats, the back of the seats were broken off from his weight."

"Won't be a tough guy to spot if they hire him to work on me," said Jack.

"He has two other guys he hires when he needs them. I'll get all the details and photos within the next day or two, including vehicle descriptions."

Jack nodded, then updated Rose on the phone call he'd received from Otto regarding Roche returning to Paris. Afterwards, he returned to his own desk and updated Laura. They then read the translation of Kerin's notes, along with those of his partner, Maurice Leblanc.

When they were finished, Jack looked at Laura and asked, "What do you think?"

"Kerin was set up to see if he had a surveillance team," replied Laura. "Walking from the café, then hanging out at a park. There had to be counter-surveillance on him."

"I'm positive there was. Goes along with Roche telling him he would only be meeting the Ringmaster once. They wanted to up the pressure. He should have ditched the surveillance team."

"Yeah. All it did was get him killed."

"That and trying to phone to warn me," Jack said bitterly.

"Obviously he was too inexperienced to know he was being set up."

"I don't know if experience would have saved him as far as the phone call goes." Jack shook his head. "If I was in that situation, I don't know if I would have acted any differently. Hope I never have to find out."

"If it's about me, I kind of hope you make the call," Laura said dryly.

"Kind of hope?" Jack raised his eyebrows. Just then his phone rang and he reached to answer it.

"Got some news you might be interested in," said Connie. "We managed to get an emergency tap on Anton's phone late last night. We got an incoming call from his brother in Paris at seven this morning."

"Surveillance put Roche Freulard on a flight from Frankfurt bound for Paris at about noon their time," Jack said. "Doing the math, it would mean Roche placed the call at four o'clock in the afternoon his time. What did they say?"

"Roche wasn't happy. Turns out the Ringmaster was going to step down and recommend he take over the organization, but all that's on hold until they get their hands on the painting. Roche isn't the only one upset. Anton said that Klaus figures he is going to be fired."

"Klaus figures right. They don't want him to know until he returns to Europe. They're probably afraid he'll do something stupid if he finds out here."

"I agree. Anyway, that was the gist of their conversation on that point. Then Roche told Anton that the Ringmaster is sending Wolfgang over to see you."

"Oh, crap," Jack muttered. "I was hoping the Ringmaster would show up in person. Wolfgang Menges was the driver when Roche rode in the back seat of a Porsche after he called me from the hotel in Frankfurt. There was a swarthy-looking guy in the front with Wolfgang. That's who I was hoping would come."

"Maybe he will later. Roche made it explicitly clear that nobody was to lay a hand on you. The idea is to get you to trust them."

"They think I have the painting in bonded storage," Jack said. "They're going to want to sucker me into taking it out. I'm going to request that Detective Otto Reichartinger, from Germany, and Kerin's partner, Maurice Leblanc, come to assist in the event others besides Wolfgang show up. They might recognize someone."

"Good idea, but there's more. I think you're going to get a call from Anton. He was told to try and check you. He's going to arrange to meet you, then have surveillance put on you."

"Perfect." Jack grinned. "I love it when a plan comes together. I'll prepare a background cover for my UC. Maybe the Ringmaster will show up after they check me out."

"You're okay with them tailing you?" Connie was surprised.

"Okay with it? I love it!"

"That makes me nervous," Connie said gravely.

Chapter Twenty-Seven

It was ten o'clock the following morning when Jack received a call from Anton. He put his finger to his lips to caution Laura, then walked into a stationery room for privacy.

"What's up, Anton?" asked Jack. "Is the boss man here from Europe already?"

"Uh, no, not yet," replied Anton. "I would like to meet you in person to talk about something."

"Trying to set me up to kidnap me, Anton?"

"No, no, no," replied Anton adamantly. "I would be happy to meet you in a public place. Perhaps a restaurant of your choice, if you like. I will come alone, but you can bring whoever you like with you."

"I see. I guess today I could free myself up for lunch, say, at twelve-thirty? I know you don't know Vancouver very well, so how about the Fort Pub in Fort Langley? Do you know where that is?"

"I do. That is ideal! Thank you."

* * *

At eleven-thirty, Laura sat in the back of an SUV, in charge of the surveillance team stationed near the Fort Pub and Grill. Half an hour after she arrived, Big Joe was spotted driving a white van with Bojan in the seat beside him. The van had dark-tinted windows along the sides and back. Moments later the van parked near the pub, and Big Joe and Bojan disappeared into the back of the van. Seconds later two men who worked for Big Joe arrived in separate vehicles and parked nearby.

Laura radioed the information to Jack, then waited.

At twelve-thirty, Jack arrived and parked his car. Sammy and Benny from Drug Section were with him and they walked into the Fort Pub and Grill. Jack was dressed casually in slacks, and Sammy and Benny wore suits and ties. They took a seat to wait for Anton when Laura called Jack.

"One of the goofs who works for Big Joe snuck over and slapped a magnetic tracker under the back of your car," she said.

"Perfect," Jack said.

"Anton pulled up, as well," she added. "He's on his way in."

Jack hung up as Anton entered and joined them at their table.

Anton swallowed as he glanced at Sammy and Benny, then gave a nervous smile. "Hope you guys aren't here to haul me away."

Jack, along with Sammy and Benny, stared blankly at Anton without answering. His face paled and he swallowed again.

The waitress arrived immediately and the four men did little talking until they'd each placed their food order. When she left, Jack gave Anton a nod. "What did you want to see me for?"

"Simply to ensure that you're willing to follow through with meeting our, uh, representative from Europe. He wanted this confirmed."

"I told him I would." Jack looked annoyed. "I don't say things I don't mean."

"I realize that, and by your willingness to meet me, it indicates that you, uh, don't have any second thoughts on the matter."

"I don't like being dicked around," said Jack. "I'm not a gofer waiting at someone's beck and call."

"I'm sorry. We wanted to make sure you hadn't vanished on us. Lunch will be on me."

"This is Thursday. The week is almost over. When will I be meeting him?"

"He is catching a flight Monday morning and with the time difference, will arrive in Vancouver Monday evening."

Jack was pleased that the meeting would take place in a few days. He wasn't pleased that the bug on Anton's phone hadn't picked it up. They were missing some of the communication between Anton and his bosses in Europe. Communication that could potentially have deadly consequences.

"I'm not sure if he would like to meet you Monday night," Anton continued. "It is a long trip and —"

"Tuesday is fine with me," said Jack. "Call me in the morning. I'll try to keep my schedule free for that day."

Forty-five minutes later they finished lunch. Jack glanced at his watch, then looked at Sammy and Benny "We better go if I'm going to get you back to work by two."

* * *

At two o'clock, Jack arrived at the first destination in his plan to enhance his cover story. He let Sammy and Benny out and then drove away.

Big Joe snapped a couple of surveillance pictures before giving Bojan a thumbs-up. He then pulled out to follow Jack at a discreet distance, aided by the laptop computer he used to monitor Jack's vehicle's movements through the magnetic tracker.

At least we know how he got rid of Clive Dempsey, Bojan thought as he glanced back at the crematorium Sammy and Benny had entered.

A short time later Jack pulled up in front of the Pan Pacific Hotel in downtown Vancouver and handed his keys to the valet before going inside.

Big Joe was only two car lengths behind and desperately radioed his two colleagues to follow Jack inside, but they were too far back in traffic. He glanced at Bojan.

"I can't do it!" exclaimed Bojan. "He knows me!"

"I know. I'll do it, but I can't park here. Drop me off, drive away, and come back in ten minutes."

* * *

Jack took an escalator up to the lobby on the second floor and saw Big Joe lumbering up after him.

Yeah, asshole. You're about as unnoticed as a chocolate cake at a diet seminar.

Upon reaching the top, Jack sauntered over to the reception desk. Big Joe cleared the top of the escalator.

"Jack!" a woman called.

Big Joe definitely saw the attractive Chinese woman on the other side of the lobby waving at Jack.

"Hey, Tina. How are you?" asked Jack when they met and gave each other a hug.

He saw Big Joe pause, then pretend to gaze over the railing at a totem pole on the lower level as he watched and listened.

"What brings you here?" Tina asked, stepping back. "Last I saw of you was when you were doing some consulting work for some international corporation."

"Still doing consulting," Jack replied. "I sold my condo a month ago and am staying here awhile. Where's your hubby?"

"John's next door at the convention center. He should be finished in an hour or two."

"I'm staying in the Pacific suite — room 2320. Pop by after and we'll catch up."

"We'd love to." Tina frowned, then said, "You're looking thin. Are you okay?" She reached out and gripped his hand.

Jack gave her hand a squeeze, then let go. "I'm fine."

"John and I have thought of you quite a bit since Molly passed on," said Tina sombrely. "We should have called you."

Jack swallowed. "I'm okay. I just need time."

"Scuttlebutt is you plan on retiring and moving to Europe or something. Is that true? Is that why you sold your condo?"

"It's true, but I'm in no hurry and haven't decided when or where yet," he said.

"You got time to sit for a moment? Maybe grab a coffee?"

"You bet," he replied. "We can go here," he suggested with a nod toward the hotel restaurant, overlooking Vancouver harbour. As they walked toward the restaurant, Big Joe waddled over and took the escalator back down to the street-level exit.

"Think it went okay?" asked Tina.

Jack smiled. "Miss Chan, there's a reason they call you the Asian Heat. You always come through."

Tina smiled. "Seems like you've been relying on our unit quite a bit lately. How did it go with Sammy and Benny? I heard you used them, too."

"It went good enough that I owe them a coffee, as well," Jack said.

Tina gave an unladylike snort. "With Sammy, I suggest you make it Canadian Club and Coke." She looked around the lobby. "This place is beautiful. Did the force really spring for you to stay in a suite here?"

"Don't I wish," replied Jack. "The hotel has been really great at accommodating me, though. An executive assistant who works here has a brother who is a member of the Vancouver City Police. She's pulled some strings to make it look like I stay here if anyone checks or leaves a message. She's also given me access to the service elevator that goes up to the luxury suites. I can use the regular elevator to go up if anyone is watching, then sneak out using the service elevator without being seen."

"What if someone goes up with you in the elevator?"

"She's taken care of that, too. There's a private lounge up top where complimentary drinks and appetizers are served for those who stay in the suites. All I would do is wander in there. The concierge knows to let me in, but would stop anyone following me and not let them enter."

Tina smiled. "Perfect."

* * *

Later that night Bojan, Anton, and Klaus sat at their kitchen table eating dinner and discussing what they'd learned about Jack.

"The Pan Pacific is one of the top hotels in Vancouver," said Bojan, chewing on a piece of barbecued steak. "I checked out the fucking suite he's staying in on the Internet. It looks out on the harbour, mountains, the city skyline … you name it. It's over eighteen hundred square feet. Even has a baby grand piano in it. This guy is loaded."

"Wish we had contacts at a crematorium," muttered Anton, skewering a mushroom with his fork to savour with the meat.

Klaus didn't comment as he sucked his canned lentil soup through a straw. Talking was too painful. He also sensed that both Anton and Bojan were distancing themselves from him. *They* do *plan on getting rid of me. The fucking wimps don't have the balls to do what should be done.* He glowered at Anton and Bojan as he concocted a course of action.

I'll show 'em. All I have to do is kidnap Jack and make him take me to the painting. If I don't get my hands on it, I can still kill him and deny it. I'm sure he has lots of enemies.

Klaus started to grin as he fantasized about how he would torture Jack, but a stab of pain hit his jaw and made his eyes water. *Painting or no painting, I'll kill that fucker.*

Chapter Twenty-Eight

It was eight-thirty Friday morning when Jack arrived at his office and listened to a voice message from Special "O" summarizing their surveillance of Big Joe Investigations. After Big Joe left the Pan Pacific Hotel the day before, he had his two cohorts watch the front of the hotel while he returned to his home office. The two cohorts went home at ten o'clock, but had returned at six o'clock in the morning. Big Joe arrived two hours later and was seen monitoring his laptop from where he was parked a block from the hotel.

"What now?" asked Laura when Jack finished listening.

"I'll talk to Rose and get her to help with a quick UC scenario."

"What am I? Chopped liver?"

"I want an older, more mature-looking woman. Not to mention, Rose isn't a trained operator. This will only be a cameo appearance. I want to save you for when I really need someone I can rely on."

Laura smiled. "No problem. You had me at *older*."

* * *

At ten-thirty that morning, Jack walked out the front entrance of the Pan Pacific Hotel carrying a brown manila envelope as the valet arrived with his SUV. Jack climbed in and drove to the Pacific Central train station. He parked and went inside. Big Joe and his team discreetly followed, with one man going inside to see Jack deposit the envelope in a storage locker.

Minutes later Jack returned to the hotel to drop of his SUV, but then walked to a nearby street corner and waited. He displayed his impatience by glancing at his watch several times.

Soon Big Joe's team saw a smartly dressed woman arrive and speak with Jack. The woman gave Jack a white envelope from her purse. He opened the envelope and partially pulled out a wad of money, then nodded and put the envelope into his inside jacket pocket. He gave the woman a key.

Big Joe continued following Jack and saw him return to the hotel. His two cohorts followed the woman and saw her retrieve the manila envelope from the train station. They followed her to the trading floor of the stock exchange, where she disappeared.

Minutes after returning to the hotel, Jack slipped out unnoticed and returned to his office.

"Go okay?" Laura asked.

"Like clockwork," Jack replied. "That should give them something to talk about."

"They'll think you obtained a company secret or supplied insider-trading information to someone." Laura smiled. "Any other plans to build your nefarious rep'?"

"Not for now. Let's catch up on the paperwork and take the weekend off. Special 'O' can babysit Big Joe."

* * *

At nine o'clock Monday morning, Jack and Laura sat across from Rose in her office as she read over the reports from Special "O." When she was finished, she looked at Jack. "What do you make of Big Joe taking his team off the hotel Saturday afternoon?"

"It's expensive to hire a private investigation team to do surveillance. The tracker is still on my SUV. If I'd gone anywhere in it, Big Joe could have always checked it out later from his laptop."

"What about yesterday?" Rose asked. "Special 'O' saw Klaus arrive in the afternoon and hang around outside the hotel wearing a hoodie."

"He's not hard to spot. Dresses like a gangster. Normally wears a ball cap that's too big for his peanut-sized cranium, and his pants hang halfway down his ass."

"He stayed until nine last night," noted Rose. "Do you think he was simply filling in temporarily over the weekend?"

Jack glanced at Laura, then shook his head. "No. I checked with Special 'O' and they said he had his car parked a couple of blocks away in a parkade. It's highly unlikely he'd planned on following me. I also spoke with Connie. Yesterday they intercepted a phone call where Anton asked Klaus what he was doing. Klaus managed to grunt out that his mouth was hurting him."

"I'm sure it is," said Rose.

"Yes, but he told Anton he was waiting in a medical clinic when, in fact, he was outside the Pan Pacific. When Anton called later, Klaus sounded angry at being hassled. He told Anton that he'd gone to a bar and met someone and that he expected he'd be going to her place — incredible as that may seem, considering he can hardly talk. Special 'O' placed him outside the hotel both times."

As Rose looked at Jack, the reason Klaus lied became crystal clear. "What are you going to do? Is he back at the hotel?"

"I checked with 'O' and they said nobody is there at the moment. Neither Klaus nor Big Joe."

"If Klaus is intent on killing you, that's the one place he knows where to find you," Rose said. "What would you do if he shows up?" Before Jack could answer she said, "That's it. You can't risk going back to the hotel. Not without having Klaus arrested to clear the way. He probably has a gun."

"Arrested? Like hell!" Jack was furious. "Do that and we'll risk burning everything!"

"What choice do we have?" Rose gave Jack a hard look. "Legally, I mean."

"I guess if I'm not supposed to hurt him, I could wear Kevlar and let him shoot me. Then run away and complain to Anton later. Maybe they would reprimand him."

"That's absurd!" Rose said angrily.

"So is telling me not to hurt someone who's attacking me," Jack replied. "Last time I dealt with him he tried to grab the shotgun and you gave me hell for smacking him."

Rose exhaled noisily. "Perhaps last time I made a mistake. What about the first time you removed his teeth? Did he try to grab the shotgun then, too?"

Jack looked a bit sheepish. "I'm sure he was thinking about it."

"Exactly!" Rose snapped.

Laura jumped into the conversation. "This is a whole different scenario," she said. "He could walk up behind Jack when he's waiting for the valet and pop him in the back of the head. Are you telling me you're willing to risk Jack being murdered over the rights of some scumbag who —"

"Cut the bullshit." Rose glared at Laura. "Insulting my intelligence won't get us anywhere. If he pulls a gun on Jack, of course, I'd expect him to defend himself — with lethal force if the situation dictates." She turned to Jack. "If you're adamant about not having him arrested, what can you do? I'm not going to risk a shootout on a downtown street."

"I agree with that," Jack said. "I'm a lousy shot, not to mention if I did shoot him, there's no way we could keep my real identity under wraps. He wouldn't be hard to outrun, though, what with his pants probably falling to his ankles."

"If you had the chance to run," said Rose wryly. "Not to mention we can't take a chance on him firing wildly. Do you have an alternative solution? Something that I can convince the brass is appropriate?"

"How about I report his activities to Anton and threaten to withdraw from any future contact with him?" he suggested. "I'm sure they would, uh, tell him to desist."

"Desist? With these guys it'd be more likely that he wouldn't exist."

"You don't need to tell the brass that," said Jack. "Besides, if you fly with the crows, expect to get shot."

"Yes, but I feel uncomfortable about setting him up, too," Rose said.

"Look," Jack said, "in an ideal situation he might go to court to be judged by twelve of his peers. In my scenario it will be his *actual* peers who judge him, and whatever decision they come to is a consequence of his actions, not ours."

"Providing we don't encourage them to commit a crime."

"That goes without saying." Jack furrowed his eyebrows in annoyance.

"Okay, as long as we're clear on that matter," said Rose. "Is Wolfgang on schedule?"

"Yes, he arrives at the airport tonight at six-thirty. He's already in the air. Otto is on the same flight. It's a twelve-and-a-half-hour trip."

"Nobody from France coming?"

"I spoke with a Maurice Leblanc yesterday," Jack said. "Today is the funeral." Again, he fought his remorse.

"It's not like you can attend, given the circumstances."

"I know. I don't believe in funerals, anyway. The last thing I need to hear is someone eulogizing a person they probably don't know and hear how some god selected him to go to a better place. The Ringmaster is not a god. Funerals make me angry."

"Spoken like a true atheist," said Rose, "and I can see you're angry."

Jack shrugged. "I am … and I am."

"I feel likewise when it comes to religion," Rose admitted. "Still, sometimes you feel a need to offer emotional support to others who do believe."

"Yeah, well, I need to look after my own mental health," Jack said, "but Maurice wanted to go, so I told him to attend. Kerin's widow, Gabrielle, also needs support, so I told him I would appraise the situation here and call him if I needed him. The next few days could make a big difference in whether I gain the trust of the Ringmaster. Let's not blow it over Klaus."

Rose grimaced.

"They killed one of us," Jack said pointedly. "I don't care if it was in France. He's still one of us. More than that, it was someone who was murdered trying to save my life."

Rose nodded. "I'm well aware of that. We all are."

"Are you?" demanded Jack. "Then why are you concerned about how they deal with Klaus? Who knows, they might simply tell him to back off. Roche said he was being recalled to Europe where they were going to fire him regardless."

Rose bit her lower lip, locking eyes with Jack. "Okay, say I go along with that. How would you do it? You can't burn the wiretap."

"Not only that," Laura put in, "but to say you saw Klaus hanging out at your hotel, there's no way you would trust them, let alone work for them. They would definitely smell a rat."

"Not if I said I knew Klaus was acting on his own."

"How can you tell them that without burning the wiretap?" asked Laura.

"Simple enough. First I would do a pre-emptive strike and detain Klaus near the hotel. Then I would meet with Wolfgang and say I knew Klaus was acting on his own."

"Why would they think you thought that?" asked Rose.

Jack looked at Laura for a response.

Laura considered for a moment, then said, "Because if Wolfgang was involved, he wouldn't be willing to meet with Jack afterwards."

"Exactly," Jack said. "Especially if Klaus was no longer answering his phone. It would be an opportunity to enhance my credibility as someone they should hire."

"What do you mean when you say a pre-emptive strike?" questioned Rose.

"No worries." Jack dismissed Rose's concern with a wave of his hand. "I'm sure after what happened that Klaus knows enough to obey my orders if I have the drop on him. Once I do that, I'll tie him up and leave him in his car for Wolfgang to collect. Rather doubtful that any violence would be necessary."

Rose stared at Jack. *I've heard that line before....*

Chapter Twenty-Nine

Upon returning to his desk, Jack had another voice message from Special "O," this one telling him that Big Joe had returned to the hotel. When he told Laura, he said, "This guy is becoming a real thorn."

"What do you want to do?" she asked.

"Tomorrow I want Wolfgang to think I found the tracker on my car before I nail Klaus. For that, I'll use Big Joe. Let's see how easy it'll be to lure him into following me. I'll get you to take me to the hotel."

A few minutes later, as they drove, Laura asked, "What about Klaus while you're busy luring Big Joe?"

"He's been watching where the valet service drops off my car. If I go down to the garage, not the valet, he won't know I'm gone. I doubt that Anton is saying much to him these days. They both sounded ticked off at each other during their last phone call."

An hour later Jack drove out of the hotel underground parking lot without Klaus realizing it and went to the restaurant where he and Laura had agreed to meet for lunch.

Special "O" reported that Big Joe, in his white van with the tinted windows, drove past the restaurant thirty minutes after Jack arrived. After lunch, Jack drove to a liquor store and then returned to the hotel. Big Joe was observed following, but an hour after Jack was back at the hotel, Big Joe returned to his home office.

That evening Wolfgang Menges arrived as scheduled. Special "O" called Jack to report that Anton and Bojan met him at the airport and took him to the Fairmont Hotel in downtown Vancouver, where he checked in.

"No sign of Klaus?" asked Jack.

"He's still hanging around the Pan Pacific. Looks more impatient every minute. Did your friend Otto show up?"

"The shuttle's pulling in now," said Jack. "Keep me posted."

Detective Otto Reichartinger had arrived on the same flight as Wolfgang but had maintained his distance. He'd taken a shuttle to the Delta Hotel, and Jack and Laura greeted him in the lobby. Otto reported that Wolfgang appeared to be travelling on his own and that he didn't recognize anyone else on the plane.

Laura glanced at Jack. "Good, maybe only one of them wants to kill you."

"For now," said Jack dryly.

"Something I should know about?" Otto asked.

"We've booked you a room," said Jack, handing him the key, "so let's go on up and we'll fill you in."

Entering the room, Otto grinned when he saw a case of Victoria Bitter beer.

"Cold ones are in the mini-fridge," Jack announced, before his face became serious. "The first one will be in honour of Kerin Bastion, who was buried today."

Three bottles of beer were opened and Laura, Otto and Jack clinked the bottles.

"To justice," Laura said sombrely.

* * *

At eight-thirty the next morning, Jack and Laura arrived for work and learned that Klaus had been staking out the Pan Pacific Hotel for the past hour. Jack called the monitor who was looking after the wiretap on Anton's phone, and learned that Anton had called Klaus that morning to tell him that Wolfgang wanted to talk with him after meeting with Jack. Klaus said he was with his new girlfriend, but told Anton to keep him updated as to when and where the meeting might take place so he could meet Wolfgang immediately after.

"Klaus wants you bad," Laura said after Jack told her about the call.

"Yeah, probably figures he'll be on a plane back to Germany with Wolfgang soon." Jack quietly added, "He doesn't have much time left."

"You mean for him to get you?"

Jack glanced at Laura, then plucked a photo of Herman Jaiger's burnt face from an envelope and looked at it. "No, I mean Klaus doesn't have much time left."

At ten-thirty, Jack and Laura returned to the Delta Hotel and were having coffee with Otto when Jack received the call he was expecting.

"What's up, Anton?" he asked.

"My boss arrived last night," Anton replied. "He is ready to meet you on whatever terms you like. He understands that you might be nervous, so is happy to oblige you in any way he can. Perhaps a restaurant for lunch?"

"I'm pleased he understands that I have some concerns about meeting you people again," said Jack. "Unfortunately something of more importance has come up. I can't possibly make it for lunch, as I have to meet someone. Perhaps I could make it for dinner."

"Perhaps? My boss has travelled a long way to —"

"I will call you back this afternoon," said Jack, then disconnected the call.

Otto looked surprised. "Why are you delaying?" he asked.

"I need to take care of Klaus first." Jack slid a couple of surveillance photos across the table for Otto to see. "He is waiting for me outside my hotel again."

"You mentioned he was a nuisance last night," said Otto. "Is that how you describe people who are trying to kill you? A nuisance?" He glanced at Laura. "I take it Klaus is not the first one to try?"

"You have no idea," said Laura seriously. "We'll tag along on surveillance to watch. Keep a sharp eye open. Others could have arrived on an earlier flight. If it is any of the men you spotted in Frankfurt, I hope you can recognize them."

"If I see them, I will know them," replied Otto confidently.

"You told me Klaus doesn't have a criminal record in Germany." Jack shook his head. "He sure *looks* like he has one. Don't you guys ever leave the coffee shop?"

"For someone like him?" Otto said contemptuously. He pointed at a photo that showed Klaus's pants hanging low on his backside. "I was speaking with a ex-con the other day when someone like that walked past. Do you know what they call guys like that in prison?"

Jack and Laura glanced at each other and remained silent.

"Easy entry," replied Otto, giving a half-smile.

* * *

At eleven o'clock Laura and Otto climbed into the back seat of a Special "O" surveillance car. Jack was seeing them off. Just as two members of Special "O" took seats in the front, another team member radioed that Big Joe was spotted parking his van a block from the Pan Pacific.

"They want to know who I'm meeting," Jack said, smiling grimly. "This should be fun."

"We'll keep our eyes open," Laura said.

Thirty minutes later Jack drove his SUV out of the Pan Pacific parkade again without Klaus noticing and went to a shopping mall. Big Joe followed and drove into the lot in time to see Sammy walk over to where Jack was parking. Sammy then left in Jack's SUV while Jack walked toward the mall, followed by Big Joe.

Once inside the mall, Big Joe saw Jack enter a restaurant, so he followed him in and sat where he could watch. Over the next hour, Jack showed his impatience by looking at his watch numerous times, as well as making several phone calls.

Eventually Jack received a call and left the restaurant. Big Joe followed and saw that Sammy had returned and was giving Jack his keys back. After the two men spoke for a minute, Jack got back inside his SUV, while Big Joe hurried to his van.

Jack's next stop was the Greyhound Bus Depot, where he entered carrying a manila envelope and moments later returned to his SUV empty-handed.

So, Friday you do a drop at the train station, and today it's at the bus depot, mused Big Joe. He saw Jack sitting in his SUV talking on his phone and waited.

Jack smiled to himself as he checked his watch. It was two in the afternoon when he reached for his phone to call Anton.

"Jack?"

"Sorry to take so long to get back to you, Anton," said Jack. "My meeting didn't go as planned. I have to meet someone who lives quite a ways outside Vancouver. I doubt I'll make it tonight, but am sure I can find time tomorrow."

"But my boss came all this way," whined Anton. "Isn't there any chance you could meet him today, if only for a few minutes?"

"Well … I'm expecting a call soon. There's a possibility that I could still make dinner tonight if I meet this person halfway. I'll call you back in about two hours."

Anton hung up and quickly called Big Joe to exchange information. "I want to find out who he is meeting that is so important," Anton said tersely.

"Think he might be selling the painting?" asked Big Joe. "It could be in the back of his SUV. He's got tinted windows — hard to see in." Movement on Big Joe's laptop caught his attention and he said, "I gotta go. He's on the move!"

Big Joe followed Jack, occasionally catching glimpses of his SUV as they drove. Twenty-five minutes later they were eastbound on the Trans Canada Highway with Big Joe doing his best to keep three or four vehicles between him and Jack.

Soon Jack passed a bus and Big Joe's monitor told him that Jack had settled in at the speed limit. He knew he could relax now. If Jack checked his rear-view mirror, the bus would provide adequate cover.

At four-thirty Jack called Anton again to apologize and say he had to go out of town, but would definitely be back tomorrow.

Fifteen minutes later a visibly angry Klaus returned to the parkade to retrieve his car. Discovering that he had a flat tire made matters worse.

Klaus was bent over, putting the flat tire into his trunk, when he felt the barrel of a pistol enter his ear.

"You been looking for me, Klaus?" Jack asked.

Klaus dropped the tire and made a grab for his own pistol in the front of his pants as he spun around. He managed to get his hand on his pistol's grip, but didn't succeed in pulling it free.

"Christ, you're stupid!" Jack yelled, grabbing Klaus's wrist to stop him while simultaneously pushing his upper body into the trunk and smashing him on the face with the butt of the pistol. Repeatedly.

Klaus was practically unconscious before he let go of his pistol. Jack grabbed it, then lifted Klaus's legs and folded his entire body into the trunk.

Seconds later Sammy and Benny appeared from where they'd concealed themselves nearby. They watched as Jack took out two zip ties and bound Klaus's hands behind his back and then his ankles, before slamming the trunk shut.

They then walked over to the Special "O" surveillance van as Laura and Otto got out.

Laura looked at Jack and said, "Rose is going to have a bird."

"The dumb bastard wouldn't let go of his gun," explained Jack.

"Now what?" Sammy asked. He gave a nod toward Klaus's car and said, "His face looks like hamburger."

"So much for your plan of leaving him in the trunk of his car to let his buddies find him later," said Laura. "Didn't you tell me that a broken jaw means there's a loss of support for the tongue? His jaw is way beyond cracked. He's liable to croak. You can't chance leaving him in the condition he's in and you can't call his friends, because in theory you wouldn't know if they put him up to it."

"I'll take him to the hospital," Jack muttered.

"How the hell can you do that and maintain your bad-guy image?" Sammy asked. "He tried to kill you. In theory, you should be putting a bullet in his head."

"I'll come up with something." Jack glanced at his watch. "Better hustle. I want to meet Wolfgang immediately after."

"You going to let him out of the trunk first?" asked Benny.

"Yes, but I'll keep his hands tied until we get there."

Otto looked at the Klaus's car, then raised one eyebrow as he looked at Jack. He shook his head.

"You okay, Otto?" Jack asked.

"I'm fine," he said. "It's simply interesting to see how other police forces operate."

"Other police forces?" Sammy echoed. "No, no. This is how *Jack* operates."

Chapter Thirty

It was five-thirty when Jack arrived at the Emergency unit of the Vancouver General Hospital. He cut the zip-tie from Klaus's wrists and went inside with him before giving him back the keys to his car.

"Consider this the last time I ever want to see you or anyone else you work with," Jack said coldly. "I'll be checking out of my hotel and tossing out the phone Anton calls me on. If I ever see any of you again, I will respond with extreme violence. The only reason you're still alive is that I know I was caught on a security camera entering the parkade."

Klaus was relieved. Not only was Jack letting him live, but the others wouldn't find out. *As far as my injuries go, I'll tell them I got in a bar fight …*

Jack left the hospital and called Anton as he walked across the parking lot to meet Sammy and Benny. "Got some good news for you," he said when Anton answered. "My meeting's over and I'm free to meet your boss immediately."

"You are?" said Anton, sounding surprised. "That's, uh, great. I'm in his room. I'll tell him."

"Put him on the line," Jack demanded.

Seconds later a voice with a strong German accent said, "Hello, Jack. My name is Wolfgang. I understand you are able to see me now?"

"Right. Where are you?"

"I'm staying at the Fairmont Hotel."

"Perfect. Okay if I come to your room?"

"Yes, that would be okay," said Wolfgang. "However, I thought that if you were worried, we could meet at some public place to discuss things."

"Me worried? Why should I be worried?"

"Well, uh, before when —"

"Consider this a test of our future relationship," said Jack. "Tell me your room number, and I'll be there in a few minutes."

"That would be fine."

"First, I will be sending over a security team to ensure my safety and check out your room."

"We mean you no harm. But if that is what it takes … by all means."

"Tell Anton to stay, but if anyone else is with you, tell them to wait downstairs in the lounge."

"It is only Anton who is with me."

"Perfect."

As soon as Jack hung up, Wolfgang looked at Anton and said, "I thought Jack was hours away? What's going on?"

Anton shook his head to show his own bewilderment as he made a call.

Big Joe tried to answer his phone, but he was in a mountainous area and the call didn't connect. He put his phone back in his pocket and grinned to himself as he thought about the invoice he'd be submitting for the long hours of surveillance.

Had he realized his tracker was on an express bus bound for Edmonton, he would have been far less happy.

* * *

Fifteen minutes after speaking with Jack, Wolfgang answered a knock on his door.

"We work for Jack," said Sammy by way of introduction as he brushed past Wolfgang. He was carrying a briefcase and was followed by Benny, who was talking on his phone.

Wolfgang and Anton stared at the two men. Both wore ball caps and oversized sunglasses. Anton recognized them as the two men Jack had used to dispose of Dempsey's body and swallowed nervously when he saw they were wearing latex gloves.

Sammy put the briefcase down, then checked the washroom to ensure the two men were the only ones there before giving Benny a nod.

"We're inside," said Benny into the phone. "Only Anton and one other man is present."

"As requested," said Wolfgang. He smiled nervously.

"I've got eyes," said Sammy gruffly. "Do you?"

Wolfgang quit smiling when Sammy and Benny both undid their jackets to reveal they each had a pistol in a leather holster on the side of their belts.

Wolfgang's face paled slightly. "Uh, yes," he replied.

"Good. Put your hands on the wall," ordered Sammy.

"Do you really think this is —"

Benny drew his pistol and spoke menacingly. "Do it!"

Wolfgang and Anton quickly obeyed and Sammy patted them down for weapons.

"Okay, the both of you take a seat." Sammy pointed to a couple of chairs as Benny put his pistol back in the holster.

Wolfgang and Anton exchanged a solemn glance, then sat down and watched as Sammy retrieved an electronic wand from his briefcase and used it to scan the room. When he finished, he put the wand back in his briefcase and nodded at Benny.

"We're finished," said Benny into his phone. "Neither one was packing and the room's clean."

A minute later Benny opened the door and Jack entered.

"Surprised to see me, Anton?" Jack asked.

"No," Anton replied as he and Wolfgang started to rise. Sammy put a hand on each of their shoulders to let them know to stay seated.

Anton looked nervously back at Sammy, then turned to Jack. "You said you were coming. Why should I be surprised to see you?"

"I thought you might've believed I was driving through some mountain pass," replied Jack harshly.

Anton's eyebrows arched in his surprise. "Uh … I don't understand. Why would —"

"Don't lie to me, Anton," Jack snarled, stepping closer.

Both Anton and Wolfgang saw the blood splattered down the front of Jack's raincoat and on his sleeve. They looked at each other in fear and confusion.

"Your lives depend on the truth," Jack hissed. He paused and stared at them to make them feel more uncomfortable.

"This afternoon one of my men found the tracker on my car when he took it for an oil change. I then stuck it on a Greyhound bus bound for Edmonton. I presume you know that because the gelatinous slob who was following me should have clued in a long time ago and is probably back in the city. Believe me, when my men speak to him, I will learn the truth, unless I hear it from you first."

Anton looked nervously at Wolfgang, who responded with a subtle nod.

"Okay, okay, I, uh, hired him," Anton admitted. "I did call him a few minutes ago, but couldn't get an answer."

"Meaning he is still in the mountains someplace," said Jack, shaking his head in disgust. "The man really is inept. You should train your people better."

"He is not one of our men," Anton said. "He's a private investigator."

"A private investigator?" Jack pretended surprise.

"You are taking security precautions," said Wolfgang, gesturing to Sammy and Benny, "and so did we."

"Oh, I am not angry about that. A little disturbed at one of my own men, perhaps." He looked at Anton. "I believe the only time you had the opportunity to put the tracker on my car was last Thursday when I met you for lunch."

Anton stared down at the floor, then nodded.

"Good for you," Jack said. "I hold no ill feelings toward you for doing that, even though it has forced me to change hotels. I had anticipated you might do that and posted a person to watch my car. This afternoon he admitted to me that he had an intestinal bug and left his post to use a washroom. I will no longer be using his services."

"So ... everything is okay between us?" asked Wolfgang, rising to his feet. "I'm Wolfgang," he added, then smiled while extending his hand. "It is good that we respect —"

"Sit down!" Jack said angrily.

Wolfgang immediately sat down.

"There's another reason I wondered if you were surprised to see me," said Jack, looking coldly at Wolfgang's and Anton's faces.

"I don't understand." Fear reduced Wolfgang's voice to a whisper.

Jack sneered at him. "You are the top guy, aren't you? The one who calls himself the Ringmaster?"

"No," Wolfgang said meekly.

"You're not?" Jack feigned surprise. "Anton told me you were his boss."

"Anton is at the same executive level as I am, but he is new to his position and is still on probation. Normally he is supervised by Roche."

"But since your arrival in Canada, which Anton told me was last night, I presume you are in charge of the people here, is that right?" Jack asked.

Wolfgang nodded.

"So you're the one who gives them their orders."

"I guess you could say that."

"Interesting," Jack mused. "You didn't try to lie your way out. I have another question for you. Knowing that you had a tracker on my car for the last five days, if during that time you wished to kill me, how would you have gone about it? Hypothetically speaking, that is."

"I have no intention of trying to kill you," said Wolfgang quickly. "Do we, Anton?" He glanced at his colleague.

"Certainly not!" Anton blurted.

"I said hypothetically speaking." Jack raised his voice. "Answer me."

"Well, uh, we know you were staying at the Pan Pacific," said Wolfgang. "It is too crowded in that area and the hotel is no doubt equipped with too many security cameras and the like for us to make an attempt on your life there. If I were to have you killed, I would simply follow you someplace, such as a mall or a restaurant, then do it when you were either getting in or out of your car."

Jack pursed his lips as he thought about it. "Sounds reasonable. How many men would you use to carry out the assignment?"

"I would use all four of us."

"Yourself, Anton, Bojan, and Klaus," Jack said.

"Yes." Wolfgang felt uneasy that Jack knew the names of all his associates, while he knew little about Jack's people.

"Go on," Jack prodded him. "Explain how. Would you run up and shoot me?"

"Not necessarily. I would have one man distract you when you opened the door of your car, perhaps by asking for directions. Then I would have another man stab you from behind if silence was necessary, or shoot you if the situation allowed it."

Jack nodded. "You may have saved your own lives."

Wolfgang and Anton looked at each other in bewilderment.

"So … your man, Klaus. You wouldn't send him to try and kill me on his own?"

"*Mon Dieu!*" gasped Anton as the reason for Jack's line of questioning became clear.

"I don't believe in any god," Jack said. "Save your prayers for later and listen. About an hour ago, Klaus tried to kill me."

"He is dead?" Anton stared at the blood on Jack's raincoat.

"Let me explain," said Jack. "After finding the tracker, I discovered he was hanging around the front of my hotel. I thought it was odd that he would risk exposure doing that when you could rely on the tracker — unless, of course, he was not made privy to that information. So it got me to thinking. Was he acting on his own? He did strike me as having a vindictive personality."

"He told me he was with his girlfriend," spluttered Anton. "Please, you have to believe me. I didn't know."

"Relax, Anton," said Jack. "I do believe you."

Anton and Wolfgang glanced at each other again as their tension subsided.

"If you had sent him to kill me," Jack continued, "I'm sure you would've been in touch with him before allowing my men to come to your room." Jack directed his attention at Wolfgang. "At first, I wondered if you intended to kill me as I walked over to your hotel, but decided you wouldn't have allowed my men into your room if that were the case. It appears to me that Klaus was acting on his own."

"He was," Wolfgang said emphatically. "We knew nothing about it."

Jack nodded to indicate he believed him.

"What … will you tell us what happened?" asked Anton.

"I approached Klaus when he returned to his car in a parkade. He was putting a flat tire into the trunk when I stuck a gun in his ear. He tried to pull a gun on me, which resulted in him losing more of his teeth, along with other facial injuries. I then shoved his body in the trunk and bound his hands and ankles together."

"He is still alive?" asked Wolfgang.

"Very much so. I drove him to the emergency ward myself. I suspect they're getting tired of seeing him. Three times in one week for the same problem must be annoying. Regardless, when I left him, he was seated in the waiting room. He'll likely be there for several hours. I also gave him his keys back and left his car in visitor parking."

"Why didn't you kill him?" asked Wolfgang.

"The parkade has security cameras at the entrance and exit. So does the hospital. If his disappearance or death results in an investigation, I will be seen as the one who took him for treatment and not the one who followed him to his car and murdered him."

"I see," said Wolfgang.

"Plus, he is your man, and therefore you are responsible for him. And quite frankly, I feel that you should be the one to, uh, take remedial action and counsel him in that regard."

"Counsel?" repeated Wolfgang. His voice revealed his deadly intent. "Oh, yes, let me assure you that he will be counselled, providing we find him. Under the circumstances, he may have wisely gone elsewhere for treatment."

Jack cleared his throat, then said, "I suspect he is not that smart, but if you do go there, it might be prudent to wait for him at his car."

Wolfgang nodded.

"I'm glad we have cleared the air," Jack said. "However, I have found this to be a long and tiring day. I suggest that you and I meet over breakfast to discuss what services I may be able to provide your company."

"Good," replied Wolfgang. "I would like to go to the hospital as soon as possible."

"I have a secure phone for you." Jack nodded at Benny, who took a phone from his briefcase and gave it to Jack to pass on. "Feel free to use it as you like. I will call you at ten o'clock tomorrow morning."

"Thank you," replied Wolfgang.

Jack, Sammy, and Benny were heading for the door when Jack turned and said, "Incidentally, Roche told me that you had a secure name to use over the phones to protect the identities of your executive members. What's yours?"

"I am simply referred to as a juggler," said Wolfgang. "Same as Roche."

"A Ringmaster and jugglers." Jack smiled faintly. "Sounds like quite a circus. I presume Klaus is your clown?"

Wolfgang's face darkened. "Was our clown," he growled in response.

Chapter Thirty-One

"I knew it, I knew it, I knew it," said Rose, glaring at Jack from across her desk.

"I had witnesses," replied Jack.

"What he said happened last night is true," Laura put in. "I had a good view from where we were parked."

"And, of course, you wouldn't bend the truth to cover up for Jack, would you." Rose didn't bother to hide her sarcasm. She looked at the coffee mug on her desk. "I haven't even had a sip of my morning coffee and you tell me this. Great way to start the day."

"It's not my fault," Jack insisted. "Check with Sammy and Benny. If not them, Otto is likely still asleep in his room at the Delta. Give him a call."

Rose shook her head. "No, the thing is, I do believe you. I'm angrier with myself for letting it happen. How do I explain it to the brass?"

"Tell them the truth," Jack said. "I was going to disarm him and turn him over to Wolfgang, but he tried to pull a gun on me. A minimum amount of physical force was applied, resulting in some damage to his jaw, which was easily injured due to a previous injury."

"Two previous injuries," Rose said.

"Okay, two, but in any event, to be on the safe side, this time I drove him to the hospital and dropped him off in case he needed treatment."

"That was awfully nice of you," said Laura, "considering the circumstances."

"Cut the theatrics," said Rose in exasperation. "What do I tell the brass when they speculate that he may try to kill you again?"

"That's been taken care of." Jack smiled smugly. "I met with Wolfgang and Anton to discuss the matter and I recommended Klaus receive counselling. They were already thinking of firing him, so I am sure he'll be sent packing." *Packing a shovel to dig his grave.*

"You recommended he receive counselling?" said Rose incredulously.

"Yes. My meeting with Wolfgang was quite civilized."

"You really expect the brass to believe that's what you said?"

"I bet they'll *want* to believe it," said Jack seriously. "Besides, it's true, so why not? Sammy's and Benny's notes will corroborate it."

"I'm sure they will." Rose said in a flat tone.

"Not only that," Laura inserted, "but Otto and I did surveillance with Special 'O' at the hospital for an hour last night while Jack met with Wolfgang and Anton. Klaus had the opportunity to bolt during that time, but he didn't. Obviously, he wasn't concerned."

"Is that right?" asked Rose, looking at Jack.

"Yes," replied Jack. "For my own safety, I wanted him watched until the meeting was over."

"That's good to know," said Rose. "Although you did it to protect yourself, the fact that he stayed is an important point in convincing the brass that he wasn't concerned for his safety." She looked at Jack speculatively. *Something stinks.*

"Something wrong?" asked Jack.

He seems so honest. Is it me? Have I become that cynical about everyone? She decided to probe in a different way. "Has there been any phone action since last night?" she asked.

"Anton did call Roche and told him what happened, but said that Wolfgang would contact the Ringmaster direct. Unfortunately, Wolfgang did not use the phone I gave him."

"So I can tell the brass that you feel safe from Klaus?" asked Rose.

"Yes. I told them I switched hotels so he wouldn't know where to look. Wolfgang and Anton don't want me dead, at least not until they get their hands on the painting. They're hoping to gain my trust so that I hang it in my villa."

"Yes, about your alleged retirement villa," said Rose. "If you think you can convince the force to spring for some villa in Tuscany, you better think again."

"I know. Getting the bean-counters to spring for a couple of martinis is usually an issue. The bad guys are paying for my travel expenses, so that should help."

"That worries me, too," said Rose. "They'll be expecting some return."

"I can handle that. You've got your masters in psychology. I'm sure you can come up with some test I can give them to start the ball rolling, then give them feedback about potential character flaws or something. After that,

I'll tell them I need to know more about who has done what in order to appraise the situation. I'm hoping to get an admission about Kerin's murder from the Ringmaster long before they question my ability as a consultant."

"What's your next step?" asked Rose.

Jack glanced at his watch. "I'm meeting Wolfgang for breakfast to talk about how I could benefit their organization. At this point, I think they would like to hire me."

"That's good," Rose said dryly, "because after I debrief the brass, it might be wise for you to have a new career prospect."

* * *

At ten-thirty Jack and Wolfgang ordered breakfast at the Dockside Restaurant, which overlooked False Creek in the heart of Vancouver. Although Jack drove Wolfgang to the location and ensured he was not being followed, as a display of trust, he had not searched Wolfgang. Outside the restaurant, Laura and Otto watched and waited in a Special "O" surveillance vehicle.

"So, Jack," said Wolfgang, once coffee arrived, "I wish to apologize for the incident with Klaus yesterday. I can assure you that he will no longer be a threat to your safety."

"That is good to hear," Jack replied. "Apology accepted."

"And you must believe that I had nothing to do with his actions," Wolfgang added.

"Of course I believe it. You wouldn't be alive otherwise."

Wolfgang looked at Jack in surprise, then smiled. "I believe you."

"You should," Jack said.

Wolfgang watched Jack take a sip of coffee. "From what I know, you're an interesting man. Uniquely talented."

"I have my moments."

"You said that if you were to consult for us, you would first do a background check and a profile of our executive members, is that correct?"

"That is of utmost importance," Jack confirmed. "Before I stick my neck out, I like to know I can trust the person I'm sticking my neck out for."

"By sticking your neck out ... I presume you are talking about things like cleaning up the mess our men made in the workshop?'

Jack nodded. "Taking care of loose ends is something I do, but usually not before I know who I am dealing with. In the matter regarding your men, I felt it in my best interests to intervene."

"I understand," Wolfgang said. "Out of curiosity, what would you usually charge for what you did?'

"Ninety-eight hundred if it was a simple as Dempsey," Jack replied. "If I had to get rid of, say, a car, or perhaps build a false trail to make someone think the person went elsewhere, then the figure would go up accordingly."

"You did take Dempsey's car," Wolfgang said.

"I had it parked near an airport alongside a river. Not a bad solution, but a far cry from making it disappear completely."

"I see." Wolfgang hesitated. "Your base figure of ninety-eight hundred seems odd to me."

"Many bank transactions in different countries have to report amounts of ten thousand and up. I am not a greedy person and that amount simplifies things for certain clients."

"I see. So, back to your profiling. How do you do that?"

"Fairly simple, actually, although because you're one of the people I would assess, I won't tell you all the secrets until such time as you have been cleared."

"Ah," said Wolfgang. "I guess that makes sense."

"What I can tell you is I would want to know everyone's background. Things like what kind of families they came from, poor or wealthy. Do they have siblings. Are they married and do they have children." Jack paused as the waitress brought them their orders, then continued, "I would ask them to complete a questionnaire designed to identify their level of intelligence and personality traits. Can they easily be deceived? Are they prone to bragging? Are they disgruntled and apt to talk to the competition or grasp an opportunity to take more than their share? Are they the type to snap under a police interrogation? Things of that nature. Then I would follow up with interviews to flesh out any problems."

"You are very professional." Wolfgang spoke matter-of-factly before biting into a blueberry scone.

"These days, so are the police," Jack said. "Cameras are everywhere, it seems, and police have scientific laboratories at their disposal." Jack enjoyed a bite of his order of Southside Huevos, then added, "Of course, it's not only the police you need to worry about. Sometimes the competition can really make a killing … literally."

"Once you are convinced that our executive level is okay, what would follow?"

"Naturally, I would need to know your business inside and out, but let me say that I have an exceptional talent for obtaining information. I have many clients who tell me things that are not in their realm of interest, but could prove extremely profitable for others."

"And your fee for such information?"

"It's negotiable and depends on how much assistance I provide. I don't expect to be paid until the venture is successfully completed."

"I am impressed with you." Wolfgang sat back and wiped his mouth, then tossed the napkin onto his plate. "However, I am not the one who makes the final decision on whether to hire you. Would you mind if I stepped away to make a phone call?"

"Not at all," replied Jack. "If there are any questions, I would be happy to speak to whoever you are calling, as well."

"That won't be necessary." Wolfgang left the table.

A few minutes later he returned. "There is someone I would like you to see right now," he said.

"Now?" Jack felt the adrenalin surge through his chest.

"Yes, at the place where you first met Anton."

"Okay."

"Does that make you nervous?"

"Not particularly," Jack lied.

"Good. Let me pay the bill and go to the washroom, and then we can leave."

Jack nodded. "Go ahead, I need to make a call myself."

* * *

Moments later, Laura started feeling exasperated as she spoke to Jack. "Are you positive?" she asked. "No backup?"

"I'm positive. I need to build trust. It's too easy for them to spot you out there. Wolfgang made a call a few minutes ago, but I don't know what phone he used. Check with the monitors in the event it was the phone I gave him last night."

"But —"

"Don't worry, I'll be okay. I'll call you when I'm clear. "

"Yeah, sure, you'll be okay. Look what happened last time. They could get the drop on you before you had a chance to draw your gun."

"I'm not packing," Jack said. "I'm trying to build trust. Gotta go."

Laura hung up and immediately dialled a different number. A woman answered.

"Who am I speaking with?" asked Laura abruptly.

"Hi, Laura. It's Nicole Purney," she replied.

Laura was surprised, but also relieved. She knew her name would come up as *private* on Nicole's display, but Nicole was good at what she did, and voice recognition was part of her job. Laura had only talked to her a few times before, but it was enough for Nicole to file her voice away in her memory.

"Calling about the new line?" asked Nicole.

"Yes. Jack is with Wolfgang at a restaurant. He says Wolfgang made a call a couple of minutes ago."

"Not on the phone Jack gave him," said Nicole.

"Anything on Anton's today?"

"Not a thing."

"I know you guys have a ton of lines to listen to, but Jack is going into a situation. Any chance you could live-monitor those two lines for me until he's clear?"

"You've got it," replied Nicole sombrely. "Hang on! The light went on for Anton's line. I'll turn it on so we can both listen, if you like."

"Please," said Laura as she strained to hear. The first couple of words spoken by Anton and another man told her that listening would not do her any good. "They're speaking in French," said Laura. "Which I can't understand."

"No worries," Nicole said. "I'll translate for you. Anton called Roche. They've greeted each other ... Roche said he was brought up to date about Klaus last night."

"By who?"

"Didn't say. Stand by ... Anton says Wolfgang is coming over with Jack ... I presume to that same acreage?"

"Yes."

"Anton says Big Joe is really pissed off, but doesn't say why. Says Big Joe is looking for revenge. If Jack isn't who he says he is, Big Joe will soon know."

"How?"

"What I'm telling you is everything we know," said Nicole quickly. "Your interruptions make it hard —"

"Sorry, I'll shut up."

"Anton says they were going to fire Big Joe, but he's anxious to make up for it and will work today for free ... the Ringmaster has set some sort of test for Jack ... Roche knows ... is telling Anton to call him back when the test is presented, as he wants to hear.... That's it. The call's ended."

Oh, man. "What kind of test?" Laura asked.

"What I told you is all there was." After a moment Nicole added, "Please let me know when he's clear of the situation, will you? Jack's a friend of the family. He and my dad have worked together."

"I know. I've worked with your dad, too. I'll keep you in the loop. Gotta go. Jack and Wolfgang are out of the restaurant. I'm going to call him."

* * *

Laura watched Jack answer her call. She knew he couldn't say much without being overheard by Wolfgang, but she was, at least, able to tell him about the phone call.

"That's too bad Nicole isn't well," Jack replied. "You should keep her company."

"Did you hear me? Their test sounds more like a trap. I think I should round up some backup and hide out nearby."

"No, I don't really believe in herbal medicine. Stick to the doctor's prescription."

Laura hung up and Otto could see the concern on her face. "Problems?" he asked. "You look worried."

"I am. Worried that Jack will be sliced into pieces with an electric saw."

"What?" Otto's mouth hung open.

"And there's nothing we can do to prevent it." Laura fought the urge to scream in frustration.

Chapter Thirty-Two

Jack drove into the yard and parked beside the three other cars belonging to Anton, Bojan, and Klaus respectively. As he and Wolfgang got out of his SUV, he saw Bojan wave to them from the side door of the workshop.

Jack felt apprehensive coming to the acreage. Entering the workshop made him feel worse. *Somehow I doubt the Ringmaster is the type to hang out in a dusty workshop.* He took a deep breath and slowly exhaled in an attempt to calm his nerves, then thought about the man who'd died trying to save him. In his heart he knew he could not back out.

He followed Wolfgang and Bojan to the back room, while Anton stood in the doorway punching numbers on his cellphone. He saw Klaus's still body curled in a fetal position on a blue plastic tarp on the floor. His eyes were closed and he was still gagged and hog-tied with duct tape. Dried blood was splattered over the tarp, and the smell of burnt hair and flesh hung in the air. There were scorched burn marks through the seat of his pants, and Jack noticed the propane torch on the workbench.

Despite knowing that Klaus was a sadist who liked burning people with cigarettes, Jack felt sickened. *There's retribution … and there's retribution. This is too much….*

"As you can see," said Wolfgang, "he will not be bothering you again."

"A brutal way to kill him," said Jack.

"We know what he did to the young lady who worked for you. We thought you would be pleased. As for killing him, I hope we didn't go that far."

"You mean he's still alive?"

"Let's find out," Wolfgang said, then delivered a vicious kick to Klaus's stomach.

Klaus moaned and opened his eyes, fixating on Jack. A subsequent moan told Jack he was pleading for mercy.

Jack glanced at Anton, who was chuckling at something said over the phone. Bojan's face was pale and it was clear that the scene before him was not to his liking. Wolfgang looked at Bojan and said, "Give me your gun."

Bojan handed Wolfgang a Glock semi-automatic .40 pistol. Jack watched Wolfgang examine it, then nod approvingly before handing it to Jack. "I'll give you the honour. Go ahead and finish him off."

* * *

Laura and Otto sat silently, listening as Nicole adjusted the volume on the audio when Anton called his brother back. She translated the call in bits and pieces as Anton told Roche what was going on.

"Jack and Wolfgang arrived … Jack is staring at Klaus … we've got him tied up and lying on a tarp. Too bad you weren't here last night when Wolfgang and I worked him over. Bojan had no stomach for it when we used the torch and had to run outside to puke." Anton chuckled, then said, "He doesn't look too good…. Okay, Wolfgang handed Jack the gun and told him to finish him off."

Laura looked at Otto, then at Nicole. She could only imagine the sickening scene that Jack had walked into. *At least he has a gun now. There's no way he can murder Klaus, so the show's over. He has to make arrests and go with what we have. Time to call in backup.*

"Anton says Jack is refusing to do it," Nicole said. "He's handing the gun back to Wolfgang —"

"No!" Laura blurted out. "This is their test!" She felt helpless as she looked at the faces of the people around her. "Look what they did to Klaus! For Jack it will be far —"

"Shh," Nicole hissed. "Anton's talking again."

* * *

Jack glanced at the gun, then handed it back to Wolfgang. "You really think you can hold something over me to blackmail me this easily?"

"Blackmail?" Wolfgang looked surprised. "No, not at all. That is not our intention."

"I told you that my first step with your organization would be doing a thorough analysis of certain people *before* acting as a troubleshooter. Or weren't you listening?"

"I was but, uh, because of what he tried to do to you yesterday, we thought you would enjoy killing him."

"You heard what I said earlier." Jack was unflinching. "It's a matter of trust. At this point I am not assured I'm with people I can trust."

Wolfgang silently regarded Jack. His look said, *And you are not trusted either.*

"Do you have something to say?" Jack asked.

"I need to call someone," said Wolfgang. "Wait here," he ordered before walking out of the room.

Jack watched him shove Bojan's pistol into his belt before taking out a phone and using it as he left the back room.

The minutes ticked by slowly. Jack heard the sound of the table saw in the front room — Wolfgang had apparently turned it on — and then Wolfgang reappeared in the back room. He walked over to the band saw and looked at Anton. "Shoot him," he said, then turned on the band saw.

* * *

In the monitor room Laura could hear her own heartbeat as everyone sat in complete silence. They'd heard Anton tell his brother that Wolfgang was leaving to call the Ringmaster. All eyes in the monitor room had automatically focused on the indicator light for the phone Jack had given Wolfgang, but it remained off. All they'd heard was the occasional sound of Anton's and Roche's breathing as they too waited.

And then came the high-pitched whirr of a power saw, and the next words they heard in the background were Wolfgang's: "Shoot him."

Only two words, spoken quickly, but played out in Laura's mind, they were in slow motion. Her body reacted with fear, as her mind highlighted and analyzed every shred of data. Then she gave a sudden involuntary jerk at the unexpected scream of a second power saw, but even that noise was not enough to deaden the sharp report of a gunshot. The second saw stopped.

Anton's comment to his brother was terse. "It's done. I have to go."

Laura grabbed her phone and pushed the memory button for Jack's phone. They all listened in silence, holding their breaths, before they heard the automated voice say to leave a message.

Chapter Thirty-Three

Jack watched Anton casually take a pistol out from the back of his belt and was relieved to see that his eyes were fixated on Klaus.

Seconds later Anton fired one shot through Klaus's temple.

Wolfgang nodded his satisfaction and switched the band saw off while Bojan left to shut the table saw off.

Jack saw that Anton had shut his phone off and immediately felt his own phone vibrate in his pocket. *Probably Laura … the timing from the sound of the gunshot and Anton hanging up is too coincidental for it not to be her … and too coincidental for me to answer without arousing suspicion…*

Wolfgang waited until the noise from the table saw ended, then looked at Jack. "Clean enough for your standards?" he asked, before smiling and gesturing at the tarp. "A simple matter to roll up and dispose of … what is it you call it? A loose end?"

Jack frowned. "Not quite up to my standards. The calibre of pistol Anton used was powerful enough to go through his head and the tarp. I am sure there is blood on the floor underneath, not to mention the possibility of the slug being there. A .22 or .32 cal' would have been better."

Wolfgang lifted the tarp by the edge, rolling Klaus's body over, and peered at the floor. "You're right," he said. He then dropped the tarp and reached into his jacket pocket, from which he withdrew a wad of money. He handed it to Jack.

"What's this for?" asked Jack.

"Ninety-eight hundred dollars," replied Wolfgang. "The going rate, you told me. Not to mention, you have performed this task for us once before."

"That I have," said Jack.

"Consider it payment for a temporary contract. If it pleases you, I am sure the contract will be extended."

Jack thought for a moment, then put the money in his pocket, before shaking hands with Wolfgang.

* * *

Laura and Otto were running to their car when Laura's phone rang.

"Hi, Laura," said Jack nonchalantly, knowing that Wolfgang was standing close enough to hear him. "It's Jack. How's Nicole doing? Is she feeling any better?"

Laura could only gasp mouthfuls of air as she tried to stop herself from blubbering.

"You sound terrible," said Jack. "Is she that sick?"

Laura's feelings went from anguish to anger. But unsure if anyone was listening to her on Jack's end, she repressed the anger and replied, "Yes, she's still in a lot of pain."

"That's too bad. Please, give her my love." He paused briefly. "The reason I'm calling is that I need to speak with Sammy. I called, but he didn't pick up." It was a lie. Jack had only pretended to call because he knew Laura would be reacting to what she heard and he needed to put a halt to it. "Do you know where he is?"

"Want me to call him and get him to call you?" Laura asked.

"Please."

"There's a lot of people I'll need to call," she added, knowing that the Emergency Response Team had been summoned, along with a host of others responding to her call for help.

"I understand that," Jack said. "Do what you have to. Does her sister, Rose, know what's going on?"

"Not yet. I haven't had time."

"Good. She's frail herself. No use alarming her until we know more."

"I take it you'll contact her yourself?"

"Yes, but not until later. Sorry to rush, but a new client has invited me in for coffee. I should go."

Minutes later Jack sat with Wolfgang and Anton at the kitchen table while Bojan made coffee.

Jack pretended to be watching Bojan, but he could sense that Wolfgang was itching to tell him something. *What now?*

Wolfgang cleared his throat and said, "Jack, there is another loose end I think you would like cleaned up. It has to do with you directly."

"Oh?"

"Klaus's car. As a result of the … encounter you had with him last night, there's a lot of blood in the trunk. If there were to be an investigation into his disappearance, you would not want the police to find his car. Particularly since, as you mentioned, you were seen driving it out of the parkade."

Jack smiled to himself. *Big Joe, you oversized baboon, so that's how you intend to check me out.*

"Well?" Wolfgang prodded him.

"No worries," Jack replied. "The car is a loose end that you are not to blame for — other than hiring Klaus in the first place. I'll look after that, as well."

"Excellent," said Wolfgang. "I expected you would."

Jack's phone vibrated and the display told him it was Sammy, so he answered.

"Laura said you were trying to get hold of me," said Sammy, careful not to say more than necessary until Jack let him know he could. "I was recharging my phone and had it switched off. She reached me through Benny."

"I need some janitorial work done again," Jack said. "Same place as last time." Jack paused, as if listening, then smiled at Wolfgang before saying, "No I'm not joking. These people might be interested in a weekly service."

"I hope not," Wolfgang whispered from across the table, before grinning.

"There is something else that needs to be cleaned up," Jack said. "Hang on and I'll tell you what I want you to do in a second." Jack then smiled apologetically to Wolfgang. "Sorry, but I need to go outside for a little privacy. If you find out my trade secrets, you won't need me."

Wolfgang inclined his head. "I understand. By all means."

Jack walked out into the yard, then said, "Okay, we're both free to talk."

"What's going on?" asked Sammy.

"Anton put a bullet through Klaus's brain on orders from Wolfgang."

"Yeah, we figured that. Laura said they wanted you to do it as a test."

"I don't think that was the only test. I'm sure the gun Wolfgang gave me wasn't loaded. He stuck it in his belt when I gave it back to him, yet told Anton to do it while he was busy yakking on the phone. Why didn't he shoot Klaus himself or have Bojan do it? Not to mention, when Anton shot Klaus, the electric saws had been turned on to cover the sound. They weren't turned on when he handed me the gun and told *me* to do it."

"Good thing you didn't try to arrest them," muttered Sammy. "Tough call to make."

"I wouldn't have arrested them even if it was loaded. They're not the ones who killed Kerin."

"I understand. Just hope the brass does."

"Big Joe has a plan to check me out," Jack said. "I think I know what it is. They want me to get rid of Klaus's car."

"Son of a bitch. Another tracker?"

"That's my guess ... and likely better hidden."

"What are we going to do? Find it and throw it back in their faces? At least they'll think we're professional and not stupid."

"If need be, but I have a better idea. You ever work with an operator by the name of Bob Aitken?"

"No, but I've heard lots about him. Didn't he retire and get a job with the Insurance Corporation of B.C.?"

"That's the guy," Jack confirmed. "He looks like Grizzly Adams, but is one of the best and smartest UC operators

I've ever worked with. I still have a drink with him once in a while. He deals with a lot of stolen cars for ICBC and has the contacts. I'll call him and get back to you."

A moment later Jack dialled Bob and explained what he wanted.

"Hell, not a problem," Bob said. "I know a place I trust to do it and keep their mouths shut. Give me Sammy's number. I'm working in Surrey today, but I've got time. I'll get things set up within the hour. In fact, I know a guy who'll lend me a tow truck. If you like, I'll borrow it and drive it myself."

"That would be fantastic. If the bad guys are doing what I think they are, I want it done right."

Jack returned to the kitchen and poured himself a cup of coffee, then sat down.

"Everything okay?" asked Wolfgang.

"Everything is fine," replied Jack. "The only thing I would ask is that your men roll up Klaus and dump him in the trunk of his car. Toss the pistol in the trunk, as well. The person I need is busy, but one of my men will be dropped off here and take the car to save time. I'll go along to ensure that things are done right."

"Sounds good." Wolfgang nodded.

"Tomorrow, let's meet for lunch," Jack suggested. "There's a popular bistro in your hotel called Griffins, right across the street from the Vancouver Art Gallery."

Wolfgang nodded again. "And with regard to the task ahead of you this afternoon … you have no worries?"

"No worries," Jack said. *Until Rose, the brass, and I-HIT find out about it….*

Chapter Thirty-Four

An hour later Laura drove to the property and dropped Benny off at the front gate. Jack met him in the yard and pointed to Klaus's car. "The keys are in the ignition," he said. "Drive carefully and don't get in an accident. I'll follow right behind you."

Jack walked to his own vehicle as Wolfgang tagged along to say goodbye.

"I'll call you around noon tomorrow," Jack told him.

"That would be good," said Wolfgang. "There are certain arrangements I need to make, and that will give me time to make them before we meet again."

Arrangements like murdering me if Big Joe gives you a report that's not to your liking, Jack thought. I've got a few arrangements to make myself. Hope they don't include arranging a bunk in my cell.

Jack was ten minutes away from the property when he received a call from Laura. She'd parked her car and was with Otto in a car being driven by a Special "O" operative.

"You scared the hell out me," she said. "We thought they shot you."

"Sorry about that."

"You should pay to get my hair coloured," she grumbled. "I'm sure it went grey."

Jack grinned. He was glad Laura had calmed down. "Settle for an olive soup? I've improved my recipe. I use Victoria Gin."

"I thought you liked Tanqueray Number Ten for your martinis."

"Victoria Gin is better … but enough of that. What's up?"

"You've got company."

Jack automatically glanced in his rear-view mirror. He hadn't spotted anyone following him since leaving the property. "Big Joe?"

"Yes. He's following about three minutes behind you."

"So he did put a tracker in Klaus's car," Jack said. "Is he in his white van?"

"No. Guess after you sent him halfway to Edmonton he figures you're on to it. He's riding shotgun with one of his guys. They're in a navy-blue Ford sedan with licence —"

"I know it. How about the other guy who works for him? Drives a silver F-150 with a crew cab."

"Yes, following right behind them."

"Perfect, I'll tell everyone it's a go."

* * *

Big Joe monitored the laptop computer and continued to give directions as they drove northwest along the

Fraser Highway. Twenty minutes later he said, "Whoa, whoa, slow down, Gordy, they're pulling over. Slow down."

Seconds later Big Joe saw Benny parking Klaus's car in a self-car-wash bay and Jack parking his SUV behind it. He immediately phoned his employee in the crew cab pickup and said, "Ralph, get in line at the bay next to them. Let me know what's happenin.'"

Big Joe and Gordy found a place to park where they could watch with binoculars. A hushed phone call from Ralph told Big Joe that Benny was washing the outside of Klaus's car, then added, "Maybe a good thing we hid the tracker under the back seat."

They didn't have long to wait before Sammy arrived in the same green van that had been used to dispose of Clive Dempsey's body.

They watched as Jack moved his SUV out of the way while Sammy backed the van up to the trunk of Klaus's car, then got out and opened both rear doors.

"Can't see what's going on," relayed Ralph, "other than the guy in the van is putting coveralls on over his suit. The van doors are blocking the view."

"Pretty damned obvious, if you ask me," Big Joe said, "but to make sure, tail the van when it leaves. If it's going to the same crematorium, it isn't far."

Two minutes later Sammy drove away in the van with Ralph following. Big Joe watched as Jack once more parked behind Klaus's car.

"Who are they waiting for?" asked Gordy.

Big Joe grunted and shrugged. They didn't have long to wait before a tow truck arrived, hooked onto Klaus's car, and drove away, while Jack took Benny and drove off in the opposite direction.

"Think it broke down on 'em, Joe?"

"Probably the ignition got wet," Big Joe suggested. "Let's follow and find out."

Using the laptop, Big Joe once more gave directions to Gordy as they followed a block behind. After a short time Big Joe said, "He's slowing down. Still northbound on 168 Street and going through Tynehead Park…. Okay, hanging a right on Tynehead Greenway and stopping alongside the road. Drive by slow and let's see what he's up to."

"Gotcha."

Big Joe's phone rang and he saw it was Ralph. "What's up, Ralphie?" he asked.

"Was like you thought. He drove straight to the crematorium."

"Good. Get your ass over here. We're near 168 Street just south of 96 Ave. Got it?"

Moments later Gordy and Big Joe drove past the tow truck. They saw the driver, a bearded, scruffy-looking individual, siphoning gas out of Klaus's car into a gas can.

"Cheap bastard," muttered Big Joe. "Okay, keep driving until we're far enough that I can watch him with the binocs."

Soon Big Joe saw the tow-truck driver pour the gasoline into the tow truck. He then took out a tool box and went back to Klaus's car, where he opened the driver's door and stood working on something. *What the hell is he doing?* Big Joe dialled Ralph again. "You drive by this time," he ordered. "Try and see what he's doin'."

Ralph drove past and called Big Joe. "He's screwing around with something in the corner of the dash."

"He's switchin' the serial number," Big Joe said. "Find a place to park and wait."

* * *

While Big Joe was waiting, Jack dropped Benny off at his own car. Then they both drove over and met Sammy in the parking lot outside the I-HIT office. Sammy tossed the van's keys to Jack and asked, "Do you mind if we stay and watch? I'm dying to see their faces."

"Suit yourselves, but I wouldn't stand too close. Connie may want to haul your asses in for interrogation. It would be better to have Isaac clear things first — if he does."

"What? You're telling me this wasn't approved by the brass? I'm aghast!" Sammy chuckled and looked at Benny. "Jack's right. Time to split."

"I'll call you later," Jack told him. "Get hold of Bob Aitkin and find a watering hole. He likes rum, preferably Flor De Caña. I owe the guy big time. The drinks are on me, so hold the tab until I get there. Give Laura and Otto a call, too. I put her through hell today."

"Will do," replied Sammy.

"It'll be a few hours before I'm done my notes, and that's providing things go down well with the brass."

"Picking up the tab are ya," Benny repeated. "Don't worry, we'll look after Bob and Laura. Take your time and make sure your notes are really thorough." He exchanged a grin with Sammy and they headed off.

Got the feeling that tonight'll be expensive, Jack thought. He pulled out his phone and called Rose.

"Here you are," she said. "I thought you would've called

earlier to find out how my meeting with the brass about what happened last night went. I take it your breakfast meeting with Wolfgang dragged on?"

"You might say that. How did it go with the brass?"

"Not bad, considering. They seemed happy that you drove Klaus to the hospital. Isaac raised an eyebrow when I told him that you later suggested to Wolfgang that Klaus should get counselling. It was okay once I told them that if Klaus was worried, he had plenty of time to leave the hospital while you were meeting with Wolfgang."

"Good. Anything else?"

"Yes. They're concerned he may try it again, especially considering that this is the third time in a week you busted him in the yap."

"I only used the minimum amount of force needed to gain —"

"Please. Maybe you did, but I've already been read the medical report."

"Oh."

"Yes … oh." Rose paused, then said, "Do you really think he'll be sent back to Germany immediately?"

"No. Are you sitting down?"

"Oh, shit," said Rose, immediately worried. "What did you do?"

"Hear me through before you yell at me. Something happened, but everything is under control."

"Talk." The edge to Rose's voice said she wasn't happy.

Jack told Rose everything that had happened. She remained silent the entire time, except for the odd mutter and to tell him to slow down because she was making notes.

Her anger surfaced when she reviewed her notes and thought about what she had to do next. "Okay, let me get this right," she said. "I'm to go to Isaac … again … and telling him that you drove another body over to I-HIT … again … of some guy who was shot in the head … again. Is that right?"

"Sounds about," Jack said thoughtfully.

"Damn it, Jack! You can't keep doing this!"

"I didn't do it. Anton shot him under Wolfgang's instructions. I only watched."

Rose acted like she hadn't heard. "The first time was one thing. Everyone thought it was a once-in-a-lifetime, on-the-job kind of thing. That was last Tuesday! Now you do it again? Then you have the gall to toss the body in a van like you were picking up a dead squirrel and drive it over to I-HIT!"

"If it was a squirrel, I wouldn't have brought it to I-HIT," Jack said.

"What you did is so absurd it's almost comical," Rose said in frustration.

"Tell me what choice I had." His tone was maddeningly even.

Rose didn't answer as she held the phone. Her eyes were closed and she massaged both temples with the thumb and fingers of her free hand.

"You there?" Jack asked at last.

"I hope not. I hope I'm home having a nightmare," she replied angrily.

"Come on, Rose. It's not like I could have stopped them. I really do think that the pistol they gave me wasn't loaded."

"Or would have stopped them even if you knew it was."

"Well … yes, you're right about that. Wolfgang and Anton are not who I'm after. On top of that, Klaus was really in bad shape. I'm sure the autopsy will show he had a lot of internal injuries. He may not have survived regardless. I actually felt sorry for him."

"You felt sorry for him? Yeah, right."

"I'm not the bad guy here, they are," said Jack defensively. "Ask the brass what they would have done. If any of them were in my shoes, there would have been two murders this afternoon. Besides, they approved it last week when I brought Dempsey over to I-HIT. How can they turn around and not approve it again? The basic circumstances are the same."

"I must be in a state of shock because I really don't know what to say or think at the moment," Rose replied. "Which is odd, because where you're concerned, I shouldn't be surprised. Maybe I'm just tired." Then she mumbled, more to herself, "I feel really tired."

"I'm asking for your support," Jack pleaded. "A good cop was murdered because of me. Don't forget that."

Jack's words brought Rose's mind back into focus. "Okay," she said, sounding reluctant. "I'll back you as usual, but I've got a couple of questions for you."

"Shoot."

Rose paused.

"I mean, go ahead."

"Have you thought of the consequences of destroying Klaus's car? Internal might suspect you were getting rid of evidence to protect yourself. They're going to be curious."

"Yeah, well, that's par for the course. They say that curiosity killed the cat, too, but I'm sure I was a suspect."

"Anyone would question that after you admitted you beat him senseless and stuffed him in the trunk of a car, then had the car taken to a car crusher the next day."

"They can access the medical records and check with the hospital," Jack said. "It will be on video, me dropping him off last night and leaving. They may even see Anton or someone picking him up after. As far as the car goes, yeah, there was blood in the trunk. If they want to see it for themselves, I'll lend them a can opener."

"I'm sure they'd appreciate that," replied Rose dryly. "One more thing, is this why Laura hasn't come back to the office? Afraid I'll tear a strip off her? Or were you stalling for time so that — again — it would be too late to stop you?"

"I gave instructions for Sammy and Benny to take Laura and Otto for a debriefing, analyze the events that took place to see if anything could have been improved upon. I felt it important that the debriefing take place while everything is still fresh in everyone's minds."

"A debriefing? Where at?"

"Yes … well, I'm not sure where. I was going to call them later. Where it is, isn't important. It's also intended as an opportunity to express emotions and to alleviate any potential post-traumatic stress."

"Yeah, I get it. A meeting where people self-medicate."

"You're right about me stalling," admitted Jack. "I was being followed by Big Joe and didn't have time to be bogged down with any red tape. If the brass knew, they might have told me to take it to the police garage for a week while they made a decision."

"You don't have much trust in your superiors, do you."

"No, but I've come to trust you. Hopefully, by telling you what I have, your response won't be something that would ruin that trust."

"Don't try to manipulate me," Rose said.

"I thought it was obvious I was teasing," Jack said honestly.

Rose paused a moment, then said, "Okay, I'll do my best to support you. You risked your life. That should count for something."

"Thanks, Rose. I knew I could count on you."

"There, you did it again. Made me feel like I've been manipulated somehow."

"You're too smart to be manipulated, which is why I trust and respect you."

"Thanks, Jack. I appreciate that."

"Rose?"

"Yes?"

"That was manipulation."

"You jerk!"

Jack chuckled. "Good luck with the brass."

"It's not me who needs the good luck," Rose declared before hanging up.

Yeah, she might be right about that.

Chapter Thirty-Five

Jack was walking through the I-HIT office on his way to Inspector Dyck's office when he spotted Connie at her desk. He decided to detour to see her.

"What's up?" she asked when he walked in.

"You didn't hear what came over Anton's phone today?"

"No. I've been out at a homicide all afternoon. Got back ten minutes ago and have about three dozen messages waiting. Why? What's up?"

"I don't have time to explain," replied Jack. "I have to see Inspector Dyck before he leaves for the day, but I may as well give you these." He tossed a set of keys on her desk, then took out his notebook and jotted down a record of the time and date he gave them to her.

"What are these for?"

"They're keys," said Jack, looking up. "They unlock things."

"Yeah, smartass. What's going on?"

"Same thing as last week. In fact, they're the same keys. The van is parked outside. I brought you another one."

"Yeah, right," said Connie in a tone that indicated her disbelief. "Not fucking likely."

"Wish it was NFL," said Jack, "but I'm serious. Also brought you this." He pulled a plastic bag that held a pistol out of his pocket, then placed it on her desk. "It's the murder weapon. Figure you might want Forensics to take a look at it."

"What the —"

"You can thank me for the help later," said Jack. "I want to make sure Dyck knows before the brass calls him." With that he turned and left her office.

"Thank you for it! You freakin' asshole!" she yelled, getting up from behind her desk. "Are you shitting me?"

Jack didn't reply as he headed for Inspector Dyck's office. He heard Connie cursing as she locked the murder weapon in her desk drawer before heading out to the parking lot.

Inspector Dyck's door was open, and when Jack knocked to catch his attention, he was waved in.

"What can I do for you?" Dyck asked.

"Brought you another one," Jack said wearily as he sat down.

"Another one?" Dyck's eyebrows shot up

"Same as last time," Jack said. "The victim's in a van outside. I took the liberty of giving Connie the keys, along with the murder weapon. Do you have a moment to talk?"

"I do now," replied Dyck grimly.

"I expect you'll be receiving a call from Assistant Commissioner Isaac shortly, but wanted to give you a heads-up. I witnessed another murder but haven't had time to do my notes yet. I'll get at them as soon I tell you what happened."

"I'm listening."

"You're aware that Klaus Eichel was waiting for the chance to kill me?" Jack began.

"I was at a meeting this morning with Rose and Isaac," replied Dyck. "I'm up-to-date on the file as of last night, where you ended up taking him to the hospital. What's happened since then?"

Jack told Dyck the details about his breakfast meeting with Wolfgang and what took place afterwards.

Dyck's reaction was calm. He didn't seem angry, but neither was he particularly pleased. He was about to say something when his phone rang. He mouthed "Isaac" to Jack and quickly answered.

"Yes, sir, he's in my office right now."

Jack listened to Dyck's side of the conversation, which mostly consisted of a repetition of "Yes, sir" and "That's what he told me, sir." The conversation droned on. During the call, Connie entered the office, and Jack put his finger to his lips and whispered, "Isaac's on the line."

When at last Dyck hung up, he stared blankly in Connie's direction.

"Sir? Should I read him his rights?" she asked, and Jack sensed she was completely serious.

Dyck looked at Jack. "Rose debriefed Isaac on what happened and suggested you receive an official commendation for the dangerous situation you faced."

"Commendation?" Connie squawked.

"Isaac told me in no uncertain terms that you will not be receiving that," said Dyck, maintaining his focus on Jack. "You are free to go, but he wants a copy of all your notes on his desk by eight o'clock tomorrow morning. I suggest you get started."

Jack felt the tension leave his body. As he left the office, he overheard Dyck say to Connie, "Make sure nobody ever gives him back the keys to that van, will you?"

Would you rather I use FedEx? Jack thought. He called Laura to let her know that all was okay before returning to his office and writing up his notes.

Three hours later he called Laura again to find out where she and Otto were. He could tell by the background noise that his tab was going to be expensive. Laura told him where they were, then said, "Hang on, Otto wants to speak to you."

"Wanted to tell you," Otto said, "that you Canadians have peculiar eating habits."

"How so?"

"Laura said she was taking me out to have the soup of the day."

"With olives?" Jack chuckled.

"Ja, das ist richtig," Otto said. Apparently realizing he had spoken German, he added, "Yes, that is right."

"You like 'em?"

"At first I didn't, but now I don't care," he replied.

* * *

It was seven o'clock at night when Big Joe met with Anton at a restaurant in Vancouver and told him what had happened.

"So they took the body out at the car wash and drove it to be cremated," Anton repeated, "but then what did you say about the car? What do you mean they stripped the VIN? What is that? My English isn't that —"

"The tow-truck driver did that after he siphoned the gas out. Stripped the VIN — means he took off the vehicle identification number. Then he probably replaced it with one taken from a wreck so if the police ever checked the records at the scrapyard, it wouldn't come up."

"I see."

"Then he towed it to a scrapyard and turned the car into a cube about the size of my lunchbox," Big Joe said. "My tracking transmitter along with it."

"Yes, you told me. Anything else?"

"No, that's about it, except … I know I said I would do it for free, but I didn't expect to lose my equipment."

Anton pursed his lips. His instinct told him to tell Big Joe to get lost, but decided that paying him may preserve the discretion that was needed. "Five hundred cover it?" he asked, pulling out his wallet.

"Cash … you bet." Big Joe grinned. "The only way to do business."

* * *

Thirty minutes later Anton met with Wolfgang in his room at the Fairmont Hotel and told him what happened to Klaus's body and car.

Wolfgang nodded thoughtfully. "I've said it before — Jack is an interesting man. The Ringmaster has said so, as well. He's a man who no doubt could be a valuable asset. "

"If his tastes were in something other than art …"

"Exactly. It's unfortunate that the painting is in bonded storage, but as the Ringmaster said, if he is truly genuine, his love for the painting will not let him keep it imprisoned for long."

"After all this, you still suspect he is not genuine?" Anton was surprised.

"As the Ringmaster told me, we are in his domain. It may all be an illusion."

"Smoke and mirrors," Anton said. "Perhaps ... but I don't think so."

"I've been told to invite him to our side of the world, where *we* control the stage." Wolfgang paused. "In the long run, whether he is genuine or not doesn't matter. He will still be killed."

Chapter Thirty-Six

It was seven in the morning when Jack picked up Laura, after having driven both her and Otto home the night before.

Upon getting in the SUV, Laura immediately shut the radio off. She scowled at Jack and said, "What time did you bring me home last night?"

"Two o'clock. Right after we dropped Otto off."

"You dirty rat," she groused. "Is that what you call looking after your wingman?"

"I tried to get you to ease off. Even suggested you drink some water, but you —"

"Shh," she said, putting her finger to her lips for emphasis, before leaning back and closing her eyes.

Jack dropped her off at the bar they'd been at the night before to collect her car and then headed for the office. He'd completed his notes but had not yet photocopied them to give to Isaac.

At seven-thirty he was at the photocopier when Rose arrived.

"Well!" she said. "Aren't *you* the punctual one."

"The trouble with being punctual is that there's usually nobody around to notice."

"Oh, believe me, you're being noticed these days," retorted Rose. "Those for Isaac?" she asked, gesturing to the copier.

Jack nodded. "I wrote them last night, but knew the door to his office was locked, so —"

"More like you were afraid you were missing out on last night's debriefing."

"Well, that, too," Jack admitted.

"First Clive's killed and then Klaus," noted Rose. "Both guys who could have identified your informant. Isaac asked me if she's safe now. I said I'd check with you."

"There was a third guy abusing her that night."

"Liam Quinn," stated Rose.

"Good memory."

"It might behoove you to remember that. I also remember that Roche Freulard told you they would never use Liam again."

"That's a chance I can't take. If they want revenge, they would use whatever means possible."

"Any other reasons I could tell Isaac?"

"Yes, it might get a little sticky if Defence goes after the angle that I forced Clive into a situation at gunpoint that got him killed."

"Or went after Klaus's recent orthodontic records," Rose said.

"Yeah. It'd better if I were to get evidence on what these guys have done in Europe and testify there. With how calm Anton was when he killed Clive and Klaus, I know they weren't his first."

"So you're concerned that Liam could be used to track down your informant?"

"That's a good explanation to tell Isaac, rather than pester him with the other details."

Rose bit her lower lip as she thought, *Jack's right. Keep it simple and use informant safety as a reason.*

"So you agree." Jack spoke matter-of-factly.

Damn it. He reads me like a book. "See me in my office once you turn in the copies of your notes. Bring your notebook, too."

"I told you everything that's in my notes," said Jack evenly.

Rose looked quizzical. "That's in your notes? Don't you mean that you told me everything?"

Jack looked at her silently and thought about the lie he'd told Klaus to keep him at the hospital. *That sure as hell isn't in my notes.*

"I see," said Rose. "Are you forgetting that I'm your boss?"

"I heard you stuck your neck out for me yesterday — suggesting I should receive commendation."

Rose frowned. "That didn't go over too well."

"Doesn't matter. The point is, you were protecting me. I like to protect you in return."

As Rose considered how to respond, Laura arrived. Abruptly, she said, "I think I'm going to be sick." And putting her hand to her mouth, she rushed off down the hall to the washroom.

Rose looked at Jack and whispered, "Morning sickness?"

"No, I suspect she consumed a bad olive during the debriefing last night."

Rose shook her head in admonishment, then said, "Meet me as soon as you drop off the copy of your notes."

At eight o'clock, Jack walked into Rose's office carrying a mug of coffee, along with his notebook. Rose and Laura were sipping their own coffees. He placed his mug on the desk and handed Rose his notebook.

"I'll read them later," she said. "I want to know what your plans are. I'm sure that'll be the first thing Isaac will ask me after he reads your notes."

Jack picked up his mug, leaned back in the chair, and took a sip, then said, "Well, the thing is, I really don't like to say what my plans are."

"Why not?" Rose instantly became irritated.

"Because then, later on, words like *premeditated* get tossed around in the courtroom," replied Jack, doing his best to keep a straight face.

Rose realized he was teasing her. "That's not funny," she said, trying to maintain a straight face.

But the stress they'd been under broke the decorum and both started to laugh, unable to stop as their joviality fed off each other.

"Do you mind keeping the noise down?" Laura muttered.

Jack felt his phone vibrate, and the moment of levity came to an abrupt end. "It's Wolfgang," he said, putting his finger to his lips.

Chapter Thirty-Seven

At noon Jack walked into the Griffins bistro and Wolfgang waved at him from a table situated under a high-arched window. Jack took a seat and Wolfgang gestured out the window at a building across the street. "I thought you would prefer to sit here."

Jack smiled. "The Vancouver Art Gallery. It's even more impressive inside."

"No problems with yesterday?" asked Wolfgang, taking a sip of coffee.

"Yesterday?" Jack pretended to be puzzled.

"With Klaus … the car," whispered Wolfgang as the waiter approached.

"Oh, that." Jack flicked his hand dismissively. "It's all been taken care off."

Wolfgang gazed silently at Jack while the waiter dropped off menus and took Jack's order for coffee. When he left, Wolfgang said solemnly. "I have spoken with my boss about how quickly you cleaned up the mess yesterday. It was ... unbelievable."

Jack caught the intended hesitation in Wolfgang's voice and the intensity in his gaze as he studied Jack's reaction. *The Juggler still doesn't trust me.* Jack gave Wolfgang a hard look. "Unbelievable?" he questioned. "Let me assure you that yesterday's loose ends are permanently cleaned up, and that you can believe. If you doubt my ability, then we should part company." *And you can kiss the painting goodbye.*

"No, no, no," Wolfgang hastened to say. "We believe you are a professional, a master, in fact, at what you do. I did not mean *unbelievable* in the way you took it. I think the words my boss used were 'unbelievably amazing', meaning we are impressed."

Jack nodded, but his face remained expressionless, leaving Wolfgang feeling unsure as to whether Jack bought his attempted cover-up.

"So —" Wolfgang clasped his hands with a smack "— I have been asked to clarify which countries you are thinking about retiring in. As mentioned before, we will cover your expenses in Europe while you search for a place, and at the same time, we'll incorporate the consultation with our representatives."

"Representatives," said Jack. "You mean the ones you call the jugglers?"

"Yes." Wolfgang smiled. "You see," he said, sounding enthusiastic, "you are already fitting in with our company."

Jack smiled politely. *Yes, convince me that we're going to be friends ... asshole.* "The areas I have been considering purchasing a villa in are the Tuscany or Umbria regions of Italy, Costa del Sol in the south of Spain, or perhaps Malta."

"Not France? Roche told me that you were considering it, as well."

Good, you took the bait. Time to enhance my artsy role. Jack paused as the waiter brought him his coffee. He told him that he'd order breakfast later. He then turned his attention back to Wolfgang. *Hope he knows less about art than I do.* "Yes, about France. Perhaps the Marseille area would appeal to me. I'm torn on that matter. On one hand, France has so many spectacular museums. The Louvre and Musée Marmottan Monet in Paris and, of course, the Museum of Fine Arts in Marseille itself. The problem is that I have not found the French to be all that hospitable to me when they discover I am English-speaking."

"I'm not so sure they are fond of Germans, either," Wolfgang replied, then grinned.

Jack smiled briefly, then furrowed his eyebrows as if in deep thought. "Perhaps France is where I should start. At one time it was foremost in my mind for retirement. I have not been to Paris for years; perhaps things have improved."

"Our offer would certainly give you opportunity to reassess things," said Wolfgang, "but I must tell you that our offer may not stay on the table for long. When could you come to Europe, and how long would it take you to complete your consultations after you arrive?"

"As far as looking at retirement property goes, I would like to spend a couple of days in each of the areas I mentioned, perhaps doing consulting work at the same time. That being said, I have to … make arrangements to satisfy certain clients in North America that I'm still contracting out to."

"We presumed that, but what time frame were you thinking?" prodded Wolfgang.

"First I will need to know how in-depth of a profile the Ringmaster wants in regard to the people being assessed. Perhaps I could meet the Ringmaster and do the jugulars in one location to speed things up."

"Jugulars?"

Damn it. Freudian slip. "Sorry, I meant jugglers, of course. I've never been to a circus and the lingo seems strange to me," he added lamely.

"You've never been to a circus? Not even as a child?"

Okay, time to make him think I've had a tough life. Give the impression that my street smarts came from surviving on the mean streets of some city since I was a kid. "My childhood wasn't much of a childhood." Jack sounded bitter. "I left home at an early age. Survival did not include the luxury of going to a circus. I take it you have?"

"A few times," replied Wolfgang, eyeing Jack curiously.

"Anyway," continued Jack, "how long I would need is dependent on the service wanted. Is it the basic background check, including close associates? Or one that would provide a psychological profile, necessitating a written test coupled with interviews?"

"That is a decision for my boss," replied Wolfgang.

"You mean the Ringmaster?"

"Yes." Then Wolfgang added, "I have said this before — you are a man of many talents."

"Ah, not really," Jack replied. "The truth is, I have contacts who assist me with certain aspects. It's more about who I know than what I know."

"Of course, but you *are* an exceptional man. I watched you when Anton killed Klaus. You didn't flinch. It struck me that you are no stranger to such an event."

Jack frowned. "Talking about something like that makes me nervous."

"I'm sorry —" Wolfgang lowered his voice and glanced around "— but there is nobody nearby to hear us."

"Please don't take this personally, but I don't know you well enough to talk so openly about such matters," Jack explained.

Wolfgang's eyes widened in surprise. He'd just realized that Jack was concerned Wolfgang may be trying to set him up to the police. "You want to search me for a wire?" he asked.

"It was Anton who put a bullet in Klaus's head under your direction, was it not?" Jack said.

Wolfgang's eyes narrowed. "Yes." Now he looked puzzled.

Jack smiled. "Your response tells me that searching you is not necessary. I was simply making a point about how easy it might be for someone to gather information that could destroy an organization. My consulting service provides protection against that sort of thing."

Wolfgang nodded slowly to indicate he understood.

"Now, back to when I can go to Europe and for how long. To begin with, for my first trip, I would like two weeks. Then, depending upon what type of consulting work is required, future visits can be arranged at a price and upon terms agreed to by your boss and myself."

"Two weeks is not a problem. I have already been authorized to tell you that we would pay for a minimum of three weeks and perhaps longer, if need be."

"Thank you, but I have other clients I wish to finish up with. Two weeks is the most I can afford to be away for the time being."

"And out of the two weeks, how much time do you think would be spent on actual consulting work versus searching for a retirement home?"

"How many profiles would you anticipate need to be done?"

"I'm not sure," admitted Wolfgang. "At the moment we have five jugglers ... but that could change. We also have people under them who may need screening."

Good, I am trusted enough to be told about some of the corporate structure. But will they trust me enough to discuss the way they conduct business, such as committing murder? Jack nodded, then replied, "It would depend on how in-depth of a profile your boss would want. As far as the jugglers go, if they were together, I would only need a day with them to get the information I need to start the ball rolling. If it is not possible to meet them all at once, then I would like to start with Roche."

"Why him?"

"He told me he didn't want to come to Canada because of recent legal difficulties. He indicated that the problem had been taken care of, but at the same time said there could be some aftermath. If he thinks that, then the problem has not been fully taken care of. As I have been involved with Roche on, shall we say, a delicate matter involving Clive Dempsey, I would feel more relaxed if I focus on him first and learn the details of his legal problem."

"I understand," replied Wolfgang. "You wish to evaluate your own risk of contamination first."

"Exactly. Then once I meet everyone it could take several months of work, depending on what I discover. Have the jugglers lived in one place most of their lives, or have they moved every couple of years?"

"Roche, Anton, and I have pretty much lived in one place, but I don't know about the other two," Wolfgang said.

"One place makes it easier. Regardless, you get my point. I need to do a preliminary assessment, which, for obvious reasons, would only be given to the Ringmaster for whatever action he deems necessary. If all goes well, my assessments may indicate no changes are necessary, or if they are, I would offer my own suggestions about how to incorporate them."

"I see. How soon could you get started?"

"I should be able to clear my calendar in about two weeks. Today is Thursday, so let's say the fifteenth of February. That's a Saturday. I know I'll be available by then."

"That would be great," Wolfgang said. "I'd planned on staying until at least the eleventh of February, so the delay of another few days won't matter. By then, Anton and Bojan will have completed their assignment and will have returned to Europe."

Jack would've liked to have found out exactly how Anton and Bojan were moving the stolen goods, but asking that might arouse suspicion. He took a sip of coffee, then said, "Once I get to Europe, if I were to meet with everyone to start with, I might be in a position to provide preliminary profiles to give to the Ringmaster before I return to Canada. That way he'd know he's getting his money's worth."

"You've already impressed the Ringmaster," said Wolfgang, "so I do not believe that is an issue." He gave Jack a warm smile. "I can assure you that you will be put up in the best hotels with the finest restaurants."

Until you get your hands on the painting. Then where do you plan to put me?

"Now, if you'd be kind enough to give me your full name and passport number," Wolfgang went on, "I will arrange to have an airline ticket available for you to leave on the fifteenth."

Jack made a grimace. "You probably won't believe it, but my last name is Smith."

"Why shouldn't I believe it?"

"It is a common name in North America," Jack replied. "So common that it's often a joke for unimaginative people to use it as a fake name."

Wolfgang shrugged. "Then it must be your real name, because I know you have imagination. I'll need your passport number, as well, to book the ticket."

"I don't have it memorized. I'll give you all the details later." Jack reached for the menu. "I'm going to order a martini to start with."

"Yes, I'll have a drink, too," said Wolfgang. "We shall toast to doing business together."

Jack smiled in response.

* * *

Rose leaned forward with her hands clasped on her desk and listened intently as Jack outlined his meeting with Wolfgang. Laura listened, too, but sat with her arms folded across her chest. Her face hardened as her concern grew.

When Jack was finished, Rose said, "So your plan is to speak to Roche and perhaps get an admission about Kerin's murder on the pretext of ensuring your own insulation from the law? Are you hoping to get it all on a wire?"

"In Kerin's notes he mentioned being scanned for a wire. I can't risk it. At least, not at the beginning. Ideally it would not only be Roche. I'm hoping the Ringmaster will also be there and trust me enough to open up. Considering what his men have seen me do, I think they would have a certain amount of faith in me."

"Perhaps even more than the brass have for you," said Rose dryly. She glanced at her desk calendar. "Europe on the fifteenth ... doesn't give us a lot of time. I know Ottawa will approve, but you're going to need to get a fake passport and arrange the co-operation of European police agencies."

"We have liaison officers stationed in Paris and Rome, so that'll help," Jack said.

"But not in Spain or Malta," noted Laura, "which are the other two places you tossed out as potential retirement spots."

Jack nodded. "I'll look into seeing what the protocol is there. Ottawa will have some kind of agreement. But regardless, I don't want a cover team breathing down my neck."

"Like hell you don't!" said Rose sharply. "If you think you can traipse around Europe by yourself with a group who murdered an officer right in front of his cover team, you better think again. You should have a team that includes the French, as well as officers from whatever country you're in."

"Having a cover team is why Kerin was murdered," Jack argued. "That, and trying to save me," he added bitterly. "It's for my own safety that I don't want anyone holding my hand every step of the way."

"Our policy would never allow it," said Rose. "If you feel that way, then you shouldn't be going." She looked hard at Jack for a moment. "Think about it. Would we allow a policeman from another country to work undercover in our jurisdiction without protection? Not a chance."

She's right of course, but policy can get you killed. Better pretend to go along with it. "You're right," said Jack. "I wasn't thinking. I'd definitely want Otto around to see if he can identify the swarthy-looking man who met Roche in Frankfurt."

"Good," Rose said.

Laura eyed Jack. *I know you. When the time comes, all you'll do is lose the cover team or send them on a wild-goose chase someplace else.*

Reading her mind, Jack turned to Rose and said, "I would also like Laura there to guide the cover team. She's experienced and knows how I operate."

"That won't be a problem," replied Rose. "Undercover is new to the French. We need someone with you who knows the ropes."

Laura looked at Rose and nodded in agreement, before glancing at Jack. *Yes, I do know how you operate. You want me to play Mother Goose and help lead them away from you. Oh, man …*

Chapter Thirty-Eight

On February 15 Jack stretched out in the first class comfort of the Boeing 747 400-passenger jet operated by British Airways. His almost twelve-hour flight from Vancouver was due to arrive in Paris at five-thirty in the evening of the following day. The RCMP liaison officer stationed in Paris was away, but his presence was not needed, as the French were more than eager to be involved.

Jack accepted the complimentary glass of champagne and exchanged a toast with Wolfgang, who was seated across the aisle from him.

Five days earlier Anton had left Canada and flown to Paris. The following day Bojan was intercepted making a phone call to arrange for home furnishings to be shipped to an address in Bulgaria. Interpol discovered that the address belonged to Bojan's parents. The day after the furniture was picked up, Bojan left Canada.

Wolfgang then gave Jack a round-trip ticket to Paris with a return date of two weeks later, along with a promise that he could extend his stay if he wished. He said that once in Paris, they would be staying at the Renaissance Paris Vendome Hotel, which, he noted, was within easy walking distance of the Louvre and the Museum d'Orsay, and only four kilometres from the Eiffel Tower. Jack was also told to charge all restaurant and bar expenses in the hotel to his room and that it would be paid for.

Laura, flying economy, had been put on an American Airlines flight that had an almost identical arrival schedule. Otto had returned to Germany ten days earlier, but made arrangements to fly to Paris to assist in the investigation when she arrived.

Jack checked out the hotel on the Internet and discovered it cost more than $700 a night. Another hotel, called Hôtel du Louvre, was reserved for Laura at a cost of $165 a night and was less than a ten-minute walk away. Otto was booked into the same hotel as Laura.

Jack grinned when he thought of the dirty look Laura pretended to give him over the discrepancy in travel and accommodation. *Love it when the bad guys pay.*

Despite knowing what hotel he was booked at, Jack agreed that the French police would put a surveillance team on him when he arrived at the Paris airport. Undercover operations seldom went as planned, but he knew it would be busy enough on arrival that the team should go undetected.

Jack had also spoken with Maurice Leblanc, who was to be part of the surveillance team. He was anxious to meet with him face to face to express his gratitude for what Kerin had died trying to do. He also wanted to visit Kerin's wife, Gabrielle, but knew the secrecy of the undercover operation demanded she not know. There was also fear it would build up her hopes that the man who murdered her husband would be caught, adding to the devastation she would feel if Jack wasn't successful.

Police forces in Spain, Malta, and Italy had been contacted and all agreed to supply a cover team for their areas. On top of that, Maurice, along with his boss, Yves Charbonneau, would assist in covering Jack in each country, along with Laura and Otto. Solving Kerin's murder was the primary objective, and therefore the investigation was under the control and direction of the French police.

The flight arrived on time, and Jack and Wolfgang booked into the Renaissance Paris Vendome at nine o'clock. Their rooms were on different floors, which Jack was pleased about. It gave him more freedom to leave undetected.

After checking in, Jack called Laura.

"You in?" he asked.

"Yes, still unpacking. Otto, Maurice, and Yves are with me."

"I saw a huge park a block from my hotel called the Tuileries Garden. I wonder if it's the same park where —"

"No. I saw it, too, and asked Maurice. Kerin was murdered in a different park. Why did you want to know?"

"Guess it doesn't matter. But every park I see makes me think of him and question what I did that night."

"It's wasn't your fault. You know that, right?"

"I know." Jack decided to change the subject. "What's your read on Yves? He'll be the one we have to answer to."

"Might be too soon to say," replied Laura, smiling at Yves, who was watching her. "Quail, did you say? Bet that was good. Wish I could have gone first class."

"You mean he's like our old boss? Staff Quaile?"

"Yes."

"Christ. Nobody could be that big of an asshole."

"Yes, you're probably right about that," agreed Laura. "First impressions and I'm tired, but Otto has some good news on finding the real owner of the painting."

"He found the owner? How?"

"Remember the old gentleman tortured in Surrey when they stole the picture?"

"Herman Jaiger."

"Yes, and he had a document of authentication from the Goldman Art Verification Agency in Paris, dated in 1933 and addressed to a Mr. Guri L. Sacher in Paris."

"Yes, there's a school at that address now. So Otto found him?"

"Not exactly. Mr. Sacher died a few years ago, but Otto found his daughter. He hasn't told her yet because he doesn't want word to get out in case it jeopardizes our investigation."

"That's fantastic. How did he do it?"

"Let me put him on and he can tell you," said Laura.

Seconds later Otto spoke. "So, you need me to teach you how to be a detective."

"Sounds like it," admitted Jack. "How did you find her?"

"We Germans have a reputation for being thorough," said Otto dryly. "Lists were kept of many of those who were exterminated during the Second World War. His name was not on any list."

"Okay …"

"The most popular country the Jews fled to was Switzerland. After making a couple of dozen phone calls and pretending I was a distant cousin interested in tracing the family tree, I located his daughter. She told me she went to Paris about ten years ago to look up the family home and discovered a school there. Her father, Guri Leib Sacher, died of old age a few years ago."

"Good work," Jack said. "When the investigation is over, we'll be able to return it."

"That's what I thought. Here, I'll put Laura back on."

"So what's the plan?" she asked.

"I'm exhausted and going to bed. I'm to meet Wolfgang downstairs tomorrow morning at nine for breakfast. He said we'd have someone joining us."

"The Ringmaster?"

"Wolfgang said he wasn't sure who'd be coming. My gut tells me it will be someone else. I don't think they're done checking me out, so try to keep the surveillance team at bay if you can."

"That might be hard."

"I don't want anyone in there on surveillance," said Jack firmly. "Don't tell the others about it and I'll call you after breakfast. If it is the Ringmaster, I'll be meeting him more than once. I've got what he wants. He's not going to dismiss me that easily."

Yeah, here it goes, Laura thought. *I'm not even unpacked and already you're telling me to ditch the cover team. Oh, man.*

"You hear me?" Jack's voice was stern.

"Yeah, I hear you."

* * *

At eight o'clock the following morning Jack went downstairs and entered Le Pinxo restaurant, situated inside the hotel. He knew he was an hour early, but he hadn't adjusted to the time difference and had been awake since five. He ordered a cappuccino, then another.

Forty-five minutes later he saw Wolfgang enter the restaurant. He was accompanied by a man who looked to be about forty-five, with thinning hair that was too black to be natural. The man was portly and dressed in black slacks and a red, V-neck sweater. A gold loop hung from the lobe of each ear. Wolfgang introduced him to Jack as Roche Freulard, and the pair took seats across the table.

Jack eyed Roche and said, "I thought you had some legal difficulties. I trust you didn't bring that problem with you?"

"I have taken the necessary precautions to ensure I was not followed," was his reply.

"Are you staying at the hotel?"

"No." Roche glanced at Wolfgang as if to question why Jack would ask.

"You're not wearing a coat and it's cold and rainy outside," said Jack, "so I presume you left it in Wolfgang's room — no doubt when you were talking about me."

Roche looked taken back, but Wolfgang chuckled.

Roche raised his hand to summon the waitress. When the young woman arrived, Roche smiled and spoke to her in French, apparently asking about something on the menu. When she leaned over to point at an item on the menu, Roche put his hand around her waist.

The waitress grabbed his wrist and flung his arm off her, then stepped back, obviously annoyed. Somewhat sullenly, Roche ordered a café au lait and a croissant. Both Wolfgang and Jack ordered omelettes and coffee, and the waitress left.

The conversation amongst the three men was general in nature during breakfast. Not until the table had been cleared and they were just finishing their coffees did Roche looked at Jack and say, "So, Wolfgang has told me that he is impressed with your abilities."

"I get by," Jack said.

"In Canada, perhaps." Roche frowned. "But we are not in Canada here."

"Guess that would explain my twelve-hour flight yesterday," Jack replied.

Wolfgang snickered but Roche wasn't amused. "What I am saying," Roche said, a tinge of anger in his voice, "is that you may be like a magician in your country at making things disappear, but how would you perform here?"

"Things disappear?" Jack repeated.

"You know what I mean. Things like a car and … what was in the trunk."

"I'd find a way. A car is easy. I could do that immediately."

Roche exchanged a surprised look with Wolfgang before asking, "How?"

"Do you have a car?" asked Jack.

"Yes. A black Peugeot parked outside."

"Give me the keys," Jack said. "It would be too easy to dispose of if you were along, as you're the owner, but let me take Wolfgang for a drive to show him how."

Roche exchanged another glance with Wolfgang, who said, "Why not? Let me see what he would do."

Minutes later Jack got into the Peugot with Wolfgang beside him while Roche stood on the sidewalk watching, first with his arms folded across his chest, then holding his hands behind his back before once more folding his arms across his chest.

Wolfgang gave a nod toward Roche. "You've made him nervous. Do you mind telling me where we're going?"

"First I need to get a pair of pliers," Jack said. "Actually, I bet I could borrow a pair from hotel maintenance."

"Pliers?" Wolfgang looked mystified. "What for?"

"I'll find an alley and loosen the plug on his oil pan to drain the oil, then take his car out for a spin. Once the engine seizes up, I'll look for the cheapest one-man tow-truck operation I can find. When the guy shows up, I'll pretend to be angry and say the warning lights were always going on and off and that the car was constantly quitting on me, but the dealership could never find the problem. I'll offer him a thousand Euros if I can watch the car being crushed today. He'll think I'll be reporting it stolen later and I doubt he'll look too hard at the paperwork."

"I bet you're right," said Wolfgang. "That's amazing that you would come up with that so fast." He glanced back at Roche, who was still watching.

"Not really. Wait and I'll go borrow some pliers." Jack began opening the car door. "Let's do it."

Wolfgang gasped. "God, no! Roche would go nuts. I think you've demonstrated your point."

"Are you sure?" Jack gestured at Roche and said, "Maybe I could get him to volunteer so I can show you how to dispose of a body."

Wolfgang laughed and moments later Jack returned the keys to Roche. Wolfgang told Roche about how Jack would get rid of a car, but when he got to the part about Jack wondering if Roche would volunteer for a demonstration on body disposal, Roche cast Jack a suspicious glance.

As they walked back into the hotel lobby, Roche turned to Jack. "I presume you're tired after your long flight yesterday. With that in mind, I will leave, but I have made a dinner reservation for eight o'clock tonight at the dining room in the Hôtel Meurice. It is one block over on the Rue de Rivoli," he said, with a toss of his hand in the general direction. "I presume you brought a suit?"

"I did," replied Jack.

"Good. Wear it. I plan on introducing you to someone."

"Someone?" Jack asked.

Roche smiled. "You will see. I suggest you get some rest. I will also give you my phone number should you need to contact me." He handed Jack a slip of paper.

"Unfortunately, I will not be joining you," said Wolfgang. "I have some matters that need looking after and will be returning to Frankfurt later today."

"So soon?" Jack frowned. "I was hoping we could all meet today or tomorrow so I could start my consultation process."

Wolfgang said, "I am sure we will be meeting soon for such a purpose."

"Yes," Roche added. "We want to give you time to look around and enjoy yourself. There will be time for work later."

So I'm not trusted enough yet.

Jack bade both men a friendly goodbye, but felt his apprehension grow as he speculated about what was in store for him tonight.

Chapter Thirty-Nine

Jack phoned Laura at the Hôtel du Louvre to let her know he was on his way over. It was arranged that everyone would meet in Otto's room, down the hall from Laura's. He also passed on Roche's phone number, but was not optimistic that it would generate any interesting calls.

He then walked over to the Hôtel Meurice, where Roche had made dinner reservations, ostensibly to see where it was located, but in reality he was checking to see if he was being followed. He was glad he did. A man and a woman tailed him, stopping to gaze around whenever he stopped.

After seeing where the hotel was located, Jack meandered across the street to the large Tuileries Garden, which contained the Louvre museum. The park, a major tourist attraction, was crowded.

It did not take him long to lose the couple, but it was almost noon before he was confident enough to go to the Hôtel du Louvre and knock on Otto's door.

Besides Otto, Laura was in the room, along with Maurice Leblanc and Yves Charbonneau.

Jack was introduced to Maurice and Yves and shook their hands. Maurice had a firm grip, which matched his athletic-looking body. Yves had a pot-belly and a red face, which Jack guessed was the result of high blood pressure, a fondness for alcohol, or both.

A moment of uncomfortable silence ensued before Jack said, "I cannot tell you how ... I'm sorry," he said, struggling to speak over the lump in his throat. He swallowed, then tried again. "Words are not enough to explain how I feel about Kerin's murder." He looked at Maurice. "I know he was your partner."

Maurice self-consciously scratched his moustache, then unexpectedly embraced Jack. Upon stepping away, he said, "We are grateful that you are here."

Jack looked at Yves. "And I know he was your subordinate. I want you to know that I will do whatever it takes to catch whoever did this."

Yves nodded.

"And his wife, Gabrielle?" Jack asked. "How is she doing?"

"As well as can be expected," replied Maurice. "She has morning sickness and ..." He stopped and gestured with his hands. "What else can I say? She wants her husband's killer brought to justice. There will be no peace in her heart until then."

Jack nodded. "I understand."

"Yes, we appreciate that you have offered to assist us," Yves said, "but in the future, I would also appreciate it if you do not intentionally lose the team I have following you."

"The man and woman following me work for you?"

"Yes."

Jack took a deep, calming breath, then said, "I thought they were working for the Ringmaster."

"No, they are my people. They were outside the hotel and saw you get into Roche's car with Wolfgang moments before, then you returned to the hotel lobby. What was that about? Why did you not tell me that you were meeting with Roche? We have been looking for him to put him under surveillance. If you had warned us, we could have arranged a team to follow him when he left your hotel. Unfortunately, there wasn't enough time."

"I met Wolfgang for breakfast and Roche unexpectedly came with him."

"I see," replied Yves. "Then it is my fault. I should have had people in the lobby."

"Don't do that," Jack said. "I spotted your team following me. What if the bad guys had also seen them? It could blow the whole investigation. I would ask that you leave Roche alone and let him bring the Ringmaster to me."

"You are a police officer," stated Yves, "and I presume you are trained in the art of surveillance. Our people are professionals, too. Criminals would not have noticed them."

"Why do you think Kerin was killed?" asked Jack.

"Someone overheard him talking on the phone. Perhaps the Ringmaster was already in the washroom. I thought you would have known that." Yves paused. "From the look on your face, it seems you don't agree with that theory."

"If I agreed, we'd both be wrong," said Jack. "I am positive that Kerin was being tested that day for the sole purpose of seeing if there was police surveillance. It was that surveillance that resulted in his murder."

"You have no evidence of that," Yves said sharply.

"I mean no offence, but I realize you are new to the concept of working undercover."

"We are not new when it comes to dealing with informants. The secrecy involved is hardly different." Yves's tone was the sort you might use with a child.

Again Jack took a calming breath. "Most informants have committed criminal acts and are well entrenched in the organization. It is different for undercover operatives, who, as newcomers, are automatically viewed with suspicion. My opinion that Kerin was murdered as a result of the police surveillance is based on my experience of having worked undercover for many years."

"Is it?" Yves scowled. "Or is it that you are looking for an excuse to pin the blame elsewhere because you feel guilty that it was you who caused his death?"

"Yves," pleaded Maurice.

"It's okay, Maurice," said Jack solemnly. "I do feel guilty, but at the same time we need to be pragmatic. Since my life is on the line, I should have a say about how close the cover team is to me."

"What are you thinking?" Yves asked. "That you will continually be on your phone telling them when to come close to you and when to move away?"

"Of course not. That is one of the reasons Laura is here. She's an experienced undercover operative and knows me well. When uncertainty arises, and I expect it will, I trust her judgement as to what should be done."

"You are in France," Yves said angrily, "and it is not you — or her — who will be calling the shots."

"I fully understand that." Jack gave a conciliatory smile.

"Sorry if we got off on the wrong foot. I was simply offering my opinion."

Yves nodded. "Tell me what happened this morning," he said coldly. "Why did you go to Roche's car?"

"They wanted to know how I would dispose of a car," Jack answered. "I told them I would drain the oil and have it towed away."

"Seems sort of silly," Yves said. "What else?"

"There was mention that Wolfgang would go back to Germany today, so with that, I suspect I will not be meeting the Ringmaster or the other jugglers anytime soon."

Yves swung his gaze to Otto. "Then you should return to Germany, as well."

"I would ask that Otto stay," interjected Jack. "He can identify the man who was in the car with Roche in Frankfurt. If it was the Ringmaster, he may be around here."

Maurice looked at Yves and said, "Otto and Laura could ride in the surveillance van with me. We never spotted the Ringmaster in the park with Kerin."

Yves gazed blandly at Maurice for a moment, then said, "Okay."

Otto and Jack caught each other's eye. Both had the same opinion of Yves.

"I gave Yves the phone number you gave me for Roche," Laura said.

Yves briefly appeared lost in his own thoughts, then returned to the moment. "Yes, that is excellent. We will have it monitored before the day is over."

"Don't get your hopes up," Jack suggested. "I'm not trusted yet, so I doubt he'll be using it."

Yves scowled again. "So what is planned this afternoon? How do you intend to gain his trust?"

"Roche told me to relax today to recover from my flight and said he would either call me or drop by my room tomorrow," replied Jack.

Yves glanced at his watch. "I have a meeting I must get to. So, what *are* your plans for the rest of the day?"

"To go back to my room and use the Internet to brush up on my knowledge of art." Jack gave a quick smile and added, "No pun intended."

"Good. We will use this room as a base of operations," Yves declared.

"You're welcome," said Otto facetiously.

Yves ignored the comment and looked at Jack. "Call us tomorrow once you know."

"You bet." Jack paused as if thinking about the situation, then asked, "If he comes to my room, do you want me to call you from the bathroom?"

"No, don't do that," Yves responded, not realizing that Jack was being less than genuine. "Wait until he leaves."

"Okay. Whatever you say."

Laura stared at Jack. *Oh, man, what are you up to?*

Chapter Forty

At eight o'clock, Jack entered the Hôtel Meurice dining room through a large arched doorway. He was wearing a navy-blue suit, a red tie, and a white shirt with French cuffs and gold cufflinks. The dining room was opulent, complete with crystal chandeliers and a mosaic floor. On the walls, rich damask drapes were pulled back to reveal arched windows.

He saw a large oval-shaped portrait over a marble stone fireplace and felt nervous. *The picture — early Renaissance? Medieval? I'm supposed to be an art collector. What if I'm asked?*

"Jack!"

Roche rose from his seat and gestured to him. He was at a four-person circular table with two women who looked to be in their early twenties.

Roche beamed with pride as he introduced Jack to Suzette and Dominique, who both rose to shake his hand.

Both women were stunningly beautiful and spoke English with only a slight French accent. Suzette, who had red hair down to her shoulders, was wearing a green dress cut low enough to expose cleavage. An emerald on a gold chain hung around her neck.

Dominique had wavy black hair that hung half-way down her back and was wearing a high-necked white blouse composed of a sheer fabric that revealed she was not wearing a bra, although a frilled panel down the front added a touch of modesty. Her skirt was black and ankle-length, with a black sash wrapped around the waist and tied in front.

Jack took a seat. "So, how do you know Roche?" he asked, looking first at Suzette, seated on his left, then at Dominique, on his right.

The question seemed to catch both women off guard, but Roche chuckled and said, "In France we say that they are my nieces."

Jack nodded. *In Canada we say that they are prostitutes.*

Roche ordered for everyone, and under different circumstances, Jack would have enjoyed the meal. It consisted of eight courses, with different wine pairings with each course. In part, it included duck *foie gras,* fish, fillet of beef, roasted partridge, and chocolate mousse cake with bourbon-flavoured ice cream.

Following dessert, Suzette and Dominique went to the washroom, at which point Roche leaned across the table and said to Jack, "So?"

"The meal was fantastic," was his reply.

"No, the women," Roche said. "Which one do you want? For myself, I will be happy with either."

"They are both young enough to be my daughters," Jack said.

Roche smiled broadly and his chest puffed with pride as he glanced around the restaurant. "Yes, I'm sure every man in here is jealous."

Jack met his gaze. "Perhaps it is a cultural issue, but neither one appeals to me."

Roche's eyes widened and his mouth briefly dropped open in surprise. "You do not mean that! Don't you think they —"

"Yes, they are beautiful," Jack acknowledged. "Perhaps it is only me, but I find it embarrassing to be seen with such young women. It makes me feel like I am incapable of attracting someone worthy of my own maturity and sophistication. These girls make it look like I have to resort to buying a prostitute or taking advantage of some young girl who, were she not a prostitute or after me for my money, must have a serious daddy complex."

"You do not want either one of them?" Roche was talking more to himself than to Jack.

"I would prefer to leave before they return," said Jack, getting to his feet. "At least that would save me the embarrassment of walking out with them. Call me tomorrow."

"I ... I am sorry. I will call you and we will go for lunch." Roche had the grace to look faintly embarrassed.

"Tomorrow I want to discuss business," Jack said. "I did not come all this way to hang out with call girls."

"Yes ... I understand."

* * *

It was ten the next morning when the Ringmaster met with Roche and learned of Jack's response to last night's entertainment.

"So I take it that afterwards you ended up having a little *ménage à trois*," said the Ringmaster coldly.

"Well, they were already paid for," Roche explained.

"What were you hoping to find out about him? The size of his penis?"

"No, but I thought you wanted him to like us and to gain his trust."

"And do you trust *him*?" The Ringmaster looked deep into Roche's eyes.

Roche swallowed. Hard. "Yes, and I believe our organization could benefit from his expertise. He is intelligent. That being said, I don't know how long it will be before he takes the painting out of storage."

"Wolfgang also seems impressed with his ability," noted the Ringmaster.

Roche nodded.

"You were also impressed with Kerin Bastion, and he turned out to be a police officer."

"Yes, but with Jack Smith, he has done much more," Roche insisted. "Kerin only pretended to rob a jewellery store. Jack handled Klaus like he was no more than a pesky fly, beating him senseless on three occasions. He has disposed of bodies through a crematorium and turned a car into a paper weight. Feats which to him seem trivial."

"Perhaps you are right, but there is one thing about him that has not been assessed. He would have us believe that he is an art collector. Is he?"

"Well, he sounds like he is."

"*Sounds like* isn't good enough." The Ringmaster's tone was sharp. "I want to find out for certain. His alleged love for my Pierrot could be a ruse to get more money … or perhaps even a more devious motive."

"I know little about art," admitted Roche.

"I realize that. For Jack Smith, we need someone far more sophisticated than the ladies you procured for him last night."

"You have someone in mind?" asked Roche.

"Yes, a woman who is his age, fluent in six languages, and an art expert."

Chapter Forty-One

Shortly after his meeting with the Ringmaster, Roche phoned Jack to arrange to meet him at noon in a small café near the Renaissance. After hanging up, Jack hesitated, then called Otto at the Hôtel du Louvre to pass on the information. The rest of the cover team were already gathered in his room.

At noon Jack entered the café and saw that Roche had already arrived. He also saw the man and women that Yves had assigned to follow him yesterday sitting at a nearby table.

"About last night," said Roche as soon as Jack sat down, "I want to —"

"Forget about it," Jack replied quickly, unsure whether the surveillance team could overhear. "What's up for today?"

"I have some good news for you. Over the next week the Ringmaster wants you to check out potential villas that you may wish to purchase prior to doing any consulting. As agreed, we will pay for your hotel and travel expenses."

"That's nice, but wouldn't the Ringmaster feel better if I did some work for him first? At least meet each other and get some of the details ironed out?"

Roche gave a dismissive wave of his hand. "You have already helped us in Canada. Don't worry about that. We trust you."

Like hell you do.

"What I think you will find even more pleasing is ... well, first of all, do you speak other languages besides English?"

"A little Spanish, but that's about it," replied Jack. "Why?"

"We are going to arrange for an interpreter to go with you. She is fluent in at least six languages, and you will be able to incorporate some pleasure while searching for your villa."

"I told you, I'm not into —"

"No, no, she is not a prostitute," Roche assured him. "She is a businesswoman. Attractive, single, about your age, but more importantly, she shares your interests."

"What do you mean ... shares my interests?"

"Well, art in particular. She loves art."

"Oh?"

"She is an expert. Her business is art authentication and restoration. You will have the opportunity to visit various museums and art galleries as you go."

Oh, shit.

"I'm sure that pleases you." Roche smiled.

"You have no idea," Jack said, trying to sound enthusiastic. "It sounds like a fantastic opportunity. I'm sure it will be an experience I'll always remember."

"Great. I'll introduce you to each other tonight over dinner at your hotel. We will provide her with a prepaid credit card for ten thousand Euros for the week, which should cover flights, food, and accommodation, but if you need more, let me know."

"That is very generous."

"It's nothing, really."

"When do we leave?" asked Jack.

"You mentioned you were interested in Marseille, so tomorrow you will go there first. As I recall, you expressed an interest in the Musée des Beaux Arts there."

"Yes, the Museum of Fine Art. I wouldn't want to miss that."

"Good. You are both booked to fly out of Paris at eleven-twenty tomorrow morning and you will arrive in time for lunch. Once you are finished in Marseille, it is about an hour flight to Malaga, Spain, and then a one-hour drive to Costa del Sol, where you also expressed interest. After that you could fly to Malta, then up to Italy to check out those areas, or perhaps save them for your next visit. Whatever you decide will be fine."

"I won't really know until I see what's available," Jack said. "I'm looking for something modest. Say in the range of two to three million Euro, cap it off at, say, four million Canadian."

"That will narrow down the selection," noted Roche. "I don't know how many properties in that high of a price range are available."

Exactly. I'll pretend to find a place I'm interested in and force the Ringmaster to meet me — hopefully before they discover my taste in art refers to the taste of crayons.

* * *

Yves glared at Jack from the far side of Otto's room. "The plan was for you to meet the Ringmaster immediately. Now you would have us travelling all over Europe?"

"It isn't my choice, either," Jack told him, "but I could hardly refuse. If I am who I purport myself to be, there's no way I would turn down such an opportunity."

Laura glanced at Jack. He had called her on his way home from dinner last night to let her know he had turned down a prostitute. *Did that cause them to be suspicious? With all the other things he has done ...*

"Something on your mind, Laura?" Jack asked.

"After everything you've done, what's it going to take for them to trust you?"

"It's no coincidence that they're lining me up with an interpreter who's an art expert," replied Jack gravely. "They're checking to see if I really am a collector, which has me worried. The only thing I know about art is what I've gleaned off the Internet in the last month. If she's an expert, she'll see right through me. I could be finished as of tonight."

"We will make sure you are well protected tonight," said Yves.

"I'm not worried about my safety tonight," replied Jack in exasperation. "It's blowing the case that has me worried."

"Perhaps you shouldn't have pretended to be an art connoisseur."

You pompous asshole. "And what would you know about undercover?" snapped Jack. "You were filling your belly when Kerin was being murdered."

Mouths dropped open around the room, except Yves's, who clenched his fists as his ruddy face turned purple. He leapt to his feet and yelled, "Yes, I was having lunch! Maybe if I had been at the park or had detailed more people to provide fresh faces, Kerin would still be alive! You think I don't know that?" His chest heaved with emotion as he glared at everyone, then his voice lowered. "There, I said it. Is that what you all wanted to hear? That I fucked up?"

The anger Jack felt turned to remorse when he realized Yves felt guilty over Kerin's murder, too. He took a deep breath, then said, "Fucking up and working undercover go hand in hand. It's all about making choices and sometimes there are consequences to those choices you don't expect. It's like a lot of police work. The harder you work, the more chance you have of fucking up."

"That's the truth," added Otto, looking thoughtful.

Jack got to his feet and said, "I'm going back to my hotel to try to educate myself more about the art world." He looked at Yves. "Dinner will be at eight in the hotel. I would ask that you not have anyone inside the hotel. There is a time for a cover team to be close and a time for them to be far away. Tonight I believe I am safe and if I am wrong or get killed, I will not blame you." He turned toward the door.

"Wait," said Yves quietly. "How do you feel about Maurice being outside in a surveillance van?"

Jack knew he should compromise. "I'm okay with that. He would be close if something needed to be done."

Yves nodded.

"Are we good?" Jack extended his hand to Yves.

Yves stared momentarily at Jack, then shook his hand.

When Jack left the room, Laura stepped out in the hall with him. "I've never seen you blow up and slam-dunk someone like that," she said. "Especially a foreign policeman."

"Guess I was an ass," Jack admitted. "I can see the guilt he's carrying. You're thinking I should go back in and apologize?"

"No, I think offering to shake hands with him was enough. That's not why I'm here. I can tell you're worried about the art expert."

"Definitely. My brain is spinning with all the different types of art, let alone famous artists."

"Didn't Roche tell you the expert is a woman about your age and single?"

"Yes, so what?"

"You're not hearing me." Laura's tone was serious. "Forget art. Sidetrack her."

"Sidetrack her? How?"

"How?" Laura was clearly surprised. She eyed Jack as if he was trying to hide something from her. "Don't give me that guff. You charm all the women you meet." She shook her head in disbelief as she recalled something, then said, "You should hear what all the secretaries say about you behind your back."

"What do they say?"

"I'm not telling you," she replied, frowning as if he shouldn't have asked.

"Why not?"

"Because if I did, your ego would go through the roof and you'd be impossible to work with. For tonight, just be yourself … well, not entirely yourself."

"What do you mean?" asked Jack.

"Try not to kill anyone."

Chapter Forty-Two

At eight o'clock that night, Otto nudged Laura, who sat beside him in the surveillance van, along with Maurice. They were parked on a street near the front of Jack's hotel, and Otto gestured at two people walking down the sidewalk.

"Yes, that's Roche," confirmed Maurice, using a camera to take pictures. "The woman with him must be the art expert."

They watched as Roche and the woman entered the hotel lobby together.

"She's a Swede," said Otto matter-of-factly.

"What makes you say that?" asked Laura.

"Blonde hair, tall, slender, pale skin, straight nose, high cheekbones, and beautiful," replied Otto. "You can tell."

"It sounds like you think you know your women."

"I do," replied Otto. "It's my mesmerizing metallic-blue eyes. "They take it all in ... or hadn't you noticed?"

Laura's face reddened. "Jack told you I said that?"

Otto grinned in response.

"That jerk. I was joking. Did he tell you I was joking?"

"It's okay, Laura," said Otto in a soothing tone. "You're only human."

"Do you like my eyes, too?" asked Maurice, batting his eyelashes.

"This is going to be a long night," muttered Laura.

* * *

Jack tightened the knot on his tie as he entered Le Pinxo restaurant. He wore his same navy-blue suit with a white shirt and gold cufflinks, but tonight had opted for a blue tie. On entering, he saw Roche talking to the maître d'. A woman with short blonde hair wearing a black, long-sleeved dress, a pearl necklace, and high heels stood beside Roche. *Simple but elegant,* Jack thought as he tapped Roche on the shoulder.

Roche turned. "Jack! Good timing." They shook hands, then Roche nodded at the woman beside him. "I would like to introduce you to Carina Safstrom."

"You're Jack Smith?" she exclaimed. Her eyes opened wide and she took a step back.

"Yes." Jack extended his hand to her. "Who ... or what ... were you expecting?" He grinned.

Carina blushed and shook Jack's hand, quickly saying, "Uh, well ... nothing. I ... I didn't see you come up behind us."

Jack could see that she was flustered. *Good. She's attracted to me.* He held her gaze a moment longer, hoping to convey that he was also attracted to her, then gave her a bemused look to indicate he doubted her explanation. "Sorry if I startled you."

She responded with a coy smile, which made him realize he'd accomplished his goal. His confidence grew.

They were led to a small rectangular table. Carina sat across from Jack with Roche beside her. After a quick look at the menu, they each ordered appetizers. Oysters in a light mushroom jelly for Roche, a salad containing goat cheese, eggplant, and black olives for Carina, and a dish of mushrooms in warm pâté for Jack.

As the bottle of wine Roche had ordered was being poured, Carina looked at Jack and said, "So, I understand that you are an art collector."

Jack felt his stomach tighten. *Here it comes.*

"Who's your favourite artist?" she asked, "and what's your favourite style?"

Any hope Jack had of charming her and keeping the conversation away from art vanished. He knew by the tone of her voice that she would not be easily sidetracked. "I love many types of art, with the exception of abstract paintings," he said, pausing to take a sip of wine. "Although I do like some abstract sculptures." He gave a lame smile. "I find it embarrassing to admit, but deep down inside, I sense I'm not a real aficionado when it comes to art."

"You're not?" Carina said frostily, before glancing at Roche for his response, which was simply to raise an eyebrow.

"Not compared to many of the collectors I've met," Jack went on. "Sculptures that are missing their heads or limbs appear incomplete or damaged to me, yet the majority of people I meet find great beauty in them."

"Like Aphrodite?" questioned Carina, her eyes fixed on Jack.

"Yes, that's one example I had in mind." Jack looked at Roche and explained, "Aphrodite may be better known to you as the Venus de Milo."

"Oh, of course. Yes," Roche muttered.

Jack turned his attention back to Carina. "Everyone seems overwhelmed with its beauty, but I must confess, it doesn't do much for me."

"What about the Winged Victory of Samothrace?" asked Carina.

Good, at least so far you're sticking to the basic Art 101 questions. Will it be the Mona Lisa next? Jack glanced at Roche again. "It's also called the Nike of Samothrace, named after the Greek goddess Nike."

Roche nodded, but it was apparent that the subject of art did not interest him as much as Carina's reactions to what Jack said.

"Beautiful to many," continued Jack, "but it is both headless and winged. I like art that seems ... well, like it speaks out to me."

"Speaks out to you? Like Edvard Munch's famous painting?"

You won't quit, will you? Edvard Munch? Oh, right. The guy who painted a picture of a person screaming on a bridge. "Yes, *The Scream.*" Jack paused, then said, "When I said 'speaks out to me,' I didn't mean scream at me, although I must admit that one does appeal to me in a rather dark way."

To Jack's relief, the appetizers arrived and everyone started to eat. The conversation about art was put on hold. For now.

* * *

Maurice grabbed the binoculars from the floor of the van and focused on two men who were strolling down the sidewalk. He cursed softly in French, then said, "One of those men works for Roche. I'm sure the man with him works for Roche, too."

Laura watched the two men as they continued down the sidewalk, occasionally pausing to peer into a parked car. Eventually they reached the van they were in, and Maurice shut off his police radio and everyone sat in silence. Laura heard them check the door handles and was glad they were locked. Equally glad for the dark-tinted windows. Moments later the two men walked away.

Maurice slowly blew out a breath. "I understand Jack's concern about our surveillance being —"

Otto interrupted him. "We have a problem," he said. "They're standing in front of the doors to the lobby and one gestured at our van ... the other is taking out his phone."

Chapter Forty-Three

Jack had barely started his appetizer when Roche received a phone call. He glanced at Jack, then said, "Excuse me. I need to take this but will go to the lobby so as not to disturb you."

Something about his glance made Jack feel uneasy, but he knew he had a more pressing problem in front of him. A problem named Carina.

"So ... we were discussing art," Carina said.

"Yes. How about you? What kind of art do you like?" he asked, hoping to get her talking about herself.

Carina smiled. "With the kind of work I do, I would have to say I like it all. To admit otherwise would not be good for business."

"Ah, yes. Roche mentioned you were into restoration."

"And authentication and appraisals," she added.

"So how do you go about doing authentication? Is it the style you look at, combined with the paint itself, along with the subject matter?"

"Yes, and technique. So tell me, what is your favourite painting?"

Good. Maybe now I'll be able to shut you up. Jack pretended to look shocked that she would ask, then shook his head in disgust. "You say you are an art expert, but by your questions I have the feeling that you are more into history."

"History? Well, of course, art is —"

"I mean, I bet you are a big fan of the Spanish Inquisition." Jack's tone was harsh.

"I don't understand," said Carina. "Why are you —"

"Never mind." Jack shook his head. "I'll tell you what my favourite painting is. It's one I obtained recently," he said emphatically. He then softened his voice and said, "It speaks to my heart." He looked intensely at Carina and added, "Actually, it does more than that. It's part of my heart."

Carina sat back in her chair, looking confused. "It sounds powerful."

"It's beyond powerful," Jack stated coldly.

"I don't understand." Carina still looked confused. "What did I say to upset you? You sound angry."

"Of course I'm angry." Jack gave her another hard look. "I don't appreciate Roche lining me up with prostitutes or —"

"Prostitutes!" Carina gaped at him. "Is that what you think I am?" She rose to her feet.

"I didn't mean you," Jack said. People at nearby tables had stopped talking and were staring at them.

Carina glowered down at Jack. "Well, for your information, when Roche hired me, sleeping with you was not part of the deal." She practically spat out the words. Then she muttered, "God, I've never felt so humiliated." She glanced around and snatched up her purse.

"I was referring to the woman Roche tried to line me up with last night," Jack explained. "Not you."

Carina looked at Jack sharply. "He tried to line you up with a prostitute last night?"

"Yes. I met him for dinner and he had two prostitutes with him. The girls were young enough to be my daughters. I was both disgusted and embarrassed."

"So you thought ... do I look like a prostitute to you?" Her expression was horrified.

"No, of course not. But when you asked me what my favourite painting is ... well, it was like sticking a knife in my heart. Coupled with last night's experience, it left me with a bad taste about the whole situation."

"What does asking you about your favourite painting have to do with anything?" she said angrily. "It seems like a normal question to me."

"Obviously, you don't know the significance the portrait has for me. I thought Roche would have told you."

"When he hired me this afternoon to be your guide and interpreter, he said —"

"This afternoon?"

"Yes, and he said you were an art collector, so naturally, I presumed you would like to talk about it."

Jack groaned. "I am truly sorry for my outburst. Your question caught me by surprise and I reacted badly. Please ... I apologize. Will you take your seat?"

Carina grimaced and fidgeted with her purse strap.

"Please," Jack repeated, gesturing to her chair. "I feel awful about how I reacted."

Carina again glanced around the restaurant, then sat down and speared a piece of eggplant with her fork.

"Do you know what Roche does?" asked Jack, hoping to smooth things over.

"All I know is he has something to do with trading precious metals on the stock market," she said, sounding annoyed. "I understand that he deals with the elite of society." She paused. "Roche indicated you may be hired as a consultant."

Jack nodded.

"What would that entail?" asked Carina in a tone that indicated she was being polite, but not particularly interested.

"My work would focus on making a company run efficiently, protect against corporate takeovers, and ensure company secrets remain secret."

Carina raised one eyebrow. "That does sound interesting. What was your formal education in?"

"I lack formal education … but make up for it with hands-on experience. Let's just say I have the ability to think outside the box." *If I don't, I end up inside a box.*

"Maybe we should get something straight between the two of us," said Carina firmly. "Roche told me that you presented yourself as an art collector, but wasn't sure if you were simply trying to impress him. He said that if you weren't genuine, his clients would easily spot you as a phony, and his company would be cast in a bad light." She paused, then added, "I wanted to find out if you were being pretentious. If you were, I couldn't see why Roche should waste money paying for us to travel around Europe."

"At least I understand your reason for all the questions," said Jack.

"I have to admit, some of my interest in you was personal."

"Oh?"

"Roche mentioned you had obtained a painting recently purported to be an undiscovered Pierrot by Jean-Antoine Watteau."

"I did," Jack said. "I believe it is authentic, but am not in any particular hurry to find out, as I do not plan to part with it either way."

"Such a painting would be a remarkable discovery, if it were truly authentic. Roche said if you ever invited me to authenticate it, he would like to know."

I bet he would.

"He doesn't have any interest in art himself," continued Carina, "so I presume he looks at it as a way to judge your credibility. The thing is, as I told him, many experienced art collectors have been fooled. There are some extremely good forgeries on the market, and that alone should not be a basis to judge your credibility, regardless of whether it is real."

Jack remained silent.

"I would love to see it sometime. If it is real … well, it would be like finding a Spanish galleon filled with treasure. Worth as much, too."

"The value of it doesn't concern me," Jack said. "It does concern me that Roche told you about it. I would prefer nobody know I have it."

"My discretion in such matters is absolute. I deal with many collectors who have rare and priceless paintings. I fully appreciate the need to keep secret."

"Hopefully Roche is of the same mind."

"I believe he is. When he told me, he cautioned me not to tell anyone."

"Good."

Carina took a sip of wine, then placed her glass down. She eyed Jack curiously. "Besides prostitutes, what else were you going to say a moment ago? You said you didn't appreciate Roche lining you up with prostitutes or … Or what?"

"Or people hired to spy on me," replied Jack.

"Spy on you!" exclaimed Carina.

"You deny it?"

"I guess you could call it spying, but I viewed it more like I was giving an overall character reference. It's not like I planned to sneak into your briefcase or read your emails or anything. He simply wants to know what sort of person you are and your degree of sophistication. I'm to give him a full evaluation in a week."

"A week?"

"Yes, but I wasn't supposed to let you know I had been asked to do that."

"It can be our secret. I don't mind that you will be reporting to him."

"You don't?" She sounded surprised.

"I would want to check out anyone *I* was going to hire."

Carina nodded. "Guess I wouldn't make a very good spy, would I."

"You did come on pretty strong, but that's okay." Jack twirled a mushroom with his fork in the pâté, then met Carina's gaze once more. "How did you meet Roche?"

"I had brunch today with a client I did some restoration work for. He introduced me to Roche."

"If your client is a collector, too bad he didn't join us."

"He had to catch a flight back to Russia this evening."

"He's Russian?"

Carina nodded.

Jack smiled, as if he knew something amusing. *Come on, Carina, take the bait.*

"What's so funny?" she asked.

"I've met a few Russians who purported to be … shall we say, cultured. Let me picture your client and you tell me if I'm right."

Now Carina looked amused. "Go for it."

"He has a large belly and a grey, walrus-type moustache. I picture him standing on a bearskin rug in front of a stone fireplace with the heads of dead animals mounted on the wall. His first name is either Boris or Ivan." Jack smiled, then asked, "How have I done so far?"

Carina grinned and shook her head. "Not well."

"Then let me add that if you were ever to see him on the beach, he would be wearing black, knee-high socks, sandals, and a Speedo."

"Oh, my God." Carina laughed. "Not even close. The man is highly sophisticated and a philanthropist of the best kind."

"Of the best kind?"

"Anonymous and not for recognition. I only know because a painting of his that I did some restoration work on was later donated anonymously to the Tretyakov State Gallery in Moscow. It happened about six years ago, soon after his wife died."

"That's too bad he lost his wife. What did she die of?"

"Cancer," replied Carina sadly. "She was a big patron of the arts and at the same time the painting was donated, a large donation was made to the Moscow Art Theatre. I know it was him."

Jack curbed any outward appearance of the excitement he felt and kept his reply nonchalant. "Okay, so I was wrong about his sophistication. How about the rest?"

"Definitely no walrus moustache or big belly. He has black hair and is physically fit."

Bingo.

"Complete opposite of what you imagined," she continued. "He's actually quite an adventurer. Scuba diving, hang-gliding … a real zest for life."

"Sounds like a bit of a risk taker."

"Perhaps," said Carina. "I admire people who have a real zest for life."

"His name isn't Boris or Ivan?"

"No. But I can't tell you his name because I have to keep that secret."

"Oh?"

"I would not divulge your name to anyone, either. At least not in regard to having a valuable painting."

"Damn, so much for trying to impress you with my psychic abilities."

Carina smiled. "You're not entirely wrong. He likes to hunt and does have a couple of stone fireplaces, but I have never seen any heads mounted on the walls."

"Aha!" Jack exclaimed. "And have you ever seen him in a bathing suit?"

"That I haven't," Carina said. "If I ever do, I'll report back to you."

Jack exchanged a smile with her in response.

* * *

Laura looked at the two thugs standing in front of the hotel, then turned to Maurice. "Do you have anyone working who's close by and on foot?"

"I have two men on standby waiting in the Tuileries Garden."

"Even better. Get them to walk over and drive this van away. Tell them to come down the street holding hands."

"Holding hands?"

"If you saw that, would you think they were police officers?" asked Laura.

"No." Maurice realized what Laura was getting at. "Still, if they drive the van away … what if Jack needs help? Where will —"

"If he needs help, he'll throw someone out a window," said Laura seriously. "You can hear the sound of breaking glass a long way away."

Maurice's mouth fell open in disbelief.

"Damn it, call them!" said Otto.

Maurice grabbed his portable radio and rapidly spoke in French.

A moment later Otto gestured toward the two thugs. "They've got company."

Maurice picked up the binoculars that hung from his neck. "It's Roche. They're all looking our way." He glanced at Laura. "There is nothing on the van to identify it. No reason for them to be doing this."

"How many vans do you see with dark windows and a curtain separating the front from the back?" asked Otto.

"Please tell me that you don't have anyone sitting in cars around the block," added Laura.

"No," replied Maurice. "After Jack's conversation with Yves, he agreed to back off as long as I watched the front of the hotel and had two officers close by on foot." He pointed out the window. "There they are. I better crawl to the front and unlock the door."

Laura saw two men walking hand in hand down the street, then pretend to unlock the van and get in.

Roche watched, also, then disappeared into the hotel lobby. The two thugs left.

* * *

Jack looked up from his appetizer as Carina leaned forward and spoke in a low voice. "I'm sorry if I was prying too much into what you like or don't like about art," she said. "For some, it's a personal issue. I obviously touched a nerve when I asked you what your favourite painting was. It is none of my business and I am sorry."

"It's okay," replied Jack. "I —"

Carina glanced past Jack, then said, "Roche is returning. Quick, before he arrives, do you still want me to be your guide? I could easily bow out. I would understand if you don't want me after the scene I made."

And have them pick someone else? "No, please, I would like to have you show me around."

Carina looked relieved. "Okay, good. But you should also know that they are paying me to evaluate your level of sophistication. I have a reputation for being ethical, so be forewarned that I will give them my honest opinion."

"I wouldn't respect you if you didn't."

"Which — because I sense you're honest — will be fun in that we can visit museums at their expense."

Shit. "Yes, that will be great." He paused. "I promise I will tell you why the Pierrot painting means so much to me."

"Only if you want to," Carina said.

"I do, but I don't want to spoil the evening by becoming emotional. If people knew, even people like Roche, it would help them understand why I am so deeply in love with it. I'll tell you tomorrow when we are in Marseille."

Carina nodded. "So everything is okay between us?"

"Yes. Let's not mention our conversation to Roche and start fresh, shall we?"

Carina smiled, then held out her hand. "Hello, my name is Carina."

"Pleased to meet you." Jack shook her hand.

"And I'm not a prostitute," she whispered, then gave a saucy grin as Roche pulled out his chair to sit down.

Jack smiled back at her. *You are my ticket to the Ringmaster.* Then another thought entered his head. *Would they extract revenge on you later?* His mind juggled that possibility. *They were the ones who hired you ... so they'd have to realize you were duped and so there'd be no reason to kill you....* He stabbed at a mushroom with his fork and put it in his mouth. He should have enjoyed the savoury flavour, but he didn't and knew why. *I'm lying to myself. They killed Kerin for no reason.*

"Everything okay?" Carina asked.

"Everything's fine," replied Roche. "It was nothing. I shouldn't have been called."

"I meant Jack," said Carina. "You were frowning," she said by way of explanation.

Jack smiled again. "I was thinking that I've never had this good of an appetizer in Canada, and was wondering why."

"Ah, the French can cook, let me tell you that," said Roche, hoisting his glass of wine in a toast.

Jack looked at Carina's face as he toasted. *I'll need to deceive you, but only for a week. You'll be long out of the picture by the time the Ringmaster is caught.*

Her eyes sparkled and she gave him a warm smile. Jack smiled back, but the unsavoury taste remained.

Chapter Forty-Four

It was midnight when Jack bade Carina and Roche good night, and an hour later when he met the team in Otto's room. He was surprised to see Yves there, as well.

"Working late tonight for a boss," Jack teased him. "Perhaps you could give my bosses back in Canada some guidance on doing real police work."

"I won't sleep until the Ringmaster is in jail," Yves explained. "Maurice called me to say that while you were having dinner, two men were checking for surveillance around the hotel and that they called Roche out to look at our van."

"So that's what that was about," Jack said. "He gave me a bit of a hairy eyeball when he left the table, but seemed relaxed when he returned."

"We had the van leave when they were watching," Laura said.

"In the future, let's get one extra room in whatever hotel I'm staying in," Jack suggested. "Preferably one that overlooks the main entrance so you'll be able to see who comes and goes. The room could be used as a field office as long as everyone takes care not to be seen. It would also make it easier for me to debrief everyone."

"I would agree with that." Yves nodded. "So how did it go tonight? Are you still scheduled to fly to Marseille tomorrow morning?"

"Yes. We're booked for two nights at the Sofitel Marseille Vieux Port Hotel. After that, it will be up to me whether I stay or continue my search for a retirement villa elsewhere. As far as tomorrow goes, they've lined up a real estate agent to take us around after we check into our hotel."

"I'll try to get us a room," said Yves. "Although I am not sure how to get one that overlooks the entrance without drawing suspicion."

"Tell them you stayed in the front of the hotel years earlier on your honeymoon and that it has sentimental value for you," Laura suggested.

Yves smiled. "That might work."

Jack nodded. "The name of the art expert who'll be accompanying me is Carina Saftstrom. She gave —"

"Ha, a Swedish name," said Otto, grinning at Laura.

"Yes, she's Swedish," said Jack, giving Otto and Laura a quizzical look.

Laura nodded begrudgingly at Otto. "Okay, so you do know women."

Otto opened his eyes wide and pointed to them, still grinning.

"As I was saying," Jack continued, "she gave me her business card. I want someone to put a trace on her phone and get a list of all her calls. She may have had brunch with the Ringmaster today ... or I guess, technically, yesterday."

"She told you that?" Laura looked astonished.

"Not in those exact words. Let me start from the beginning."

When Jack was finished, Otto said, "The swarthy-looking man I saw with Roche in Frankfurt looked more like a Spaniard or an Italian, not Russian."

Maurice said, "Perhaps you saw someone else. The Russian has to be him — but who is he?"

"He's definitely a good possibility," replied Jack, "and for now I will go under that assumption. Her call history may give us a name."

Maurice nodded, then wrote down the phone numbers from Carina's business card.

"Tonight she's staying in a hotel that sounds like the Hotel of the Little Louvre," said Jack.

"The Hotel de Lille Louvre," said Maurice. "It's about a kilometre away. A modest place, perhaps fifty Euros a night, but reportedly clean."

"Guess the money associated with valuable paintings is for the owner and not those who evaluate or work on them," said Jack. "Her home base is in Zurich, but she also uses answering services, which are the other numbers on her card."

"Paris, Rome, Stockholm, London, and Zurich," Maurice noted from the business card. He handed it back to Jack.

"Which means our man from Moscow likely used her answering service in Paris to contact her," Jack said. "Either that, or through her email address. Still, it would be nice to find out who she's phoning."

"A list of who she calls won't be a problem," Yves said.

"Who calls her through the answering services *is* a problem. If we check those, word may get back to her."

"She told me he had to catch a flight back to Russia this evening," Jack told him.

"We could check the manifests and come up with a list to run past the Russian police."

"I would be a little worried about checking with the police in Russia," Jack said. "There's a lot of corruption there, and if this guy is as rich as I imagine, he'll have connections. I don't want to risk it, especially if I can draw him out in another week on my own."

Yves breathed out audibly. "I understand, but speaking of risk, what about Carina? What if she puts in a bad report on you?"

"We cross that bridge when we come to it." Jack glanced at Laura. "I think I can befriend her enough that she won't say anything too detrimental."

Laura nodded knowingly.

"Maybe she'd help us if she knew the truth," suggested Maurice.

Jack shook his head. "I prefer she not know. It could change her demeanour around Roche and I doubt she'd stand up to questioning. These people are violent. The less she knows about me, the better. I don't want her ever seen as having intentionally helped me."

"Even if she wanted to co-operate, I doubt she'd want to give up her profession and spend the rest of her life living under a false identity," Yves added.

"I wouldn't mind if inquiries were made about her with the Swiss police," said Jack, "providing it could be done without her knowledge. I'd like to know more about her.

Anything I can use to distract her while getting her to like me might help."

"Pretend to share common interests to gain her trust," Otto put in.

"Something you do to attract women?" Laura asked him, pretending annoyance.

"With these eyes?" Otto pointed to them again. "Not necessary."

"Yeah, yeah." Laura snorted. "How could I forget?"

"Are you sure you don't want inquiries made in Russia?" asked Yves.

"No," Jack said. "His prominence in Russian society may result in word getting back to him. Besides, I already know a lot about him. He's a philanthropist, an art collector, his wife died of cancer, he's a bit of a risk taker, and he's a sportsman who likes to hunt."

"There was nothing sporting about how Kerin was murdered," said Maurice bitterly.

Everyone nodded silently. Jack continued, "The point is, I've got plenty to work with to help me befriend him."

"You shouldn't have any trouble portraying a risk taker." Laura's tone was dry. Then she turned to Yves. "How about I make the inquiries regarding Carina? I've worked undercover with Jack for years, and a woman's point of view about her background may prove useful."

"Why not?" Yves said. "You'll likely have as much influence with Interpol and the Swiss as I do."

"She was born in Sweden," Jack said, "but her parents moved to Zurich when she was a child. Her father and mother both worked in the chocolate industry. She mentioned she went back to Stockholm and lived with her aunt and uncle for five years while she went to university. Then she moved back to Zurich, but often returns to Stockholm. Besides English, she's fluent in German, French, Italian —"

"All three of those are official languages in Switzerland," Yves said, "although English is common there, too."

Jack nodded. "On top of that, she also speaks Russian and Spanish."

"I'll contact Interpol tonight," Laura said. "Have them check with Sweden and Switzerland."

"She's a smart woman," noted Otto, "as well as beautiful. You should enjoy the coming week."

Jack nodded agreement, but his eyes said otherwise.

Laura knew what he was thinking. *Don't worry about it, Jack. She's a big girl and it won't be the first time some guy has lied to her. Besides, it's only for a week, then you can send her on her way.*

Chapter Forty-Five

The following morning Carina arrived at Jack's hotel in a taxi, and then the two of them headed for the airport. The eleven-twenty flight from Paris to Marseille was on time.

Their conversation was mostly small talk until they were airborne, and then Carina said, "Roche gave me a rough figure of what you are willing to spend on a villa. There aren't a lot of places in the high-end price range you gave, but the agent said she had two places to show us this afternoon and four tomorrow."

"Sounds good," replied Jack. "I'm still suffering jet lag and that's plenty to see for now."

He sensed that Carina was studying him. *What now?*

"Roche never gave me any idea of what, uh, special features you're looking for," she said, "or any concerns you may have."

Concerns? Right. It's hard for homes to have the perfect conditions for paintings that museums can have, but what are the basics? He stifled a yawn, then said, "Well, as far as concerns go, I would want a high-tech security system, along with the proper controls in place to ensure there are no excessive levels of cold, heat, dryness, or moisture."

"Spending that much money, you would expect to be comfortable," said Carina. "That goes without saying."

"Of course, but it's also for my personal property."

"Ah, yes, of course. Your art collection." She sounded as if she hadn't thought of it.

"Yes, that," Jack said. "I realize a home can't duplicate a museum. What is it they strive for? Twenty-one degrees Celsius and forty-five percent humidity?"

"Yes, exactly."

"Naturally, I would also be wary if there were signs of insects. I would expect the structure to be sound in that regard. I would hate to awaken in the night to the sound of lice or moths eating away at the frames and canvases of my collection."

"You wouldn't believe how often that happens," said Carina. "Even if the insects don't attack the paintings, their droppings contain acid that can damage the paint."

"Which, I suppose helps keep you employed," Jack suggested. "Hope you don't carry a jar of bugs around with you."

Carina laughed lightly. "No, but I can see your profession as a consultant causes you to think of innovative ideas to improve one's profit margin."

Okay, Carina, time to put you in your place. Jack's voice hardened as he asked, "Is that enough testing in that area, or do you have more questions?"

Carina's face reddened. "I'm sorry. Was I that obvious?"

"Yes. I wish you would tell me when you feel the need to do that. It would make having a conversation with you more pleasant if I knew you were being honest."

Carina hung her head in shame. "I know. I'm sorry. I told you I would make a lousy spy. I hate this. I want it over and done with."

"Really? It's like an all-expenses-paid holiday."

Carina twisted her body to face Jack. "It's not that," she said.

"Then what?"

"It's ... it's that I like you, and it bothers me a lot that I am supposed to report on you. You're right. This should be a fun trip, but how can we relax? You'll never trust me enough to —"

"It's okay," said Jack. "I told you before, I expect it. It won't change who I am. I don't need to work for Roche. Their offer is a matter of convenience, because I would still like a little something to do when I retire. More for its entertainment value than anything. Also, if I'm not suited for Roche's organization, it would be better to find out sooner rather than later. You'd be doing me a favour. In a way, it's like you're working for me."

"Working for you?" Carina smiled.

Jack forced a smile in return. *You have no idea.*

"I hadn't thought of it that way," she said. "So you really don't mind?"

"Not as long as you're honest. It's people who intentionally deceive that get under my skin." *That was hard to say with a straight face.* "I like you, too. I sincerely hope that when your report goes in, no matter what you say, we can still be friends."

Carina squeezed his hand. "Thank you for understanding. It makes me feel less guilty." She added, "Guess I can report that you are honest and exceptionally understanding."

It's nice you feel less guilty, he thought.

* * *

Jack and Carina arrived at the Sofitel Marseille Vieux Port Hotel at one-thirty in the afternoon and checked in.

Their rooms were side by side and Jack had barely entered his when Carina knocked on his door.

"Have you seen it?" she asked excitedly.

"Seen what?" Jack ignored an incoming text message on his phone.

"The view! We are overlooking the harbour! It's beautiful."

"I thought you'd been to Marseille on several occasions."

"Yes, but not in places like this." She giggled. "I feel stupid. You are used to this lifestyle, and here I am, checking out your character. It's me who needs lessons in culture. Anyway, I better unpack and call the real estate agent, then we can go eat."

As soon as Carina went back to her room, Jack checked his message and learned that the temporary field office was in Otto's name three floors below him. Laura had a room in the New Hotel of Marseille, which was one block away, as did Yves and Maurice, who were sharing a room.

Jack texted back that they would be going out with the agent this afternoon, that he felt safe, and that he didn't think it was necessary to have a cover team tag along. Moments later Laura sent him a text saying that

Yves would check with his contact at the local police station and would consent to Jack going on his own if the
real estate agent was legitimate.

* * *

The agent apparently was who she purported to be,
and that afternoon she took Jack and Carina to two different villas. Both were beautiful, complete with swimming
pools, spas, and fabulous views. Jack took his time exam-
ining each place so that it was too late to go to any art
museums once they returned to their hotel.

At eight that evening, Jack went with Carina to the hotel
dining room, which overlooked the harbour. He ordered a
bottle of wine to enjoy as they waited for their entrées.

"So, we have four places to look at tomorrow," Carina
said as she reached for her wineglass and took a sip. "It
shouldn't take long and … this isn't a test," she said, looking
seriously at Jack, "but if we are done in time, do you want
to visit the Museum of Fine Arts here? It's quite renowned."

"That reminds me," said Jack, intentionally bypassing
her question. "I've been meaning to explain to you why
the painting I obtained recently means so much to me.
I'm still embarrassed by how I reacted last night."

"Don't be. As I said, sometimes art is personal and
there is no need to explain what you feel to others. It is
what it means to you that matters."

"Thank you, but I want you to know. Perhaps it would
be best if Roche knew, as well."

"Don't worry about him. Art doesn't interest him."

"No, but he told me he has a friend who expressed an interest in purchasing it."

"A friend?" Carina stared at Jack for a moment, then said, "I wonder if it is my Russian client? Roche never said anything to me about it."

Jack shrugged. "I don't know, could be. Roche never mentioned his name. The thing is, it would be better if they understood why I am so passionate about it. It would also make me feel better if you understood why I became so emotional last night and acted rudely."

Carina nodded. "Okay, if you wish."

Jack briefly thought about the points he wanted to make. *The Russian loves art, he lost his wife, and the painting means something special to him.* He cleared his throat. "You know Pierrot was always portrayed as a hapless clown who was too trusting."

"Yes, often seen as a naive."

"My wife was like that," Jack said forlornly.

"You were married? Children?"

"Twelve years," replied Jack. "We wanted children but weren't able to conceive."

"You're divorced?"

Jack glanced down to display the grief he pretended to feel. "My wife drowned two years ago last month," he said.

"Oh, my God. I'm sorry."

"The thing is, her personality was so much like Pierrot," said Jack. "I even teased her about it. She was too trusting. The type who wanted to bring home a homeless person for Christmas dinner. She'd give money to beggars, even though I told her it would only go to buying drugs. She would tell me I didn't know that for sure."

"I am so sorry," Carina repeated.

"It was her gullibility that got her killed." Jack spoke quietly. "We were staying at a resort in Mexico. She was out for an early-morning walk along the beach with a woman she'd met the day before. Normally, I would have gone with her, but I had a touch of food poisoning and was staying close to our room." Jack swallowed, then continued. "The waves were really big — she wasn't much of a swimmer and the woman she was with didn't swim at all. There was a young man out in the water not far from shore. He was flailing his arms and screaming to his girlfriend that he needed help. The girlfriend was lying on a lounge chair and there was nobody else around. Turns out she was passed out drunk and didn't even hear him. My wife jumped in and tried to swim to him."

"Oh, no." Carina put her hand up to her mouth.

"The undertow was too strong." Jack fell silent for a moment, then went on, "The thing is, the young man didn't know she was trying to rescue him. He swam back to shore himself. He was also drunk and was trying to tease his girlfriend because she was ignoring him. They took off when they realized what happened. I never even found out their names."

Carina stared opened-mouthed at Jack.

"Yes, she was a fool," said Jack, "but she was *my* fool and I loved her very much."

Carina's eyes filled with tears. She reached for her purse and pulled out a tissue.

"It was on the anniversary of her death that I discovered the painting." Jack sounded more matter-of-fact. "It was like she'd given me a sign that she was still with me." He paused. "That sounds stupid, I guess. I'm an atheist, after all. I know it's only my emotions that make me feel that way."

Carina dabbed at her eyes. "Six years ago my husband, Denzler, died in a car accident." Her voice was shaky. "I know exactly what you're going through." Abruptly, she uttered an apology and rushed to the ladies room.

Jack stared blankly after her. *I can be a real asshole sometimes.*

Chapter Forty-Six

An hour after dinner Jack bade Carina good night and went to his room. He texted Laura, who was waiting with everyone else in Otto's room below.

> *Back in room. Nothing new to report. Expect tomorrow to be same. Will tell C we'll go to Spain. I'll book hotel. Check with Spaniards to see what hotel they recommend.*

Laura replied back immediately with:

> *OK Everyone exhausted. Going back to my room. TTYL*

Jack turned on the television and lay on the bed for half an hour, then cursed to himself and quietly slipped out of his room.

Laura answered her phone and realized Jack was calling her from the lobby.

"Can I see you?" he asked.

"Now? I'm in my pajamas."

"You wear pajamas?" Jack was surprised.

"I do when I'm not home," replied Laura, sounding defensive.

"Well don't take them off on my account," he said.

His humour was forced, and he knew she knew it and a moment later she let him into her room. He took a seat on the only chair while she sat on the bed and listened as he told her the lies he'd fed to Carina over dinner.

"What happened after she went to the ladies room?"

"She was in there quite a while. When she came back, I could see she'd tried to fix her makeup, but her eyes were still all red and puffy. Then she apologized for running off." Jack took a deep breath and released it. "I feel like shit. When I told her that story it was to ingratiate myself with her, and by extension, the guy in Moscow. I didn't know she'd lost someone."

"It's not like you were trying to upset her. Things happen."

"Wish the Swiss or the Swedes had gotten back to us," Jack said. "Those are the sort of details I'd like to have known about."

"It's only been twenty-four hours. I'll check with them again tomorrow."

Jack nodded.

"Did you talk about her husband later?"

"A little. Seems he ran a company that made orthopaedic appliances and parts for the body."

"How long was she married?"

"Nine years. No kids."

"Well, you did what you had to do."

"Know what makes me feel worse?" Jack asked.

Laura shook her head.

"For a moment, when she told me that she'd lost her husband, I thought okay, good, you're probably vulnerable. I'll be able to romance you and you'll completely forget about going to any museums. Yup, wrap you around my little finger and keep you there until I get to the Ringmaster. It's like nothing else matters."

Laura gazed at Jack without any expression.

"What kind of a person thinks like that?" he demanded. "I even slipped it in that since obtaining her portrait —" Jack paused. "Yes, I referred to it as *her* portrait, as if I was talking about my dead wife. I told Carina that it's the only portrait I can think about and questioned whether any other art would ever hold any significance to me now." He shook his head in disgust. "She swallowed it all, hook, line, and sinker."

"You weren't thinking of her. You were thinking of catching a cold-blooded murderer."

"I was thinking like an asshole is what I was doing." Jack pushed himself to his feet. "Sorry to have unloaded on you. I needed to get a woman's perspective. I was wondering if you'd be upset with me."

"For what? Lying to a woman? Guys do that all the time for a lot less of a reason."

"Yeah, I know."

"You only need to be with her for a few more days. The week will be over before you know it."

Jack nodded. "Thanks for listening. I'll let you get to sleep now."

Laura got up and said, "Let me say something before

you go. You're worried about her vulnerability. That isn't how assholes think."

"Yeah, thanks." Jack knew he sounded cynical and dismissive.

"Don't dismiss my words like I'm some airhead," said Laura hotly. "Sometimes, like now, you *are* an asshole, but with Carina you were only doing your job."

Jack sighed. "Sorry. I didn't mean to … your opinion means a lot to me. It's why I came to talk to you." He paused, then added, "Sometimes the job sucks."

"No doubt about that, but there's one more thing to consider. Carina's husband died six years ago in a car accident. That's too bad, but she can get on with her life. She already has. Think how Gabrielle feels and the pain she must be in. She's pregnant and her husband was murdered only last month. Focus on that. Catch the Ringmaster and you can always apologize to Carina later. If you don't catch him … well, think of the pain Gabrielle will be in forever. What you are doing needs to be done. I'm glad it's you and not some other guy who probably would take full advantage of her."

Jack nodded again. "Thanks. I mean that. What you said is something I thought, too, but somehow I feel better hearing it from you and not my own brain trying to placate my conscience. I'll catch you later." He turned to leave.

"Let me give you a hug before you go," said Laura. "I think you could use one."

"No way." Jack glanced at her over his shoulder.

"How come?"

"Because you look too sexy with those little bunnies all over your pajamas. They put horny thoughts into my brain."

Jack ignored the pillow that bounced off the back of his head as he left.

Chapter Forty-Seven

The following morning Jack entered the hotel restaurant and joined Carina at her table for breakfast. When he sat down, she said, "I received a call from Roche an hour ago, asking how everything was going."

"And how *is* it going?" Jack gave her a friendly smile.

"I told him that I don't think you're a phony. He seemed happy to hear that."

"That's nice. Glad you feel that way about me. Did you talk about anything else?"

Carina nodded reluctantly. "He asked me if I had brought up the subject of your Pierrot. When I said we'd talked about it, he wanted to know if I had offered to authenticate it for you. I told him that you weren't concerned with having that done and explained to him why the painting means so much to you."

"That's fine," said Jack. "You seem concerned. Is there something else?"

"I hope that you are not angry with me for telling him what happened to your wife."

"I told you I wanted him to know."

"You said you did, but at the same time … well, it seems so personal. I don't want you to think that you can't trust me."

"I have to admit, I'm not trusting by nature, but I sense I can trust you."

Carina smiled. "Thank you."

* * *

The real estate agent arrived at nine o'clock and by mid-afternoon Jack had seen all the properties that were available. He and Carina were dropped back off at their hotel.

"Still early," said Carina when they entered the lobby. "Anything you would like to do? There are a few good museums in the area."

Jack grimaced. "I'm sorry, but I found last night's conversation regarding my wife and the Pierrot stressful. I would prefer we skip any museums for the time being."

Carina nodded sympathetically. "I understand."

"Instead, let's go for a walk so I can get a feeling for what the place is like."

"It's only ten degrees," said Carina. "Not too cold for you?"

"The weather here in February is about what it's like in Vancouver in February," replied Jack. "I'm used to it, but if you think it's too cold, I could go on my own."

"No, I'd like to go for a walk with you."

"Good. When we come back, after we clean up, we could go for a drink. Then I would like to see if the two of us can actually have dinner together without any heavy conversation."

Carina nodded. "Sounds like a good idea to me. Any thoughts for tomorrow?"

"I've seen enough here. Let's head for Spain. Maybe catch a late-morning flight to Malaga, and from there, it's only an hour's drive to Costa del Sol. Before our walk, how about you book us on a flight, and I'll go to my room and find us a decent hotel?"

"Great. I've already contacted a real estate agent there. I'll call him, too."

Jack returned to his room and called Laura, but kept his voice to a whisper.

"First things first," said Laura. "I heard back from the Spanish police. They recommend you book the Hotel Claude Marbella and will supply a four-man team if we request it."

"Won't know until we get there and see if any bad guys show up," said Jack. "What else do you have?"

"You were right about the phone number Roche gave you to contact him. It hasn't been used once."

"No surprise. I'm not trusted."

"I did hear back from Interpol. The police in Zurich have done some background on Carina. She's highly respected in her field. Also does volunteer work with a children's charity for abused or impoverished children. She helps them through art therapy."

"Anything on her husband?"

"His name's Denzler Bussmann."

"Carina goes by Safstrom."

"They were married, but she kept her maiden name — probably for professional reasons. As far as her husband goes, there's no criminal history. He died in a car accident in Mullheim, Germany, which is about an hour and a half from Zurich. The police in Zurich will check to get the details."

"Good. Text me the name of that hotel in Spain."

* * *

Late that afternoon, Jack and Carina went for a walk. When they came upon an elementary school, Jack reached into his pocket and removed a handful of coins.

"What are you doing?" Carina asked.

"Making some kids happy," he replied before throwing the coins into the schoolyard. "It's a nuisance taking change on the plane, and think how excited some little tykes will be when they find money in the schoolyard tomorrow."

Carina smiled as she imagined a bunch of excited children running around looking for the coins. She looked at Jack. "You're a nice guy, do you know that?"

"Not really. The teachers will probably find it first."

"Now you sound cynical," she teased.

"Cynical?" Jack paused, as if thinking about it. "Maybe. When I smell flowers I do look around to see where the coffin is."

"That's terrible!" Carina gave him a playful push on his chest.

* * *

That night they had dinner in a restaurant called Chez Michel, within walking distance of their hotel.

When they returned to their rooms, Carina kissed Jack on the cheek and told him she had really enjoyed herself that day, then said good night and entered her room.

* * *

The next two days spent at the Hotel Claude Marbella in Malaga, Spain, went as planned. The cover team did not spot anyone suspicious, and Jack and Carina went with an agent to look at more properties, but finished by four o'clock each afternoon.

Jack knew there were several museums in the area, but Carina never mentioned it, suggesting instead that they go for a walk and repeat the ritual they'd started in Marseille: a walk, then cocktails, then dinner.

On the second day in Malaga, the weather was again about ten degrees Celsius, but a breeze made it feel colder, especially near the ocean. As they walked, Jack was conscious that Carina had wrapped an arm around him. When she bade him good night, she pressed her hand to his back, urging him closer, then kissed him on his lips.

The third day it was Sunday, and they took the flight to Malta. Laura, Otto, Yves, and Maurice were on a later flight that would arrived a couple of hours later.

Halfway into their trip, Carina turned to Jack and said, "So far you don't seem overly excited about any of the properties we've viewed."

"I'm still taking it all in."

"I've got an real estate agent lined up to meet us at ten o'clock tomorrow morning at the hotel," she said.

"Good. I'm interested to see what Malta has to offer."

"You also mentioned Tuscany or Umbria as possibilities."

"Yes, I believe the Italians have a real zest for life. I also love my wine," he added with a wink.

"Both those regions appeal to me, also," Carina said. "In the last couple of years I have been checking those areas out."

"You have?"

"Yes, and I would really like to show you around there."

"I would like that, too, but I don't think think Roche plans on letting us extend our time together past Malta. Then you have to do the 'report,'" he said, making quotation marks with his fingers.

"That's easy," Carina said. "I'm going to tell them that you're a hard guy to get to know and that I need at least another month to check you out."

"Don't do —"

"Or maybe a year would be better," she said, smiling and giving Jack's hand a squeeze. He squeezed back and she remained holding his hand. "I'm only joking," she said. "Well ... sort of." With that, she snuggled closer to Jack and went to sleep.

They arrived in Malta at ten o'clock at night and it was midnight when they checked into the Hilton Malta. Jack's room was two rooms down the hall from Carina, and they agreed to meet for breakfast at ten in the morning, when the real estate agent was to arrive.

The following morning, an hour before breakfast, there was a knock on his door. He put on his hotel bathrobe, and when he opened the door, there was Carina, also wearing a hotel bathrobe. She was grinning.

"You look happy," he said, gesturing her inside. "What's up?"

Carina looked as if she was holding a secret. "Roche called me a few minutes ago. He wanted to know where we were and how things were going."

"What did you tell him?"

"Well, first of all, I told him things were going pretty well and suggested that because there's still at least three thousand Euros left on the card, we go to Tuscany for a couple of days before I 'report' in." As Jack had done earlier, she drew quotation marks in the air with her fingers.

"And?"

"He said no."

Jack's face sagged as he pretended disappointment. "So then what? Did you give him your impression of me over the phone?"

"A little, but wait until you hear the good news. First he wants to meet us both in person. On Wednesday we are to fly to Reggio Calabria, to meet him."

"Reggio Calabria?"

"Yes, it's opposite Sicily on the mainland. The bottom of the boot, as they say."

"Ah, yes," Jack said, "but why there? I want to look at places in northern Italy. Wouldn't it be —"

"There are people you are to see in Reggio, but wait. The good news is that I'm to stay there, too, for a couple of days while they meet with you!"

Jack nodded.

"And then they'll hire you and —"

"Roche said that?" Jack interjected.

"He didn't say that. I have to meet with him first, along with some others … but then I know you'll be hired."

"That would be nice."

"They will. All that's left is my recommendation. And that's a given."

"Thank you," Jack murmured.

"So that gives us today and tomorrow here," continued Carina, "but the *really* good news is that after a couple of days in Reggio, you and I will be free to continue on our way to Tuscany!"

"Really?" Jack feigned enthusiasm.

"Yes! My contract will have ended, but we can use the rest of the money on the card. I won't be getting any more calls from Roche, because you'll already have been hired. We'll be able to relax and have fun without your feeling as if you're under a microscope."

"Wow … I don't know what to say."

"Well, you'd better make sure you don't make me angry in the next two days," Carina said jokingly as she headed for the door. Then she stopped and turned to face him. "I'll book the tickets to Italy and meet you downstairs for breakfast. Maybe we can finish early today?"

"Maybe."

Jack was sipping coffee when Carina joined him. "All arranged," she said. "We fly out at one-forty Wednesday afternoon and arrive in Reggio at five-fifty. I called Roche back to let him know." Carina then gestured to a man in a suit who entered the restaurant. "Bet he's our real estate agent."

Carina was right in her assumption, and the man joined them for coffee while Carina and Jack ate their breakfast. Before they were finished, Jack received a call from Roche.

He was pleased to see that the call display was a different number than the one Roche had given him in Paris.

After exchanging niceties, Roche said, "I was speaking with Carina earlier this morning."

"So she told me." Jack caught Carina's eye from across the table. "We are to meet you in Reggio in two days."

"Yes, I have made reservations at a hotel for you. I will pick you up at the airport myself."

"Thank you."

"You have made quite an impression on Carina," said Roche. Jack sensed the curiosity behind the statement.

"That's nice to hear," Jack replied evenly, smiling at Carina.

"In a surprisingly short time," added Roche.

"Perhaps, but listen, I'm talking with a real estate agent at the moment, so …" Jack did not want to delve into his relationship with Carina.

"Fine, I'll see you soon." They disconnected.

After breakfast, Jack returned to his room and sent Laura a text with Roche's new number, along with their itinerary, before joining Carina and the agent in the lobby.

They spent the day looking at different properties. At five o'clock they were looking at the last villa of the day when Jack received a text, asking him to call Laura. *She's contacting me while I'm on a UC? What the hell is going on?*

Chapter Forty-Eight

"Excuse me, I have to make a call." Jack left the agent and Carina in one room in the villa while he went to another room to call Laura.

"I'm clear to talk," he said when Laura answered. "What's up?"

"Nothing life-threatening, but I thought you should hear. The number you gave us for Roche is good. He's using it."

"What did you get?"

"When they hooked up, there was a call in progress. Roche was talking to a Russian. We caught the tail end of it. Right after that, Roche made three more calls. All short. Ones to Anton and Wolfgang telling them to go to Reggio tomorrow and call him when they arrived. The third call was to someone named Giuseppe, saying it was a go and to make hotel arrangements."

"That's all he said?" asked Jack. "Make hotel arrangements? Not for how many people or which hotel?"

"No, it's obvious he had spoken to all of them in earlier calls that we missed. We've got a copy of the recording. Thought you might want to hear the one involving the Russian."

Jack glanced in the other room at the agent, who was directing Carina's attention to the ocean view. "Go ahead, let me hear it." Seconds later Jack heard the conversation.

"… is business. I won't arrive until ten-thirty the next night," said a man in English with a heavy Russian accent.

"Too bad," replied Roche.

"It is what it is. You and the rest can have fun while you wait. Kill a pig for me."

Jack felt himself tense. *Are they talking about me?*

"We will eat it Friday when I get there," the Russian went on.

"I've never gone boar-hunting before," said Roche, "but Wolfgang says he has been to Giuseppe's before. He said it is easy."

Jack grinned when he realized what they were talking about and continued to listen.

"It is. They don't shoot back. Not like the pigs in Chechnya."

A chuckle from Roche.

"So this Mister Jack Smith … you think she is in love with him?" the Russian asked. "What did she say?"

"You should have heard her," replied Roche. "She sounded like a schoolgirl in love for the first time." He then changed his voice to mimic a girl. "He is so wonderful. He is so smart. He is so nice. He is so sophisticated."

"They have only been together one week," the Russian said.

"I know. I wonder if he feels the same about her," Roche said musingly.

"She's beautiful. How could he not?" the Russian growled.

"You sound angry," Roche noted.

The Russian was silent for a moment, then said, "Who is this man that she would fall in love with him so fast? What do we know about him, other than he makes things disappear. Everyone else has family — good collateral should something go wrong. Jack Smith appears to be a lone wolf. I don't like it." His tone was harsh. "Has he clouded her judgment?"

"I don't know."

"She said he was sophisticated. Is that in regard to art?"

"I don't know."

"I don't know, I don't know," the Russian mocked.

"But I don't."

"I will speak to her when I arrive." The Russian sounded matter-of-fact.

"The question will be, do we trust him or not?" stated Roche. "If we are to open up to him and tell him things …"

"I will talk to her and see what she says."

Jack heard a click and then Laura came back on the line. "When I first heard about the pig bit, I —"

"Me, too, but I think it's legit," Jack said. "I don't like what they said about Carina."

"No, but still, it sounds like everything is coming together."

"Connect with our liaison officer in Rome," Jack said, "and tomorrow you and the rest of the team fly to Reggio to be there in advance. Sounds like lots of bad guys will be there, so make sure things are prepared. I don't mind if surveillance is done at the airport to confirm that Roche shows up, but after that, leave it to me. I'll contact you after I check in at the hotel. If they spot surveillance following us to the hotel, the gig will be up. In the meantime, I'll be safe enough with Carina on my own."

"I agree with you there," replied Laura. "I knew you could charm the pants off her. Figuratively speaking, of course."

"Don't even go there," Jack muttered. "Her trusting me is no longer a problem. The problem will be whether the Russian trusts her. You heard what he said … and how he said it."

"I can't see how you could have played it any differently."

"Yeah, well, anyway, I did my research before coming to Malta. There's a museum of fine arts here. I think I better go there with her tomorrow. At least it will give her something to tell the Russian."

"You're taking a chance."

"Once in the museum, I'll sidetrack her if she starts to get technical."

"How will you …? Never mind. I think I know."

"Yeah, as if I wasn't a big enough jerk already." With that, Jack hung up.

Carina stopped talking to the real estate agent when Jack returned. "Everything okay?" she asked.

"It will be okay," he said smoothly, "but I have to straighten out a consulting problem back in Canada. With the time difference it is only morning there, which means I'm going to be on the phone half the night." He paused, shaking his head, then looked at Carina. "You should have dinner without me tonight. I'll be ordering a sandwich or something from room service. I'll need to work without distraction."

Carina looked crestfallen.

"I can certainly take you back now," offered the real estate agent. "Then we can start again tomorrow."

"I'm sorry —" Jack met his gaze "— but I've seen enough of Malta to know I am not interested in purchasing property here."

"Oh … I am sorry to hear that," replied the agent.

Jack looked at Carina and said, "I would like to take tomorrow off and spend the whole day with you, if that's okay? I have some ideas in mind to make it a day I hope you'll enjoy."

Carina perked up. "I would love that!" she said. Then she kissed him on the mouth.

Jack held the kiss long enough to display interest, then glanced at the agent and said, "Perhaps we should be going."

* * *

That evening Jack stayed in his room after promising Carina he would meet her for breakfast at ten the next morning. He spent the time on the Internet studying the various pieces of art on display in the Museum of Fine Arts in Malta. The more he studied, the more he realized how little he knew about art.

At midnight he went to bed, but sleep eluded him for another couple of hours. He thought about Natasha and Mike and Steve and wished he could call home, but did not want the phone record on his hotel bill. He didn't use his own phone, either, because it would be too risky in the event it fell into the wrong hands.

Then he thought about Carina, and the Russian's words played over in his mind. *Has he clouded her judgment?*

Everyone else has family — good collateral should something go wrong. One word in particular bothered him. *Collateral. How long before they look at Carina as my collateral?*

He sighed deeply. *Gain the Ringmaster's confidence fast and cut Carina loose immediately. Make it sound like I don't give a rat's ass about her.*

Chapter Forty-Nine

At nine-thirty the next morning Jack spoke briefly with Laura and learned that she and the rest of the cover team would depart for the airport at noon and arrive in Reggio Calabria that evening, which would be a full day ahead of Jack's and Carina's arrival. The liaison officer in Rome had arranged for a team of police officers from the Italian national police force, the Guardia di Finanza, to assist them.

"Did you discuss surveillance?" asked Jack.

"Yes, there is good news and bad," she said. "The Italian police agree to give you lots of freedom without breathing down your neck."

"Good. And the bad news?"

"They agree to give you lots of freedom because they're reluctant to make inquiries or do much for fear of it getting back to the various Mafia families who control the region. They figure they'll be in a better position to re-evaluate once this Giuseppe is properly identified."

"I'm happy with that. Once I check into a hotel there, I'll contact you."

* * *

Half an hour later Jack went to the hotel restaurant and found Carina waiting for him. She immediately rose and gave him a hug and a kiss.

"Are you finished whatever it is you had to do last night?" she asked as she sat back down.

"Pretty well," Jack said. "I worked until about midnight. I may have to make another couple of calls in the next day or two, but nothing that will take long."

"And your plans for today?" she asked. "You said you had some ideas, but never told me."

"How about after breakfast we go for an invigorating walk, then take a taxi and go on a wine tour for lunch. After that, I would like to visit the Museum of Fine Arts. It's reputed to be excellent."

Carina's face brightened. "I'd love to see it!"

"Once we're done with the museum, we could come back, freshen up, and find a nice restaurant for dinner."

Carina smiled. "It sounds absolutely perfect!"

"Good."

"Will you let me pick the restaurant?" she asked.

"By all means," he replied.

"I was bored last night after you abandoned me and decided to check out some restaurants on the Internet. There's a place called the Bacchus restaurant that I thought looked good."

"The Bacchus it is," Jack said.

* * *

The afternoon went as planned. By three o'clock they had been to four wineries, and although Carina was far from swaying on her feet, she was in a joyful and playful mood by the time they entered the Museum of Fine Arts.

"What is your first impression of this one?" Carina was gazing at a watercolour of a harbour filled with boats, a city in the background.

"My first impression was, and still is, one of outstanding beauty," Jack replied.

"I agree," said Carina. "It is exquisite how the artist, Turner, managed to capture the almost mystical feeling to the cloud, or rather, the fog swirling in. Is that what caught your attention?" Her rapt gaze remained on the painting.

"No, I think it was the look of surprise, followed by the astounding beauty," Jack said as he stared at Carina.

Carina looked startled when she realized Jack's eyes were on her, not the painting. She giggled. "How much wine did you have?"

"I hadn't had any the first time I met you."

Carina pursed her lips, hoping it would stop her from blushing.

"Let's move on," said Jack. He waved his hand in the direction of several other paintings. "Although I like some sixteenth- and seventeenth-century art, a lot of it is based on religion and depicts biblical characters, which I do not care for. I like paintings such as the one over there by Bernardo Strozzi." He gestured to a painting farther down the wall. "I believe that one is entitled *The Piper*. The fact that the character in the painting is playing a musical instrument represents fun to me; but on the flip side, I also like works that represent hardship, such as *Les Gavroches,* the sculpture of street urchins in Barrakka Garden here in Malta."

"Ah, yes," Carina said.

"It was done in the early twentieth century by a local sculptor named Antonio Sciortino and —" Jack's face lit up. "I've an idea. Barrakka Garden is less than two kilometres away and I've yet to see the sculpture in person. Do you want to go? After the wine it seems stuffy in here. I could use some fresh air."

"I'd love to go, especially as it's a sculpture you like," said Carina, taking his hand.

Twenty minutes later they stood gazing at the statue and Jack said, "So, what is your first impression? Do you like it?"

"Like it? I love it. I look at these three bronze children and it makes me want to take all the change from my purse and throw it into a schoolyard."

"Where on earth did you come up with an idea like that?" asked Jack.

Carina smiled. "Oh, from some guy I met. I can't remember his name."

* * *

That evening, before leaving his room for dinner, Jack checked out the Bacchus restaurant on the Internet. It was reputed to be the most romantic restaurant in Malta. *Of all the trips I have been on, the guilt trip is by far the worst.*

* * *

The restaurant lived up to its reputation. Its soft lighting and rustic stone walls gave it a warm, intimate ambiance, and the food was delicious. Their conversation flowed easily.

Carina cut a piece of halibut, but then paused to look at Jack. "I'm still embarrassed by what I said the first time I met you in Paris."

"What you said?" Jack grinned. "You mean when you said, 'You're Jack Smith!'"

"Yes." Carina blushed. "God, I must have sounded like a schoolgirl. I tried to cover for it, but I could tell by those big blue eyes of yours that you saw right through me."

Jack took a bite of his roasted rack of lamb. "I kind of thought you were interested in me."

"Kind of thought? I may as well have hung a sign around my neck saying Available on Request."

Jack chuckled. "It wasn't that bad, but tell me, why were you so surprised?"

"Well, I'd asked a few questions about you. Roche told me you collected art, but he also said he suspected you had a rough childhood and likely raised yourself — in dangerous or perhaps gang-run neighbourhoods. He said you were a tough guy. I pictured you with a bald head covered in tattoos and scars, a crooked nose from being broken often, and a missing earlobe."

"If you learn to run fast, those things don't happen," he said.

"Perhaps ... but I have a feeling that you can handle yourself."

"Well, Roche is right about one thing," said Jack quietly. "I did have a rough childhood, thanks to my dysfunctional family, and have seen more than my share of bad things on the street."

"In Zurich I volunteer to help kids from such families."

"You do?"

"I try to encourage them to get into art. It's good therapy."

"Better than drugs," noted Jack.

"That's for sure. Do you have brothers and sisters?"

"Not anymore," he said sadly. "I used to, but they didn't fare as well as I did. It's too hard to talk about."

Carina nodded sympathetically, took another bite of halibut, then smiled wistfully. "I wish I'd known you when you were a child. I can picture you with those big blue eyes and a mop of ruffled hair."

"Oh? From your response when we first met, I thought you preferred me as a man."

Carina blushed, then reached for her wine. "You got me there," she admitted, then took a long sip.

"Tell me about yourself," said Jack. "What was your childhood like?"

Carina looked blankly at Jack for a moment, then said, "I'm embarrassed to tell you. It was the complete opposite of yours. I was an only child and spoiled beyond belief. I always got what I wanted. Private schools, even my own horse."

"Born into money; it must be nice."

"No, it wasn't that my parents were wealthy. They worked incredibly long hours and I think spoiling me eased their guilt for being gone so much. My mother died of cancer when I was in university, and my father died of a heart attack a few months later."

"I'm sorry."

"Thanks, but I managed okay. My aunt and uncle in Stockholm sort of adopted me after that. It was my uncle who walked me down the aisle when I got married."

"That's really nice," Jack murmured.

Carina paused to reflect a moment, then said, "Enough of the past." She reached for her wineglass and lifted it. "Here's to new beginnings!"

"To new beginnings," Jack repeated, his smile warm as they clinked glasses.

* * *

It was nearing midnight when they returned to the hotel. At the door to her room, Carina turned and kissed Jack passionately on the mouth. Moving her lips to his neck, she whispered, "Would you like to come in?"

"I ... I'm sorry," Jack said softly. "I've only known you a week. I haven't been with anyone since ... since it happened."

"You're still in love with your wife, aren't you?"

Jack nodded. "Yes ... I am and I always will be."

Carina's eyes moistened and she looked down.

Jack swallowed, then said, "I'm sorry. I didn't mean to imply that your love for your husband was any less than —"

Carina put a finger on Jack's lips to silence him. "It's okay. I've had more time to heal ... and more time to be lonely. You are the first man I have asked to come to bed with me since my husband died." She shook her head. "Just my luck that you would turn me down."

"I'm sorry. It's ... I don't know. I want to ... but my mind feels frazzled when I'm around you. I feel guilty that I've only known you a short time and worry that I'm on the rebound or that this is just a sort of shipboard romance. I need time to know that what I feel is real."

"I understand," she said softly. "I'm not blaming you. When I toasted to new beginnings tonight, I didn't mean that we needed to rush into things. I know how I feel about you and believe you are worth waiting for. I am hoping that in time, you will feel the same way about me."

"Thank you for understanding."

She kissed him on the cheek and said, "You wife was lucky to have had you as her husband." She turned and unlocked her door, but as she entered, she glanced back and said, "Call me when you're up." Before Jack could reply, she looked at his crotch and added, "I meant up out of bed, of course." She gave a mischievous smile and closed her door.

Chapter Fifty

At five-thirty the next day, Laura, Otto, and Maurice were scrunched into the back of a surveillance van with an Italian police officer by the name of Paolo. They were parked in a lot across from the main entrance to the Reggio Calabria airport.

They saw a black BMW with a bumper sticker advertising a car-rental agency arrive and park in the same lot, then watched the driver get out. "That's Roche Freulard," Otto and Laura said in unison.

Paolo immediately used his police radio to alert the rest of the surveillance team, including Maurice's boss, Yves, who was a passenger in another surveillance vehicle.

"So far, so good," Laura whispered, still watching as Roche stood by his car, looking around.

"What's he waiting for?" Paolo wondered aloud while taking photos.

Soon a red truck arrived and parked behind Roche's car. The driver unwound the window.

"Italy's answer to the Hummer," said Paolo, admiring the truck while continuing to take photos. "The Lamborghini LM002, more commonly known as the Lambo Rambo."

Otto squinted at the driver, then grabbed the binoculars for a closer look. "That's him! He's the guy I lost on surveillance in Frankfurt. The one who was in the front seat with Wolfgang when Roche was in the back."

"I don't understand," said Paolo. "Who is he?"

"Roche called Jack from Frankfurt and the call was traced to a hotel," Laura explained. "We think the one they call the Ringmaster was with Roche. Right afterwards, Otto spotted Roche and two other men leaving the hotel. One man was Wolfgang Menges, who later came to Canada and met Jack. The other guy was never identified."

"So this guy may be the boss?" Paolo asked.

"We don't know," Laura replied. "At the time, he seemed like a good possibility, but that was before we learned about the Russian. All we have is a witness who described the killer as having collar-length black hair and hairy hands."

"He definitely has the black hair," said Otto, still peering through the binoculars. "I can't see his hands, but I'm thinking he's Italian. Okay, he's leaving and Roche is walking away. I can't see the licence plate."

Paolo used his police radio to notify another surveillance vehicle, who reported that the Lambo Rambo had parked near an airport exit, with the driver waiting behind the wheel. Moments later they learned that the truck was registered to a Giuseppe Carbone, with an address in Reggio Calabria.

"I will check our database to find out what we know about him." Paolo punched in numbers on his phone.

Roche had gone into the airport and it was reported he was waiting at Arrivals. A few minutes later Jack and Carina arrived and were greeted by Roche. At the same time, Paolo received a call back about Giuseppe Carbone. When he hung up, he said, "To our knowledge, Carbone is not yet a made member of the black hand, but is working hard to become one. Many of his relatives are made members. He has been arrested many times for things like extortion, armed robbery, and a sexual assault, but has never been convicted. No doubt because of the influence of the black hand on witnesses, or perhaps the judiciary."

Maurice glanced at Laura and said, "The black hand may be better known to you as the Mafia."

"I'm familiar with the term," Laura said. "It extends to Canada, as well. Particularly Montreal. Unlike the States, who have the Sicilian mafia, in Canada they tend to be from Calabria. Either way, they are still known as the black hand when it comes to manipulating things."

"Sometimes in Germany, the blue hand reaches out and slaps the black hand," Otto put in, then grinned.

A few minutes later they watched as Jack, Carina, and Roche came out of the airport with their suitcases and then departed in Roche's car.

"I wish to confirm that you do not want surveillance to follow?" Paolo glanced at Laura.

"Right," Laura said. "Jack will contact me once he gets to the hotel, but how about a loose surveillance on Giuseppe in the Lambo Rambo? If there's any chance of being spotted, have your team break off."

Paolo gave the orders, but minutes later received a report that Giuseppe was discreetly following Roche's car and keeping an eye out for anyone else who was following. It was also reported that he was using his own portable radio, and it was surmised that there were others assisting him with his counter-surveillance.

"Tell everyone to break off," Laura ordered.

"Already done," Paolo said.

* * *

Jack sat in the front seat of the BMW beside Roche, while Carina sat in the back. As they drove, Jack noticed that Roche was continually checking his rear-view mirror and side mirrors, and felt his stomach tense as he stared out the window. *Please, don't let there be any police surveillance.*

After driving for a few minutes, Roche turned off the main route and drove around for several blocks in an area where there were mostly apartment buildings.

"Sorry, I seem to have taken a wrong turn," said Roche by way of an apology.

Like hell you did.

Minutes later Roche found his way back to the main route. Jack glanced in the side mirror and saw a set of headlights rapidly approach from behind, then slow down to follow them. *Damn it! If that's the police …*

Roche checked his rear-view mirror and it was obviously he'd seen the lights, as well. Jack pretended to clear his throat and reached across to tap Roche on the side of his leg. When Roche glanced at him, Jack gestured with his head at the side mirror and the headlights following them.

Roche nodded, then used his phone and made a call. Seconds later the headlights behind them flicked to high beam and back to low beam. Roche smiled and looked at Jack. "It's okay, my friend."

"Something wrong?" asked Carina.

"No," said Jack. "I'm simply not used to the traffic. In Canada it's not so crowded."

"Trust me, I will get you to your hotel safely," Roche assured them.

Trust you? NFL.

Moments later they arrived at the E' Hotel and went to reception to check in. Jack noticed that his room, which was on the second floor, was only for one night. Carina's room, on the fourth floor, was booked for four nights.

Jack gave Roche a quizzical look. "Only one night for me?"

"Yes," Roche confirmed. "Tomorrow we will be taking you to meet some people for a two-day adventure. Then we will bring you back to this hotel on Saturday."

"An adventure?" Jack asked.

"A colleague has a lodge about a three- or four-hour drive from here. It's used for hunting wild boar. It will be a good place to get to know each other."

Jack recalled what Carina had told him about the Russian who had introduced her to Roche. *He's a sportsman and likes to hunt.*

"Do you like to hunt?" asked Roche.

Jack nodded and said he did. *Oh, yeah. Going out in the bush with a bunch of bad guys with guns should be fun. What could possibly go wrong?*

"Coming from Canada, I suppose you have shot grizzly bears and moose," continued Roche.

Jack cleared his throat. "I enjoy hunting, but have never killed a moose or a grizzly bear. I've only hunted smaller game."

"Good." Roche smiled and patted Jack on the back.

Two-legged animals mostly.

"It will be fun," said Roche.

Carina looked at Jack. "You like killing animals?" she asked.

"Sometimes."

Carina wrinkled her nose in distaste.

"We'll talk more about it over dinner," said Roche. "I've never hunted before, but it sounds exciting. Check in, then meet me in the restaurant in half an hour. There will be some colleagues, the executives of our company, who will be joining us for dinner."

"Are they also going hunting?" Jack queried.

Roche nodded. "Yes, except for one who has been delayed. He'll arrive tomorrow night and join us at the lodge on Friday."

Yes, the man from Russia who wants me to have collateral.

"Once he arrives, we'll have a meeting to go over what everyone has accomplished within the last year, as well as to set new goals," Roche went on.

"And will I be a part of ...?"

"That's the plan," said Roche.

Jack nodded and outwardly showed no emotion. *Perfect!*

"Carina, may I have a word with you?" Roche gestured for her to move farther away from the reception desk so they could talk in private. She obliged, and Jack saw them whispering to each other as he dealt with reception. Roche then gave a curt nod and went to the restaurant.

"Everything okay?" Jack said as he joined Carina on the way to the elevator.

Carina's face revealed her displeasure. "He told you to join him in half an hour. But I'm to meet him as soon as I drop off my bag in my room."

"That's reasonable," replied Jack. "He won't want me there when he's asking you questions about me."

"That I understand, but tonight is to be only for the men. They want to get to know you. I feel like I have to say goodbye now."

"I'll be back on Saturday," Jack said, pushing the button for the elevator. "Depending, of course, on what you tell them about me."

"I think I'll tell them that they could save expenses tonight if you and I shared a room." Carina cast him a quick glance.

"You know I'm not ready for that yet. I need —"

"I was only joking … well, sort of," Carina admitted.

Jack nodded and they stepped into the elevator.

"Do you really like hunting?" she asked as the elevator started its ascent.

"Not really," Jack said. "I've never shot a pig before, wild or otherwise. What is it Winston Churchill once said? Dogs look up to men, cats look down on them, but pigs just treat us as equals."

Carina smiled.

"I've always had a soft spot in my heart for pigs," Jack went on. "They're intelligent animals."

"The little ones are cute. Maybe you won't shoot anything. Simply go along for the fresh air."

"Then again, I hope we get something," he said, grinning. "I love roast pork."

"You ass!" she said, giving him a playful punch on the arm.

The elevator stopped on the second floor, but before Jack could get off, Carina held the button to keep the door open while wrapping her other hand around his neck and kissing him passionately. Seconds later a loud buzz in the elevator indicated the door had been held open long enough.

"Promise me you'll hurry back on Saturday," she said. "I don't want our new beginnings to be me sitting alone."

"I promise. I also have a favour to ask."

"Anything."

"It would sound better if you did not share the feelings we have for each other with Roche or any of the others. It could reflect upon the value they place on your assessment."

Carina smiled. "The feelings *we* have for each other. So you feel the same way. I was beginning to wonder."

The irritating buzz in the elevator continued and Jack wasn't sure what to say, anyway, so he smiled apologetically and stepped into the hall. "See you downstairs in half an hour, Carina."

Once in his room, Jack immediately called Laura and gave her the name of his hotel, then listened as she passed on the name to Paolo.

"We're booked into a hotel called the Grand Excelsior," Laura said. "I've been told it's just a five-minute walk from your hotel."

Jack told her about the plan to go hunting, as well as the business meeting scheduled to review everyone's accomplishments and goals for the year. Any expectations he had of Laura being excited about his attendance at the meeting were soon put in perspective — Laura's perspective.

"You're going out to kill some little pig?" she cried. "Or worse yet, orphan a bunch of little pigs?"

Jack knew that Laura's love for animals sometimes surpassed what she felt for people. "I don't expect I'll shoot anything. I think it's more a guys-bonding kind of thing."

"I've seen that picture before," said Laura sternly. "A bunch of guys boozing it up and carrying guns."

"Yes, it sounds like the Drug Section Christmas party," Jack joked. "Should be fun."

"It's not funny, Jack."

Jack became serious. "I suspect the Ringmaster likes to hunt. I need to show an interest."

"How do you feel about attending this so-called executive meeting on Friday?"

"I feel okay with it."

Laura was silent for a moment, then said, "They put counter-surveillance on you from the airport."

"I saw. I was worried it was our people."

"Don't worry about our people," Laura insisted. "All is good, except that Giuseppe has Mafia connections. Tread carefully."

"Always. Anything new over Roche's phone?"

"A couple of calls to Anton, Wolfgang, and Giuseppe. Nothing of interest. It was about picking you up at the airport and meeting downstairs for dinner." She waited a beat, then asked, "So what do you want done?"

"Have someone check in here tonight and see if we can identify the Russian when he arrives tomorrow. Don't do it yourself. A second Canadian showing up after I checked in would be too coincidental. Not to mention, if Anton's here, he'd recognize you."

"For sure."

"Tonight I'm meeting the bad guys downstairs for dinner. If our Russian friend does the same thing with Carina tomorrow night, I'd like you in there to see if you can hear something or read anything from his facial expressions."

"The phone tap indicated he wouldn't arrive until ten-thirty at night," noted Laura.

"Schedules change. Maybe he'll catch an earlier flight."

"Gotcha."

"I also want a loose surveillance put on Carina throughout the day. I doubt they'll be doing any counter-surveillance on her, so it shouldn't be difficult."

"Do you suspect her of —"

"No."

"Then you're thinking more for security reasons," Laura said. "The Russian talking about having collateral bothered me, too." She waited a beat, then said, "It's not like they would need to drag Carina kicking and screaming off the street. We might not be in a position to know if she's about to be harmed."

"If something goes sideways with me, scoop her up," Jack said sombrely.

"Right … and how will we know if something goes sideways with you?"

"I'll call you."

"Oh, I see," Laura scoffed. "You would say, excuse me, bad guys, don't shoot me yet. I need to make a phone call first. Yeah, I'm sure they would go along with that."

"Damn it, Laura!" Jack couldn't contain his annoyance. "What am I supposed to do? The next two days are crucial. We need her to convince the Russian … but if something goes wrong I don't want her being harmed because of it. Come Saturday I'll break up with her one way or the other."

"Yes, but how will I know if things do go sideways?" Laura persisted.

"Like I said, I'll call you if the situation turns ugly," Jack replied.

"And if you can't?"

"Then I'm probably already dead and they won't have any reason to go after Carina."

Chapter Fifty-One

Jack entered the restaurant and had barely taken a couple of steps when a man shouted, "Hey, Canada!" He saw Wolfgang wave at him from the far side of a table where he was sitting with Roche and Anton.

Jack approached and Wolfgang rose and gave him a warm handshake. On the near side of the table sat Carina and a man whom Wolfgang introduced as Giuseppe. Jack shook his hand and noticed that there was very little hair on it. *Strike you off the list.*

Jack looked across the table. "Hello, Anton. Nice to see you again."

Anton nodded, but Jack saw by his eyes that he was not pleased to have Jack there. *Perhaps something to do with me taping his eyes shut or putting a gun to his head and threatening to blow his brains out. Or was it the threat of cutting him up in a band saw that makes him dislike me?*

Jack took the free seat beside Carina and felt her briefly squeeze his leg. She gave him a reassuring smile.

"Carina has been speaking highly of you," Roche said.

Jack smiled and nodded to indicate he heard, but wondered how cognizant Roche was of Carina's feelings for him.

"Perhaps she even thinks as highly of you as Wolfgang does," Roche added, giving Wolfgang a jab with his elbow.

Wolfgang grinned, then raised a glass of red wine in Jack's direction and said, "You may have impressed me a little with the, uh, consulting work you did for us in Canada."

"A little?" Giuseppe said. "What about you, Anton? Were you impressed … a little?"

"What does he know?" Wolfgang chuckled. "I think he had his eyes closed half the time Jack was around."

"This is not the place or the time to be discussing work," Roche said. "We are here to have fun tonight. Everyone drink, and let's order. I'm hungry."

A waiter was summoned, and Jack and Wolfgang each ordered pasta, while the others ordered swordfish. The wine continued to arrive at the table and Jack was pretty sure that they wanted to get him drunk. Of course, that meant they'd get drunk, too.

Anton, in particular, as time went on, appeared to have difficulty locating his mouth. The front of his shirt had collected a growing number of food and wine stains.

Giuseppe talked about the hunting lodge he owned and laughed about the times hunters were chased by the wild boar. "Happens especially if the boar is wounded," he said. "They can be dangerous."

"I'm sure Jack could handle them," Wolfgang slurred. "Couldn't you, Jack? Probably smack 'em in the teeth with the butt of —"

"I'd prefer to shoot them," Jack interrupted him. He glared at Wolfgang.

Wolfgang took the hint and quit talking. Jack watched as he chased the last morsel of pasta around his plate with a fork, then captured it and popped it into his mouth.

Carina was quiet during the meal and stopped drinking after her second glass. Once the plates were cleared, Jack felt her squeeze his leg one more time, then she announced that she was tired, but would see them off in the morning. The men concurred that everyone would meet at nine o'clock for breakfast.

"We will leave the hotel around ten tomorrow morning," said Giuseppe as Carina walked away. "Also, it is cold in the mountains, might even snow. We will shop for some warm clothes along the way. I have some winter coats at the lodge, but you might like to buy your own warm shirts, pants, boots, and heavy socks."

Jack nodded. "Thank you. I'll need to shop. Leaving at ten doesn't give us much time once we have breakfast."

"We go through a town on the way called Bianco," Giuseppe said. "My cousin has a store there. Don't worry. It is already paid for. Whatever you want."

"Oh, that's very nice of —"

"I am looking forward to hunting boar with you," Anton said in a voice that sounded menacing.

"And I with you," Jack replied cheerily. "I've never hunted pigs before, but I presume by your appearance that you're to be the decoy?"

There was a burst of laughter from Roche, Wolfgang, and Giuseppe, but Jack knew by the look of hatred on

Anton's face that he had made a blunder. Undercover work is about befriending people, not making enemies.

Jack cleared his throat, then looked around the table. "So that you don't get the wrong idea," he said, "I should tell the rest of you that Anton is one of the bravest men I've ever met. I had a gun to his head and threatened to cut him up with a band saw, yet he refused to tell me where the stash was hidden. Even when I fired a gun beside his head, he didn't flinch." *Actually, he was too terrified to move.*

Anton glanced at the sombre faces of his colleagues as they reflected on what Jack had said.

Jack raised his wineglass toward Anton. "I salute you. You've got *balls.*"

The hatred vanished from Anton's eyes and he shrugged modestly. He met Jack's gaze, giving a slight nod and smile to show his appreciation.

Jack nodded in return. *Good. Just reeled you in, dumb-ass.*

Chapter Fifty-Two

It was midnight when Jack returned to his room and called Laura. After she told him that one of Paolo's men had obtained a room on the second floor overlooking the front entrance to the hotel, Jack updated her. When he told her they would be stopping in Bianco to shop at Giuseppe's cousin's store, she relayed the information to Paolo.

"Okay," she said, when she came back on the phone. "Bianco is about an hour-and-fifteen-minute drive from here. Paolo says the only place he thinks there would be boar-hunting is in the Aspromonte mountains. Translated, it means 'rough mountains.' On days when the roads are good, you can go from the sunshine of the coast and be skiing an hour later."

"Good," replied Jack. "Sounds like you'll have a rough idea where I'm headed. Maybe suggest to Paolo he send a couple of his guys to Bianco to see where I go from there."

"He's already said he would, but now the bad news. From Bianco, once you get into the mountains, there are myriad back roads, rivers, and mountains with little traffic this time of year. It's been a popular region for the Mafia to hide people they kidnapped or took prisoner. He's not sure if they still use that area, but he knows there's no way they could follow you without being seen. If the roads are bad, which they often are, you could be looking at a three- or four-hour drive once you leave Bianco, depending on where they take you."

"Lovely," Jack said.

"I hate these situations," said Laura.

"Well, *my* good news is I think I impressed everyone at the table tonight. I don't feel any bad vibes at all. Not even from Anton, who started off with a bit of a grudge."

"Just a bit? After what you —"

"I think I smoothed it out. Just had to stroke his ego."

Jack heard Paolo talking to Laura in the background, then Laura muttered, "Crap."

"What now?" Jack asked.

"Once you're in the mountains, you can't use a cellphone in a lot of the areas — at least, not without driving for up to an hour to find a spot that works."

"Like I said, I feel pretty good about the situation. I'll tell the bad guys that I have to take care of business in Canada and will need to make a few calls. Eight in the morning in Vancouver is five in the afternoon here. So I'll try to touch base around five."

"And if we don't hear from you, what then? We won't have a clue where you are. Damn it, Jack, they could even shoot you and say it was a hunting accident. With Giuseppe's connections he wouldn't even be charged with —"

"I know. I thought of that, too."

"Well?"

"Well what? It's not like I have any choice. Same as Kerin when he tried to save me. He had no choice, either."

* * *

At eight-thirty the next morning, Jack went into the restaurant for breakfast, hoping to catch Carina alone and remind her not to disclose the feelings she had for him until after he was hired. She was in the restaurant, but so was Roche.

Jack saw Carina smile at him, then grimace and discreetly nod toward Roche. It was evident she was hoping the two of them could be alone, too. It made him feel better that she did not display any obvious signs of affection toward him.

Shortly after Jack sat down, Wolfgang, Anton, and Giuseppe arrived. When breakfast was over, Jack, Roche, Anton, and Wolfgang checked out of the hotel. They said goodbye to Carina in the lobby and then Giuseppe drove them to Bianco.

It was two in the afternoon by the time they bought clothes at the store owned by Giuseppe's cousin and groceries at another store. Then, just as Paolo had predicted, they headed into the Aspromonte mountains. Traffic on the mountain roads became scarce.

Forty-five minutes out of Bianco, they came to a small town called Sant'Agata del Bianco. On the outskirts of the town, Giuseppe pulled into a driveway of a home set amongst a grove of trees.

"My brother-in-law's place," he explained. "Wait here. I won't be long. If you need to make any calls, do it now because once we get to my lodge, the phones won't work."

"I'll have to make a call tomorrow night around five o'clock," said Jack. "How far do we have to go yet?"

Giuseppe glanced up at the sky, then said, "If it doesn't snow, we'll be at my lodge in another hour. Sometimes you can get a signal about halfway there, but not always."

Jack and Wolfgang both got out of the vehicle to use their phones, and Giuseppe went to the house, where he was greeted by a bearded man dressed in a wool lumberjack shirt, cargo pants, and green boots. He had two dogs with him, one a pit bull and the other a hound. The man eyed Jack briefly, then grabbed the dogs by their collars and disappeared back inside with Giuseppe.

A real hillbilly, Jack thought as he wandered back up the driveway to call Laura. Wolfgang was within listening range, but was busy talking on his own phone.

Jack decided not to chance whether or not Wolfgang could hear him, so he chose his words carefully. "Sorry to wake you," he said when Laura answered. "Guess it's early where you are." He paused, then said, "Where am I? Passing through some little town in Italy called Sant'Agata del Bianco. It's cold and windy. Feels like it's gonna snow."

"Okay for me to chat?" she asked.

"You bet."

"Paolo says the team saw you heading out of Bianco but decided not to follow."

"That's great. I mean that." Jack glanced at Wolfgang and saw him hang up and get back inside the truck.

"They also did a loose surveillance on Carina," continued Laura. "She went to a jewellery store and bought a man's ring. Gold with a blue sapphire. She ordered it engraved and went back a few minutes ago and picked it up."

"I'm clear to talk now," said Jack. "Any idea what was engraved on the ring?"

"Yes. It was in English and said *New Beginnings.*"

"Christ," Jack muttered.

"I thought that might mean something to you." When Jack didn't respond, she said, "At least you know she'll give a good assessment about you to the Russian."

"Yes, but I hope to hell she doesn't show him the ring. If she does, I may as well buy her one and have it engraved with the word *collateral.*"

"She's going to be upset when you dump her."

"I'll use the ring as an excuse and say I feel like I'm being rushed into something."

"Guess that's nicer than telling her you're married with two kids."

"Anything on the Russian yet?" Jack asked to change the subject.

"Paolo looked into some flight manifests, but there are several Russians listed. I told him not to risk making inquiries as we'll likely identify him when he arrives."

"I agree. It's not as though it'd make a difference at this point." He glanced at the house and saw Giuseppe emerge with four rifle scabbards. "Gotta go. I'll call you tomorrow around five o'clock. Hopefully by then I'll have met him."

"Don't make any pig noises in the bush," Laura said, then hung up.

Jack approached Giuseppe as he was putting the rifles into his vehicle. "There are five of us and only four rifles," he noted.

"I have killed enough boar," Giuseppe explained. "If someone wounds one and it comes at me, I've got this." He flashed open his jacket to reveal a pistol stuck in his belt.

A minute later they drove out of Sant'Agata del Bianco, and fifteen minutes after that Giuseppe turned down a road consisting of two ruts that meandered in and around the mountainous slopes. Forty-five minutes later they came to a long, barren stretch where the road cut through a meadow. At the end of the meadow were some small, wooden buildings backing onto a densely forested area.

"Welcome to my lodge," Giuseppe said as he drove up and parked in front of a larger building that had a wall of sheer rock on one side and a steep gully on the other that plummeted down to a raging river.

"I own 144 acres," he added as they got out of the truck. He pointed toward the forest and said, "The boars are in there. If you go to the end of my property, the river on one side meets up with the mountain on the other. There's no place for the boar to go at that point and they know it."

"Sounds easy," Roche said. "Chase them to the end where they can't escape and shoot them."

Giuseppe smiled. "You will find it's not that easy. About eighty acres is forest. There is plenty of room for them to sneak past you."

"So we may not be eating roast pork," Wolfgang said. "Hope you brought enough food."

Giuseppe shook his head. "If we are not successful by noon, I will return to my brother-in-law's place. He has two dogs. One is what they call the bay dog. It tracks the scent and howls when it finds the boar. The other dog is known as the catch dog, and once the boar is found, it will clamp its jaws onto the boar's face or ear and hold it until we arrive and kill it. I don't like to use the dogs unless it is necessary. With them we could kill a boar within an hour, but using the dogs is …" He looked at Jack and asked, "What is the expression? Fishing in a barrel?"

"Shooting fish in a barrel," Jack replied.

"Yes, thank you, that's it. However, either way, we will not go hungry." He then pointed to a building on the left and said, "That's the bunkhouse. The other is the kitchen. There's a shed behind the kitchen where I have two all-terrain quad bikes. When we do get our boar, you will appreciate not having to carry it out."

"Looks like quite the setup," Jack said.

Giuseppe nodded. "I have generators on the porch behind the kitchen with a line to the bunkhouse. They are good for ten hours of running time at fifty percent power. You will have light, heat, and water from a well for a hot shower. There are sleeping bags in the closets between the bunks. The bunkhouse isn't locked, so everyone go make yourselves at home while I start the generators."

"Not locked?" questioned Jack. "Don't you worry about stuff being stolen? Especially your quads or your generators."

Giuseppe looked taken back. "This is my land and my property. Everyone knows that. If anyone did such a thing … well, let me say they would not dare." He slid his index finger across his throat.

In other words, you're king in this neck of the woods. Jack went with the others to the bunkhouse while Giuseppe took a jerry can of gas out of his truck for the generators.

The bunkhouse had a door at the front with a small window adjacent to it. Inside were three double bunk beds down each side separated by a double closet between each bunk. At the far end of the bunkhouse, Jack noted, were shelves on one side and a bathroom on the other.

Jack laid claim to one of the beds nearest the bathroom, then decided to use the facility, which had a sink on the left, and toilet and shower stall on the right. A window above the toilet faced the kitchen, Jack discovered, and he could see Giuseppe pouring gas into a generator. Between the bunkhouse and the kitchen were benches placed around a firepit.

When Jack returned to his bunk, they suddenly heard the hum of the generator, and Wolfgang flicked on the lights.

It was five o'clock by the time everyone had stowed their clothes, put sleeping bags on the bunks, and gone next door. Jack entered the kitchen through the front door and saw that it was spacious, with windows on both sides and two picnic tables standing end to end down the middle of the room. In the back a counter extended partway out to separate the cooking area from the seating area. A rear door led onto a back porch.

"Welcome," said Giuseppe as they entered. "Don't worry about taking off your boots. It's too cold for the ground to be muddy, so you're not likely to track anything in. I have a vacuum in the shed if I need it." He glanced out a window at the darkening sky. "Is there anyone here who has not fired a rifle before?"

"I was a sharpshooter in the military," Wolfgang said.

All eyes turned to Jack. "I can handle a rifle," he said, then looked at Roche and Anton.

Both admitted they'd never used one. "Only pistols," Anton said.

Giuseppe nodded. "I was going to take you out and do some target practice, but it is getting dark. We will do it in the morning. It is light by eight o'clock, so if we have breakfast around seven, it will work out."

Everyone took a seat at one of the tables. Giuseppe poured them each a glass of wine and set out a plate of black olives before making spaghetti. After they'd eaten, Giuseppe looked at Jack and said, "I have a chore for you. Being from Canada, I think you will know how to do it."

"I'm listening," said Jack.

"While I clean up, I would like you to go outside and start a fire in the pit. There is firewood on the back porch and matches on the counter."

Jack nodded and Wolfgang went with him, while Roche and Anton remained to assist Giuseppe clean up in the kitchen. Jack found a hatchet and Wolfgang hauled several armloads of firewood over to the pit, where Jack used a chopping block to make kindling. The fire was well underway when the rest of the men joined them.

The evening went without incident. The men sat around the fire sipping wine until ten o'clock, when a light snow began falling.

"It is good," said Giuseppe, holding his hand out to the snow. "We will not need the dogs tomorrow."

* * *

Surveillance at the E' Hotel indicated that Carina had gone to her room. Maurice, Yves, Otto, and Laura then snuck into the room on the second floor that one of Paolo's men had booked, which overlooked the front entrance of the hotel.

At ten-forty-five Paolo received a call saying that a man with a Russian accent had deplaned from the ten-thirty flight and was renting a Jeep. He was described as clean-shaven with short black hair touched with grey at the temples. He was wearing a three-quarter-length fur coat.

Paolo shut the lights off in the hotel room and they waited.

Thirty minutes later a man driving a Jeep drove slowly past the entrance of the hotel, obviously looking for a place to park. Minutes later he walked into the hotel with a suitcase, unaware that he was being photographed from above.

"How about I slip down to the lobby on the pretext of asking for a wake-up call or perhaps to look at a map of the city?" Paolo suggested.

"Go for it," Laura said.

Minutes later Paolo returned. "His name is Yakov Kadnikov. He's built like a bear with a strong, thick neck."

"A Russian bear," Laura said musingly. "The killer was described as being stocky. How about his hands?"

"I'm not sure." Paolo paused. "His skin is pale and the hair on his hands is black, but not as thick as I have seen on some men."

"In daylight, against white skin, it may look more so," Yves said.

"Did you get his room number?" Maurice asked.

"No, but I rode up with him in the elevator and he pushed the button for the fourth floor." Paolo looked at

Laura. "I will sleep here tonight and detail a surveillance team to be watching his Jeep by six o'clock tomorrow morning. Is there anything else you would like?"

Laura shook her head. "Let's call it a night and regroup at eight in the morning."

"This time in my room at the Grand Excelsior," volunteered Maurice.

Everyone nodded in agreement. Otto and Laura left, taking the stairs to the lobby, where they checked to ensure it was clear before heading out on the five-minute walk back to their hotel. So as not to jeopardize future surveillance possibilities, Maurice and Yves gave them a ten-minute lead to eliminate any chance of their being seen together. They used the elevator.

* * *

The thing about elevators is that the empty shaft between floors does little to block the sound of the voices of people waiting at the elevator doors.

Hearing French spoken in Italy was not uncommon, and that alone did not arouse the interest of the Ringmaster. What did arouse interest, when the elevator stopped on the second floor and two men stepped in, was the abrupt silence that followed.

The Ringmaster watched as one of the men self-consciously scratched his droopy moustache. *A moustache that twitches like a tarantula dancing on his lip.*

When the elevator stopped in the lobby, Yakov smiled at Carina, gesturing with his hand. "After you."

Chapter Fifty-Three

Jack awoke to the sound of the toilet flushing. He looked at his watch. It was 5:45 a.m. When Giuseppe emerged from the bathroom, he got up.

"Good, you're awake," Giuseppe said in a hushed voice.

"I'm going to have a shower," Jack whispered.

"When you're done, wake the others. I'll start making breakfast."

Minutes later Jack adjusted the hot-water heater to high and turned on the shower, but stood outside the stall for a moment to let the water warm.

The window behind the toilet was open a crack, so he opened it further to look out. The snow from last night hadn't amounted to much more than a light covering. He watched Giuseppe refilling the generators as he thought, *The Ringmaster should arrive today. What will happen then? Will I be trusted?*

Steam was billowing out from the shower stall as he stepped inside. He was just closing the shower curtain when he saw headlights through the window. Someone was arriving. *Did Giuseppe decide to have his brother-in-law bring the dogs?*

A moment later Jack was rinsing shampoo out of his hair when the shower curtain was ripped open.

"You bastard!" Carina screamed. Her face was contorted with rage.

Jack's mouth gaped open as he took the scene in, or tried to. Giuseppe stood behind Carina and someone else was behind him. Then he saw the pistol in Carina's hand. Watched her raise it, as if in slow motion, and point it at his face, then pull the trigger.

* * *

The phone woke Laura from a sound sleep.

"There is a problem," said Paolo sombrely. "My surveillance team discovered that Yakov's Jeep is gone."

"Maybe he decided to get an early start." Laura glanced at the alarm clock on her bedside table. *Not quite six.*

"A very early start," Paolo replied. "It rained last night for about an hour, starting at two. The spot where the Jeep was parked is wet. He had to have left before then."

"You're telling me he travelled all day yesterday, didn't book into the hotel until almost midnight, then took off within two hours?"

"Yes. It does not seem right."

"No kidding it's not right!" Laura couldn't hide her fear. "What happened?"

"I don't know."

"Something must have happened."

"I called my men in Bianco and they are watching for the Jeep, but I think it would be past there already."

"I'm calling Interpol to get whatever we can on Yakov. In the meantime, call the others and we'll meet in Maurice's room."

"Will do," said Paolo.

Laura hung up, then gave a start when the alarm clock rang. When she set the alarm, she'd thought the clock was charming. It was silver with a large, circular face and had a small silver handle mounted on top. She didn't view it as charming now. *Has time run out for Jack? If not, how much time do I have to save him?* Her hands fumbled in a failed attempt to shut off the alarm, and she didn't succeed until she mashed the clock into her pillow. Then she reached for her phone.

Interpol in Ottawa listened to her urgent request for whatever details they could immediately get on Yakov Kadnikov.

"You work with Corporal Jack Taggart," said the woman from Interpol.

"Yes. How did —"

"I'm Constable Jane Martin. I was on duty the night the French police officer tried to warn him." Her voice trembled as she asked, "Is there anything you can tell me about how that is going? Have the French arrested anyone?"

"Not yet. The information I'm seeking is in regard to that. Jack is missing again and things aren't looking good. Please get back to me as soon as you can."

"It might take an hour or two," Jane said. "I'll do my best."

At seven o'clock, Laura arrived at Maurice's room at the same time as Paolo. Otto and Yves were already there, both grim-faced.

Maurice nervously scratched his moustache as he told how they'd gotten on the same elevator as Yakov and Carina when they left the hotel.

"You didn't think to tell me about it?" said Laura angrily.

"They've never seen me before and Maurice kept his distance from Kerin the day he was killed," Yves explained. "I don't think the Russian leaving has anything to do with seeing us in the elevator."

"Maybe they were leaving when you saw them," Otto suggested.

"No, they weren't wearing coats," Yves said. "I saw them heading into the bar as we left."

Laura looked at Paolo. "Do we know if Carina is still at the hotel?"

"No."

"Have someone call her room and then if she answers, pretend to be a wrong number," said Laura. "If she doesn't answer, try again in a couple of minutes in case she's in the shower."

Paolo reached for his phone and said, "I'll have someone check the restaurant, as well."

Several minutes later Paolo was informed that Carina did not answer her phone and was not having breakfast.

Oh, man. "I should be getting a call back from Interpol shortly about whatever they can find on Yakov," Laura said. "This may turn into a long day. I suggest we get something to eat. We may have a long drive ahead of us. Depending on what we find out, I think we should get to Sant'Agata del Bianco and find someplace to watch the road."

"And what do you hope to see?" Yves asked.

"If the bad guys drive out of there without Jack, we'll know he's dead." Laura's tone was grave. "Otherwise, we need to sit there and wait until we hear from him."

Yves and Maurice decided to remain in the room, while Laura, Otto, and Paolo went for breakfast at the hotel restaurant.

The coffee Laura drank only fuelled her already jittery nerves, and she could only eat one of the two pastries she'd ordered. Barely a word was spoken amongst the three of them until eight o'clock, when Laura received a call from Jane in Ottawa saying she had some information about Yakov.

"Give me a minute to get to a better location," Laura said. Glancing at Otto and Paolo, she whispered, "Interpol. I'm going back to my room."

"We'll pay the bill and meet you in Maurice's room," Otto said.

As soon as Laura was back in her room she dug out her notebook and recorded what Jane told her, which was basically that Yakov was known to the police as a gangster and reputed to deal in stolen property and guns. He wasn't considered high enough in the criminal empire for the police to have made him a priority.

"Maybe if they'd worked on him, they'd discover otherwise," said Laura cynically. "Anyway, thanks, I better —"

"Hold on. The report you requested from the police in Zurich concerning Carina Safstrom and her husband, Denzler Bussmann, just came in."

"Yes, they were going to check with Germany. Bussmann died in a car accident there."

"Apparently it wasn't an accident," Jane said. "They believe it was suicide. No skid marks on the road and a good impression of the gas pedal on his shoe when he hit a bridge abutment."

"Well, that's too bad, but —"

"Hang on, I'm still reading. The report contains information from the Swedish police, as well."

"Carina Safstrom said she lived with her aunt and uncle in Stockholm for several years. I put in a request that they check their records, too."

"Let me give you the gist of this," Jane said. "Bussmann had fallen for some type of Ponzi scheme where he invested all his money and lost it in the scam. The guy who ripped Bussmann off took at least fifty-five other people for their life savings. He was a Swede. His name was Noah Akerman."

"Was?"

"He was murdered in Sweden a year later," Jane went on. "They had a suspect, but he was a well-known gangster who died of cancer shortly after." Jane's voice rose in pitch. "Guess who the gangster was!"

"I don't —"

"Carina's uncle! He ran a criminal network that spanned most of Europe."

Laura felt like her brain had been put on spin dry. *Carina took over the family business.*

"There's more," Jane said. "The Swedish police pulled a newspaper clip on Bussmann's funeral in Stockholm to try and identify people who attended. A newspaper photograph confirmed that the aunt and uncle were there for it."

"It was in the newspaper?"

"Yes, it looks like Bussmann was a popular person in the community. He belonged to something called Clowns Without Borders and performed at many hospitals, schools, and retirement homes."

Seconds later Laura was on her way out the door.

* * *

While waiting in Maurice's room for Laura to return, Otto, Maurice, and Yves speculated on whether or not Yakov was the Ringmaster.

"Black, collar-length hair, stocky, hairy hands," Otto said. "That was all?" He looked at Maurice. "Nothing else?"

"No. I have a copy of the witness report in my briefcase and will read it to you." He pulled out a document. "It's in French, but I will translate."

Otto glanced at the report and saw that it was a copy of a handwritten statement written in French and signed at the bottom. He did not read French, but there was something he did see. "The name at the bottom of the report," he said, pointing to it. "Maria Popescu, with what looks like a date of birth and passport number underneath it."

"Yes, that is the witness who saw the killer run away," replied Maurice.

"Maria Popescu is Romanian," said Otto.

"Yes, so was her passport."

"Do you have a list of the five Romanian passports that were stolen?" asked Otto. "The ones Jack found hidden with the drugs and the painting?"

Maurice's eyes revealed his concern, then he tore through his briefcase and pulled out a file and compared the numbers of the stolen passports in Jack's report to the passport number of the witness. He looked dumbfounded. "Maria Popescu was using one of the stolen passports." He stared at Yves. "I remember seeing the witness in a patrol car being interviewed. She had long black hair, thick plastic glasses."

"A disguise that included a wig," Otto said. "I'm going to get Laura."

* * *

Laura was about to knock on Maurice's door when Otto opened it in front of her.

"Carina is the Ringmaster!" she blurted.

"I know," Otto replied.

Laura stared at Otto. At the moment she didn't care how Otto knew. Her thoughts were on what a psychopathic killer would do after being romantically betrayed.

Chapter Fifty-Four

Jack deflected Carina's arm with his forearm and the bullet shattered a tile on the wall behind him. At the same time he delivered his fist with a knuckle twisting finish to her face, smashing out her upper teeth and breaking her nose.

Fuelled by adrenalin, the blow was powerful enough to hurtle Carina backward like a rag doll into Giuseppe. The pistol flew from her hand, deflected off Yakov, and clattered across the floor all the way to the sleeping area, where it slid under a bunk.

Yakov rushed to pick it up, while screaming for Wolfgang, Roche, and Anton to get out of his way.

Jack took the only exit available, leaping onto the toilet, shoving the window all the way open, and diving naked onto the snow-covered ground. He scrambled to his feet, slipping in the snow, then dove behind the bunkhouse where he could not be seen. He looked at the darkened forest looming a short distance in front of him. *Darkness is my friend.*

While the other men raced out the front door of the bunkhouse, Giuseppe sat Carina on the edge of a bunk and tipped her head back. He saw the gaping holes where her front teeth had been as blood poured from her broken nose and ran down the sides of her mouth.

"No," she screamed, pushing him away. "I want him," she spluttered as she got to her feet.

Outside, the sounds of yelling told them that Jack had made it into the forest.

"Don't worry," Giuseppe said as he followed Carina outside. "There is no place for him to go. I'll get a flashlight."

Moments later Giuseppe's flashlight picked up Jack's trail. It was easy to follow in the snow and revealed that he'd run to the chopping block before heading into the forest.

"He's got the hatchet," said Wolfgang.

"Yes," Yakov concurred with a snicker, "but maybe he doesn't know that you shouldn't bring an axe to a gunfight."

"You think this is funny, Yakov?" Carina snarled.

"No, I'm sorry. I only mean that he will die. I have a pistol, and he has only —"

"Shh, listen," Giuseppe said. "See if we can hear him. Please, everyone be quiet."

The group stopped moving and stood silently at the edge of the forest.

* * *

In the forest Jack discovered that the ground around the base of some of the larger trees was bare of snow. His gut reaction told him to put as much distance as he could between himself and the people trying to kill him, but it was too dark to see. And twigs and branches, brittle from the cold, snapped too loudly for his location to go undetected.

He heard the voices of his pursuers and rather than run, he wondered about going on the offensive. *Yakov has the pistol. If I can get it....* He circled back from the direction he came, trying to leap from one bare spot of ground to the next to hide his tracks, but skinned his ankle on a rock, leaving spots of blood, as well as footprints in various patches of snow. The people following him had quit talking and he knew they were listening.

Guess it's now or never. He crouched behind a tree near the edge of the forest and waited. Soon he heard them talking again, in English, their words easily heard over the crisp mountain air. He had to grit his teeth to stop them from chattering, and his body was trembling. *Fear or cold? Probably both.*

A flashlight beam cut the darkness, following the tracks he'd left when he first entered the forest, but then the group stopped again and the flashlight danced around both sides of the tree he was hiding behind. He held his breath. *Shit ... steam from my body, wet from the shower ... will they see it?* The flashlight beam moved to another tree and he knew he'd been lucky this time.

"I ... I think I need to sit down for a moment," he heard Carina say in a shaky voice.

"I should get you to a doctor," Giuseppe said. "There is one in Sant'Agata del Bianco." Jack saw the flashlight beam skirt the trees again, then heard Giuseppe say, "It is foolish to try to find him in the dark. He could circle around or attack one of us from behind. We should wait until day-break, which isn't far off. There's nowhere he can escape to, and he will be seen if he leaves the forest."

"Are you sure?" asked Roche.

"Positive." Giuseppe responded. "I will give you the rifles and the ammunition before I leave. If he comes out of the forest, he will be an easy target. I will also give you the keys to the quads. If he tries to run across the meadow, you can easily drive circles around him and shoot him whenever you felt like it."

"I would enjoy that," said Anton.

Jack heard Giuseppe address Carina again. "Let me take you to the doctor. We have time."

"Okay, but I'm not staying there," said Carina. "I want to be the one to put a bullet up his ass." She paused. "Unlike Paris, a bullet to this bastard's head would be too kind."

You rotten bitch.

"Once you see the doctor, I will stop at my brother-in-law's and get the dogs," said Giuseppe. "If Jack hasn't died of the cold, he will wish he had once the pit bull grabs him by his balls. Then you can do to him whatever you wish."

Jack unconsciously squeezed his legs tight together. *Maybe falling off a cliff into a rocky gorge would be a preferable way to die.*

"Come." Giuseppe urged. "If we leave now we will be back shortly after daybreak."

Jack heard the group move away, but remained where he was for several minutes in case someone had stayed behind. The cold caused him to shake uncontrollably, and when he heard the truck start, he peeked around the tree. As Giuseppe and Carina drove away, he saw Wolfgang carrying the rifles into the kitchen, followed by Roche, Anton, and Yakov.

Jack stared at the bunkhouse. There wasn't a lock on the door and the bathroom window was still open. He wondered about trying to sneak in to get his clothes. The light in the bathroom had been left on, as well as an outside light over the bunkhouse door. *It could be risky.*

However, he could see through the kitchen window that Wolfgang and Yakov were keeping vigil on the bunkhouse and could see the entrance, as well as the open bathroom window. *Scratch that idea.* He then focused his attention on the shed behind the kitchen. It was not visible to Wolfgang or Yakov.

Moments later he crept up to the back of the shed, then stayed close to the building as he made his way to the door, so that his footprints would not be so obvious. Once he reached the door, he glanced at the kitchen. A window overlooking the porch was open slightly and Roche and Anton were now making breakfast.

Jack opened the door to the shed. There were no windows and it was pitch-black inside. He hesitated, then decided that someone looking out from the bright light inside the kitchen may not see if the door to the shed was left cracked open, which he had to do if he were to see even a little.

He started to search the shed, just using his hands to feel. He felt along a workbench and found a toolbox. Inside was an assortment of screwdrivers, pliers, and some duct tape. He decided the hatchet he carried would make a better weapon than a screwdriver.

The duct tape. Do I wrap myself up like a mummy? Yeah, that ought to give them all a good laugh before they kill me. Not enough tape, regardless.

He continued his search, and any hope he had of finding an old pair of coveralls or boots vanished, but he did find a large burlap bag. He used the hatchet to tear holes in the bottom of the bag, then pulled it over his head like a sleeveless T-shirt that hung to his knees. *Talk about being half in the bag.*

Next he wrapped some of the tape around his feet. He was about to leave the shed when he stumbled into a shop vacuum cleaner. To him, the noise of the collision was like a bomb exploding, and he peeked out the door to see if he'd been heard. Roche was cracking eggs into a frying pan and had not looked up. The sound of the generators had drowned out the noise.

Jack breathed a sigh of relief, then a new plan formed in his mind. He unscrewed the hose from the vacuum cleaner. Taking it with him, as well as the hatchet and roll of duct tape, he crept onto the back porch, where he found the funnel Giuseppe had used to put gas into the generators.

The light from the kitchen window shone across the porch, but the area directly below the window was in shadow. He sat down and ripped off strips of duct tape to fasten the funnel to the hose. The cold had made his fingers feel like sticks of wood, as the blood in his limbs receded to protect his vital organs. He knew that hypothermia caused confusion in thinking and made for poor decision-making. *Hope this plan isn't a result of that.*

He glanced at his feet, bound with tape. *I can't feel them. Did I wrap them too tight? How can I tell when I can't feel them?*

The door beside him burst open and Roche stepped onto the porch, barely an arm's length away. Jack looked up at him and then at the hatchet he held between his knees. *Can I grab it in time? I feel so numb… I can't even feel it … what if it falls? The hose! He's almost stepping on it!*

"Can you smell this, Jack?" Roche yelled at the forest. "We're having eggs and coffee!" He fanned the door a couple of times. "Sure is warm in here!" He laughed, then stepped back inside and closed the door.

Ten minutes later, mission accomplished, Jack crawled off the porch on his hands and knees, then stumbled back into the forest. Once there he got to a position where he could see Wolfgang and Yakov still sitting in the same spot, drinking coffee and eating while they watched the bunkhouse. Roche and Anton sat opposite each other at the adjacent table.

Jack glanced up at the sky and saw the sun briefly illuminate the top of a mountain peak before it clouded over.

How much time do I have? Will it be enough? Maybe I should try to do some exercises to stay warm. I feel so tired. Gotta stay on my feet or I will go to sleep … and never wake up.

Chapter Fifty-Five

Two hours had passed, during which Jack had mostly crouched behind some bushes in an effort to draw his legs inside the burlap bag for warmth. He kept an eye on the kitchen window, occasionally looking at the palm of his hand and then his knees. To stave off the cold, he had tried jogging on the spot. He recalled falling against the rough bark of a tree and gouging himself. *I'm not bleeding. I am invincible. Hypothermia causes difficulty and confusion in thinking. But I'm not bleeding — that's gotta be good....*

He looked at the kitchen again. *Something's different. It's daylight now, but I knew that. There's something else. One, two, three ... Wolfgang isn't there.*

He automatically tried to grip the hatchet tighter, but could no longer feel his hand and had to look to ensure he was still holding the thing. He tried to flex his fingers one at a time, but they remained gripped on the handle. *Bet I have to carry it around the rest of my life, which I guess won't be all that long.*

He saw Giuseppe's truck arrive and park in front of the kitchen. *Hey, Carina, how ya doin'? Did you get new teeth? Boars' tusks might be good, instead of teeth. They'd suit you better…. Ha ha, real funny, Jack.*

* * *

Giuseppe had barely come to a stop when Carina turned to him. "Give me your gun and let them loose," she said, gesturing to the dogs in the rear. "I hope the pit bull's hungry."

Giuseppe handed her the pistol and said, "I've seen that dog in action. It can take down a wild boar without a problem. If Jack is still alive, he won't be for long." He then glanced at the kitchen and tapped his horn, before saying, "I'll go to the bunkhouse and get some of Jack's clothes to use as a scent before letting the dogs out. Today will be a day to remember."

"A day I am looking forward to," Carina said fiercely.

On getting out, Giuseppe swung his gaze toward the kitchen again, then gave Carina a puzzled look.

She returned it, furrowing her brow. "Go check," she ordered, tightening her grip on the pistol.

A moment later Giuseppe opened the front door to the kitchen and looked inside.

* * *

In the forest, Jack stumbled forward. *Okay, let the shit hit the fan while I get some real clothes before becoming an ice sculpture.*

* * *

The first thing Giuseppe saw was Yakov, sitting with his back slumped against the table. Beside him he saw Roche, face down on the table in his own vomit. Across from him, Anton was slumped over, his head and arm on the table. Wolfgang was on the floor under the table with his arm stretched out toward the door.

Giuseppe called to Carina for help, then rushed inside and tried to drag Wolfgang out by the arm.

Carina reached the kitchen in time to see Giuseppe drop Wolfgang and collapse on top of him. "Giuseppe!" she screamed. "Get out of there!" He did not respond and she stepped back in horror. Then a flicker of movement near the bunkhouse caught her eye. She turned and saw Jack, looking like he was wearing a brown dress and staggering into the bunkhouse like he was drunk.

"You!" she screamed.

Jack had barely made it to his bunk when Carina raced in and fired a wild shot in his direction. As she paused to take aim, he fell forward into the bathroom and kicked the door shut behind him. She heard him stumbling and trying to get to his feet as she reached the door. "Not this time!" she yelled, then fired a shot through the door.

Jack's plan was simple. He stood beside the sink with the idea that when Carina opened the door, she would look to the window over the toilet, thinking he had escaped through it again. Then he would slam the door into her, knock her over, and grab the gun.

Perhaps if he had not been suffering from hypothermia it might have worked, but his breathing had become slow and shallow, and what his foggy brain told his body to do was not what he could accomplish, at least not with the speed he needed.

Carina opened the door and a glance at the mirror behind the sink revealed Jack's whereabouts. She swung the pistol around for another shot when he lurched against the door. She stepped back, but was struck by the door and pinned with her chest against the door frame. Her left arm and head were still inside the bathroom and she turned her head sideways to look at him.

"Drop, drop," Jack managed to gasp.

Carina struggled to get her other hand with the pistol past her body for a shot, but Jack used his weight to keep her pinned.

"I shed drop it," he slurred.

Carina glared at him from eyes encircled with blackened bruises from her broken nose. "Fuck you," she seethed. "I killed one cop in a bathroom, so watch me do it again."

Jack realized she was about to fire a shot backward over her shoulder and ducked as a bullet came through the door where his head had been. She squirmed to adjust her aim as he took a step back, still pushing on the door with one hand, before swinging the hatchet.

The sound of crunching bone and a gurgling noise told him he had succeeded. He'd aimed for the top of her head, but instead struck her on the side of her face below her left eye. Despite hearing the gun fall to the floor, he kept his grip on the hatchet and stared at her face.

Her mouth gaped open and she coughed, spraying blood. Her left eye was distorted, but her other eye remained fixed on his face.

"Welcome to the Bates Motel, bitch," he said, barely containing his rage. He then stepped back as she fell into the room. He watched her body shudder and convulse with a few more bloody coughs, then become still. He looked out the window toward the kitchen. The generator was still running and the vacuum-cleaner hose was still feeding exhaust from the generator into the kitchen window. *It can wait.*

Leaving the burlap sack on, he wrapped a blanket from a bunk around his head and torso, hobbled back and forth in the bunkhouse until he felt his body start to warm. He knew that warming his extremities immediately could cause him to go into shock. It was a slow process, but eventually he headed for the shower.

Chapter Fifty-Six

It was eleven o'clock in the morning when Jack drove around a bend in the road and was finally at a place where he could make contact with Laura's phone.

"Hey, it's me," he said. "I'm free to talk."

"It's Jack!" he heard her call out, then say to him, "Where the hell are you?"

"Settle down," he said. "I didn't shoot any little pigs. Neither did anyone else."

"Where are you?"

"I'm driving Giuseppe's truck and am guessing I'm about fifteen minutes out of Sant'Agata del Bianco. Are you still in Reggio?"

"I'm not upset about the pigs," she spluttered. "We're in the Aspromonte Mountains looking for you! We found out that Carina is the Ringmaster!"

"Yes, I figured as much," Jack said.

"She saw Maurice last night and we were afraid she

recognized him," Laura went on. "She took off soon after with … You figured as much? Did she show up there?"

"Yes, and she wasn't happy."

"What did she say to you?"

"It was more the body language that caught my attention. I've been around long enough to tell by a woman's hands when she is angry."

"By her hands?"

"Yeah, like when they're holding a gun."

"Damn it, Jack, this is no time for jokes."

"Sorry, I feel giddy," he replied in a high-pitched voice.

"Giddy? We figured you were dead. Paolo is driving like a maniac along icy roads. Hang on." She paused. "He says we're also about fifteen minutes out of Sant'Agata del Bianco."

"On the opposite side from me," Jack said rapidly.

"What's going on with Carina?"

"She has what I would call a split personality. Mind you, it might've been me who gave it to her. I split her head open with a hatchet." His voice was still high-pitched.

Laura realized the reason for Jack's odd-sounding voice and black humour. He was fighting to maintain control. For undercover operatives, maintaining control in a conversation became a natural habit, but in this case, she knew he was fighting to control his own emotions. Often, when you're fighting for your life you're too busy to think of the consequences. It's after the event is over that shock and the *what ifs* set in as your mind tries to cope with the horror you endured.

"Wolfgang, Roche, Anton, and some guy called Yakov are dead, too," Jack continued in a shaky voice. "I'm still alive, though. Damn near froze my balls off, but I'm still alive. Don't know why anyone would want to join one of those polar bear clubs. I gotta go. I wanna phone Natasha. Let her know that … well, that everything's over."

"Jack?"

"Yeah?"

"Don't phone her yet. Wait an hour. You need to calm down."

"What do you mean? I'm fine."

"Hey, tough guy, it's *me* you're talking to. Don't lie. Carina may be dead but it's not over until —"

"Yeah, the fat lady sings."

"No, until the nightmares stop. Which from my experience of working with you might be never."

Jack's sigh was audible, then he said, "I'm okay."

"No, you're not. I can hear it in your voice. Natasha knows you a lot better than I do. If you don't want her to worry, wait until you've calmed down."

A few seconds passed in silence, then Jack said, "Laura?"

"Yes?"

"Thank you."

Laura smiled grimly. His voice sounded tired, but she knew he would be able to cope with the reality of their world. He always did. So did Natasha, for that matter.

* * *

It was Monday morning in Vancouver when Staff-Sergeant Rose Wood walked into Assistant Commissioner Isaac's office and took a seat. He was reading a report, but looked at her over the top of his glasses. "Anything further to add to what you told me on Friday?" he asked.

"Yes, Corporal Taggart was cleared to go by the Italian police. Forensics verified everything happened the way he said it did. He acted in self-defence."

Isaac leaned back in his chair and folded his arms across his chest. "What about the men he gassed with carbon monoxide?"

"They ruled that as self-defence, too," replied Rose.

"I knew this would happen," replied Isaac, shaking his head. "I wasn't the least surprised."

"Sir, it really was self —"

"I'm sure it was, but to kill all of them?"

"Not all," Rose said. "Bojan Buchvarov was arrested in Bulgaria."

"The fellow who was shipping the drugs and stolen jewellery to his parents' address?"

"Yes."

"Lucky for him," said Isaac dryly. "I also have a question concerning the story Carina Safstrom told Taggart about some Russian philanthropist whose wife died of cancer and was connected to the theatre and the arts. An original report from you indicated he might have been the Ringmaster. Could he have some of the stolen paintings? Or was he just someone Safstrom made up to deceive Taggart?"

"That has since been checked out. That man does exist and was someone who Carina Safstrom had restored paintings for. He's a well-known philanthropist and his only connection with Saftstrom was that he hired her do some restorations for him. The man is said to be totally honest. Safstrom did lie to Jack about him, but only by saying that was how she met Roche Freulard."

"I see. So where are Taggart and Secord now?"

"Laura arrived home last night. Jack put in a leave request and went to Paris to —"

"Paris! After all this? I want him back here immediately, and tell him to make sure he pays for his own ticket!"

"Sir, he went to pay his respects to Gabrielle Bastion. She was Kerin's wife. He thought he should —"

Isaac put up his hand for Rose to stop, then said. "I'm sorry, I should have clued in. Do you know when her baby's due?"

"She had it Friday night. A girl."

"Tell Taggart to take whatever time he needs." Isaac's voice sounded gruff, but his eyes were moist. "Consider it official business. You may go."

* * *

It was ten o'clock Monday morning in Paris when Maurice dropped Jack off at Gabrielle's apartment building.

"Aren't you coming in?" Jack asked.

"I saw her Saturday night while you were still in Italy," Maurice replied. "She asked if she could talk to you alone. She feels she would get to know you better that way."

"Her English —"

"Is better than mine." Maurice smiled. "Call me when you want a ride."

Moments later Jack was buzzed into the apartment building. Gabrielle stood waiting for him in the doorway holding her baby, swaddled in a pink blanket. She invited him inside, where she offered him a coffee. He accepted and tried to hide his discomfort when she passed him the baby to hold while she made the coffee.

"Her name is Camille," Gabrielle said.

"Beautiful name for a beautiful baby," Jack said, fighting to overcome the anguish he felt.

Gabrielle looked at him. "Are you married? Do you have children?"

"Yes. My wife, Natasha, and I have two sons. Mike is nine and Steve is eight."

"Then you should be used to babies," said Gabrielle, "but I can tell you don't feel comfortable, so tell me why."

Jack nodded. "I'm sorry. Your husband died trying to save my life. I don't know what to say."

"You seem like a nice man," Gabrielle said. "Mind you, I know it would not have made any difference who you were or what you did."

"I don't understand."

Gabrielle looked surprised. "You should. You're a policeman. So was Kerin. He would have risked his life to save a wino in an alley if he thought the person was in danger. Isn't that what police officers do? Serve and protect us? All of us?"

Jack nodded.

"That was what Kerin was doing — the same as you. I loved my husband and respected what he did. I want you to know that I respect you, as well, and do not blame you for what happened. I know you would've done the same for him. From what Maurice told me, I know you already have."

"Thank you."

Gabrielle paused, looking at Camille. "Her eyes are open. I think she's smiling."

Jack gazed down at Camille and felt Gabrielle rest her hand on his shoulder, as she stroked Camille's chin with her other hand. Somehow the weight of her hand on his shoulder alleviated the weight he felt in his heart.